IMPLANT

A British murder mystery with a little slice of horror

RAY CLARK

Published by The Book Folks

London, 2020

© Ray Clark

ISBN 978-1-913516-97-0

www.thebookfolks.com

"If I were asked to answer the following question: 'What is slavery?' and I should answer in one word, 'Murder!' my meaning would be understood at once. No further argument would be required to show that the power to take from a man his thought, his will, his personality, is a power over life and death, and that to enslave a man is to kill him. Why, then, to this other question: 'What is property?' may I not likewise answer 'Theft!'"

Pierre-Joseph Proudhon

Chapter One

The sound of the incoming call broke the silence in the station.

Maurice Cragg, the desk sergeant, glanced up as PC Gary Close reached for his mobile and answered it.

Under normal circumstances, he would not allow personal calls at work, as was the right of any employer. But there were a number of overriding factors that gave way to his leniency. Not the least of which was the fact he was engrossed in a serial on BBC Radio 4, a lost classic from the archives recently discovered. The fact that it was also three o'clock in the morning on Monday, meant the small community police station of Bramfield had little or nothing to actually do.

Also, he liked Gary Close. Close was pretty slim, around six feet tall, with dark brown hair and a rugged complexion that had at some point suffered the effects of teenage acne. Despite being only nineteen, he was no stranger to bad luck. His father had been killed when Gary was eleven. His best friend had died of a drug overdose about four years ago, in extremely strange circumstances. Three months ago, he broke his leg playing Sunday League football, and had returned to work following only a two-month convalescence. And to top it all, his mother Christine had recently been diagnosed with what seemed like an inoperable brain tumour.

Cragg sighed. God, he felt sorry for that lad. But for all that, he had the makings of a damn good copper. He was dedicated, willing to go the extra mile to help out. He'd make detective someday, if his temper didn't have the better of him.

"What do you mean, three hours?" demanded Gary.

Cragg glanced up again, slightly irritated at the interruption but concerned by Gary's tone.

"Who is this?" shouted the PC.

Cragg lowered the volume on the radio, taking a keener interest.

Gary moved the phone away from his ear and glanced at the screen. "Number withheld," he said to Maurice. He raised the mobile and tried to continue the conversation. "Hello?" Gary lowered the cell. "He's gone."

"Who has?" Cragg asked, leaning forward in his armchair. They were currently in the back room of the station, which resembled someone's sitting room. They had a table and chairs, a three-piece suite, a wooden floor with an assortment of rugs, and wallpaper that must have ceased production in the 1950s.

"That's just it, I don't know."

"Well, what was he on about, three hours?"

"When I answered, he just said 'you've got three hours left.'"

"To what? He didn't say anything else? He didn't hint towards anything?" asked Cragg, trying to assess whether or not it was serious. In the background the only thing he could hear was the continuation of his serial at a much lower volume.

"No," replied Gary.

"Did you hear anything else, any background noise? Cars, phones ringing, a party going on somewhere?"

"No, nothing. That's what was unsettling me."

"A hoax call, maybe?"

"Could be, but you'd still expect to hear something else, wouldn't you?"

Cragg glanced at his watch. "Perhaps not, especially at this time of a morning. No hint then as to what was going to happen in three hours? Or where?"

"No."

"Did you recognize the voice?" asked Cragg.

2

"No."

As Cragg was about to ask another question, the station phone rang.

"Bloody hell," said Cragg. "Not much chance of a relaxing end to the shift, is there?"

He answered after the third ring. Before he could say anything, a concerned voice spoke.

"Is that the Bramfield Police Station?"

"Yes, sir," replied Cragg. "How can I help you?"

"It's *me* that can help you. I live in the town, in a flat above one of the shops at the back of the Market Square, on Spital Street opposite Armitage's."

"The hardware store?"

"That's the one."

"Can you tell me your name, sir?"

"Jones, Richard Jones."

"What about the hardware store?"

"Well, it's three o'clock in the morning, and there's a light on in the shop."

"I appreciate your concern, Mr Jones," replied Cragg, who knew Richard Jones pretty well; he worked nights at the furniture warehouse a couple of miles outside the town, which would explain why he was still up. "Maybe old Armitage can't sleep."

"Maybe he can't, but he's hardly likely to leave the front door wide open, whatever he's doing."

Chapter Two

Alex Wilson was awake, of that he was sure.

But it was hard to tell because he couldn't see a thing. Wherever he was, it was pitch black. He'd often heard the saying, and had also been in circumstances where it had been dark, but not completely fucking black like it was now.

Alex was more than concerned; the first waves of paranoia were creeping in.

For one thing, he couldn't move. Every time his brain sent a signal to either his arms or his legs, nothing happened. Equally frightening was that he had tried several times to shift his position, even in the slightest way, without success. He couldn't even *feel* his arms or legs, or in fact his entire body.

Did he still have it?

Don't be fucking stupid, Alex! You must at least still have your body. Otherwise, how would you be able to think things out? The blood must be circulating towards your brain and at least allowing some rational thought.

Unless, of course, his head been removed from his body and he was wired up to machinery which produced thoughts *for* him.

Alex decided he wasn't going there. That was irrational!

He tried to work out whether he was horizontal or vertical, but even that seemed impossible.

Maybe that bastard, Lance Hobson, was testing out a new drug, something that wasn't street legal, to see what kind of effect it would have.

That would obviously take time, which was another puzzle. How long had he been in his current situation? He had no way of working it out. Even if he *could* move his arm and check his watch, he wouldn't be able to see it because of how dark it was.

As his thoughts were becoming clearer, he tried as hard as he could to remember the last conscious thing he'd done. He conjured up a picture of meeting Lance Hobson in the car park in Bramfield, outside the public toilets adjacent to the church. But he had no idea when that was.

He suddenly had a vision of his flat. He was in the kitchen, heating up a pan of soup. He had no recollection however of eating it.

Alex sighed. It was bloody hopeless.

Chapter Three

"It's okay, lad. I can dispatch a car if you like."

"Where are the others?"

"Further north, at Rudson, investigating an attempted break-in."

"You could give them a call and see how they're doing. If they're nearly finished, let 'em know I'm going, and maybe they can meet me there later. After all, we don't know what this is yet, and it'll only take me a few minutes to walk round."

"If you're sure," said Cragg.

"Course I am. Anyway, the doc said I needed the exercise for the leg."

Gary put his helmet on and stepped out the station front door. The sky was still dark with little cloud and no breeze. The road was quiet: no traffic, no people, not even a brave fox.

The station was situated on Old Bramfield Road, to the north of the town, going towards Bursley Bridge and eventually Harrogate. Armitage's place was in Carpenter's Alley, behind the Market Square, at the foot of The Shambles. He estimated it would only take about ten minutes to walk, despite his leg.

It took less than a minute for the bloody thing to start aching – an annoying pulsing sensation.

The accident was still very clear in his mind. They were playing a team from Ilkley. One of their defenders was known locally – and nationally, he shouldn't wonder – as 'The Monster'. He'd been sent off more times than any other player in the league, and that was probably the sole reason why Ilkley Town hadn't been promoted. Maybe their manager would see that one day.

The Bramfield defender, Steve Preece, had supplied the perfect cross for Gary. The goalkeeper was the only man to beat, and Gary reckoned it wasn't much of a problem. Where The Monster had come from was anyone's guess.

Gary went down like a sack of spuds, even heard the break. He hadn't felt any pain at first. He couldn't remember the exact point at which he *had* felt pain, but it had more than made up for his initial lack of it.

Gary approached the crossroads in the town centre and turned right on to Wheelgate, passing the shops. He hadn't seen any people on his walk, and passed only a couple of vehicles approaching from the south side; one of them was a bus with no passengers.

He turned left on to Finkle Street, and his thoughts were once again with his mother.

She had a type of brain cancer called glioma. He remembered the day when she had suddenly started having epileptic fits, right out of the blue. With progression, she'd had more, and had then grown forgetful.

She was so frightened. So was he, come to mention it. He'd lost his father; he wanted to hang on to his mother.

Gary approached the old library, which led to The Shambles. As Armitage's hardware shop came into view, he could indeed see the light burning in the window, and the front door open.

He glanced behind him and noticed Richard Jones with his pushbike, standing outside The Golden Lion pub. The man waved, wheeling his bike towards Gary. He was dressed in an old trench coat and trousers. Gary reckoned his age to be mid-fifties.

He turned his attention to the old hardware store. It had been a part of the community for as long as he could remember. In fact, the sign above the shop told him it had been established in 1939.

It was a long-fronted building made from different shades of brick, indicating when and where it had been extended. He suspected the main door at the far right side was not the original entrance, which was probably the more central one now used as a window display. To reach the shop you had to walk down four huge concrete steps, with a slope for wheelchairs running down the middle. To the far left was a cycle rack, and a huge potted plant. On the corner of the building an old-fashioned gas mantle was fixed to the wall, unlit.

Gary was about to tell Richard Jones not to come too close when movement caught his attention. About thirty feet in front of him, where the shop ended and a wall separated it from the public toilets and the car park beyond, someone had stepped back into the shadows.

At least, he thought someone had.

Chapter Four

Alex Wilson still had no idea what was going on, or the length of time he'd been wherever he was. In fact, he had no idea how long he had been awake: it could have been minutes, it could have been hours.

It was still pitch black, but whatever thoughts he'd harboured about his possible non-existent carcass were disappearing as feeling had begun to return.

And fucking hell did it hurt!

His first sensation was pins and needles overtaking his entire body, as if the circulation had been stopped and then started again. All his limbs had felt heavy, and he'd felt sick. Within minutes that had turned to pain, proper pain, and the level was increasing with each passing second.

But he still couldn't move. Not fully anyway. He knew there was something hard against his back, and it felt like his arms were stretched out. The slight movement he *was* allowed seemed to create a gap between the hard surface and his limb. But that was as far as he could go. The same could be said for his legs, a little movement and no more, as if his feet had been pinned, but by what he could not see because it was still too dark!

Furthermore, something was stopping him opening his mouth. It wasn't a gag, and it hadn't been taped up, but he still couldn't open it. He could only breathe through his nose.

What the hell was going on?

He'd managed to work out that he was vertical, because if he moved his head, it hung forward very easily and it preferred to stay there. Returning it took an effort, and it wouldn't have done if he'd been lying down.

Had Lance Hobson given him something? Was he under the influence of some new and untested hallucinogenic drug that only Hobson knew about? Was he a guinea pig?

If it *was* a new kind of drug they were going to knock out, they had better do something with it. People wouldn't come back for more if they suffered symptoms like these.

Hobson was a dangerous bastard, a very rich, dangerous bastard who had everything simply because he had everyone else do his dirty work. Wasn't that the way with the people at the top of the drug chain? They never sullied their own hands.

Alex went into a spasm as his whole carcass was wracked with a pain equivalent to nothing he'd ever felt before. It filled his entire body from head to foot, as if someone had pulled his fucking nerves through his skin and plugged them into the mains.

Alex twisted and writhed and still could not break free of whatever held him in position.

As his body calmed, he could feel himself bathed in sweat. He was shaking, and although the pain had subsided, his hands and feet continued to throb incessantly.

And then he heard something that momentarily distracted his thoughts.

Footsteps from above.

Chapter Five

After telling Richard Jones to stay outside and keep an eye open for his colleagues, Gary stepped inside the shop.

Armitage's hardware store was a shrine to the past, and seemed to stock everything anyone would need: tools, paint, varnish, wood, and tiles. If you could name it, old Armitage had it. Moving from the doorway into the main area was like walking through a tunnel. Display boards on either side were crammed full with Hoover bags and belts and other accessories. In front of him was a stand with gardening products and implements, ranging from plant food and compost, to small trowels and forks.

He moved forward slowly, peering into the shop. From his vantage point, he could not see anything untoward. He listened carefully for any movement. There was nothing.

He glanced to his right and saw the counter in front of the back wall of the room. On the extreme left side, near a window – looking out onto what he presumed would be a back yard – was a lift-up hatch, which was down at the moment. Behind the counter he saw a cabinet with hundreds of drawers with brass handles on them. God only knew what they contained.

A range of smells pervaded the building, comfortable aromas that DIY enthusiasts would soak up every time they entered. The fragrance of pine was the strongest, and beneath the frame holding the lumber, the excess shavings supported the fact. He could smell polish, and linseed oil.

A sudden movement caused Gary to jump, which in turn made him lose his balance. From there he crashed backwards into a stand with dustpans and mops and buckets and other cleaning materials. The sound seemed louder than anything he had ever heard in his life, one that could have woken half of Bramfield.

Mops, brushes, and buckets fell to the floor all around him, along with brand-named containers like Flash and CIF Cleaner. As he was about to move, one struck the corner of his eye. He lost his temper and yelled an obscenity.

"Are you okay in there?" shouted Richard Jones from the shop doorway.

Gary allowed the dust to settle before he quickly found his feet, desperate to keep the man from entering.

"I'm fine, but don't come in. It could be a crime scene."

As he glanced around, he realized what had caused him to react like a tit: the appearance of his own reflection in a mirror.

Disgusted with himself, he straightened his uniform and ran his hands up and down his body, clearing the wood shavings from his clothes.

Once he'd calmed down, Gary approached the counter. As he glanced down, he saw an A4 sized piece of paper. He could make out writing. He reached into his pocket and withdrew his mobile, using it as a torch. He read a message.

> *Time to play a game*
> *The clock is ticking*
> *But time's not on your side*
> *And neither am I*
> *What are you waiting for?*

Gary hadn't the faintest idea what was going on, or whether or not any of what he'd seen was serious. It could be an elaborate prank.

What happened next removed those thoughts. Gary jumped as an old-fashioned monitor on the countertop to his right came to life. What he saw caused his stomach to swell.

He grabbed his police radio and contacted Cragg.

Chapter Six

For Alex Wilson, a number of things happened in rapid succession. A wave of pain coursed through him like an express train, so severe and so shocking that the end result was a loss of control of his bodily functions.

As he fought for composure, he realized something else. He must have been naked, because although he could smell what he'd done, he didn't feel anything clinging to his body.

With that thought, Alex felt a chill. There was no wind, no draught, but he was still cold.

He came to the conclusion that whatever predicament he was in had nothing to do with Lance Hobson. So maybe it was a rival gang. Perhaps someone had muscled in on his turf, tried to take the drug trade away from them. Happened all the time.

Maybe they had Lance Hobson as well.

Above his head he heard a crashing sound, followed by a bang and a clattering before one final thump sounded out, as if something had fallen onto the floor.

Why? Who was up there? *What* was up there? Where the fuck was he? A box? A container? Was he in a room, or a cellar?

Alex raised his head, and lots of light suddenly bathed the space he was in. He winced, the pain too much to bear momentarily, blinking furiously a few times his vision finally focused.

The room he was in was long and angular. The bricks were old, but in good condition. The building did not have any damp. It was full of boxes, trade names he recognized: Stanley, Draper, Spear & Jackson.

He realised why the smell had been familiar. He glanced upwards and saw a trapdoor, with steps leading down into the cellar he was in. He was underneath his uncle's shop, the hardware store in the town.

Why? What was happening? Who had put him here?

His uncle wasn't capable and would have no reason to. He doubted it was Lance, and he couldn't think of anyone else who could have done so.

Checking to see if he was, in fact, naked, he was shocked at what had been done to his body.

He had his back to the wall. He noticed he was not standing on the floor, but supported a foot or so above it, crucifixion style. He glanced slowly at his hands and feet, or at least as much as his head would allow from the angle he was at. Each limb had the head of a huge screw protruding from its appendage, and lines of blood trailing to the concrete below him, intermingling with his own waste. That was why he had been allowed a little movement from his arms and legs, but not his hands and feet. He also noticed two plain white envelopes a few inches above each hand.

Terrified, Alex fought hard to keep his stomach under control, remembering his mouth was blocked.

He allowed his eyes to scan his body. In the area of his abdomen, he noticed a wound with fresh stitches, but there were no other marks, cuts, grazes, or bruises on his body.

Alex moaned. He had never been so petrified in his life. But he figured it wasn't over by a long way.

Suddenly he felt a sharp, stinging sensation underneath his skin, directly behind the wound.

Chapter Seven

Gary ran out of the shop shouting into his police radio, trying to contact Cragg. PCs Robin Nice and Steve Graham pulled up in the squad car they had been using following the investigation of an attempted break-in at Rudson. Richard Jones was standing near the bicycle rack in front of the shop, which he'd casually made use of.

"What's wrong?" asked PC Nice. He was slightly older than Gary, very tall and dangerously thin, but pretty fit despite his appearance.

"Don't go in there," replied Gary. His radio crackled.

"Come in," said Cragg on the other end.

"Why? How bad is it?" asked PC Graham. He was senior member of the three, as tall as Nice but much broader. He played rugby.

Gary ignored the question, speaking into the radio. "Sir, I think we need some real back-up."

"Is it that bad?" asked Cragg.

"I don't know," said Gary. "It's a mess."

"What's a mess, Gary?" asked Cragg. "Calm down and tell me what you've seen."

Graham and Nice glanced at each other. Nice placed a hand on Gary's shoulder. "Do as he says, calm down."

"Somebody's definitely playing games," said Gary. He went on to explain everything.

"It is a real body?" asked Cragg.

"Looks real enough to me. I'm calling a crime scene. We shouldn't be trampling all over it and we need some back up here. I think this is out of my league."

Gary hoped he hadn't destroyed any evidence when he'd fallen over. PCs Nice and Graham had puzzled expressions, as if he'd lost his mind. Richard Jones moved nearer to them, as if he was part of the squad.

"Where is this body?" asked Nice.

"I've no idea," replied Gary.

"What?" asked Graham. "It isn't actually in the shop?"

"I need to talk to Sergeant Cragg," said Gary. "This looks really serious to me."

"Who's that?" asked PC Graham, pointing to the wall beyond the shop. Nice followed the line of his finger, peering into the semi-darkness.

"I can't see anyone."

"Well, I'm sure I did," Graham replied, before taking off in that direction, heading toward the car park and the public toilets.

Gary thought it might be the person he'd seen on his arrival at the shop and asked Nice to check around the back. He glanced around. The town was waking up. Lights in windows above premises were coming on all over the place.

"Gary?" asked Cragg. "What's going on?"

"Graham thinks he's seen someone near the public toilets in the car park. I've asked Nice to check out the back of the shop."

Nice and Graham returned and said they hadn't seen anyone. The rear of the premises was clean and all locked up.

"Someone's gone to a lot of trouble here, sir. The message on the counter said time was running out and then the screen lit up and I saw the body."

"And the person on the screen is still alive?"

"Yes," replied Gary, "but his body has been crucified to a wall, and it's been stitched up and I can see blood, and he was shaking like a shitting dog. If this is a game, it's a sick one."

Cragg sighed, then grew silent.

Chapter Eight

Detective Sergeant Sean Reilly aimed the car down Horsemarket Road, and then onto Spital Street. On the right they passed a car park in front of a church, and on the left a group of shops and pubs. He brought the vehicle to a halt in front of another squad car parked at The Shambles.

Detective Inspector Stewart Gardener jumped out of the passenger seat and closed the car door. From what he'd seen so far, despite the early hour, the town was picturesque: quaint streets and rustic shops.

The scene that greeted him did not fit into any of those categories.

There were four people waiting for him, three police officers and one civilian, standing in front of a small hardware shop with a light on.

Gardener withdrew his warrant card as Reilly came to stand next to him.

"DI Gardener and DS Reilly, Major Crime Team. Which one of you is Gary Close?"

"I am, sir," replied the young PC. As he walked towards Gardener and extended his right hand, the detective couldn't help but notice his limp.

"Have you just done that?"

"No, sir. Broke my leg about three months ago, playing football."

"Nasty," said Reilly, glancing around.

"You're the attending officer, Gary? What time did you arrive?"

"About three-thirty."

"Was there anyone else here at that time?"

"Only this man." Gary pointed and introduced Richard Jones.

"Why were you outside the shop, or in fact in the town at such an early hour?"

"I work the night shift, sir, at the furniture factory outside the town."

"And you were just coming home?"

"That's right."

Gardener studied the man, wondering where he'd seen him before.

"Did you see anyone else?"

"No, can't say I did, but I never do at that time."

"Did you go into the shop?"

"No, sir."

As long as Gardener had been on the force, he'd learned to trust his judgment with people. They'd have no trouble with Richard Jones.

Reilly was wearing his usual attire of brown bomber jacket and jeans, and had his arms folded across his chest. He'd so far chosen to say very little. Gardener sensed he was studying the place. Nothing much escaped the Irishman.

As the detective glanced around the town, he noticed that the early starters in the business world were coming to life, the butcher and the baker to name but two.

He turned his attention back to PC Close. "What did you see when you arrived, Gary?"

"Nothing much, sir. The town was pretty still. I didn't pass anyone on the way down here. Richard Jones had reported the incident. He was standing across there, outside The Golden Lion, with his bike. The front door of the shop was open, and there was a light on inside."

"Have you checked anywhere else, round the back for instance?"

"I didn't, but they did." He pointed to PCs Nice and Graham.

"And you are?" Gardener asked. Both men acknowledged the senior officers and introduced themselves.

"And you didn't see anything you considered unusual?"

"No, sir," both men replied in harmony.

Gardener turned back to Close. "Have you seen anyone suspicious lurking around, Gary?"

The young PC didn't answer straight away. Gardener picked up on it instantly.

"Why the hesitation? Is there something you're not telling us? Or don't want to?"

"It's not that, sir. It's just, I can't be sure whether I actually saw someone or not. And when PC Graham arrived, he thought he had too, but when he checked the area, he didn't find anyone."

"Then let's widen the search, shall we? Sean, take both PCs with you, search the toilets and the grounds of the church."

Gardener watched all three of them leave before speaking to PC Close. "Suppose you describe what you saw in the shop, Gary."

By the time Close had done so, Reilly and the two constables had returned with their mystery guest.

"Who's this, Sean?"

"Wouldn't talk to me, boss. Maybe he's shy."

Gardener asked Gary Close if he knew him. "Yes, it's Jackie Pollard, local drug dealer. Or one of them, at least."

"Is he, now? What have we been up to, Mr Pollard?" Gardener asked the man.

"Out for a walk. Couldn't sleep."

"Look at the trouble your walk has caused us," replied Gardener. "We're going to have to talk to you now, Pollard. I hope you'll be a little more reasonable when we ask our questions."

"You're the one being unreasonable. I haven't done anything."

Gardener wasted no more time with the dealer. "You two, Graham and Nice, take him to the station and throw him in a cell. I'll question him later."

"You can't do that," shouted Pollard.

"Says who?" Gardener asked.

"I know my rights."

"Good, then you'll know why we're detaining you."

"As a matter of fact, I don't. You have nothing to hold me on." Pollard had found some self-confidence that Gardener didn't like.

"Try burglary on for size, Mr Pollard. We've been called to investigate commercial premises in the middle of the night. The door is open, and you're found nearby. We're lifting you for burglary until you can prove otherwise."

He turned to his sergeant. "Sean, caution him." Gardener then nodded to the two PCs to take him away. Ignoring Pollard's protests, Gardener turned and walked towards the shop. Reilly followed.

Inside, Gary Close explained that the shop was exactly as he'd left it.

"Did you disturb someone, Gary?" Gardener asked, glancing at the mess.

"Only myself, sir. I thought something moved over that side of the shop, and I fell over into that lot. Turned out it was my reflection."

Reilly laughed. "What do you do for an encore, Gary?"

Gardener grinned. "Don't worry about him, he'll grow on you."

All three moved further in, toward the counter. Gardener glanced at the note. He had no idea what it meant. He studied the monitor, which now appeared dead. It was very old, cube-shaped, in gunmetal grey with a grille on the side. He couldn't see any buttons. It had to have worked somehow. He leaned over, but saw nothing to prove his theory.

"How was the monitor operated?" Gardener asked Close. "Could you see?"

"No, sir, I didn't really check, to be honest. I was more interested in what it was showing me."

"Did the body on the screen move naturally?"

"How do you mean?" asked Close.

"Did it look staged, like a film?"

Close appeared to think about the answer, casting a doubt in Gardener's mind. Finally, he replied. "It didn't look like a film."

"So you don't actually know if any of this is real, son?" asked Reilly.

"It looked real to me, sir."

Gardener figured the young PC's body language of shifting his hands and feet around meant he was now doubting what he'd seen.

"I understand, Gary," said Gardener, "but in all honesty, we're MIT. We should really only be called out if you *find* a body."

Close appeared disappointed but stood his ground. "I know what I saw, sir. Something about all of this doesn't sit right with me, and I still think I did the right thing in calling it out."

Gardener nodded. "Okay, we're here so we may as well have a look."

Gardener glanced over the counter and noticed the trapdoor in the floor, held in place by a padlock. "Sean, what do you make of that?"

The Irishman leaned over. "Why would you want a padlock on a trapdoor?"

"My thoughts exactly. What do you think he has down there?"

"Cash? Some of these old school guys don't trust the banks."

"Can you blame them, the mess they've made of the economy?"

"I can't imagine anything of any value down there, sir," said Gary Close. "Most of the old shops in the town have deep cellars. We have problems with flooding."

Gardener threaded his way behind. As he crouched down, he recognized the padlock as an expensive model attached to what resembled a bomb-proof hasp with round-headed bolts.

He stood up and peered around the shop, noticing an ABUS stand full of padlocks. He searched behind the counter and spotted a discarded packet tucked behind a small stool, a hard plastic, shrink-wrapped one that had been cut open to obtain the lock it had obviously housed. He picked it up.

The packet informed him it was an ABUS 190 series, which had a high-strength steel body that could not under any circumstances be bolt-cropped. It was also a combination lock with a 4-digit pin number, re-settable to one's choice of code using a special security key, preventing anyone from changing the combination at a later stage.

"Looks like there's definitely something private down there, Sean. Question is, what? Does the owner keep his takings down there? Or his really expensive stock?"

"Or has somebody else put something down there that they don't want us to see?" asked Reilly. "What about bolt croppers, boss?"

"According to the packet, not a chance in hell."

"Do you want to try, anyway?"

"Okay, grab a set off the stand over there."

Reilly put on gloves and did as Gardener asked. By the time he'd finished, he was sweating, and there wasn't a mark on the lock.

Gardener glanced at Gary Close. "Have you heard anything from down there? Any noises?"

"No, sir."

"Who owns the shop, Gary?"

"Mr Armitage."

"Does he live here?

"No, sir, I think he lives on the south side of the village – about a five-minute walk."

"Right, we'll need to speak to him."

Gardener was about to speak again when a pinging sound came from behind him. He turned, glanced down, and noticed a flashing light coming from underneath the counter.

He reached into his inside jacket pocket and produced a pair of gloves. Slipping them on he bent down and retrieved a phone: the screen indicated a message had come through.

Gardener pressed a button and read the message.

Rearrange the dear nun: it's where you should be!

Chapter Nine

Gardener read the message two or three times before showing it to his partner. "Any thoughts?"

Reilly said nothing, he simply studied what was on offer.

Gary's mobile suddenly chirruped. He answered.

"Are you still at the shop, lad?" Cragg asked.

"Yes, sir."

"I've just had some information through that you need to know—"

Cragg completed his sentence, but Gary's mobile was cutting out. The only words he caught were "station" and "landline".

"Sorry, sir, what did you say?" Gary asked Cragg.

"I said, the suspicious call made to your phone at three o'clock came from a landline, the one in Armitage's shop."

Gary glanced at Gardener and told him what Cragg had said before thanking him and terminating the call.

The SIO thought about everything that had happened so far. A strange call, a message, a video feed on a monitor and, finally, another message.

He stepped around the side of the counter, surveying the shop, before finally slipping outside for a breath of fresh air.

Reilly joined him. It was growing lighter. They were going to have to act if they wanted to close things down. The fact that dawn was breaking meant the town would be full of people before too long. A fancy car drove by and the occupant paid them little attention. Gardener noticed it had a private plate, and asked Reilly to jot the number down in his pad.

"I have a friend…"

"Apart from me, you mean?" said Gardener, smiling.

"I never actually included you."

The senior officer appreciated the working relationship that he and Reilly had. No matter how serious the situation there was always banter between them. It helped.

Gardener glanced at the phone and then his partner. He summarised what had happened before saying, "Someone's controlling us, Sean. He wants us here for a reason."

"Backs up the fact that what Gary saw on the monitor was real."

"I'll give it the benefit of the doubt."

"I have a friend," said Reilly, continuing with his earlier statement. "Very good at crosswords, and I remember him telling me how to interpret the clues." Reilly pointed to the retro mobile that Gardener still held in his hand. "'Rearrange the dear nun.' He means shuffle the letters around to make another word. If we do that, it might help us decide what to do next."

Gardener wasn't happy. He knew at the moment it wasn't a full-on investigation: that there was no body, but he was trapped here because it *could* be serious — so he had to do something.

He stared at the phone, willing himself to figure it out. The light-bulb moment came when he thought about the trapdoor.

"I've got it."

"Go on," said Reilly.

"The trapdoor, jumble up the letters, and you get the word 'underneath'."

"Sounds good to me."

"Might be a trap when we get down there. What if he's rigged the place with explosives?"

Reilly hesitated but still answered positively. "I don't think he has. He wouldn't run us ragged just to blow us up. He wants us to find the answer."

"To prove what?"

"At the moment," replied Reilly, "I don't know, and I don't care. I'm going back into that shop, the one that's full of tools. I'll grab an angle grinder and grind that fucking lock off. At the end of the day, boss, if there is someone down there then our first duty is to preserve life."

Gardener didn't think about anything else. "You're right."

Before entering the shop, he ran over to the pool car and searched around for an item he desperately needed – a Faraday Bag. It was slightly bigger than a Walkers crisp packet and made of a shiny metal foil. The phone was bound to be part of an ongoing case, but until the tech boys could download all the information, he would have to treat it as live. The bag would allow him to read the contents without altering it. If another text message came in and forced the last one to drop off, no one would be very pleased.

Once inside the shop, Gardener slipped back around the counter. Reilly found what he wanted before ripping apart the box.

"Christ, Sean, couldn't you find a bigger one?"

Reilly laughed, connected the blade to the machine, plugged it in and set to work.

Within five minutes the job was done. The padlock was no longer a problem, and access was theirs.

Chapter Ten

Gardener slowly lifted the hatch.

The first thing that hit him was the smell, the unmistakable sour stench of bodily fluids and blood.

As he carefully dipped his head into the room, he noticed a number of cardboard boxes. They had all been neatly stacked according to size, and the floor was very clean, as if it had been swept regularly.

"Sean, pop back to the car and grab three scene suits, will you? Judging by the smell it's serious."

Reilly returned and within minutes they were suited and booted. The Irishman nodded and took the first tentative steps into the cellar below. Gardener followed, with Gary Close in tow.

The room was lit. On the wall opposite the opening, the naked body of a man had been crucified, using pretty big screws from what Gardener could see. His head dropped towards the floor, and his body hung limply upon the cross.

Gardener wondered if he'd been alive while he was being fixed to the wall.

Reaching the corpse – and he was pretty sure by now that the man *was* dead – would not be a problem. The rustling of the paper suits created an eerie atmosphere as they made their way to him. Gardener could hear the distant sounds of traffic outside.

"Jesus Christ," said Gary Close, bringing his hand to his mouth.

Reilly turned. "Do that outside if you're going to."

Gardener approached the body very slowly. He could see no signs of life; the man's chest was not rising and falling, and he could hear no breathing. Then again, he wouldn't: the victim's lips had been sewn together.

"There must be a mirror in here somewhere, Sean."

One was soon found and passed over. Gardener held it under the victim's nose. He then tested for a pulse, which confirmed the man was very definitely dead.

With Reilly one side and Gardener the other, they searched the room for something that might give them a clue as to what had happened. Peering at the body, Gardener noticed puncture marks in his arms.

"Is he a user, Sean, or has this been done to him?"

"I think he's a user, boss. Look at the veins. There's a bit of damage where he's tried to find one. If someone had done that, I'm pretty sure it would be more clinical."

Gardener stared at the small, sutured wound in the area of the abdomen. "I wonder what the story is there."

Reilly leaned in a little closer. "It looks fresh. Do you think someone is harvesting organs?"

"I hope not, but it's a big business."

"Dangerous as well."

"And a lot of misery to go with it, especially with the rampant poverty in some of the lesser-developed countries."

The DS studied two white envelopes placed against the wall above the victim's hands. "What do you make of these?"

Gardener was itching to take them down and see what they revealed, but he was reluctant to contaminate the scene any more than they already had.

"They're obviously significant. But I think it's time we called in the team. Let the SOCOs do their job. We need to find and speak to Mr Armitage, and set up an incident room, the closer the better. So the station at Bramfield will be our best option."

"We'll also need to call in your friend and mine," said Reilly. "Good old Fitz, and his bespoke body removing friends."

"God help us," replied Gardener, smiling. Despite Fitz's offhand manner, he was very probably the best Home Office pathologist in the country.

Reilly turned to Gary Close. "Don't happen to know him, do you?" Gardener lifted the head of the deceased.

"Yes," replied Gary Close. "His name's Alex Wilson. He lives in the flat above the shop. Albert Armitage is his uncle."

Chapter Eleven

Gardener had spent the last hour bringing his team up to speed, with actions including an inner and outer cordon around the shop and a chat with the two officers from Bramfield – PCs Nice and Graham. Everyone else had been given door-to-door duties. By the time they were leaving, Steve Fenton and his team had run the scene tape around the area.

He now studied the police station as Reilly brought the pool car to a halt outside.

It was a huge building that resembled a town hall, or a Methodist church. There were four steps leading to the front door, flanked either side by Grecian pillars, with mock battlements. Above the front door was a wrought iron canopy with potted plants that suggested the second storey was still in use. The windows were old-fashioned wood, not double-glazed, and the exterior was surrounded by lamps with gas mantles, which was probably more for effect.

Once inside, Gardener smelled lavender and furniture polish, and saw a middle-aged cleaner hard at work. She simply smiled as he passed.

Gardener and Reilly flashed their warrant cards and introduced themselves to the desk sergeant.

"Good to meet you at last, Mr Gardener, Mr Reilly. I've heard such a lot about you." The desk sergeant offered his hand. "I'm Maurice Cragg."

"Maybe we'd best leave now, then," replied Reilly.

Gardener sensed Cragg was close to retirement. His features were solid and dependable, and the detective suspected that was probably a good measure of his character. He had close-cropped, iron grey hair, and a hard, rugged complexion – his face pock-marked. He was stocky, but not fat.

Gardener asked if there was somewhere they could talk, and Cragg took them through to the back room. He mentioned that although he was officially off-duty, he had no wife and family to return home to, so he was happy to put in an extra few hours to help.

Gardener and Reilly explained what they had found so far, and the fact that he would like to take over the station for the investigation.

"What can you tell us about Old Man Armitage, Maurice?"

"He's a bit of a legend round these parts. Been running that business most of his life. Shop belonged to his father. He came into the business when he was fifteen. It's a very old-fashioned place, run in an old-fashioned manner. You won't find any computers in there, keeps everything in his head."

That wasn't what Gardener wanted to hear. It would certainly slow down the investigation.

"So he's not likely to be involved in this, in your opinion?" asked Reilly.

Cragg's expression could have frozen an active volcano. "No, Mr Reilly, not a chance."

Gardener noted his opinion. "Okay, Maurice let's get things sorted here and maybe you can give him a call. He needs to know what's happened and we need to speak to him."

Chapter Twelve

Graham Johnson lost his concentration for only a couple of seconds, less than the time it took to blink. The blade of the screwdriver slid forward, bounced into the guts of the phone he was working on, then somehow jumped clear and scraped across the ball of his left index finger.

"Bollocks!"

Graham hurled both screwdriver and phone across the room, where it bounced off a bench and disappeared behind the rest of the mess in the shop. That was the third one he'd ruined, and it wasn't even ten o'clock.

What the hell was wrong with him?

After he'd checked his finger and decided he would live, he glanced in the direction of the items he'd thrown. He'd never see them again. The benches were covered with hard drives, keyboards, tower carcasses, speakers, and monitors.

Some would ask how he could ever find anything in such a godforsaken place. Finding time to clean would be a bonus. But business was booming, and it was all his. Everyone that came to him did so through word of mouth. He was very good at what he did, and he didn't rip people off.

If his work was so profitable, why then did he not hire himself a cleaner, his mother had asked on more than one occasion. The answer to that one was pretty simple. Who in their right mind would want to attempt to clean up the mess he'd created? He had spent years making it; it'd probably take even longer to fully straighten out. That aside, though, he valued his privacy, and didn't relish the intrusion into his work environment.

It wasn't as if he couldn't put his hands on any of the things he really wanted. That's what surprised most people. Customers often entered, and the expression on their faces was one of such distaste that he could almost read their minds. They were trying to invent an excuse to leave: wrong shop; I've left my wallet at home; I don't think you'll have what I'm after. He'd heard them all. Within minutes however, he could overcome even the most awkward interaction with his devastating repartee and his charming manner.

Graham glanced at his watch and made his way to the back of the premises, deciding it would soon be time for his morning cuppa and a daily dose of the pop quiz on the radio. He'd have no problem finding that; it was the one item he refused to throw around no matter how foul his mood.

Graham eventually returned to the shop with tea and biscuits. He located a free stool and switched on the radio. The station was midway through playing one of his favourite oldies, *We're Through* by The Hollies.

The bell to the front door pinged, and in walked two likely lads carrying a laptop. They were of school age – though why they weren't attending classes today, he had no idea. Neither one of them could have weighed more than seven stone wet through. Both were wearing T-shirts, with faded denims that had vertical slits all the way down. Both had ginger hair and wore glasses.

The song on the radio finished and the DJ announced the quiz was about to start.

"You do know what time it is, don't you?" said Graham to the pair. The brothers glanced at each other and then said "No" in unison, leaving Graham to ponder if the rest of their meeting would be spent the same way. He lifted his biscuits and pointed towards the lads as if he were holding a loaded shotgun.

"It's quiz time. But if you guys behave yourselves, I'll let you stay. If you manage to answer the questions correctly, I may even let you have a biscuit. And if you answer one that I can't, then you can tell me why you've brought the laptop in."

The brothers glanced at each other with concerned expressions, perhaps wondering what to make of the idiot with the biscuits.

"Do you understand the rules, boys?" asked Graham.

"Yes, sir," replied one, nervously.

"Good, then let's get started."

Graham edged up the volume. The DJ had finished talking to his contestants and started on a first-round question, which was considered easy. "How is Elaine Bookbinder better known?"

Graham pointed to the brothers. "And your answer is?"

The brothers were clueless. They simply shrugged their shoulders.

"It's Elkie Brooks," said Graham, delighted that he was right when the DJ confirmed the answer.

The brothers relaxed for the rest of the quiz and earned themselves two biscuits each. All three had laughed about what they did and didn't know, though that wasn't much in Graham's case. The final question however, earned the ginger ringers – as he'd nicknamed them – some real respect, because Graham was stumped.

"Whose stabbed head appears on the front cover of her first solo album?"

Excitedly, one of them shouted, "I know that." He even put his hand in the air.

"Go on, then, clever-clogs," replied Graham.

"Debbie Harry. My dad has that album."

"Give that man a medal," shouted Graham, switching off the radio. "So, now you've redeemed yourself, and eaten half my biscuits, let's get down to some serious business. What's wrong with the laptop?"

Expressions grew serious. "We don't know," said one.

Graham pulled out a job sheet. The shop may have a resembled the aftermath of an explosion, but he still worked to a system, and that meant crossing the 't's and dotting the 'i's.

"Okay, suppose you guys take it from the top. Tell me your names, addresses, and phone numbers. I'll take down all the details, and we'll see what we can do."

Although he'd discovered they were called Richard and Roland, he couldn't tell them apart to save his life, so he didn't address either of them personally. After he'd filled in the form, he continued with the questions.

"So where and when did you start to have problems?"

They seemed to take it in turns to answer. "Yesterday," replied one of the boys.

"What happened?"

"We were on the Internet," said the other.

"Doing what?" asked Graham. Neither wanted to answer that one.

"Come on, you'll have to tell me eventually. You know I'll find out anyway."

"It's not our computer, mister."

"What? You mean you've stolen it?"

"No, it's our dad's."

"And where's your dad?"

"Away on business."

"Till when?" Graham asked.

"Saturday."

"And let me guess, he has no idea you've been using it."

"Well, he knows, he said we could do our homework on it."

"But you weren't using Google for the answers, were you?"

"Not really."

"So come on, out with it. You'll have to tell if you want me to fix it." Graham offered them another biscuit each and finished his cup of tea. "Have either of you been on sites you shouldn't have?"

With a defeated expression and a lowering of heads, they admitted they had.

"Which ones?"

They reeled off a whole load of names that he wasn't happy with, but at the end of the day it appeared to be straightforward porn. "And I'm not going to find anything illegal on here, am I?"

"What do you mean?"

"Anything involving children or animals?"

"No, no, honestly, mister, there's nothing like that." Both of them had spoken at once and completely out of sync, so it sounded like a jumbled mess.

Graham believed them. "Okay, so you were surfing the Net, looking at boobs and things, and then what happened?"

"It just stopped working."

"Stopped working, how?"

"It started playing up, flickering screen, funny sound," said one.

"Then it just went blue and started buzzing," said the other.

"Oh my God, you didn't get the Blue Screen of Death, did you?"

Neither seemed to have a clue what he was on about, obviously not as up on computer talk as they had imagined.

"It looks like it," one replied.

"That could be serious, guys. Even if I can fix it, I doubt very much I'll be able to get it back to its original state without your pa knowing. Something will be different, and it won't be long before he finds out. And it won't be cheap."

"He's gonna kill us," one said to the other.

Chapter Thirteen

By the time Gardener and Reilly had made some headway, the residents of Bramfield were going about their business. All except Armitage's, that was.

To his credit, George Fitzgerald, the Home Office pathologist, had arrived within half an hour of Gardener's request, and so too had most of his team. Once he'd briefed Fitz and was happy that the scene had been secured to his satisfaction, the scenes of crimes officers had been given specific instructions to tear the place to bits.

Albert Armitage had visited the premises and handed over the keys: he'd said he would see Gardener and Reilly at the police station once he had informed his wife of what had happened. Although technically a suspect, the officer in charge didn't for one minute think Armitage would do a runner. He did, however, send a junior officer with him.

From the station, Gardener had made phone calls: one to the FSS at Wetherby, requesting a scientist; one to MIT – the HOLMES operators – to meet him at Bramfield police station to set up an incident room.

Maurice Cragg greeted them as they walked in.

"You'll be needing a cup of tea, sir?" Cragg asked, although it was more a statement.

"Breakfast as well, Maurice, if you can sort something out for us."

"I certainly can. There's a bakery about fifty yards from the station. One of the lads can take an order for us all and nip down there."

Gardener hadn't realized how hungry he was until then. He'd pretty much jumped out of bed and left the house within ten minutes. His shirt, suit, and tie had all been pressed and hanging ready, but food had not crossed his mind.

"Thank you." Gardener passed over ten pounds. "I'll have something healthy, and whatever you and Sean are having. Whilst junior runs out for the order, can you show me around?"

"Certainly," said Cragg, with a puzzled expression.

"I'd like to run the investigation from here. I've called in the HOLMES operators. We'll need a room with sufficient trunking, and enough power sockets for all the internal computers. And a separate room for the investigation team, which we'll also use for briefing and debriefing."

As Cragg was about to leave, another officer appeared. Gardener hadn't seen him earlier. He stood about six foot four, had a trim frame with short dark hair, blue eyes, wire-rimmed glasses, and a pencil-line moustache. He spoke with a Welsh accent.

"Sergeant Williams, sir. The daytime desk sergeant," said Cragg.

Both men shook hands, and Williams said he would be happy to do anything he could to help.

Gardener turned to Cragg. "Maurice, are you okay to stay a while longer? I really would like to try and keep the original team together for as long as I can."

"I told you before, sir, it's not a problem. I don't have to rush off."

Cragg showed Gardener and Reilly a large conference room at the back of the building that could not be seen from the front. It was about twenty-foot square, with a linoleum floor, four desks, plenty of power outlets, and even a screen and projector. It was sufficient for what they needed. Reilly said he would stay there to greet the HOLMES team and start the proceedings.

Cragg showed Gardener another ground floor room, which he could use for his own team, some of whom had already started arriving.

"What's upstairs?" asked Gardener.

"We use the upstairs mostly for storage, sir," replied Cragg. "We have files in a couple of the rooms, and we have another room for all the usual rubbish you collect. The cleaner keeps her stuff there."

A young constable appeared with everyone's breakfast. There were two dozen sandwiches, all of which smelled mouth-watering but no doubt contained enough cholesterol to kill a dinosaur. Gardener spotted his healthy option almost immediately: a fruit cocktail, plus a granola and yoghurt mix.

He asked for them to be taken to his incident room. Once breakfast was over, all his team – along with Cragg – gathered there with him.

Gardener stood at the head of the group in front of a blank whiteboard.

It took him twenty minutes to describe in detail the scene as he and Reilly had found it. Only when he'd finished, did he open the floor to questions.

"Is there any information about Alex Wilson yet?" asked Frank Thornton, probably the most experienced officer he had. Thornton was tall and lean, and reminded Gardener of a POW. His hair was never free of dandruff.

"No. PC Close identified him. We know he lived in the flat above the shop, which is owned by his uncle, Albert Armitage. Sean and I will be speaking to the old man shortly."

"He's just arrived, sir," said Cragg. "I've shown him to an interview room and given him a cup of tea."

"And he's involved with drugs?" asked Bob Anderson, Thornton's partner, perhaps his complete opposite. Bob was well fed, well read, married with children and grandchildren, but equally as dependable.

"PC Close said he was. Which reminds me, where is Close?"

"He's here as well, sir," said Cragg.

Gardener picked up a felt pen and started to create an ANACAPA chart, which would help show all the connections and relationships between each scene once HOLMES started throwing out information. He labelled Scene 1 as the basement, Scene 2, the victim, and Scene 3, the shop. As an afterthought, Wilson's flat became Scene 4.

"You mentioned a wound, sir," said Colin Sharp. "Any ideas?"

Gardener knew Sharp would pick up on that. He was probably the most dedicated member of the team. Sharp had proved invaluable in the last two major investigations; he was very thorough and had an unrelenting passion for digging into a person's past.

"At the moment, no. Sean and I discussed it, but until the pathology report lands on our desk, we have no idea whether or not he's been in hospital recently, and if he has, what for."

"But it's doubtful," said Sean Reilly. "If he had, it's bloody likely he'd still be in there."

"I'm having some photos run off, so before you go, take a copy with you. Someone will have the chance to visit the local hospitals in the area. There can't be that many. Show them the photo, and ask if anyone recognizes him as having recently been admitted. We might get lucky. However, there are a number of high priority actions to be getting on with."

Gardener glanced at Sharp. "Colin, I'd like you and Dave Rawson to head the investigation on the shop. It's going to be a long, drawn-out affair, because old man Armitage didn't have a computer, nor an electronic till."

"Christ! Is he running Beamish?" replied Rawson, the team's biggest individual. He was a rugby centre forward for one of the local squads on his spare weekends. He had short black hair, a beard and moustache, and strong square teeth.

"You might well wonder by the time we've finished. Anyway, I want you to identify the last customer, the top ten regular customers, and anyone purchasing items connected to the inquiry. By the time we've finished it should *look* as if the shop has been run on computers."

"Any news about what was in the envelopes near the victim?" asked Thornton.

"No, but I've told SOCO I want them as soon as possible. I'm hoping we can see them before you lot leave here."

Gardener turned his attention to Paul Benson. Despite only being twenty-three, Benson had been with Gardener for six months, and was proving to be an asset, not the least of which because his girlfriend, Natasha, was a legal secretary.

"I'd like you to head the team conducting a house-to-house of Bramfield. I want a list of all the locksmiths and tradesmen in the area, and get someone to talk to all of them. Have they used the shop recently? Have they bought anything connected to the inquiry, or done jobs for anyone that they might think is connected?

"Patrick, I'd like you to join Paul Benson and his team, but before you do, Sean will give you the registration of a fancy black car that was seen early this morning in Bramfield. Find out who it belongs to and pay them a visit. See what they were up to so early. Could be nothing, all very innocent, but I want to know."

Patrick Edwards was the junior member of his squad: a twenty-one-year-old fresh-faced constable who had an earring in one ear that no one was pleased about. Gardener felt that he would make good one day.

Gardener turned to Thornton and Anderson. "Can you two start looking into Alex Wilson's life? You know the drill, find out everything you can about him.

"Hopefully, we'll build up a victimology of Alex Wilson. Find out who his friends and family are, if he has any. We'll check his computer and bank accounts as well, if he has any of those, and we'll look at pre-convictions.

"Whilst you lot go about your actions, Sean and I are going to interview Albert Armitage and Jackie Pollard. I think Pollard most definitely will be a known offender. We picked him up at the scene of the crime a little after four o'clock this morning. He looked as if he'd been there quite a while, but he claims he hadn't. It's a safe bet his prints will be all over everything. He's also a known drug dealer. We'll interview him after we've spoken to Armitage."

Gardener turned to Maurice Cragg and introduced him to the rest of team.

"Maurice is local to the town and the station and has been here all his life. Make good use of him. He probably knows everything there is to know about everyone. In other words, Maurice is your local human search engine. He might even let you call him Craggle."

That raised a laugh, which pleased Gardener. So far, there had been very little to smile about. He felt as if he'd put in a full day already, and they hadn't yet reached lunchtime.

"And Maurice, in my absence, will you please look after the ANACAPA chart? Sean and I have a lot to get through today, and I'd appreciate it if I could entrust that task to you."

"Be my pleasure, Mr Gardener," replied the desk sergeant, who seemed to be really enjoying himself, as if the unusual incident had brightened up his life and given him a purpose.

A knock on the door interrupted the meeting. Cragg opened it, and Gardener recognized one of the SOCOs. He held out four clear, sealed packets.

"Mr Fenton, sir, said you needed these as soon as possible."

Gardener thanked the officer before he left. Inside two of the clear wallets were the white envelopes that had been pinned to the wall close to Alex Wilson.

Gardener didn't know whether to feel pleased or not. They might mean a boatload of extra work before they had even started. The problem might then be the amount of men he would be allowed to work on his other tasks.

He asked for his team to come up to the board as he opened the envelopes and pinned their contents to it.

It was Sean Reilly who spoke first. "That one's easy enough, boss. It's a tarot card. I think it's The Fool."

Gardener sighed. The investigation had now taken a wrong turn, not that there was ever a right one.

"Okay, we'll talk about that later. And the other?" he asked.

No one spoke. Expressions remained blank.

The card was oblong, approximately three inches by two, and featured a character by the name of Inspector Catcher. He was wearing a trilby, was clean-shaven, and what could be seen of his hair was dark. He stood with a stance of authority, and wore a long plain overcoat. He was holding his arm out, and in his hand, he held an ID card. A little balloon from his mouth said 'You're Nicked!'

Gardener showed his team the reverse side of the card, which had one word in the centre, 'Murder' in a fancy font, with an hourglass underneath and a patent number.

It was plain to see that no one had a clue what the card was, or what the hell it belonged to.

Chapter Fourteen

After his team had left, Gardener realized it would not be an easy case to crack. But then, were any of them?

Reilly was in the corner of the room on his mobile. Gardener asked Cragg if he could arrange another round of tea for them both. As Cragg returned with the tray, Reilly concluded his conversation and flipped the phone shut.

Gardener and Cragg sat, and Reilly joined them. The room was clean and pleasant, with large windows affording a good view of Old Bramfield Road. On the walls hung prints of the town from bygone days. The cleaner had placed a couple of dishes of potpourri on the window ledges.

"What do you know about tarot cards, Sean?" asked Gardener.

"Not as much as Laura."

Laura was Sean's wife, and Gardener had almost as much respect for her as he had for his partner. She was a terrifically independent woman, and had probably been as much help to Gardener as his sergeant following the death of his own wife, Sarah.

"And you know what she's like," continued Reilly. "She can talk for Ireland."

"And you can't?" replied Gardener.

"Yes, but all my conversations make sense."

"That's a matter of opinion."

Reilly scoffed. "You used to be such a wise man."

Gardener laughed. "That was before I started working with you."

"Anyway," replied Reilly, having the good grace to know when he was beaten. "I described the card in detail."

"And?"

"The tarot is a set of cards used for divination. They give an insight into the unknown, predicting the future."

"So we could add clairvoyants to our list of suspects?"

"Maybe. Laura explained that there are different sets of cards. There's Major Arcana, which is what we have, and Minor Arcana, which look like playing cards. They all have meanings, either upright or reversed. Though what our suspect had in mind, I'm not sure."

Gardener sipped his tea. "We might find that out when we know Wilson a little better."

Reilly continued. "The upright meaning signifies beginnings, most probably of journeys. Could be mental, physical, or spiritual."

"Judging by what Wilson has gone through, I'd say it was all three," replied Gardener. "And the reversed meaning?"

Reilly referred to his notepad. "Impulsive action, ill-advised risks, rash decisions. Foolishness, gambling... the list seems endless."

"All of which describes Alex Wilson," offered Cragg.

Gardener thought for a moment. "So, could we be looking for someone who knew the victim, and is pointing out problems he's had with Wilson's personality? Maybe he's justifying his actions – to himself – for something that happened in the past? An incident that involved a bad decision Wilson made, in keeping with the card's meaning?"

"Probably," replied Reilly. "Once we know what's going on, we might find the card fits Wilson perfectly."

Gardener stood up, put his hands in his pockets and stared at the second card on the board, 'Inspector Catcher'.

"What about that one?"

Reilly joined Gardener. "I've no idea, boss. I haven't seen anything like that before."

"Looks like a card from a board game to me," said Gardener.

"That card up there isn't from any board game I've ever seen," said Cragg, "and I've seen most."

Gardener turned to face the desk sergeant. "But how many board games are there on the market?"

"Nothing that's new, boss," Reilly replied. "Most games are electronic these days, and usually online."

"I want copies of that card for the next meeting in the incident room."

"He could also be telling us something else," offered Reilly. "Like the fact that Wilson got away with something big in the past, and we didn't put him away."

"You may be right, Sean. Maurice, what do you know about Wilson?" Gardener asked, finishing his tea.

"A bit of a waste of space. He didn't just live above the shop, he also worked for Armitage. Part-time, mind. He was hot-headed, argumentative; didn't think things through. I reckon he used drugs as well as sold 'em, because he was always edgy around people. Could never stand still, or sit still, for that matter. One of those people who constantly shook his leg. Would drive you bloody mad when you were interviewing him. He was always trying to make a fast buck, bend the rules wherever he could.

"From what I can gather his parents disowned him years ago; it was a bit of a family secret. Never did find out what for. Armitage took him on because no one else would. Nobody would employ him. Blood's thicker than water. I suspect old Armitage didn't want to see him out on the street."

"No hints about the family secret?" asked Gardener, convinced that drugs – more than anything else – would be the likely reason.

"There were rumours, of course, but nothing definite. He's got previous. First time we saw him was on a robbery charge, with violence. There were a spate of 'em on chemists in the area, Bursley Bridge, Ilkley, Bramley.

"Anyway, he broke into the one in the town here, about seven year ago. The old chemist was still working. In the back room, stock-taking, had the lights in the shop switched off. Wilson got a surprise. The old man put up a good fight, but he finished up with busted ribs, a broken jaw, and lost the sight in one of his eyes. I reckon Wilson took him for dead.

"He did a stretch in Armley, which is where I reckon he met Lance Hobson. We've arrested Wilson a couple of times since, selling drugs to schoolkids, dealing in the local pubs."

"Who's Lance Hobson?"

"He's the main man, the real dealer. From what I know, Wilson was Hobson's runner – gofer, if you like. So the big man might well be behind all this."

"A disagreement, maybe? Perhaps Wilson was trying to take over?" offered Gardener.

"I doubt it very much, he hasn't got the bottle," replied Cragg. "But the other one you've dragged in, Pollard, he's a different kettle of fish. He's big enough to take Hobson on. And there's been rumours that he wants to."

"Does he now?" replied Reilly. "That's interesting. Could be one reason why Pollard was at the scene."

"Criminal returning to the scene of the crime? Pollard might well be our man," said Gardener. "If he wants to take over Hobson's empire, what better way than to take out the people on the inside? Where can we find Hobson?"

"I'm not sure," replied Cragg. "He lives in a big house out near Harrogate. I can get the details for you. Tell you the truth, I haven't seen him for a while."

"Please, Maurice," Gardener replied. "Get me everything you can on all three, Hobson, Pollard, and

Wilson. And find out who they shared cells with, if you can. Sean and I are going to talk to Old Man Armitage. I think we've kept him waiting long enough."

Cragg headed for the door, when Gardener stopped him. "Just one more question. Do you think the old man knew about the drug habit?"

"I've no idea, sir. I don't think he's been working for his uncle all that long. But I do have it on good authority that he was using the company van for his ill-gotten gains of late. Like I said, blood's thicker than water. Maybe the old man was trying to straighten him out."

"Someone certainly has," replied Reilly.

After Cragg left, Gardener used his mobile phone to call Fitz to see if there was any news on the post-mortem. The pathologist's assistant said he was still working on the body. Gardener put his phone back in his pocket.

"What do you think, Sean?"

"Same as always, boss. It's an open playing field."

"I know what you mean. Too many people fit the bill. I don't like the tarot card, but I can't for the life of me see why a clairvoyant would want to kill Wilson."

"The other way round might have fit better. Someone as rash as Wilson having their fortune told might not like what they hear. I reckon that would be enough reason for him."

"Maybe, but it's unlikely someone of Wilson's calibre would want to know in the first place."

"Doesn't strike me as your traditional drug killing," offered Reilly.

"An old man who runs a hardware shop doesn't really fit the bill either. He's far too old to have carried out that one. Without help, anyway."

"I wouldn't disagree with that."

"There is one other possibility," said Gardener.

"Go on."

"The stitching. It's clean, looks reasonably professional..."

Cragg popped his head round the door and interrupted the two detectives.

"Thought you might like to know, the computer's just pulled up pre-cons for Jackie Pollard. Amongst other things he was a trainee doctor, thrown out of the NHS for stealing drugs.

Chapter Fifteen

Albert Armitage was already seated by the time Gardener and Reilly stepped into the room they were using to conduct interviews. Gardener would have preferred more comfortable surroundings for the old man, but they had decided to use a standard cell with recording equipment. Other than a table and four chairs, there was very little else.

Armitage stood, raised his hand and tipped his hat. "Good morning to you, Mr Gardener."

He was dressed in a camel hair coat that seemed as if it had been bought only yesterday, but Gardener thought otherwise. He was the same height as him, but more chunkily built, with grey hair, grey eyes, and a grey moustache. Although he had a nose and a mouth like everyone else, his face seemed featureless. His gestures, however, said to Gardener that they probably had a real character on their hands.

"You too, Mr Armitage."

Both detectives shook hands with him before taking a seat.

"I apologise for the hospitality," said Gardener. "You are not under arrest, but we would like to record the conversation if you're okay with that."

"I have nothing to hide, Mr Gardener," replied Armitage, his arms folded.

Armitage removed the expensive camel hair coat and was now dressed as if ready to open his shop. He wore a beige-coloured smock that bore the stains of his trade: grease, paint, and oil to name but a few. Underneath the overalls, Gardener noticed grey trousers, and a pair of black brogue shoes.

"I appreciate that," said Gardener. "It's possible you'll say something that we might later have to come back to."

"No doubt I will, Mr Gardener. I must say I wouldn't like your job."

"There are times when *we* don't like it, but it's not all doom and gloom. We have our fair share of rewards along the way."

Armitage simply nodded, as if there was little else to add. For a seventy-year-old man, he was doing well. His grey hair was still thick and wavy. He had very few lines on his face. From what Gardener could tell, his teeth were his own. His physique suggested he didn't miss many meals either. Not that he was fat, more hale and hearty.

Gardener started the tapes and introduced Reilly, then asked Armitage about his life and the shop.

Armitage turned the tables almost immediately. "Mr Gardener, are you going to tell me what's happened?"

"In good time, Mr Armitage."

"You drag me out of bed quite early this morning and I've been here for some time now, but you don't tell me what's going on? I think that's a little unfair."

"To be fair, you're here of your own free will. We haven't kept you, but we do have good reasons for not telling you anything at the moment," replied Reilly.

"I'm sure you do," Armitage said with a sigh.

He kept his arms folded. Gardener suspected he was holding up well and would probably continue to do so, even when he found out who and what was in his basement.

"You can see for yourself, Mr Gardener. My place would be well-suited to *Last of the Summer Wine*, or *Open All Hours*. It's a very old-fashioned place, and it's run the way I like it. The way my father used to run it before me."

"How long has the business been there?" asked Gardener.

"Since 1939. Despite being old enough to join the war effort, my father was not fit. He was turned down by the Army. That was a blow to him. He wanted to serve king and country. He told me many a time that he and my grandfather used to talk often, and it was *his* father's dream to run his own business, selling tools and everyday items. Stuff that people were always going to want. When my grandfather died, he left my father a tidy little nest egg, enough to buy that place and live out the dream."

"When did you join him?"

"When I was fifteen, straight out of school. It's all I've ever known, and I know it well."

"Has it always been you?" asked Gardener. "No partners?"

"No, sir, always me."

"You made a reference to running it just the way you like it. I take it by that you mean you like the old-fashioned methods? I notice there are no computers."

"Don't need computers, Mr Gardener. I come from good stock, with good memories. I know where everything is, and what I have in there. I keep my stock records on cards, not a computer."

"Where are they?"

"The big cabinet with all the drawers, behind the counter."

"I thought as much. Your suppliers, you know them all well?"

"All of them, by name."

"Any problems with them?" asked Reilly.

"What do you mean by problems?"

"Anything. Faulty stock, late deliveries, the usual sort of thing."

"It's the nature of the business, Mr Reilly. You're always going to face things like that, but we're all adult enough to get over them. I've been dealing with my suppliers for years. We know each other well enough to sort things out amicably."

"What about your customers, Mr Armitage?" asked Gardener. "Do you know those as well as your suppliers? Do *they* talk things over when there's a problem?"

"What are you getting at?" replied Armitage, leaning forward.

"I'm not getting at anything. You're helping me with my investigation, and in order to do that I'd like you to answer my questions."

Armitage sighed. "Once again, usual run of the mill stuff. You can't run a business without it. If we sell faulty goods, we replace them, without question."

"Okay, so there are faulty goods now and again. Any disgruntled customers?"

"Not my regulars, they understand as well as I do. New customers may not be so patient."

"And on that subject, have you had many new customers that would cause you concern for any reason?"

"None that I can think of."

"Anyone asking strange questions that don't fit with the business?"

"That could mean anything," replied Armitage. "Someone asking for directions wouldn't really fit with my business, but I wouldn't have a problem with it."

"I meant something more specific. Maybe it was a bad example. What about people asking for strange or unusual tools?"

Armitage thought for a moment, but had to eventually say that he could not recall anything.

"Any recent disagreements you can think of regarding pricing, or the returning of a faulty article?"

"Like I said, Mr Gardener, we replace faulty goods immediately. As for pricing, well, you're always going to have competition. But I like to think I sell quality goods, charge a fair price, and offer a good service. Anyone who thinks any different is quite at liberty to shop elsewhere, but we won't fall out over it."

"I presume you have a lot of trade customers," said Gardener. "Any of them have accounts with you?"

"Only the ones I can trust. You have to remember, Mr Gardener, it's a small business. I can't afford to let too many people have credit."

"And those that have settle on time, do they?" It was only the second question Reilly had asked.

"Yes."

"Any financial problems?" asked Reilly.

"Do I look as if I have financial problems, Mr Reilly?"

"Never can tell, Mr Armitage."

"I don't pay myself unreasonable bonuses. So, if you want a straight answer, no, I do not have any financial problems."

"It's a nice spot you have there, Mr Armitage," said Gardener. "Ideally placed for all the local business and the passing trade. Anyone approached you wanting to buy the place?"

"As a matter of fact, there are a number of companies that have shown some interest, especially for when I decide to retire. In fact, one of my trade customers said he would like first refusal."

"Before you go, we need a list of those customers, in particular the one who's interested in taking it off your hands."

"Certainly. Are you going to tell me what this is all about now?"

"Who has keys to the shop?"

"Just me and Alex, apart from a spare set my wife keeps for emergencies."

"Is the building alarmed?"

"Yes."

"Who knows the codes?"

"Same again, me and Alex and my wife."

"Alex Wilson? Your nephew?"

"Yes, have you spoken to him?"

"No."

"Well, when you do, tell him I'd like a word."

"When was the last time you saw him?"

"Back end of last week, lazy little tyke."

"And how did he seem?"

"Same as always. He's a bloody airhead, can't keep his mind on any one thing for too long. You have to keep at him if you want a job done."

"Did he seem nervous about anything?"

"You obviously don't know him," replied the old man. "He was always nervous."

"Any idea why?"

"He's always been like it. You get used to it after a while."

Gardener knew the time was fast approaching when he was going to have to break the bad news to the old man.

"What do you keep in the basement?"

"Mostly empty boxes, some excess stock, nothing else."

"You have no safe down there? No money, or anything of any financial value?"

"No. Do you mind if I have a cup of tea, Mr Gardener? It's dinnertime, and I'm partial to a mid-day drink."

"Not at all," he turned to Reilly. "Can you organize that please, Sean?"

"What did your last slave die of?"

"Answering me back," replied the detective.

Reilly laughed but did as he was asked.

"So, to come back to the basement. If you have nothing of any value down there, you wouldn't need a padlock, would you?" Gardener said.

"Not at all."

"So, you definitely didn't use one?"

"No."

Gardener produced the empty box from the combination padlock he'd found on the trapdoor, sealed in a forensic bag.

"Do you recognize that, Mr Armitage?"

"Looks like one of mine, top of the range job as well. An ABUS 190. There should be four in stock. Where did you find that?"

"On the floor of your shop behind the counter. The lock itself was attached to the trapdoor. The hasp had been fixed with round-headed bolts, the nuts underneath."

It was the first time Gardener had seen an expression of concern on Armitage's features. "That was on the trapdoor leading to my basement?"

"I'm afraid so."

"Well, it's not my doing, Mr Gardener. For the first time in thirty years I actually took a break this weekend. Me and my wife went to visit my sister. She lives on the east coast, Whitby. She'd been nagging us to go for long enough. My wife reckoned it was high time I relaxed a little. So, whoever did that had to have done so between Friday and Sunday."

"Can you give us your sister's details, address, phone number?"

"If I need to."

Reilly returned with teas and a plateful of chocolate Hobnobs. Gardener glanced at them. "You've just had breakfast."

"That was ages ago. Anyway, I'm a growing lad, so I am."

"Which way?"

Gardener glanced at Armitage and passed his tea over. "Sorry, please carry on."

Armitage did so. "See what happens when you take time off and leave the place to someone else? Wait till I see that bloody nephew of mine. I'd like to know what he knows about this."

"When exactly did you last see him?"

Armitage thought for a moment. "That would have been Thursday night. He should have turned up for work on Friday, but I saw nothing of him."

"Does he normally take days off without your consent?"

"He's family. He feels he has a right to."

"Does he ever contact you when he is off?"

"Sometimes, but he's not that far away, is he? You've had a good look around my place. I suspect you know by now where he lives."

"Did you try and contact him on Friday?" asked Gardener.

"I knocked on his door a couple of times, but there was no answer."

"Try his mobile?"

"Only once. It went to answer-phone. 'Leave a message.' I left him a bloody message alright."

"Was he supposed to open the shop on Saturday?"

"Yes."

"Did you check to see if he had?"

"It was my first weekend off in thirty years. Quite frankly I could afford to lose the trade if he wasn't there. What I couldn't afford to do was upset my wife. You've not seen my wife when she's angry, have you?"

Gardener could guess.

"When did you return from Whitby?"

"Sunday night."

"Did you check to see if he was around?"

"No, it was a bit late. Has something happened with Alex? Has he been up to something I should know about?"

Gardener avoided the question and pressed on. "Does he have a track record for getting up to no good in your absence?"

"I reckon you've done your homework, Mr Gardener. He has had his problems."

"And you've stuck by him when others wouldn't. We do happen to know that he had a disagreement with his parents, but we don't know over what. Can you tell us anything?"

Armitage sipped his tea, as if he was buying time till he thought of an excuse. Or working out how much to actually tell them. Gardener knew what people from close-knit communities were like. Family secrets stayed buried for generations.

Armitage put his cup back on the table. "Someone hasn't missed an opportunity to talk, have they?"

"It's a small town."

"Well, I don't feel inclined to air my dirty washing in public. Let's just say he brought the family name into question."

Gardener felt the old man needed a gentle little nudge. "You do realise anything you say here will be treated confidentially?"

"I dare say it will, but what about a little quid-pro-quo? Isn't it time you told me what was going on? It is my shop."

Gardener glanced at his partner.

"It's your call, boss. He'll have to know sooner or later."

"Know what?" asked Armitage, leaning forward. "Has he done something to my shop I should know about?"

"There has been an incident, Mr Armitage, and we fully intend to tell you everything, but if you can bear with us a little longer? We'd like some background on Alex. How long has he worked for you?"

"About a year, maybe a bit longer."

"What does he do?"

"Well, he's not full time. I employ him for three days a week, but he has the use of the flat above the shop rent free, and he gets the van. He serves in the shop now and again. He runs to and from the suppliers to collect stock when I need him to."

"Does he have a girlfriend?"

"Not that he's talked about."

"Does he have many friends in general?"

"Couldn't tell you, we don't socialize much. But one or two of them have come into the shop to see him."

"What are they like, his friends?"

"Pretty much like him. Not the best dressers in the world. Some of them don't have jobs, but they still do okay. Beats me, that one."

"None of them seem unusual?"

"In what way?"

"Pushy, threatening behaviour? Are they all there?"

"Most of them seem pretty normal. Some of them are what I'd call 'out of his league'."

"What do you mean?"

"Suited and booted. One comes to mind, well dressed, a bit flash, big car. I've seen the casual exchange of money. I turned a blind eye. I suppose it's his little problem, but I think things are under control now. He doesn't like to talk about it, and I don't push him."

"Do you know his name, this friend who's out of his league?"

"I've heard the name 'Lance', that's all."

Gardener made a mental note to pursue that one. He had to mean Lance Hobson. Gardener intended to track that man down.

"A little problem?" pushed Reilly, sitting a little more to attention.

"Yes, Mr Reilly. We all have them. It was one of the reasons his close family disowned him a few years back. They couldn't cope with the shame. Chucked him out. I suspected things got worse. I do know he spent a bit of time in prison, but they do say you shouldn't do the crime if you can't do the time. I squared up one or two of the debts, and then took him under my wing. I think it's all behind him now. He's got it under control."

"Let me get this straight," said Reilly. "You know what he's up to, yet you turn a blind eye?"

Gardener had to admit he was surprised. Armitage had seemed as straight as a die. He figured they would learn something, but he never expected a revelation of such magnitude.

Reilly pushed on. "You employed him, put a roof over his head, practically gave him everything he needed to operate, and you call it a *little* problem?"

"Well, what would you call it, Mr Reilly? We all make mistakes. Learning from them is the important thing."

"Selling drugs to school children is classed as a mistake in your books, is it?"

"Drugs?" Armitage said.

It was the second time Gardener had seen such an emotional response. He now realized that they had not been talking about the same thing. So, what the hell was the other problem?

"Who's talking about drugs?" asked Armitage.

"We are," said Reilly. "What are you talking about?"

"Gambling."

"Gambling?" repeated Gardener.

"Yes, Mr Gardener, gambling. Our Alex has a betting addiction. Horses, dogs, online bingo, you name it, he'll put money on it. Like I said, I squared up one or two of the debts and then gave him a home and a job, which is why I thought it was under control."

Gardener suddenly wasn't so sure that Armitage would be able to take what they were going to say.

"Would you care to elaborate on this drugs business?" asked Armitage. "Are you going to tell me something that I need to prepare myself for?"

The moment had come.

"Mr Armitage," said Gardener, softly. "I'm afraid I do have some bad news for you. There *has* been an incident in the shop, and it does involve your nephew Alex."

"Go on," pushed the old man.

"I'm really sorry, but we found Alex this morning in your basement."

It took a little time for the dust to settle and the penny to drop. "Dead?" Armitage asked.

"I'm afraid so."

"How?"

"We don't know the details yet, but from everything we've pieced together it would appear to be drug related, which is why we wanted to see how much you knew before we told you."

Armitage stayed silent for a few moments. Gardener noticed his eyes turn a little red-rimmed, coming to the conclusion that there was no truer statement than the one Cragg had made earlier about blood being thicker than water. For all his nephew's wrongdoing, Alex Wilson was still Armitage's family, and probably pretty close judging by the emotion.

"Would you like some time to yourself?" Gardener asked.

Time did pass before he replied. "No, Mr Gardener, I would much rather press on and get this whole nasty business out of the way, so that when I leave here, I know I'm done."

"If you're sure."

"I am, but I just hope there are not too many more questions."

"Not really, no. Do you know someone called Jackie Pollard?"

"I've heard the name, but that's all. Is he another of these druggies?"

"Let's say he has more than a passing interest. I just wondered if there had been a connection between him and your nephew."

"I couldn't tell you," replied Armitage. "How long has it been going on, Mr Gardener? The drugs?"

"We can't tell you just yet. I'm sure you're aware he's done a couple of stretches in prison?"

"Yes, but I thought that was robbery and violence, all of which I put down to his gambling addiction. You're going to tell me different, aren't you?"

"The first term may have been what you thought, the others don't appear to have been."

"So he must have been at it years," Armitage was talking to himself. "Why the hell didn't someone tell me? I could still have helped, but I would have sought a professional. There's a very good surgeon near to where I live, Dr Sinclair, he would have helped. He deserves a knighthood, that man, especially for how he's helping Gary's mother."

"Gary?" asked Gardener.

"Gary Close. I feel sorry for that young man."

"Is his mother ill?"

"Brain tumour from what I hear, but she's in the best possible hands."

A silence descended in the room.

Gardener rose from the table. "Mr Armitage, I'm sorry to have broken the news to you. I think it might be best if we leave you for a short while to gather your thoughts and come to terms with your loss. If you'd like someone to accompany you home, please just say."

Armitage nodded.

Before Gardener reached the door, he turned to face the old man.

"Just one more thing. We'd like to hold on to the shop keys a little longer, at least until we've finished our investigation."

"That won't be a problem, Mr Gardener. You can keep them forever, for me. I won't be setting foot back in the place. Wife's been nagging me for years to retire. I reckon now's as good a time as any, don't you?"

Chapter Sixteen

Gardener and Reilly were back in the incident room after the SIO had introduced himself to the officer in charge of HOLMES, a man named Mike Sands.

"What do you think, Sean?"

"I think the whole thing has been well planned, judging by what the old man had to tell us."

"I agree. Somebody's been watching the shop for a while. Had to have known Armitage was away for the weekend."

"Not only that," said Reilly, "he knows Alex Wilson very well. Think about the tarot card and its meanings."

"I have done, Sean, especially the reversed meanings. He was impulsive, took risks, made rash decisions. He was a fool, and gambling was involved."

"Most of which was backed up by Cragg. He said Alex was a waste of space, hot-headed, argumentative, didn't think things through."

"He also said he was edgy around people. Armitage confirmed the gambling. Everything we've found out this morning was covered by the tarot card."

"In other words, that card tells us just how well the killer knows his victim."

"Looks that way to me," said Gardener. "The killer obviously knows the victim well, but is he trying to lead us astray?"

"Make us *think* there's a darker side to it?"

"Possibly. It might all hinge on what's inside Alex Wilson's mouth, if anything. Why was it sewn up?"

"Who's to say there's anything in the mouth? What's behind the suture might be more important."

"If there's nothing inside the mouth, why sew it up?"

"To keep him quiet?"

Reilly had a point. Gardener was itching to read the pathology report, but he knew Fitz well enough to know you couldn't hurry him. It was a specialized job. Fitz was the best he'd ever come across. He could be cranky, but he was good at what he did, and Gardener had worked with him for more years than he cared to remember. That alone allowed the old man some liberties.

Gardener's thoughts were distracted as Sergeant Williams knocked and entered the room carrying a file.

"Got some interesting reading on Jackie Pollard, sir. We took his outer clothing for a fibre match from the scene, and gave him a black light scan. We also gave him a live scan for fingerprints, not that it was necessary. He's well known to us. The SOCOs lifted his prints and put them into FISH, which then loaded them onto NAFIS. He was definitely inside that shop. We're still waiting on fibres."

"Thank you..." Gardener hesitated. Cragg had introduced Williams but not given a first name. Gardener asked.

"David, sir. Everything we have on Pollard is in the file. He definitely has form, sacked as a trainee doctor and taken to court by the NHS for stealing drugs."

"Was he sentenced?"

"Yes, but he had it reduced by his brief, Wilfred Ronson."

"Not that old soak," replied Reilly. "He's more twisted then a corkscrew."

Gardener smiled. They'd come across Ronson before. He was a solicitor who seemed to specialize in cases that very few other people would touch. Stood to reason he would represent drug dealers. It was common knowledge that he was a drunk and he was bent, but the latter had been almost impossible to prove.

"Is there any connection between Alex Wilson and Wilfred Ronson?" Gardener asked.

"I believe so," said Williams.

"Thought there might be. Who was the arresting officer when all this happened?"

"Peter Browne," replied Williams. "But that was a long time ago, and I'm afraid Browne is no longer with us now. Died of a heart attack about three years ago, brought on by the drug dealers of this parish, I shouldn't wonder."

Gardener was disappointed. Reading the file probably wouldn't tell him everything he wanted to know. First-hand contact was always better; you usually picked up gut feelings, which were not always in the report.

He suddenly remembered the packaging from the padlock that he'd shown Armitage. He passed it to Williams.

"Can you get that tested for prints?"

"Yes, sir. Any rush?"

"Yes, I'd like to know if Pollard's are on there. It would be nice to have the results before we finish interviewing him."

"Not a problem, I'll get straight on to it. Oh, and before I go, we've also included the data from Pollard's phone in the file. You'll find that extremely interesting."

Gardener turned his attention to the file.

At thirty-eight, Pollard was older than the detective had first imagined, so the offence he'd committed as a junior doctor was quite some time back. The kind of drugs he'd stolen fell mostly into the category of prescription tablets, but he'd also lifted amphetamines, and even morphine. Gardener knew all too well how saleable the latter was.

The report covered the interviews he'd had in custody, and the fact that Ronson had attended every single one of them. It was interesting to note that Pollard would not say a word without Ronson present. And even with his solicitor there, he had not told anyone why he had committed the offence, despite the obvious reasons.

The value of the cache was probably somewhere around five thousand pounds net, and none of it had ever been recovered. The court records informed Gardener that the drugs were mostly smuggled out, although there was also evidence of fraud. The original sentence had been ten years, but Ronson had managed to reduce it to five.

The file contained evidence that he was still dealing while in prison, where Pollard sustained a very serious injury, one that nearly caused the loss of his right eye. The usual thing, it happened in the shower room late one night, and no one saw anything. Both prisoners involved were isolated afterwards.

Following Pollard's release, he had not served another prison sentence, but what he'd been doing since was anyone's guess.

Gardener passed it to Reilly and started to update the ANACAPA chart himself.

"This is interesting, boss," said Reilly.

Gardener finished with the chart. "I think I know what you're going to tell me."

"The incident in the showers?"

"Yes. Seems our friend Pollard was muscling in on an existing drug scam inside, trying to take over."

"And look whose patch it was."

"Lance Hobson."

Chapter Seventeen

Gardener and Reilly sat opposite Jackie Pollard. The Senior Investigating Officer judged his height to be around six foot two. He had piercing brown eyes – well, one of them was – and a head of thick black hair. Despite knowing about the eye problem, Gardener couldn't help but concentrate on it. The scar was now nothing more than a two-inch white line. He also registered that the man only had half an index finger.

"I'm not saying anything without my solicitor." Pollard was on the attack immediately, tapping on the table in front of him.

"Quite right, son," said Reilly. "I don't blame you."

Gardener nodded, and Reilly slipped out of the room and back in again almost immediately with a cordless phone.

"There you go," he said, placing it on the table.

Pollard hesitated before speaking again. "I'm going to show you two up for the amateurs that you are. I haven't done anything."

"Why the solicitor, then?"

"Because I don't trust you. Have you got my mobile? I need the number."

Gardener fished one of Wilfred Ronson's business cards out of his pocket, instead of the one that Williams had given him.

"No need, Mr Pollard, we already have the number for you."

The change of expression was minimal, but Gardener noticed. Maybe he'd managed to rattle Pollard earlier than he'd anticipated.

When Pollard made contact, he asked to be put straight through to Ronson. There was a pause before his expression changed again, to one of concern.

"Well, where is he?" he asked. "When's he due back? Wednesday's no good to me, sweetheart, I need him now."

Whoever he was speaking to had obviously explained why that was not possible, and Pollard ended the conversation by demanding that Ronson call him first thing Wednesday morning. He replaced the receiver and was about to make another call when Gardener interrupted him.

"Not so fast, you know the regulations. One call only."

"You're wrong, I'm allowed at least two."

"Unless I believe that we may be able to prevent injury or death to someone else. Now put the phone down."

Gardener switched on the tape recorder and introduced everyone in the room.

"I've told you, I'm not talking without my solicitor."

"Who isn't available," replied Gardener. "Would you like a duty solicitor?"

"You must be joking," smirked Pollard, continuing to tap on the table. He seemed fairly cool, but Gardener suspected that feathers were about to be ruffled.

He rose from his seat. "In that case, you can stay here until Wednesday morning and we'll talk to you then. If he returns."

"You can't do that!" Pollard was on his feet.

"Sit down," ordered Reilly.

"Yes we can," said Gardener. "We'll apply to the Superintendent for an extension." He headed for the door.

"I haven't done anything," shouted Pollard.

Gardener turned. "Talk to us, then. Last chance!"

Reilly also stood up, prepared to leave.

Pollard sat down and sighed. "Okay, you win. I'm innocent, and you'll soon see that. Quicker we get this over with, the quicker I get out of here."

Both detectives sat back down, and Gardener once again introduced everyone for the benefit of the recorder.

He placed Jackie Pollard's file face down on the table. He also removed Pollard's phone from his suit pocket – sealed in an evidence bag – and dropped it onto the floor near his seat.

"Right, Mr Pollard. What were you doing outside the shop?"

"I've told you, I was out for a walk."

"That's right, you said you couldn't sleep."

"So why do we need to go over it again?"

"Because I'm having a geographical problem," replied Gardener. "You see, you say you were out walking in Bramfield at four o'clock in the morning, yet you live about eight or nine miles away in Holt Park."

"I didn't say I lived in Bramfield, I just said I was out walking. I'd been staying with friends."

"You've actually got some, then?" asked Reilly.

"Unlike you, I haven't blown all mine up."

Reilly laughed. "Quite the comedian," he said to his partner. "Let's see if he's still cracking jokes when we've finished with him."

Gardener continued. "Well, before you go, you won't mind supplying the name and address for us to follow up."

Pollard stretched back in his chair and yawned. "Don't think the husband will take too kindly to that, if you get my drift."

"That's not my problem," replied Gardener. "Back to the shop. How long had you been out walking?"

"A few minutes. I was coming across the car park when I saw you lot arrive."

"So you hadn't been near the front of the shop?"

"No."

"You never noticed that it was open?"

"How could I?"

"And you never went inside?"

Pollard shook his head, inched forward, and rested his elbows on the table. He was dressed in a plain black T-shirt, dark blue jogging bottoms, and black plimsoles. Standard issue custody clothing.

"This is getting boring."

"Oh, I am sorry," replied Gardener, picking up the file and pretending to study it.

Reilly turned to Gardener. "We can't have that, now, boss. You must watch your manners and change the subject. With no solicitor present, we don't want him claiming harassment now, do we?"

"Not at all, Sean." Gardener switched his attention back to Pollard.

"Nasty scar you've got above the right eye. How did you get that, Mr Pollard?"

"You do know this is illegal?" said Pollard.

"What is?" Gardener asked.

"No solicitor."

"No it isn't, and it's your choice. Let's get back to the scar."

"It was an accident."

"How did it happen?"

"I slipped."

Gardener noticed that Pollard's answers were becoming shorter.

Reilly took over. "Have to watch those wet floors in Armley, son."

Pollard said nothing, so Reilly continued.

"Ten-year stretch, you must have been a bad lad."

"Five, actually."

"Let's cut to the chase, Jackie, lad. We know all about the stretch in Armley, so we do. You were sentenced to ten years for stealing drugs from the NHS. You were very lucky that you had a solicitor almost as bent as you who managed to knock it down to five with good behaviour, though God knows what that constitutes from a drug dealer."

Gardener continued. "While you were in there, you thought you could continue with your nasty little trade. But then you met Lance Hobson."

During the silence that followed there was a polite knock on the door. Sergeant Williams appeared and asked if he could have a word.

Gardener noted that Reilly was leaving the room for the benefit of the tape.

Reilly quickly returned and called Gardener over to a corner, where he informed him that the SOCOs had found Pollard's shoes matched the same pattern as footmarks lifted off the floor inside the shop. But there were no fingerprints of any description on the padlock packaging.

Pleased, Gardener returned to his seat. "Let's talk about the NHS."

"It's in a terrible state. That's the government for you."

Gardener leaned forward. "Let's forget politics and small talk. As you said, the quicker you answer our questions, the quicker you can leave."

Pollard smiled. "I thought you picked me up on a burglary charge, yet you come in here asking all sorts. So far, none of it to do with the charge I'm here for."

"How observant. NHS, what were you doing for them?"

Pollard sighed and sat back, arms folded. For a short while, Gardener thought he had decided to shut up shop, so *he* maintained the silence as well.

"I started as a junior doctor."

"Interested in that sort of thing, are you?" asked Reilly. "Anatomy?"

"Well, I must have been."

"Were you specializing in anything?" asked Gardener. "Any particular field?"

"To start with, it was general medicine. My mother died when I was ten years old. My father was a bastard, a drunken bastard..."

Gardener had not expected the change of attitude. Pollard was cooperating, so he didn't interrupt.

"He used to beat me whenever he got the chance, no fucking reason. I spent that much time repairing myself, I started to enjoy it, found something rewarding in it." Pollard stopped talking for a moment before adding, "How sad is that?"

"So what made you want to continue?"

"My mother. I realized after a while that he must have beaten her, too. She often had cuts and bruises, which she used to tend to herself. She taught me a little bit of first aid. The interest went from there. I read books, and thought maybe it would be a good idea to become a GP."

"Which hospital did you apply to?"

"St. James's, where else?"

"How many years did you train for?"

"About five. Started as a junior doctor, passed through a training grade to house officer, and spent a lot of time in general surgery."

"So, what the hell went wrong?" asked Reilly. "Sounds to me like you had a damn good career lined up. Why did you blow it?"

Pollard sighed heavily. "Why does anyone blow it? Money's crap, hours too long. I got greedy. I was introduced to another side of the medical world. Saw just how rich I could be with only half the effort."

Gardener brought the subject back to the hospital. "How would you describe your surgical skills?"

"Pretty good. They were training me to be a surgeon. They even expected I'd study further, become a member of the Royal College of Surgeons."

Gardener figured he'd struck gold, not insofar as having the killer handed to him on a plate, but he reckoned he'd found a subject that Pollard would talk about freely and without losing his temper. However, he had what he needed, so now it was time to change things. From the file he'd read, he knew the rest, and preferred to tackle another subject.

"Tell us about Lance Hobson."

Lighting the touch paper was how Gardener would describe the difference. From Pollard's expression, there must have been some real hatred between the two of them, suggesting that Cragg had been right when he reckoned that Pollard wanted to take over the patch.

"What do you want to know?"

"Whether or not you know him, for a start," replied Gardener.

"Of course I know him, and you know that. You already know that he was behind the incident in the showers."

"And that was because?"

"We didn't see eye-to-eye."

"I doubt you'd see eye-to-eye with anybody," said Reilly. "You've only got one good one."

Pollard ignored the jibe, but his expression could have halted a tsunami.

"Is that because you both wanted the same territory?"

"I'm not a drug dealer," said Pollard.

"The records show different, Mr Pollard. You've been inside for stealing drugs, a net value of over £5,000 to my knowledge. None of which was ever recovered."

"Once a dealer, always a dealer," Reilly continued. "Come on, Jackie lad. What's the crack with Hobson, if you'll pardon the pun? Who supplies who?"

Pollard leaned forward and started tapping the table again. Gardener also noticed one of his legs was shaking. A clear sign he was agitated.

"I do not work for Hobson, or with him."

"Is there a money problem, then?" asked Gardener. "The connection between you two – does one of you owe the other money?"

"What the hell is this? Why are you asking questions about Lance Hobson?"

Gardener switched topics again. He knew he had Pollard irritated, and felt he needed to keep the pressure on.

"Know anyone named Sonia?"

"Pardon?"

Gardener made a point of rifling through the file before asking again.

"Sonia. Do you know anyone named Sonia?"

"I don't think so."

"Strange," said Gardener, lifting Pollard's phone from the floor, placing it on the table. "Judging by your phone records, I'd say you know her very well. Sonia Knight."

Pollard remained quiet.

"Come on, Jackie lad, you're being less than honest with us. If you don't tell us the truth, it'll take much longer to sort this mess out. And do you know what I'm thinking?" Reilly deliberately left the question unanswered, waiting for Pollard.

"Do tell me," he finally replied.

"That if you're not telling me the truth over Sonia Knight, you probably haven't told us the truth about anything else we've asked you."

Gardener leaned forward. "And you know what that means, don't you? We'll have to keep going round in circles until we're completely satisfied. And you might never get out of here."

"Don't want that, do you, Jackie lad?" said Reilly, grinning.

Pollard pointed half an index finger at Reilly.

"Stop taking the piss, Irishman."

"That would look more dangerous if it was a whole finger."

Pollard stood up fast and his chair crashed to the ground, but the Irishman was much quicker.

"Sit down, Pollard! We've told you once already." Reilly held Pollard's stare, and the ex-con finally picked up the chair and sat back on it.

"You stand up once more, and we're out of here," said Reilly. "And you can wait for your solicitor. Do you understand me?"

Pollard nodded, and Reilly mentioned it for the benefit of the tape.

Gardener wasted no time. "Sonia Knight."

Pollard's foul mood continued. "It doesn't matter who she is."

"Oh, but it does," said Gardener. "It matters to me and DS Reilly, and we want to know what you know about Sonia Knight. Who is she?"

After some time, Pollard answered. "She's the friend I've been seeing in Bramfield. You know, the one whose husband won't like me giving out the details."

"You're lying, Pollard," said Reilly.

"What?"

"I said you're lying. We know damn well that she doesn't live in Bramfield."

"And so do you," said Gardener.

"Well, if you know that, why do you need me to tell you?"

"One more chance," said Gardener. "And believe me, I am not bluffing when I say we're out of here until Wednesday."

Pollard hesitated, and Gardener eased his chair back a little.

"Okay, okay. She's Lance Hobson's girlfriend."

"See," said Reilly. "Didn't hurt, did it?"

"What's the connection between you and Lance Hobson's girlfriend?" Gardener asked.

"We're good friends, nothing special."

"It will be if Hobson finds out."

"He's not going to, is he?"

"I wouldn't put money on that," said Reilly. "Now, stop lying. Why are you seeing her?" When Pollard didn't answer, Reilly continued.

"Is it because you want revenge for what he did to you in prison? Is he muscling in on your territory, Jackie lad? Maybe you're not seeing Sonia Knight in the way that she thinks. Maybe you're using *her* to set *him* up for something. Take over his patch."

Pollard shook his head repeatedly, and Gardener knew they were on to something.

"Or maybe," continued Reilly, "you're setting them both up. You intend to get rid of them both. That way there's no opposition."

"What vivid imaginations you two have."

"Comes with the job," said Gardener. "It's very difficult dealing with scum day in, day out, without some of it rubbing off." He decided to switch topics again to keep Jackie on his toes. "What about Alex Wilson?"

Pollard seemed a little more alert. "What about him?"

"I've just asked you that."

"What are you talking about? I don't know anything about Wilson."

"Yes you do," replied Gardener. "You're at it again. I've already told you we have your phone records here."

Gardener held up the file. "We know you've been talking to Sonia Knight. We know she's Lance Hobson's girlfriend. We also know that Alex Wilson has a connection to Lance Hobson, and so do you. What we're struggling to piece together is why your phone calls from Sonia Knight have dried up. She hasn't called you in a month. Until last night, that is. The very night that we find Alex Wilson's body at the shop, and you outside it."

Gardener had lit the touch paper again.

"What?"

The fear in Pollard's eyes told Gardener everything he needed to know. The man was very definitely guilty of something, and it would only be a matter of time before he could determine what.

"What are you talking about, Alex Wilson's body?"

"Let's finally come full circle back to the shop, shall we? I've given you every opportunity to do so. Didn't think I'd leave it, did you, Mr Pollard?

"You told us earlier that you hadn't been in the shop. You were lying to us. We have evidence. Fingerprints, although in your case not all of them, shoe prints, and now Scenes of Crime tell us there is a fibre match from your clothing. Do you still maintain that you have not been inside?"

Pollard remained silent.

"We know for a fact that Alex Wilson is dead, because we found his body in the cellar below the shop."

"Very nasty, that was, Jackie lad," said Reilly. "Looked to me like he'd met with a terrible accident."

"Bits of him were missing," said Gardener. "Areas that had been stitched up..."

"Just a minute." Pollard was on his feet quickly, and the chair fell over once more.

Reilly was soon up as well. "We've told you, no more standing. Pick that chair up, and do it now!"

The cocky attitude had all but left Pollard as he quickly did what he was told. "I've killed no one."

"Doesn't look like that to us," said Gardener. "From the information we have, we reckon you've been plotting something with Sonia Knight, something involving Lance Hobson's right-hand man, Alex Wilson. She takes a month out, and then phones you to tell you it's all on, and you do the deed."

"It's not like that," shouted Pollard.

"No, maybe it isn't," replied Gardener. "Maybe you've already done away with Knight, and that was someone else phoning you tonight."

"I haven't done anything to Sonia Knight. How many more times? I haven't killed anybody." Pollard stared at them.

"Go on," said Reilly.

"I haven't seen Knight for a month. I have no idea where she is. She suddenly stopped contacting me. I don't know, maybe Hobson found out, and he's sorted her out."

"In which case, you'll be next," said Reilly. "Maybe we should stop worrying, boss. We'll just leave Hobson to sort this scum out for us."

"I'm not so sure, Sean." Gardener glanced at his partner. "Hobson couldn't have butchered Alex Wilson. Why would he? They were close friends."

"Which leaves us with you again." Reilly stared at Pollard.

"It's not me, I swear. I might be a lot of things, but I'm not a murderer."

"So, what were you doing outside the shop, and who called you on Knight's phone?"

"I don't know," shouted Pollard, slamming his fists on the table.

"What did they say?" demanded Gardener.

"Not much. They just said if I went to the shop, I would see something to my advantage."

"And you believed them? Just like that?"

"Not really, no."

"Why?" Gardener asked.

"Because it wasn't Sonia. Well, yes it was her, it sounded like her, but..."

"What the hell is that supposed to mean?" asked Reilly.

Gardener didn't give him the chance to answer before he asked. "Was her voice live, or recorded?"

"How do you mean?"

"Simple enough question. Did you have a conversation with Sonia Knight? Or did she say what she had to, and then cut it short?"

Pollard was thinking. "She only said what she had to."

"Nothing else?"

"No."

"You mean your phone rang, you answered, she told you she'd meet you outside the shop, and then ended the conversation?"

"Something like that. I can't remember exactly."

"Didn't you try to phone her back?"

"No... yes... I don't know, that was when you lot turned up."

"Bullshit!" said Reilly. "You've told so many lies you don't know what you're saying."

"Doesn't it strike you as odd?" Gardener asked. "You plot to take over Hobson's business with Sonia Knight, and then you don't hear anything for a month, and then out of the blue she phones you and tells you to meet her at the shop?"

Pollard said nothing. He was obviously trying to calculate how much trouble he was in by having agreed to talk without his brief.

"Which leaves you with three options, Mr Pollard," said Gardener. "Either Knight is setting *you* up, she's changed her mind, or you got to her first and engineered the rest. Which is it?"

"I have not killed anyone!" Pollard screamed, slamming his fists on the table again. He ran his hands through his hair. He was obviously panicking, but Gardener still felt he hadn't told them everything he knew.

Gardener stood up. "Try looking at this from our point of view. You want revenge on Hobson. You collude with Sonia Knight, but then she decides to go quiet and could very well be missing. Alex Wilson is dead, and you're found at the scene. You're the common denominator, the catalyst, shall we say? That leaves you in a whole stack of trouble. You'd better pray that Ronson doesn't extend his vacation."

Gardener glanced at the tapes. "You'll be with us a lot longer than you thought, Mr Pollard. Interview terminated at 14:00 hours."

Reilly switched the recorder off and collected the tapes. On his way out, Gardener stopped, then turned and walked back to the table.

"Just one more question. We were talking to Maurice Cragg earlier, and he made a comment that I didn't pay too much attention to at the time. But in light of recent information, I'm now very curious."

Pollard glanced at Gardener but said nothing.

"He said he hadn't seen Lance Hobson for a while. So, when was the last time you saw him?"

Pollard didn't answer, but something in his expression told Gardener that was one of the things he was still holding back on. The SIO suspected when they did find out, Pollard would be singing like a canary.

Chapter Eighteen

Iain Ross pulled his car to a halt outside 15 The Mount in Bramfield and switched off the engine. With perfect timing, his mobile rang. The display informed him that it was his secretary, Fiona Barton.

"Hello?" he answered.

"Mr Ross, I'm so sorry to bother you, your wife phoned, said you'd had a visit from the police."

"Really? Is everything okay?"

"They just wanted to ask you a few questions to help with their inquiries, but they wouldn't say what it was about."

"Did they leave a name?"

"Yes, Patrick Edwards. He said he would call back, but if you were in the vicinity of the station in Bramfield, would you mind calling in."

Ross glanced at his watch. He *could* pay a visit, but it would all depend in what condition he found Christine Close. In all honesty, he wasn't expecting good news.

"Was he by himself?" Ross asked.

"Yes, Mr Ross, he was."

"Okay, Fiona, it can't be anything serious, so please don't worry. Once I've finished my house call here, I should have time to see them before afternoon surgery."

Ross glanced at Number 15 once more. It was a two-storey semi-detached with UPVC windows and doors, and a grey slate roof. The garden was neatly trimmed, with a water feature and a bench and a short wall with wrought iron framework.

He'd decided to make an unscheduled call after what he'd witnessed in the early hours of the morning. Considering her deterioration over the last three days, he suspected it wouldn't be long before he would have to hospitalize her.

He collected his medical bag and left the car, exchanging pleasantries with one of the neighbours who happened to pass the gate before he reached it.

The front door opened before he'd shut the gate and headed down the path.

Gary Close ran out dressed in a blue T-shirt and jeans, with nothing on his feet. Ross could see that he was on the verge of tears, very probably a breakdown. His expression was one of surprise.

"Why are you here, Mr Ross?" asked Close. "Where's Mr Sinclair?

Ignoring his question, Ross asked, "Gary, what's wrong?"

"It's me mam. Quick, please, I think she's dying."

Ross entered the house and went straight into the living room. It was clean and tidy and spacious. The walls were decorated with emulsion in two-tone pastel colours; different shades top and bottom, divided by a border. Everything matched, the carpet, the curtains, the light shades, even the cushion covers. The only unpleasant factor was the smell, but that couldn't be helped.

Christine Close had once been an attractive thirty-eight-year-old woman with a head of glossy, shoulder-length black hair, and firmly defined features both in face and body. She was now little more than a skeleton, whose hair and complexion had taken a serious battering due to her grave condition.

His first glance told him she was losing her fight.

Less than six months previous she had been diagnosed with a glioma. Unlike other cancers, a glioma grows in the confined space inside the head, and is particularly damaging because it sprouts and spreads within the brain. Each year, approximately eighteen thousand people are diagnosed with glioma. Most die within twelve months.

Ross placed his medical bag on the floor. Talking to Christine would be impossible because she was having a seizure, her third in three days. Her arms and legs were contracting. She was biting her tongue, and had suffered a loss of bladder control.

"Please, Mr Ross, do something."

"It's okay, Gary. I can give her something to help, but we do need to talk." Ross bent down and prepared the only thing he could, ten milligrams of diazepam.

"Gary, can you please hold your mother's arms? I understand that this really is unpleasant for you, but the quicker we treat her, the quicker we can arrange for something more intensive."

Gary did as he was told but continued to ask questions.

"Will she have to go into hospital?"

Ross injected the diazepam, and then used his phone for an ambulance. Luckily, the Bramfield hospital was only round the corner, so the vehicle would not be too long. The problem, however, was that they were not equipped to deal with her.

Within five minutes the medics were walking through the door, and Ross told them exactly what had happened. He gave instructions to take her directly to the Ross & Sinclair Foundation, which was on the A660, between Otley and Burley in Wharfedale. Ross said he would follow in his car.

He turned his attention to Gary while they were preparing Christine.

"I'm sorry, Gary, I didn't answer you. Yes, I'm afraid your mother *will* have to go to hospital."

"But surely she'll feel much better here. She has her sister to help while I'm working."

Ross guided the young PC into the kitchen and sat him down at the table. "It's for the best. While she's at home, we can't give her the care and attention she needs and deserves. And look at what it's doing to you and your aunt. You're both worn out with it all."

"I'm okay, Mr Ross, really I am. We're coping."

"In a fashion, young man, but look at you. Have you looked in a mirror lately?"

Gary hung his head, as if he was ashamed.

"Gary, please listen to me. You asked where Mr Sinclair was and why he wasn't here. I'm afraid your mother's condition isn't something he can help with. He's not a neurosurgeon. But he has relayed everything he knows about your mother to me and he's asked me to take her case personally, as a favour to both him and you. I want to continue to do my best for your mother, really I do, but I can't do that here at the house. Are you aware that I was here in the early hours of the morning?"

Gary obviously wasn't due to his shocked expression.

"Your aunt didn't tell you, did she? And I don't blame her. She was trying to protect both of you, just as I am."

"Why were you here?" asked Gary.

"Your aunt thought your mother was having another fit. Gary, your mother has had a fit every day this week. What she has is very serious. I've allowed her stay at home much longer than I should have done, but it really is for the best that we put her into the clinic, where she'll receive professional, round the clock care."

Gary broke down and wept openly. The neurosurgeon understood his feelings. Gary thought that because he was a policeman, he would be able to take care of her. He'd repeatedly begged Ross's partner, Robert Sinclair, to leave her at home where he could keep an eye on her, and so could everyone else in the family. They took it in turns, covering the twenty-four hours between them. But they were not professionals. Gary obviously now felt he had let his mother down.

But she wouldn't know. Right now, Ross knew she wouldn't be conscious of anything around her, and experience told him that there was every possibility she would not come out of the latest seizure. But he did not have the heart to tell the young PC, whose world started and ended with his mother. God knew he'd been long enough without a father.

Gary Close raised his head. "Is she going to die?"

Ross felt completely hollow. What could he say? "I'm going to do my best for her, Gary, as I've always done."

The young PC gripped the surgeon's arms. "But Mr Sinclair said all her treatment would make her better. He said it."

"Gary, I understand how you're feeling right now. What was said to you at the time was she would have a much better chance of fighting and surviving with the right treatment. We gave her the best that money could buy."

Ross paused. He was going to have to be really careful with his next sentence. "Sometimes, it isn't enough."

He noticed the change in Gary so he continued. "But listen to me. We're a long way from over yet. Your mother is a fighter. She's not going to give up, and neither am I."

The medics called Ross to the living room. They had made Christine Close comfortable and had installed her into the ambulance. Gary joined them.

"Would you like to go with her in the ambulance, Gary?"

"Are you coming?" His eyes were like saucers. He must have been petrified.

"Yes, of course. I'll follow in my car."

"Where are you taking her, round the corner?"

Ross realized that even though he'd instructed the medics to take her to his own private clinic, Gary would never have heard him say that, not the world he was living in right now.

"No, she's coming to my clinic. They can't treat her round the corner, they're only equipped for minor injuries."

Gary grabbed Ross by his arms again. "But, Mr Ross, it's miles away. She doesn't know anyone. She'll be frightened when she comes round."

"Gary, please, it's for the best. We can see to her needs much better. She has been before. She knows us, and she'll soon get to know everyone else. By the time she leaves my clinic, we'll all be on first name terms."

Gary seemed to accept what he was saying and started to limp towards the ambulance.

Ross noticed and asked if his leg was okay. He'd known about the football injury and the operation that had followed.

Gary nodded but didn't say anything.

In his car, Ross phoned the Foundation and asked them to prepare a private room, supplying the details of the patient he was admitting.

Within ten minutes, after breaking every speed limit in the neighbourhood, the ambulance pulled up outside the Ross & Sinclair Foundation; a very modern, tinted glass and steel building constructed to the highest standards.

The glass was so dark it was almost impossible to see inside.

Two nurses, two doctors, and a gurney were ready, and Christine Close was wheeled into a private side room. It resembled a small country cottage living room, with beams on the ceiling and dark oak skirting, equipped with everything you would expect in your own home: a TV, DVD, hi-fi, small fridge, tables and chairs, and a cupboard. It was en suite. The only addition not found in a home was the state-of-the-art medical equipment.

While the staff made Christine Close comfortable, Ross walked through to his private office. It was also finished in dark oak, with bookcases floor to ceiling containing an extensive collection of medical texts. He had armchairs, coffee tables with copies of *The Lancet* in view, and a large desk with a PC. The room had an open fire, which was currently set with logs and ready to light at the strike of a match. It was also en suite.

He stood against the fireplace, leaning against the hearth with his arms open, defeated. Between them they had done everything they could to save Christine Close's life, but it didn't seem to have been enough.

Before he had time to even consider what course of action to take from here, the door opened and Robert Sinclair entered. He was slim like Ross, due to an excessive workout routine. He had wavy grey hair, and was currently dressed in a blue suit, white shirt and blue tie, and expensive leather shoes. Judging by his expression, he was extremely concerned by what he'd seen.

"How is she?" asked Sinclair.

"Not good," replied Ross.

"Is she conscious?"

"No."

"Where's Gary?"

"He's keeping vigil outside the room."

Sinclair sighed. "I'll be honest, I know it's more your field but I don't think she'll recover from this. The fits are too frequent."

"Don't berate yourself, Robert. We've done the best we could."

"It's not enough, though, is it?"

"You know as well as I do, however we'd have treated her, it would never have been enough. And let's be honest, she's had the very best."

"And I want it to stay that way. Whatever she needs in the time she has left," said Sinclair, "she gets it, and so does Gary. I'll pick up the tab."

Chapter Nineteen

Gardener and Reilly were back in the incident room. Maurice Cragg had joined them; so, too, had Sergeant Williams. Patrick Edwards had completed his little task, and was also with them. Information from his team was being filtered back at a steady pace, because the ANACAPA chart was starting to take shape. Crime scene photographs were pinned to it.

"The fancy car with the private plate, R1 OSS, belonged to a doctor, sir," said Patrick Edwards. "Iain Ross, he lives in Burley in Wharfedale."

"What make of car was it?" asked Reilly.

"A Mercedes."

Although he was no expert when it came to cars, he had not seen one as sporty as that little number. "What model is it?" he asked.

"An SL 400, sir," replied Edwards. "It's a real piece of equipment. A coupe, top of the range."

"Okay for some," said Gardener. "Did you go and see him?"

"Yes, but he was out. His wife was home. Apparently he was on a call here in the town. She also confirmed that he was in Bramfield in the early hours of the morning, attending to Christine Close."

"That's Gary's mum, isn't it?" Gardener asked Cragg.

"Yes, sir, she's seriously ill, by all accounts."

"Armitage mentioned something about that."

"He's well known around these parts, sir," replied Cragg. "A damn good doctor, as is his partner, Robert Sinclair, and *he's* no stranger to tragedy. They have a private clinic, very successful."

"Brain tumour, isn't it?" asked Gardener. "How's Gary coping with all this?"

"Bloody well, if you ask me," said Cragg.

"Is she still at home?"

"No, sir. Gary phoned earlier to say she'd been taken to the clinic."

Gardener made a mental note to speak to Gary Close. God knew if anything happened, Gary was going to need some help, and though Gardener realized it was not his place, he could make sure a word in the right ear would have the desired effect. He remembered all too well the effect of the death of a close family member: your world could crumble instantly. A picture of his late wife Sarah entered his head.

Eager to continue with the investigation, Gardener asked Williams if he had copies of the Inspector Catcher card found at the scene. The sergeant nodded and passed them over.

"Okay, Patrick," said Gardener. "I want you to join Colin Sharp at the shop. I'm sure he'll have his hands full. Before you go, take a copy of this card with you, and see if you can find out anything. I'm sure there's a toy shop in the town."

"I'm on it, sir." Edwards left the room.

Gardener briefed Cragg and Williams on what he and Reilly had discovered while interviewing Jackie Pollard.

"I thought I hadn't seen Lance Hobson for a while."

"Did you find an address for us?"

"Yes, sir." Cragg handed Gardener a slip of paper from a notepad.

"According to our files, Hobson started when he was twelve – stealing cars, breaking and entering. Did a couple of stretches in a young offender's institute. Got into the big league when he was about eighteen, delivering parcels and prospecting youngsters. Seems he shared a cell with Alex Wilson when he spent time in Armley for violent assault."

"What about Sonia Knight?"

"She's another piece of work, sir," replied Cragg. "She lives with Lance Hobson; runs his empire, so to speak. Used to be a duty nurse at one of the private care homes out near Harrogate. I forget the name, but I'll have it before long."

"Interesting," said Reilly. "Another one with medical knowledge?"

"Possibly"

A knock on the door captured the attention of everyone in the room, halting the conversation.

The CSM, Steve Fenton, entered. He had with him two Faraday bags containing two phones, only one of which Gardener had passed him earlier in the morning, as well as a file folder of what Gardener hoped was his findings.

"Come in, Steve."

"Before I start, you're not going to like this. Can I grab a coffee?"

"We have no objection to sharing our coffee," said Reilly.

"Not that, you lunatic."

"Just for that you can only have coffee. No biscuits, mind."

Fenton turned to Cragg. "I should keep your biscuits under lock and key, if you haven't already lost them all."

Cragg smiled and Gardener laughed.

"What have you got for us, Steve?"

Fenton was as tall as Gardener. He weighed around twelve stone, and his features were similar to his SIO. He had short black hair, a rugged complexion, and maintained a reasonably slim physique. Gardener had long since become accustomed to Fenton's eyes, which differed in colour from day to day. The contact lenses had confused him, at first.

Fenton took a sip of coffee and sat down, arranging his treasure trove in order. He held up a clear plastic bag. "This is the good news."

"What is it?"

"A piece of torn cloth, from a pair of Levi's by the look of it. I know it's only small, and probably bloody hard to follow up on, but it's something. We found it in the cellar. About halfway down the steps, there's a nail sticking out. You'd have to be unlucky to catch it, but someone has."

"Excellent," replied Gardener. "Let's get someone on that," he said to Sergeant Williams. "I know it's laborious, but leg-work is like that. It can also be invaluable. Get someone to call on all the local clothes shops, see if anyone recognizes it."

"Could be more difficult than that, sir," said Cragg. "Bramfield is a market town. We might have to speak to the traders, see if they can shed some light. Trouble is, they're not always around."

"That's assuming whoever did it bought them locally," offered Williams.

"It's also possible that it doesn't belong to our suspect at all," said Gardener. "Might be from a pair of Alex Wilson's jeans."

"Sorry to disappoint you, Mr Gardener," said Williams. "But it's possible the torn piece hasn't come from Pollard's clothes either. He was wearing black trousers."

"He was when we picked him up, Sergeant, but I suspect Wilson has been down there for some time, a few days, maybe. So it is still possible that Pollard is our man." Gardener turned to Fenton. "What about prints from the cellar?"

"Only Wilson's and Armitage's so far, sir. None that belong to Pollard, or anyone else that we can find, for that matter, but it's going to take time to go through the entire scene."

"Have we got Armitage's prints on file?" asked Gardener, struggling to believe the old man could have any previous.

"I asked if he'd mind," said Cragg. "Only so as we could eliminate him from the investigation.

Gardener was beginning to like Cragg. He would have been pleased to have him on his team.

"Okay. David," he turned Sergeant Williams, "can you organize a warrant for the search of Pollard's premises? I want his clothes, his computer, and anything else connected to the investigation."

Gardener turned to Fenton. "Wilson's clothes will be easy enough to gather. They should all be in his flat. What else have we found there?"

"Nothing," said Fenton.

"What do you mean?"

"According to Thornton and Anderson, Wilson's flat is empty. Like his phone, everything in his life seems to have been cleared. There are no clothes, no bedding, no towels, or anything personal. No drugs, no cleaning materials. Absolutely nothing. Someone's done a real job on wiping him out."

Gardener glanced at Reilly, but said nothing.

Fenton continued. "The only thing in the flat is a computer, which was probably his, but that's also been cleaned. In fact, the hard drive has been completely removed."

Gardener stood up and paced the room a little. "What the hell is going on here? Maurice, can you ring Armitage and tell him we're sending a car round? I'd like him back at the flat as soon as possible."

Gardener addressed Fenton again. "So, if there *was* something on his hard drive that linked him to his killer, the killer probably knew about it?"

"Either that, or he was taking no chances," replied Fenton. "Maybe you should speak to Thornton and Anderson later on, see what they have found out."

Gardener glanced at the Faraday bags. "Two phones?"

He picked up one of the bags.

"This phone was Alex Wilson's. Like his computer, memory completely wiped, except for one text message. It's short and sweet, and threatening: a little knowledge is a dangerous thing – especially in your case."

"Where did you find that?" asked Gardener.

"In the basement, not far from Wilson's body."

Gardener sat down. Whoever they were dealing with had a high level of intelligence and had been very thorough.

"Any idea where the text came from?"

"According to the search we've done, Sonia Knight."

"Her name keeps popping up," said Gardener.

"Maybe she's engineering everything," suggested Reilly.

Cragg shook his head. "If that's the case, she must be working *with* someone. I don't think she has what it takes to arrange what we've found so far."

"Maybe it's Hobson," said Reilly. "Maybe she's been feeding him everything that Pollard's been up to, and together they're going to sort things out."

"But where does Alex Wilson fit in, Sean? Why would Knight and Hobson butcher him, if their target is Pollard?"

"Maybe he knew something about them," offered Cragg. "Stumbled on something that would implicate them both, which might mean another sentence in Armley. Or at the very least, something he could clue Hobson in on."

"You could be right, Maurice. Especially as the phone's been wiped," said Gardener. "We need to find those two, and pretty fast."

"It is still the same SIM card, isn't it?" Reilly asked Fenton.

"According to the records, yes."

"What about the other phone, the one we found in the shop?"

"Here's the interesting thing. That's Lance Hobson's. The text you got on that one also came from Sonia Knight's phone."

"Has the memory on that one been wiped?"

"No. We've recovered all sorts of messages and conversations that have been recorded and saved. Most of them between Hobson, Knight, and Wilson, but there are others on there as well."

"Okay, I want a full report on all those conversations, and all the text messages. Everything you can find on that phone, I want," said Gardener. "Have you made a list of all contacts?"

"Yes, it's all in the file. But there's something else you might find interesting. All contact between Hobson and Knight dried up about a month ago. There have been plenty of missed messages on his phone from other people, but the first contact Knight made with Hobson in a month was this morning. Probably the message you received in Bursley Bridge."

"Which suggests that either Knight and Hobson are plotting this together…"

"Or someone else is behind it, and he's taken them both out already," said Reilly.

"Possibly," replied Gardener, "but why the message from Knight this morning?"

"To throw us off the scent," offered Reilly.

"There's something very strange going on here," said Gardener. "We have one corpse, the involvement of two people who are nowhere to be found, and only one suspect, and nothing that adds up.

"Okay, Maurice, make the call to Armitage. We'll pick him up and take him to Wilson's flat. After that, we're going out to Hobson's place to see what we can find there. And somewhere during all that, we need to find time to call on Fitz and get the results of the post-mortem.

"Steve, carry on at the shop and see if you can find anything else. And put together a list of all the missed messages on Hobson's phone, so we can do a follow-up. Maurice, when you've called Armitage, I'd like you and Sergeant Williams to update the ANACAPA chart and start going through the list of contacts from Hobson's phone. I need to know what's going on here. The deeper we get, the less information we have."

Chapter Twenty

Robert Sinclair opened the front door and stepped into the plush-panelled hall, sighing loudly. A long, demanding day had taken its toll, and it was far from over. He had two more appointments for his private afternoon surgery.

The floor beneath his feet was parquet, complimented by pale Persian rugs. His walls were wood veneered to a height of three foot. Most of the expensive wallpaper above the dado rail was hidden by a variety of framed oils. There were two portraits, one his late wife, the rest landscapes. The paintings continued up the sweeping staircase and onto the landing above.

The huge Victorian mansion had been left to him in a will by an eccentric aunt. He'd spent some serious money on renovations, which had allowed him to set up his own private surgery. During the refurbishment, Sinclair had discovered that the house had vaults, one of which was large enough to accommodate a wine cellar, which he'd filled with a good stock of fine wines from around the world. In the basement, he'd had a fully functioning operating theatre installed for emergencies.

His housekeeper entered the hall from the kitchen, and in the background, he heard a voice on the radio. He knew from experience it would be Radio 2; she was an avid listener.

"Oh, Mr Sinclair, how are you? You've had quite a long day today."

"I'm fine, Miss Bradshaw," replied Robert, not wishing for any fuss. He simply wanted to finish his timetable, take a shower, and relax in a reclining chair with a glass of Vida Nova.

"Well you don't look it, if you don't mind me saying."

"And I thought I was the doctor. I must be training you too well."

She smiled. "You know what I mean, Mr Sinclair. You work too hard and too long, and you need to take better care of yourself."

He knew she meant well, but sometimes she was intolerable. Still, he put his briefcase on the floor and held her shoulders and smiled back. It didn't hurt to be civil.

"And you fuss too much, Miss Bradshaw."

"Well, if I don't, who will? Now, have you had your lunch?"

It was pointless lying because she knew his daily routine to the minute.

"No, but..."

"Mr Sinclair, that's unforgivable. I'll prepare you something now."

"Ah, ah," he cut her off before she went too far. "It's too late, Miss Bradshaw. I still have a lot of work to do, and two more patients to see."

She was about to protest, but he held up a finger. "Please, not another word. My digestive system won't take it. Afternoon tea with a couple of oat-based biscuits will be fine."

From her expression, he knew she didn't like it, but also knew better than to argue. He was pleased to see her retreat to the kitchen.

He picked up his briefcase and went into his study, where he calmly launched it into a chair at the other side of the room, then clenched his fists.

"Shit!" He was absolutely gutted by how fast Christine Close had deteriorated.

He dropped down into the chair behind the desk, and for one split second, could have swept his hands across the top of it and pushed everything to the floor, such was his anger. He hated to lose control of any situation; more importantly, he hated to lose a patient. But you couldn't have one without the other.

Sinclair placed his elbows on his desk and rested his head in his hands.

Miss Bradshaw knocked and entered the study carrying a tray with herbal tea and oat biscuits, which she placed on the desk.

"Are you sure you wouldn't like anything else, Mr Sinclair?"

"No, thank you, that will be fine. What time are the Bonewells due?"

"Four-thirty."

He glanced at his watch. "Perhaps you'd be kind enough to make them some tea, and explain I'll be a few minutes late."

"Of course."

She turned to leave the study, but he called her back.

"Miss Bradshaw? If I could have my evening meal at seven o'clock precise, please?"

She nodded and left the room.

Sinclair's thoughts returned to Christine Close. No matter how good a brain surgeon Iain Ross was, he could not save her. When Christine had first come to see Sinclair six months previous, she had been an NHS patient at St. James's Hospital. Her symptoms had been severe headaches, nausea and vomiting, all for no reason she could think of.

Unhappy with two opinions, she had tried a completely different surgery altogether, and had even sought out herbal remedies and acupuncture, to no avail. Two months later the symptoms became much more severe, resulting in seizures and cranial nerve disorders.

Sinclair's housekeeper, a close friend of Christine's, had suggested she seek his professional opinion. He'd consulted with Ross and within twenty-four hours the neurosurgeon had diagnosed a high-grade glioma, for which there was no known cure.

There were many anti-cancer drugs around, none of which were cheap. Ross had suggested bevacizumab, and a cytotoxic drug called irinotecan, to be given intravenously every two weeks for a six-week cycle.

But there they had a problem: each six-week cycle came with a price tag of £5,000.

NICE, the National Institute of Clinical Excellence, deemed the treatment not suitable for the NHS because of a lack of evidence for its effectiveness. And because it was too expensive. The local Primary Care Trust's Exceptional Treatments Committee also made a similar decision, and so too had the hospital.

Not without influence, Sinclair was the chairman of the hospital's Drugs and Therapeutics Committee. He realized that new treatments were usually expensive and had very little evidence behind them, but he also argued that you were in a chicken and egg situation. How can you obtain the evidence if you didn't try them?

He made the decision to issue the treatment anyway.

That was three months ago, and the first six-week cycle actually saw a distinct improvement for Christine Close. Both mother and son were happy, until Gary had had his accident. The pressure and the love for her son proved too great and, much to the annoyance of Iain Ross, she missed one of the two-week cycles. Which, in his opinion, was why they were in the position they were in today.

He glanced across the desk and saw the picture of his beautiful late wife, Theresa. The photo had been taken before their son, Adam, had been born, nineteen years ago. How young and glamorous and carefree she had been then; a whole life ahead of them, to do what they wanted, when they wanted. No worries, no troubles. He soon grew bitter, as he had come to realize that life couldn't stay that way, and hadn't done.

No matter how much he hated losing, he simply had to accept defeat once in a while.

After all, neither he nor Ross had been able to save Theresa.

Chapter Twenty-one

Hobson tried to move, but found it impossible. Something was restricting him, even his head. Irritated and frightened, he studied his surroundings, realizing that the room he was in today was different from the one he was in yesterday. He had no idea if it was even the same building.

He was in a cellar or basement, an underground chamber of sorts, as there were no windows. The floor was concrete, the walls bare and unpainted. In one corner he saw a central heating boiler with pipes running up through the roof. He figured it must work, because he was reasonably warm. And he shouldn't have been, because he was naked. He tried to move, succeeding only in twisting and hurting his back. He needed to quit worrying and start thinking.

His body was trapped in a huge wooden frame. His hands and legs had been fed through big thick beams that resembled railway sleepers. Above them, sticking out at angles, were a series of levers. Because of his limited vision, he could not see beyond that, nor how his hands and legs were restrained.

He glanced downwards. Underneath him was a large bucket, obviously for waste. In front of him was a computer monitor, which at that moment was not switched on. A tower unit and keyboard sat on a shelf built into the wooden frame. A foot away from his mouth he could see a microphone.

Who had him, why, and what they were doing, was a complete mystery. He hadn't even seen anyone.

He thought back over the time he had been held captive. To his recollection, it had been approximately four weeks. The last thing he could physically remember was returning to his car at The Harrogate Arms, a beautiful old building on the outskirts of the town, ideally situated to conduct his business. He could not remember leaving, only waking up in a strange and uncomfortable room with a bed, and nothing else. He had been chained to the wall, and had a bucket for a toilet within easy reach. He had also been fed and watered, but not in vast amounts. All of which had been placed in the room while he'd been asleep.

Another thing that had concerned him was his state of health; he had grown progressively weaker in the time he had been imprisoned.

The first seven days had been fine. His problems had started during the second week, where he had suffered serious headaches, and pains in almost all of his joints. For a while he'd thought he'd been forced to take the drugs from which he'd made a prosperous living. He also worried that his food had been contaminated, or that he was coming down with something.

The last week, however, had made him take stock of how serious his condition was. He'd started vomiting and, yesterday, he'd had to put up with bloody diarrhoea. Seeing where he was now, he doubted very much that drugs or food were responsible. Nor did he think he was coming down with anything natural. To top it off, during the course of the last few days, a constant hammering and banging and drilling had driven him almost to the point of madness, as apparently his captors must have been making the very thing he was trussed up to now. At one point he had heard conversation, indicating there was more than one person involved in his abduction.

Without any warning, he felt as if a red-hot poker had been shoved inside of him. Every nerve end burned as if he'd been connected to the mains. Hobson arched his back, his body pulling as taut as the frame would allow. He screeched, his voice hoarse and raw. As the pain subsided, his stomach started to rumble. He knew all too well what that meant.

He desperately wanted to know who had him, and why. The only connection he could make was drugs. There were enough dealers out there, all wanting a slice of the action, each as nasty as the next.

One thing Lance did know was that if the bastard ever made the mistake of letting him go, he wouldn't live very long.

Jackie Pollard came to mind. That man had wanted his territory for some time now. And he also craved revenge for what had happened in Armley all those years ago. He'd never trusted Pollard.

But if Pollard had him, how had he done it? Who had he been working with? And did he have Alex and Sonia, or were they working with him?

No, he couldn't see that. Couldn't accept it. Neither of those two would ever sell him out, so the only conclusion he could count on was that Pollard had all three of them.

Hobson's body had been so wracked with pain, he hadn't realized that something within his environment had changed.

He raised his head a little. It was a small but very significant change.

The computer monitor had come to life.

Chapter Twenty-two

Gardener and Reilly found Fitz sitting at his desk, in an office that was extremely tidy. Folders were neatly stored and labelled and within easy reach. A midi hi-fi sat on a shelf behind him, currently playing something classical, but Gardener had no idea what.

On his desk, next to his computer, sat a fresh cup of coffee, which he'd no doubt made using his expensive machine. If Gardener's memory served him right, the coffee maker had been a gift from Mrs Fitz, priced at somewhere in the region of £600. Apart from a couple of prints on the wall and a framed photograph of his wife, the only other decorative item in the office was a plaque, above and behind Fitz's head which read: *Hic Locus Est Ubi Mors Gaudet Succurrere Vitae.* 'This is the place where death rejoices to teach those who live.'

Gardener liked Fitz because he had a no-nonsense attitude. He wasn't afraid to tell you what he thought, despite your rank. He'd never forgotten the first time they'd met. Fitz had given his car keys to a young, fresh-faced PC – whose SIO was the legendary Alan Radford – and asked him to fetch a parcel from the boot of his car. Fitz immediately opened the package, and to Gardener's horrified amazement it had contained a human heart. He'd felt nauseous for the rest of the day.

George Fitzgerald had an almost encyclopaedic knowledge of his profession, something he'd been practicing for nigh-on forty years. He could – at any given point – quote from almost any criminal file in history when prompted. He had a tall, lean frame, with a wrinkled complexion. Half-lens glasses perched on the end of his nose, which he constantly cleaned due to his work. How they managed to stay on was beyond Gardener.

Gardener sensed the pathologist was very tired. Fitz ran his hands down his face in an effort to wipe away his fatigue. He finished his coffee, reached behind, and reduced the volume of the music.

"How are you getting on?" he asked.

Gardener sat down, pretty tired himself. He gave Fitz a brief summary of the case and the problems it had so far caused.

"Would you like a coffee? It's fresh."

"I'd love one. What about you, Sean?"

"Count me in. I need something to keep me awake. God knows when this day's going to end."

"Sounds like we've all had a bad one," said Fitz, pouring and passing the drinks.

"It's been a bloody long one," replied Gardener. He glanced at his watch. He'd been up and on the case for sixteen and a half hours straight, and what they had so far achieved had been very little: one body, a number of possible suspects, and no evidence to pinpoint the killer with.

Fitz took a mouthful of the coffee. His expression said to Gardener that it was the only thing he'd had today that pleased him.

"What have you got for us?" Gardener asked, hoping the pathologist would provide something positive before they had the final incident room meeting.

"I've been working most of the day on your corpse. Finished about four o'clock and started making the notes. I'll send you the full report through in a couple of days, but there is something we need to discuss that might focus your mind for the next few hours."

"Hours?" questioned Reilly. "That doesn't sound good."

"Depends which way you look at it," said Fitz. "Might not be what you want to hear, but it'll certainly intensify your investigation."

Fitz pointed to his desk. "Ever seen one of those?"

Gardener followed the line of his finger to the object sitting on his desktop. It was a round disc approximately an inch-and-a-half in diameter, and half-an-inch thick. The centre was made of alloy, which seemed to be encased in a white plastic material, with a very long and narrow plastic tube attached to it.

"No. What is it?"

"It's an implantable insulin pump."

"Something to do with diabetes?" asked Reilly.

"Have you been force-feeding him fish?" Fitz asked Gardener.

"I'm not privy to his diet, that's usually constructed and sent straight from NASA."

"Would you listen to the two of you? And will you stop talking about me as if I'm not here? You can hurt a man's feelings, so you can," Reilly said.

"It's unlikely with a skin as thick as yours."

Gardener laughed at Fitz's remark. A joke from the pathologist wasn't a bad sign.

Fitz continued. "That's exactly what it was for, originally. It's an insulin-delivery device that can be surgically implanted under the skin of someone who has diabetes. The pump delivers a continuous basal dose through a catheter into the patient's abdominal cavity. Patients can also self-administer a bolus dose with a remote-control device.

"They were first tried in the 1980s. In America they are still classified as investigational devices, only accessible in clinical trials. They've been available in Europe for quite a number of years."

"And you're telling us this because?" asked Gardener.

"Alex Wilson."

"Was he a diabetic?"

"No."

"Then what?" Gardener asked.

"When I opened him up this morning, I paid particular attention to the abdominal area. The surgical stitching was very recent, fresh, clean, and could only have been performed by a professional. But there was nothing missing. This device," Fitz held up the pump, "or should I say, modified device, had been placed inside his body. The long thin tube had been inserted directly into the largest vein available."

Gardener leaned forward and studied the pump.

"Was it full of insulin?"

"Not at all," replied Fitz. "We're going to have to wait for the toxicology report to be absolutely certain, but there are a number of things I can tell you to be going on with.

"Firstly, it's difficult to say with any certainty what killed Alex Wilson, because he was a known drug user and some of the damage to the major organs will most likely be the effect of whatever he was taking. However, I have found traces of sodium hydroxide in this pump."

"Which is what?" asked Gardener.

"You and I would know it as caustic soda, a household chemical used for unblocking drains. It's a very strong alkali. It attacks metals. Turns fat into soap, which is how it unblocks sinks. It burns skin and damages eyes.

"In this case, the caustic soda was released by the insulin pump. The pain would have been horrific. It damaged the blood vessels, the blood, and then went on to attack the organs that receive the most blood: the liver, stomach, brain, heart, and kidneys. This pump is almost certainly what caused Alex Wilson's demise."

Gardener sat back and sighed heavily, trying to work out how and when that had taken place. "Alex Wilson went missing on Thursday night. I think it's safe to assume that he was back in the cellar on Sunday at some point, or the very early hours of Monday morning. Would that be enough time to do what was done?"

"Certainly, if you knew what you were doing," said Fitz. "And I think there's enough evidence to support the fact that whoever did this was very good at his job."

"So, it had to be someone with medical knowledge," said Gardener.

"Looks that way," said Fitz, rising and pouring another coffee. He offered a refill for the two officers, but both declined.

"Where can you get these things? Is the name of the manufacturer on it, or a model number?"

"Under normal circumstances, yes, we should be able to see that kind of information. They always have a serial number. But, as I said, this one has been modified, and the serial number has been erased."

"And there's no manufacturer's name on it?" Gardener asked.

"No," replied Fitz. "It was probably with the serial number."

"Sounds like our man knows what he was doing. More evidence to suggest a medical specialist," said Reilly. "Any idea who makes them?"

"I'm sorry," replied Fitz. "I deal with dead people, and they have no use for them. It's pretty specialized, but I'm sure some of the doctors at St. James's Hospital would be able to enlighten you."

"There's more to this story, isn't there?" Gardener asked. "You mentioned a modification?"

"Yes. I understand that these pumps are externally programmable. This one has been changed in such a way that it will deliver the substance when it's told to."

"Told to?" repeated Gardener. "How?"

Fitz rifled through a folder on his desk.

"It has a SIM card in it. This thing is working through Bluetooth. It's a technology that allows your computer, monitor, mouse, keyboard, PDA, or anything else with a Bluetooth chip to communicate by radio instead of cables.

"In order to get rid of the cables, companies developed infrared.

"But then things went a step further, and they developed Bluetooth. The devices simply need to be within ten metres of each other. They work by using radio chips. When a Bluetooth device detects another one nearby, it automatically links to it."

Reilly leaned forward. "Like mobile phones?"

"Definitely," said Fitz.

Gardener digested what the pathologist had told them, considering the implications. "So, it's possible that the text to that phone in the shop could have set off the SIM card in that pump to deliver its lethal compound?"

Fitz leaned forward and rested his chin on his hands. "I was coming to that. I think it's very possible."

"And the fact that these things are externally programmable means all this could have been set up and timed to the last second."

"As near as."

Gardener pondered the situation, the way that both he and Reilly had been manipulated. Dragged into solving clues with an unknown time limit, with the possibility their killer may not have been anywhere near the scene of the crime.

"Could we have saved Alex Wilson? The original message gave us three hours."

"I wouldn't think so," replied Fitz. "Even if you had managed to work out the meaning of the message within the time limit, assuming you reached Wilson by six o'clock, all you would have done was watch him die. By that time, it was too late. The compound was charging around his body, and there is no antidote."

"Why were his lips sewn together? Was there anything in his mouth?"

"No, nothing," replied Fitz. "To try and keep him quiet, probably, so as not to alert you lot to the fact that he was in the cellar. The pain that Wilson would have felt is probably beyond describing. The holes in his hands and feet where he'd been crucified were elongated. That man desperately tried to pull himself off the wall. He was in the cellar of a shop in Bramfield, but you'd probably have heard his screams half a mile away."

"Wonderful," said Reilly. "The killer obviously knows that we wouldn't want to rush into a trap in the cellar, but we'd do what we could to save someone who was in trouble."

"Quite." Fitz sat back in his chair and finished his coffee. "You might want to consider that there's more than one person involved."

"That thought had crossed my mind," said Gardener. "I think there's too much here for one person. I would think that one half of the duo has medical knowledge. Could be a doctor, a chemist, maybe even a student. The other half is an electronics expert, IT man, maybe. Someone who's pretty clued up with technology if you take the Bluetooth chips, the SIM cards, and the externally programmable pumps."

Gardener glanced at his watch. "Look, Fitz, thanks for all your help. At least it gives us another direction in which to take the investigation. We need to get back to the incident room and discuss all the developments."

"And I need to get back to my wife before I have to find myself a solicitor."

Gardener laughed, knowing full well that the elderly pathologist and his wife had a cast-iron marriage. He picked up the implantable pump and placed it in the clear bag alongside the SIM card. He headed for the door, but stopped and turned.

"Just one more question. Do you know a couple of surgeons called Robert Sinclair and Iain Ross?"

"Ross is consultant neurosurgeon at St. James's Hospital?" replied Fitz. "I certainly do. Why do you ask?"

"No reason, really. It's just that he's personally involved with one of the officers at the station. A young PC whose mother has a brain tumour, something called a glioma?"

"Very nasty. A glioma is an extremely serious tumour, very few people survive those," replied Fitz. "If Iain Ross is on the case, then she couldn't be in better hands. I've known him for years. He and his wife are fans of the opera, and we have met on a number of occasions. Sinclair is also a very good surgeon, but he's not in Ross's class. But he's had more to deal with in his personal life."

"How so?" asked Gardener.

"The two of you share something in common – losing your wife in tragic circumstances."

Fitz's phone chimed as he was about to explain. He answered, and it was immediately obvious he was trying to console a wife who had his tea in the oven and wondered how much longer he'd be. Fitz asked if she would hold for a minute.

"If I were you, I'd pay them both a visit. Especially Ross. He's a genius, been practicing medicine since the age of sixteen. He has a list of awards as long as your arm. He's the man you need to talk to with this case."

Chapter Twenty-three

Gardener and Reilly arrived at the Bramfield police station much later than anticipated. Inside, the lobby was light and warm, and Gardener could hear the voices of the officers going about their business. The aroma of fresh coffee and a mixture of different foods reminded him he had barely eaten since his breakfast.

"Christ, that smells good," said Reilly. "Listen, boss, do you fancy a curry or something after the meeting?"

"Something sounds nice, even if it is a curry," replied Gardener.

Cragg appeared from a back room with a tray of cups. "Good to see you, sir. We're all here. Most of the lads are in the incident room already. Plenty of tea and coffee available." He made his way across the lobby to the conference room as if he'd been a part of Gardener's team forever. Gardener was about to follow him when he noticed Gary Close also emerge from the back room, a mug in his hand.

"Sean, can you tell everyone I'll be there in a few minutes? I want to talk to Gary."

"Sure thing, boss."

Gardener intercepted the young PC and asked if he had a minute and somewhere they could talk. They ended up sitting in a couple of old armchairs in an area where Gary and Cragg spent much of their time on the night duty.

"Are you sure you want to be here, Gary?" Gardener asked.

"What do you mean, sir?"

"I know about your mum. Cragg mentioned a problem, and Armitage told me a little more. Sean and I have just been to see the pathologist, and he told us of the severity of her condition. I'm truly sorry to hear about it, which is why I asked if you are sure you want to be here."

Gary stared at Gardener as if he had misunderstood.

"I don't know where I want to be, sir."

"I understand. I also realise that being here may in some way help you to cope. Is this the first time she's been hospitalised during the course of her illness?"

"Yes, sir."

"How have you managed until now?"

"Over the last few weeks my aunty has looked after her while I've been at work. Now she's..." Gary almost struggled to say the word, but he regained his composure. "Things will be a little easier. But I just couldn't sit there, watching her. There's nothing I can do."

Gardener leaned forward. "Going into hospital doesn't mean that she isn't going to come out. It probably means that she needs more specialist care to help her get over her latest setback. I don't want you to think that you're failing in your duty towards your mother because this has happened."

"I know what you mean, sir."

"But I do want you to promise me that if things get any worse, you'll tell me. Please don't keep it to yourself. I can't help you if you do."

From Gary's expression, Gardener felt that he had gained the officer's trust, which was exactly what he wanted. All his team knew that in spite of being the senior officer, he was also their friend, and there wasn't anything he wouldn't do for any of them should they find themselves in a difficult position.

"Don't take the whole weight of this on your own shoulders. I know what it's like to lose a loved one. My wife died in my arms on the streets of Leeds. I still blame myself for what happened, although I am aware that nothing I could have done would have prevented it. And it was only through the help of my friends and close family that I got through it. We're all here for you."

Gardener stood up to leave. "I have to get back to the incident room. I simply wanted you to know that *I* know about your unfortunate circumstances, and I may have to mention it during the meeting."

Gary Close stood up as well and offered his hand. "Thank you, sir. I won't let you down."

Gardener shook it and smiled. "Before we go in there, Dr Fitzgerald, my home office pathologist, tells me that doctors Sinclair and Ross are on the case. You know them well?"

"Yes, sir. Sinclair sorted out my leg when I broke it in a rugby match about three months ago."

Gardener decided to leave it there. "Okay, let's go and discuss what we've all found out today."

As he and Close entered the incident room, his team was still deep in conversation. He noticed that the ANACAPA chart had grown during his absence, which meant Maurice Cragg was taking his duty seriously. The desk sergeant was another member of staff that he wanted to have a talk with; he was concerned about the hours Cragg was putting in. But for all that, he seemed as fresh as a daisy. In a room full of people, however, the most amusing scene was his sergeant, Sean Reilly, with a coffee in one hand, a wrap in the other, and a cake of some description on a plate to one side of him. God only knew how he stayed so slim.

Gardener grabbed a cup and had a sip of tea before addressing them.

"Okay, lads, if we can have a bit of hush, please? It's been a long and tiring day, and I suspect when I tell you what Sean and I have discovered, it isn't about to get any better.

"Colin, Dave, let's start with the shop. What have you found?"

As the senior of the two officers, Colin Sharp opened the folder in front of him and consulted his notes.

"Well, it's been hard going, sir, but we're getting there. Most of the paperwork has been put into some sort of order, and the HOLMES lads are starting to pass back the results. Six customers have shown up as having bought padlocks and had extra keys cut. We've managed to speak to all of them. The padlocks they purchased are basic, nothing like the one we found on the trapdoor. They're mostly for sheds and oil tanks. None of them have been bought by locksmiths."

Rawson took over. "We do have a list of the locksmiths, but we haven't spoken to all of them. We've identified the top ten customers, and none of them have bought padlocks, or anything else connected to what you found in the cellar. The last customer in the shop was a man called Phillip Hammond. Recently married, he bought everything he was likely to need to do up his new home for his wife and their expected child."

"Where is the house?" asked Gardener.

"It's a two-up-two-down on Wentworth Street," said Sharp.

"And you're quite happy that it's all above board? The man is who he says he is?"

"Definitely," replied Rawson. "He doesn't look as though he knows one end of a screwdriver from the other. He's a chef. But from what he's said, his stepfather is a bit of an enthusiast, so he's helping them."

"Okay," said Gardener. "Keep at it, maybe the locksmiths will reveal something when you speak to them."

"Yes, sir," replied Sharp. "We'll carry on first thing in the morning."

Gardener nodded and turned his attention to Benson. "Paul, what do we have from the house-to-house of Bramfield?"

"Something that might be worth pursuing. I spoke to a Mrs Shaw who rents the flat above the flower shop in the town, not far from Armitage's place. She was awake during the early hours of Sunday morning, not Monday, so this is the night before."

"What time?" Gardener asked.

"About two o'clock. She couldn't sleep, and decided to make herself a cup of tea. When she heard a door slam, she gazed out of the window and saw a white van parked near the shop. She was too far away to see the number plate, but she noticed that one of the brake lights wasn't working."

"Did she say which one?" asked Reilly.

"She thinks the driver's side, but she wasn't too sure."

"It's a start. What about the CCTV, did it reveal anything?"

"Not much, sir. It did catch the van, but the angle was all wrong to see the plate."

"Get the IT lads on to it, see if they have software that will give us a better view."

Gardener noticed Maurice updating the ANACAPA chart.

Gardener glanced at Thornton and Anderson. "I gather you two had a shock at Wilson's flat."

"You can say that again," replied Thornton.

"The place has been totally emptied," said Anderson. "There's nothing left: no clothes, no personal items, no phone. But I spoke to Steve Fenton and he reckons they found Wilson's phone in the cellar."

"Yes," said Gardener, "but I believe he had a computer in the place."

"Yes," said Thornton, "but the bloody hard drive was missing so whoever has done this knows what they're doing."

"We've had the place dusted for prints," said Anderson, "but it's clear so far, and I don't think we're going to find much."

"Anyway," offered Thornton, "we're still trying to piece together his last movements and build up a network of friends."

"And enemies," said Anderson, "and we reckon there will be plenty of those."

Gardener sighed. It was early days and the work was always hard in the beginning. "Keep at it."

He addressed them as a team again. "I gave Patrick Edwards a task this morning, to find out who owns the fancy car that drove by around five o'clock. It belongs to Dr Ian Ross, an eminent neurosurgeon at St. James's Hospital in Leeds. From what I can gather, he even has his own clinic, which he shares with one Robert Sinclair, another surgeon. Both are very highly spoken of by everyone."

Gardener glanced at Gary by way of an apology. "Ross was attending an emergency call to Gary's mum. Some of you know that Christine Close has been suffering of late with a brain tumour. For those of you who don't, it's serious, and Ross, after making another call this afternoon, has placed her in his own clinic.

"The point I am coming to here is that we have learned something from our own Home Office Pathologist this evening which confirms that we are looking for someone with medical skills. Sean and I are going to talk to Dr Sinclair tomorrow to see if he can help us further with our inquiries. With that in mind I'd like Edwards and Benson to go and see Ross to see what he has to say about the things we've found.

"But Fitz has thrown another spanner in the works, because he thinks we may be looking for more than one person."

Gardener went on to explain the meeting with the elderly pathologist and what he'd found inside the body of Alex Wilson, the modified implantable insulin pump – which he held up for all to see – and the fact that it had contained a SIM card.

"Colin, we're going to arrange for an enlarged picture of this, and I want you to take it around all the hospitals in the area and see if they can offer any advice on it. Do they recognize it? Would they know the manufacturer? Do they have any like it in their own stock? Are they all accounted for, or are there some missing?"

"Will do, sir, but there isn't much to go on."

"I know, Colin, but we'll settle for anything they can offer. If our killer is using these, they must have access to them. Maybe it's a doctor, a nurse, or even a chemist. Perhaps someone who works for the manufacturer who has a grudge. Maybe it's someone who works in a warehouse. The possibilities are endless, but if they can shed any light at all it would help."

Before passing it over, Gardener asked Reilly if he could find any tech lads who could handle his request for photocopies. He wanted the actual pump to show to Sinclair.

"As for the SIM card, we now have to broaden the search. We have to identify the card. Once again, we need to find the manufacturer. Are there any marks that will help us? Maybe someone can start by searching Google. After that we need to speak to electronics experts, people who work on phones, computers – just about anyone involved with these things."

Frank Thornton put his hand up, as if he was in class.

"Frank?" asked Gardener.

"There's a computer shop in Bursley Bridge, right opposite the station. We'll go tomorrow, maybe he can help."

"Okay," Gardener continued. "Whoever did this is good enough to manipulate technology to their own advantage, which is why I think we may be looking for two people. I'm not saying a doctor isn't capable, but you have to ask yourself, would a doctor really have the time?"

Gardener moved over to the ANACAPA chart. It was growing. An array of names had been linked to the three scenes they had started with. Photographs of the crime had been pinned to the board, as well as some of the evidence such as the cards found in the cellar. Despite the lack of anything solid, he still felt like they were going somewhere.

He pointed to Alex Wilson's name on the chart. "This man is going to be a real problem. As Thornton and Anderson have just said, his flat was empty."

"You think he was planning on going somewhere?" asked Rawson.

"No. But whoever did this to him obviously had that idea. We brought Armitage in to have a look, and he was shocked. He said that there wasn't much to begin with, but whoever had been in there had totally emptied the place. As we've heard, the only item left was his computer, and the hard drive had been removed.

"That suggests to me that someone had been watching Wilson very closely, and perhaps knew that whatever was on that hard drive implicated him. I want you guys who have been on the house-to-house of Bramfield to go back and ask further questions of the residents. Whoever did it, had done so between Thursday night and Sunday night. Now you know as well as I do, when you first call on people they don't remember a great deal, it usually takes a day or two to sink in and then they start to remember other things. So call back."

Gardener nodded to Reilly, who took over.

"Because of that, we have very little on Wilson." Reilly nodded to Thornton and Anderson. "This might help you two. We know he has pre-cons. We know that he had a gambling addiction according to his uncle, so maybe that's a starting point for his affairs. Did he have a credit card? Did he use the bookies in the town, or maybe those a little farther afield? Internet gambling, maybe?

"What we also know, that his uncle didn't, was that he had a drug problem. Someone was supplying him with drugs, and he was selling. Now that's a big can of worms we've opened.

"We interviewed Jackie Pollard this afternoon. He was found at the scene. We know that he was training to be a junior doctor, and that he's also a drug dealer. We need you to find out as much as you can about Pollard. Sergeant Cragg has some notes for you lads to look at, but we need a lot more. Check out his background, his financial status, everything. We want to know everywhere he's been for the last month at least, the last week especially. More important, what was the link to Alex Wilson?"

"Is he our man, do you think?" asked Bob Anderson.

"Let's say that we're not completely satisfied with what he's told us," replied Gardener. "Two more names came out of that little conversation, which could implicate Pollard and leave him in it up to his neck."

Gardener briefed his team with everything he had on Jackie Pollard, Lance Hobson, and Sonia Knight, and how the two men met up inside. He also voiced his theories regarding the disappearances of Hobson and Knight.

"No one has seen either of them for at least a month. The interesting thing here is the phone in the shop this morning was Lance Hobson's, and the message it received came from Sonia Knight's."

Colin Sharp drew Gardener's attention.

"If the call to Hobson's phone came from Sonia Knight's phone, surely it couldn't have been Pollard. We had him locked up."

"Good point, Colin," Gardener replied. "But at the moment, we can't rule anything out. You know as well as I do how fast technology is moving. I'm pretty sure there are some phones that can send a delayed text message."

Colin Sharp nodded and Gardener continued.

"Knight has been calling Pollard regularly for quite a while, but a month ago, all calls and texts stopped. Then last night he received a message to go to the shop in Bramfield, where he would find something to his advantage."

"Was he set up, do you think?" asked Sharp.

"Maybe," replied Gardener. "Then again, maybe he's the one doing the setting up. Maybe he wants revenge. Hobson's business was cutting into his so much, he's prepared to stick his neck out for it. You see, Sean and I went round to Hobson's place today, in Harrogate. There was absolutely no sign of life. It's as if Hobson and Knight have disappeared off the planet."

"Why would they do that?" asked Frank Thornton.

"That's what we want to know. As Sean said, we've opened a real can of worms now. At the moment, we don't have a clue who's organizing all this, but Pollard is swearing his innocence."

"What do you think?" asked Sharp.

"I'm not sure what to think, Colin. All I know is that he's implicated somewhere along the line, but whether or not he's actually murdered Wilson and made Hobson and Knight disappear is another matter. You guys can all read body language well enough to know when someone's guilty. Pollard definitely seemed shocked at hearing of Wilson's death, and did quite a bit of shouting when he thought he was being fitted up for it."

"He could be a good actor. Does he have a brief?" asked Paul Benson.

"Oh, does he," replied Reilly. "Only Wilfred Ronson."

"Oh, Christ," said Colin Sharp. "He's more twisted than a spiral staircase."

"Precisely," said Reilly.

"Have you spoken to him?"

"No," replied Gardener. "Pollard made his phone call, only to find that Ronson was on holiday and will not be back until Wednesday. So Sean and I are going to the office tomorrow to find out exactly where he is, why he's on holiday, and whether or not we can find anything that implicates him in all of this.

"Something will tie these men together. I've no idea what, where, or even when, but even if we can find only one answer, it may put us well on the way to solving the rest of the puzzle."

"But with the exception of Pollard, none of them seem to have any medical experience, and maybe not even an electronics background," offered Bob Anderson.

"You could be right, Bob, but once we've dug a bit deeper, we may find something that will contradict what we think. And as far as Pollard is concerned, I've asked the super for a twelve-hour extension. His time runs out at four o'clock in the morning. I for one don't intend to be around, but I suspect that as the information comes in tomorrow, we'll need to speak to him again."

"I've made up a folder of photos for the rest of the team, sir," said Cragg. "We've got plenty of mugshots of Hobson and Knight. Maybe they can use them to see if anyone's seen anything."

"Thanks, Maurice, much appreciated."

Gardener turned his attention to Patrick Edwards. "Anything on the card I gave you this afternoon?"

"Nothing, sir. There's only one toy shop in the area, and he didn't have a clue. He reckons it's from a board game of some kind, but no idea what."

"Okay." Gardener held the card aloft and glanced at PC Close. "Gary, in view of what's happening at the moment, I think it best if you stay pretty local to the station, so what I want you to do is see if you can find out any information about this Inspector Catcher card. Try the Internet first. If you come up with anything positive, pass the details to Maurice, who can then get in touch with either Sean or myself. We'll assign someone, or follow it up ourselves."

Gary Close nodded, and Gardener suspected he appreciated the gesture.

"Sean and I are pretty sure that the tarot card was left there simply as a means of telling us that the killer knew the victim better than we do." Gardener nodded to Sean, who told them everything Laura had told him earlier in the day.

"Can I just add something else, sir?" Cragg asked Gardener, who nodded in reply. "The monitor in the shop, the one that Gary saw Wilson on, won't be any help to us."

"Too old?" inquired Gardener.

"Well, apart from that the insides are fried. Looks like the bit of work it did in the shop was the last bit it was ever going to do."

"Thanks, Maurice," said Gardener. He addressed the team again. "Possibly the work of the electronics genius. Maybe he set it up to do its bit and then fry itself so we couldn't get anything from it. It's probably far too old for us to check out but we'll get the details if we can and it might be worth bearing in mind."

When he'd finished, Gardener glanced at his watch. It was after ten o'clock. Despite knowing that police work was not a nine-to-five job, he didn't feel he had any right to keep them any longer.

While each man was leaving, Sean Reilly handed out the photos they would need to help them with the next day's assignments.

Gardener went over to Maurice Cragg, who was still updating the ANACAPA chart. "How are you, Maurice?"

"Right as nine-pence, sir," said Cragg, turning to speak to the SIO. "I'm going to have another drink, and then finish all this."

"Maurice, I really appreciate the time and effort you're putting in, but please don't overdo it. You've worked some hours today."

"Oh, don't worry about me, sir. We Craggs are made of tough stuff."

"I've no doubt, but I'd hate to see you come to some grief because you're not getting your rest."

"Oh, I take rest breaks when I need them. And as I said to you earlier, there's nothing to rush home for these days."

"No Mrs Cragg?"

"Not anymore, sir."

Cragg didn't elaborate, and Gardener didn't push. He felt there was a lot more to that story, and it may be best left for another time.

"Okay, Maurice. Well, if you need to speak to me or you need any help, don't hesitate to ask."

Gardener turned and saw the room was empty save for his partner.

"Ready for that curry, now?"

Chapter Twenty-four

When Reilly brought the car to a halt outside the station on Park Street, Gardener jumped out and glanced around.

Bursley Bridge was a typically elegant, small Yorkshire town; a pleasant mix of residential homes sharing space with business premises. Opposite was a pub called The Station Hotel; to the left, a row of stone cottages, and to the right, an art gallery, a computer repair store, and a model shop.

He turned and studied the station. To his right he saw gates leading to the car park. The entrance was to his left, flanked by LNER information boards and a small post box in the wall underneath a window. Gardener noticed a man pushing letters into the small post box despite the activity.

Standing near the steps leading into the station was a man around sixty years of age. He'd lost most of his hair, had a bulbous nose and wore thin wire-rimmed glasses. He was dressed in a black business suit, and carried a briefcase and an umbrella. He was overweight, but his posture was erect, militaristic. Judging by the way he went on the attack, so too was his manner.

"Are you the police?" he asked, pointing his umbrella at them.

Gardener and Reilly both flashed warrant cards. Before they had a chance to say anything, the man started again.

"What the bloody hell is going on around here?" He spoke slowly and through gritted teeth.

"Who *are* you?" Gardener demanded.

"Giles Middleton, General Manager."

"Like you, Mr Middleton, I have absolutely no idea." Gardener continued walking as he was talking, trying to show Middleton that he neither had the time nor the patience for his pomposity.

"I'd like some answers to my questions, young man."

"So would I," replied the SIO. "And at this moment, mine are more important than yours."

Gardener pointed to the station entrance. "You see that tape there?" Such was his annoyance at the intrusive little man he spoke very slowly, a trait he'd had all his life. Shouting the odds was not his style. When Gardener became really upset, he would talk very slowly and with care so that he made sure you understood every one of his words.

"That means no one but my sergeant and I are allowed beyond that point. You stay at the bottom of the steps and you do not come into the station. Do you understand?"

Middleton pointed again. "Now you look here–"

"Do you understand?" repeated Gardener.

Middleton opened his mouth.

"Say one more word, and I'll arrest you for causing an obstruction." Gardener turned and met PC Robin Nice, one of the officers he'd seen outside the shop in Bramfield the day before.

"What do you have for me?"

"Female, mid-to-late twenties."

"Female?" repeated Gardener. "Any identification?" His heart sank. He could only think that they had finally discovered Sonia Knight.

"No," replied Nice.

"Where is she?"

"The waiting room."

"Is she conscious?"

"Yes she's conscious, but I get the feeling she'd rather not be."

"Why?"

"You need to see for yourself."

Eager to stop wasting time, Gardener and Reilly followed Nice onto the platform, noticing PC Steve Graham waiting at the top of the ramp. On their left was a ticket booth, a frame to stand by, a poster advertising the services and timetables of the trains, and a plaque presented to the residents of the town for opening their doors to evacuated children in World War II. On the right stood a London & North Eastern Railway board with timetables, and more plaques. Before turning left to the waiting room, Gardener glanced to his right, along the tracks. He wasn't sure what he expected to see, but everything appeared normal.

But it wasn't, was it?

Nice told them that no one had been inside. The door was open, and Gardener glanced beyond.

The girl was naked, sitting in a chair. Her arms were behind her, her legs intertwined with the chair's. As Gardener could not see any restraints, he quickly came to the conclusion she had somehow been bonded to the frame so she couldn't move. The chair was high-backed, like those found in most dining rooms, only taller. A plain white envelope was pinned to each wing. But for the girl in the chair, the room was bare.

Closer scrutiny revealed the female was completely hairless, her head, between her legs, even under her arms from what he could tell.

Her lips had also been sewn together, like Alex Wilson's.

"Is this how you found her?" he asked Nice.

"Middleton found her. Called us immediately. Obviously, she can't speak, but I have the feeling she hasn't been conscious very long."

"Have you tried to speak to her?"

"Only a couple of questions that she could have nodded or shook her head to, but she hasn't communicated at all."

Gardener and Reilly quickly suited and booted, using the scene suits they had brought with them, and stepped gingerly into the room.

The girl's complexion was ash grey, and she was lean and fragile. As he slowly walked towards her, she opened her eyes so wide that he thought they were going to fall out. Her body started to shake, thus demonstrating the means by which she had been held in place.

She had been glued to the chair.

Gardener had never, in all his life, seen someone so frightened. He couldn't begin to imagine what kind of an ordeal she had suffered.

Apart from the stitching to the lips, he could see no further scarring, which he hoped was a good sign. The girl tried to move from the chair, but it was impossible. The chair scraped along the floor as she retreated a couple of inches. Gardener sensed that she was trying to move away from him. As he drew closer, he noticed the female jerk her head ever so slightly down towards the floor.

"I want you to do something for me," said Gardener. "If you can't move, please blink your eyes once."

The girl calmed a little, and blinked to indicate that was the case.

"Is your name Sonia Knight?"

She blinked once. She then tried to move her head again, blinking furiously as she did.

"Something's rattling her, boss," said Reilly.

The Irishman leaned further forward, and Sonia Knight pushed away with her feet so hard the chair nearly went over. Reilly grabbed the leg to prevent that from happening.

Knight was growing extremely agitated. She opened her eyes as wide as she could, and angled them down as far as they would go, glaring down at her side. Gardener slowly stepped around the chair. Strapped to it was a mobile phone.

At precisely that second it rang, and all hell let loose.

Sonia Knight jumped as hard as her situation would allow, the chair leaving the floor by at least six inches. Even though her lips were sewn together, she let loose a spine-tingling mewl. Gardener sensed that if it had been at all possible, she would have screamed loud enough to wake the dead. He stepped back very quickly.

The phone rang again, and Sonia Knight frantically tried to part company with the wooden frame.

She must have succeeded in some way, because Gardener heard a tearing sound, and the skin on her arms gave a little. He glanced down, noticing how far it had actually stretched despite the fact that it was still connected to the chair. A bloodstain marked the area. Sonia Knight was lathered in sweat, her body shaking violently.

"Sean, call an ambulance. If we don't do something soon this is going to be fatal."

Gardener reached out for the phone, and Sonia Knight flinched, struggling to keep out of his way. He put his hands up in surrender. "It's okay. Please, try to keep still. I'm not going to hurt you."

As soon as Reilly called the emergency services, the phone strapped to the chair chimed again. It rang only once, but that was enough.

Sonia convulsed, and with a stomach-churning, ripping sound she managed to free her limbs. Splashes of blood landed across the floor and splattered both officers. The chair shook so hard it left the floor a number of times, but no matter how hard she tried, she could not remove herself completely.

Sonia brought her hands to her mouth with arms that were torn red-raw, her fingers trying to work at the stitches binding her lips. Gardener reached out to stop her, to try and calm her and keep her from hurting herself further.

As he restrained her, a picture entered his mind of the man they had seen when they arrived.

"Oh my God, Sean." He glanced at his sergeant. "That man we saw outside posting letters. Go and see if he's still around. Take the car if you have to, but find him."

Reilly left without question. They had worked together for so long, that when Gardener asked him to do something even in a situation so intense, he did it without question. He knew his superior would have a bloody good reason.

Gardener reached down and grabbed the mobile attached to the chair, but it didn't move. It was held in place by a fancy round bracket that covered all of the buttons, which in turn was held in place by two screws drilled into the wood,

He called out to Steve Graham. "I need a screwdriver."

Graham suddenly disappeared as if by magic.

"What the hell is going on?" asked Nice.

"We need to get the phone away from the girl."

"Why?"

"No time to explain," replied the SIO. "Just trust me."

Gardener wondered where the ambulance was. He noticed Sonia Knight was shivering. It had to be shock, because he doubted she was cold. He removed his suit jacket, intending to cover her, for what use it would be.

The phone rang again. And kept ringing.

Knight hit the roof. The pain barrier must have been indescribable. She jerked hard against the chair. He heard another ripping sound, and one of her legs came free, the wound so severe he could see bone.

More blood and further muffled screams invaded the enclosed space. Even with her mouth sealed, the girl was capable of a sound so guttural, it had to have emanated from deep within her bowels.

Knight put her hands to her mouth, then her head and her ears. The poor girl seemed to have no idea what she wanted to do. She stood up on her one free leg and tried to shake the chair free.

Still the phone kept ringing, accompanied now by a siren outside, closing in on the small country railway station.

Nice entered the room in an effort to try and restrain Knight. She proved to be a real handful, as if in some bizarre, surreal parody of a dance with him. Graham approached with the screwdriver Gardener had asked for. Knight quickly lashed out and caught him square on the jaw, sending him back towards the waiting room door. The screwdriver fell out of his hand and rolled towards Gardener. Still the phone kept on ringing, and Knight continued screaming behind the stitches, skipping all around the room, trying to put distance between herself and the chair, regardless of the pain.

A paramedic appeared in the doorway, the expression on his face one of complete disbelief.

As the phone rung on, Gardener suddenly realized it must have been tampered with, so it would continue to do so without diverting to the messaging system. That meant if she was in the same situation as Wilson had been, it would continue to create the most unbearable pain for her. He had to stop the bastard ringing.

Suddenly, Sonia Knight finally released herself from her prison. She had literally torn free of the chair, which fell to the floor with a clatter. She turned her back to them. Her body glistened with blood and raw muscle, resembling a freshly skinned carcass hanging in a butcher's window.

Gardener noticed that the mobile phone had abruptly stopped ringing during the confusion. But no sooner had that thought entered his head, when it started again.

Sonia Knight turned back around and fell to her knees with her arms in the air, her hands clenched in fists. Her screech of agony was heard in full, her pain so great, she had torn her mouth completely open. Gardener couldn't tell which was her bottom lip, and which was the top.

But it was the view inside her mouth that would be the stuff of his nightmares for a very long time to come.

Chapter Twenty-five

Robert Sinclair stepped out of the shower in his en suite bathroom, and quickly dried himself down.

He loved the summer months, when he could rise at five-thirty, slip into a jogging suit, and go for an early morning run. His house bordered the stream, so he usually left via the back garden and onto the bank.

From there, he ran all the way into Bursley Bridge, which was approximately a mile and a half. Once around the town, through most of the streets, and finally back to his house on the path that bordered the main road.

In the winter months he had a different procedure. His training was undertaken in the gymnasium he'd had built, complete with treadmill, cross-trainer, and a variety of weight machines. As far as he was concerned, his body was a temple, and should be treated accordingly.

Sinclair loved routine. Always had. He liked his breakfast at seven-thirty, to start work at eight. He had an hour at two for something to eat, and then worked through till six. He ate an evening meal – prepared by his housekeeper – at seven, and eventually retired for the evening around ten o'clock. As a trainee doctor, it had never been possible. Given the position he held now, treating private patients, it was much easier to dictate the times and terms on which he would see them.

Having dried and changed into casual clothes, he went down into the kitchen, pausing only once on the staircase to check the time on the grandfather clock. He stepped into the kitchen.

He was ready for the most important meal of the day, which was usually something healthy. Miss Bradshaw never let him down. However, the expression on her face told him that his routine today was about to go AWOL, something he would find difficult to deal with.

"Oh, Mr Sinclair. Dr Ross has just phoned from the clinic. He wants to speak to you immediately."

Sinclair knew better than to question his housekeeper, because Iain Ross would not have told her anything. The only reason he would call so early was because they must have suffered another setback with Christine Close. Something he didn't relish hearing.

Sinclair sipped his green tea.

"Here, take this," said Miss Bradshaw, passing over a small container. "I know you'll want to leave immediately, but it's very important that you eat."

"Thank you. I really had better go. It must be urgent." Robert Sinclair left the kitchen, went upstairs, and changed into a suit.

Twenty minutes later he was walking into the Ross & Sinclair Foundation. He headed straight for his office, where he found Iain Ross waiting for him. The surgeon was immaculately dressed in a pale blue designer suit with white shirt and blue tie. He was standing by the fireplace.

As always, the logs and paper were set, ready for someone to strike up a match.

"Robert," said Ross. "Good to see you. Thank you for coming so quickly."

"Is it Christine?"

"I'm afraid so."

Ross poured a fresh coffee from the machine in the corner of the room, offering one to his colleague, who declined. "She had two more seizures during the night. I'm afraid she's unconscious. But she's been given pretty large doses of phenytoin. She's comfortable."

Sinclair had asked Ross to administer the best treatment available, in the hope that it would have bought her some more time. He'd known from the start that he could not guarantee anything. Nothing he did now would work, apart from sedatives and anti-epileptic drugs.

"Is she on a ventilator?"

"Yes," replied Ross.

Sinclair sighed heavily. The end was in sight. The machine would help her to breath, but the question was, for how long? Someone would eventually have to make the heart-breaking decision of turning the ventilator off. And the only person who could was Gary.

Sinclair didn't think he was strong enough yet. Gary needed to know, but, for the moment, he would rather keep the details to a minimum.

"Has Gary been in to see her?" he asked Ross.

"Not yet," replied Ross, sipping his coffee.

"In that case, when he does show up, will you bring him straight into the office? I need to be careful with this one."

"Would you like me to tell him?"

"No thank you, Iain. I think you've done enough already."

Ross left and Sinclair sat in a chair at his desk, his head in his hands.

Chapter Twenty-six

Gardener stood facing Andrew Jackson's office door at St. James's Hospital. Reilly had taken a seat. They were waiting for the doctor's answer regarding Sonia Knight's condition. He didn't hold out much hope.

Since leaving the railway station, everything had been a blur. The only way for the medics to transport Sonia Knight was to silence her completely with a sedative, something they were reluctant to do because they had no prior knowledge of her condition. In the end, it had been Gardener who had made the decision. Without it, they were never going to be able to do what was necessary.

Before following the ambulance, he had called out SOCO and ordered the place to be completely sealed and ripped apart, much to Giles Middleton's utter horror.

Gardener turned to face his partner, and once again inquired about the man they had seen posting letters. "You couldn't see him anywhere?"

"No, boss."

"Can you remember anything about him?"

"Not really," replied Reilly. "Only his clothes. A long, dark green wax jacket and black boots. Never saw his face."

"Me neither," replied Gardener.

It was possible he was clutching at straws. The man could have genuinely been there posting letters. But it seemed odd.

"I shot a look in both directions. Had to make a decision. I reckoned he was local, ran past our car and up to the cottages opposite. So I knocked on a few doors, annoyed some people because of the early hour, but I didn't come across him. By that time I knew I'd made the wrong choice."

"Wasn't your fault, Sean. If we'd had more men, we could have split up and done a thorough search."

Reilly stood up and joined Gardener near the door. "I took the car around the town after that, but it was obviously too late."

"It's not easy to drive and look at the same time, is it? He could have been anywhere by then. If he'd been down one of the side streets, you'd have had no chance anyway."

"Are you convinced he's our man?"

"Not really, but I can't see why else he would be there," replied Gardener. "It's just too coincidental."

"I'm inclined to agree. Perfect spot to watch us go in, and then send a signal to the victim's phone. Once the pandemonium started, he could just do one."

"Call me paranoid," said Gardener, "can you remember how many cars there were when we pulled up?"

"I think so." Reilly pulled out his pad and opened it to the page where he had registration numbers. "There were only four, these are the numbers."

Gardener chuckled as he removed his own pad from his jacket pocket. "We've been working together too long."

"Tell me about it."

They compared notes and the vehicle details were the same.

"So, if the same amount of cars were there when we arrived and left, it's possible that he *is* local."

Reilly thought for a moment before responding. "I didn't check the car park of the pub opposite."

"Could be our answer."

"They do bed and breakfast. He could be a guest."

"Give Colin Sharp a ring, Sean. Tell him whatever he's doing, or thinking of doing, drop it and get himself around to the pub. Question the landlord, and get a list of all guests staying there at the moment. Then call the rest of the squad and tell them to meet us at the station at nine o'clock prompt."

Gardener popped his head around the door and glanced into the corridor. He saw empty gurneys, a nurse pushing a patient in a wheelchair, another holding a clipboard whilst talking to a matron. But there was no sign of Andrew Jackson.

"I can't say I heard a car engine while we were in the waiting room," said Reilly. "But to be honest, with all the racket she was making, a jet could have crash-landed on the street outside and we wouldn't have heard it."

Gardener checked his watch. What the hell was keeping the doctor? They had heard nothing about Sonia Knight's condition, or if she was even alive.

"She must have been in some serious pain, considering what was in her mouth."

"What did you see, boss?"

Gardener suspected he would never forget what was in Sonia Knight's mouth as long as he lived. He wasn't even sure if he could adequately describe the image.

"Wires... lots of them."

"Wires?"

Gardener turned to face him. "Yes, Sean. Wires. Don't ask me to explain what the hell was going on, but her mouth seemed to be full of wires. And there was something in the middle of them, a capsule of some sort, with the wires extending from it."

"Could you see where the wires were going?"

"No, it all happened so quickly.

"Was it another one of those pumps?"

"I don't think so." Gardener put his hands in the air, almost in defeat. "But it could have been. It could have been anything."

Gardener walked over to Andrew Jackson's desk, staring at the mess. His PC was barely visible under a mountain of letters, files, and stationery – the only bit of colour was a collector's magazine of some description. But if it was true, what he'd heard about the amount of hours that NHS doctors had to work, he could see why they didn't have time to clean up after themselves. The only other item visible was a framed photo, which he took to be the doctor's wife and two children.

Reilly broke his train of thought.

"You know what that means, don't you?"

"What?" Gardener asked, turning to face his partner.

"It can't be Jackie Pollard."

Gardener sighed.

"It still doesn't mean he isn't involved. He may not have been pressing the buttons on the phone, but he sure as hell could have instigated it."

"I don't doubt you, boss. Lance Hobson and Jackie Pollard *could* be in it together. What I don't understand is why?"

"That makes two of us. It's pretty unusual for drug dealers to collaborate. They're normally tearing each other's throats out, trying to gain superiority."

"We need a full background check on Hobson," said Reilly. "Maybe he's our electrical genius, and Pollard is the medical man."

"You could be right. Whatever happened to Knight took a lot of arranging, and a fair amount of time. She's been holed up somewhere for a month. Enough time to carry out what we saw today."

"Pollard operates on them, and Hobson puts them into place?"

"If that's the case, Sean, where the hell is Pollard doing it? You need expert equipment to carry out operations like he's doing."

"Maybe we'll find that out when we search his house."

Both men fell silent for a few moments.

"I've just thought of something else," said Reilly.

"Go on."

"How much do they trust each other if they *are* working together?"

Gardener smiled. "That's just what I was thinking. Let's face it, they're both a nasty pair of bastards. Each of them must have a hidden agenda."

"Which throws up another question. Where does that bent bastard Ronson fit in?"

"Maybe he has an agenda as well. A background check on him might turn up something of a surprise."

"It's like human Sudoku," said Reilly.

At the mention of the puzzle, Gardener remembered the cards pinned to the wings of the chair. They were obviously very important, and he was desperate to find out what they meant.

The office door opened and Andrew Jackson walked in. He was taller than Gardener, slim with a very rugged complexion, possibly an indication of too much work and not enough rest. His hair was ginger, combed forward from the middle in an effort to disguise his premature balding. Underneath the open white smock and stethoscope, he wore a pair of grey chinos, a white shirt with a grey tie, and a pair of black slip-on shoes. His voice was mellow, and his accent clipped.

"Thank you for being patient, gentlemen. Come with me, there's something I'd like to show you."

"Where are we going?" Gardener asked. "Is she still alive?"

"Please." The doctor indicated for them to follow him out of the office.

Both men followed Andrew Jackson down a white tiled corridor and into a side room.

The body of Sonia Knight was laid out on a gurney. A thin sheet covered her naked and hairless body. Despite the horrors she must have experienced, she seemed more at rest than anyone Gardener had ever seen.

He was disappointed. The killer had struck again. They'd had a living person in their grasp, but were unable to keep her that way.

Before approaching Knight, Jackson turned to face the two detectives.

"Have you any idea what the hell is going on here?"

"Let's say we're in the middle of an investigation, and to be quite frank, I'd prefer to ask the questions," replied Gardener, trying not to cause offense.

None seemed to have been taken.

"Mr Gardener, I don't know who's responsible for this abomination, but I've never seen anything as barbaric as this in all my practicing years."

Andrew Jackson opened Sonia Knight's mouth to allow both detectives a better view. Gardener leaned in close. In the centre of her mouth was a small object no bigger than a matchbox. It was silver in colour, and almost the same shape as a beetle. On top of its body was a small, clear plastic sheath, into which all the cables were connected.

"Am I seeing things?" asked Gardener. "Or does every one of those cables in her mouth run into every one of her teeth?"

"You're not seeing things. Each tooth has a cable inserted into its centre."

"And what's that in the middle, the silver thing?"

"I'm not sure." Andrew Jackson picked up a small round mirror on the end of a steel rod – the type used by dentists – and placed it in Sonia Knight's mouth.

He moved around very carefully, as though the wires would detonate at any moment and blow them all to Kingdom Come. After drawing in a couple of deep breaths and clicking his tongue a couple of times as he examined the object, Jackson stared at the detectives.

"It's an ICD."

"Pardon?"

"I'm sorry, to give it it's full title, it's an implantable cardioverter defibrillator."

"Which is what?" asked Gardener.

"A battery-powered electrical impulse generator, which is implanted in patients who are at risk of sudden cardiac death. It's programmed to detect cardiac arrhythmia, and to correct it by delivering a jolt of electricity."

"So, it's different to an implantable insulin pump?" Gardener asked.

"Very. Where did you learn about those?"

Gardener straightened. "From the last person who'd met the monster we're chasing. How does it work?"

"They constantly monitor the rate and rhythm of the heart and are able to deliver therapies by way of an electrical shock."

"In other words," inquired Reilly, "it can start the heart if it stops?"

"Yes," replied Jackson. "Or the other way round, if you're devious enough. And someone has been, looking at this lot.

"ICDs normally include wires, which pass through a vein to the right chambers of the heart, usually being lodged in the apex of the right ventricle. The most recent development is the subcutaneous ICD, which is what we have here. Current state-of-the-art electronics and batteries have enabled an implantable device to deliver enough energy to defibrillate the heart without the need for a lead in or on the heart. This prevents the risk of lead-related problems or dangerous infections. They are normally positioned just under the skin, outside the ribcage."

Gardener digested the information before firing off an order at the doctor. "Cut it out."

"Pardon?"

"Take it out of her mouth."

"I'm not sure I should..."

"This is a murder investigation," said Gardener. "And you're helping me with my inquiries. Now cut it out."

Jackson obviously thought better of any further objections and did as he was told. The procedure lasted five minutes. When he'd finished, he laid the device out on a bench.

"Do you recognize it?" Gardener asked.

"In what way?"

"The manufacturer? Do you use them here in the hospital?"

Andrew Jackson donned a fresh pair of gloves and examined the small unit, before holding it out to Gardener.

"There should be a serial number here, and a name. As you can see, someone has removed it. What's this all about, Mr Gardener?"

"Pain, I should think. Judging by what you've told me, one of these things can deliver quite a shock."

"Good God," he said, turning back to the body. "What kind of a monster are you hunting?"

The doctor leaned in closer to Knight and peered into her mouth.

"Every one of those wires is connected directly into her teeth. And her teeth have been filled, which means he must have placed them on the ends of the nerves. Jesus Christ! The poor girl must have hit the roof."

"She did," said Gardener, still reliving the scene. At the time he had no idea what was causing the pain, or how severe it must have been. Now that he knew, he still couldn't imagine it.

"I'll ask you again, do you recognize it?"

"Why do you keep asking me that? What do you mean?" asked Andrew Jackson.

"Just that. Do you recognize this device? Is it something you would you use in the course of your duty?"

"A heart surgeon certainly would, but I'm not a heart surgeon. If you're asking me whether or not it came from this hospital, I couldn't say, but I will make some inquiries. There are a lot of manufacturers of these sorts of device, and they all differ in some way."

"I'd like you to do that, and tell me as soon as you know."

"Are you implying that a doctor from this hospital could be responsible for such a hideous crime? Quite frankly, I find that hard to believe. Doctors save lives, not take them."

"Would you agree that to do something like this," continued Gardener, "you'd need extensive medical knowledge? In fact, that it would require surgical skill to use the device in this manner?"

Jackson did not seem to want to answer his question.

"Well?" Gardener pushed.

"Almost certainly."

"Which can only lead us to believe that not all doctors save lives. Now do something else for me, split that device open, on the bench."

Jackson did so without question.

"Good God! What the hell is that?"

"A SIM card, Dr Jackson, which is exactly how it's working. Someone has modified the defibrillator to accept a signal from a mobile phone, at which point, your little energy module would crank out a massive electrical discharge to the nerves on Sonia Knight's teeth."

Gardener slipped on a pair of gloves, collected the device, and turned to leave. Before reaching the door, he stopped and turned to address Jackson once more.

"Like I said, not all doctors save lives."

Chapter Twenty-seven

Gardener was sitting in the incident room waiting for his squad to arrive, with a multitude of thoughts all fighting to emerge victorious. The first concerned PC Close. From the information he'd learned yesterday, he doubted very much that Christine was going to come out of the clinic, but they would all have to deal with that when it happened. He felt he was right to put Close on station duties, and thankfully, he had the perfect job for the troubled officer.

He had thought about the white van, and tried to make a list of the manufacturers he knew. The fact that it was a large van made things easier; there were not that many model variants. One question he had forgotten to ask was whether or not there were any logos on the side. Gardener suspected one of his team would have said so if that had been the case.

When it came to suspects, he didn't have many in the frame. Gardener was reminded, however, of something Alan Radford, his superior officer of many years ago, had taught him: never rule out anyone. What you thought about a person was immaterial; it was cold, hard facts that mattered, and damn good powers of deduction that could piece those facts together.

With regard to Pollard, Gardener had to be careful that he wasn't putting the drug dealer in the frame simply because there was no one else. Although he had some medical knowledge, Gardener still wasn't completely satisfied Pollard was their man. He did suspect, however, that the man *was* more than capable of making Hobson and Knight disappear. He hoped the search of Pollard's house being conducted at that moment would turn something up. Without at least something to back up his suspicions, they really couldn't keep Pollard much longer.

The electronics angle had brought fresh light to the case, but also added further problems. The fact that someone else might be involved only increased their caseload.

The door to the incident room opened, and one by one his officers rolled in. Maurice Cragg was amongst them and, at the very back, one of the SOCOs with the envelopes that had been pinned to the chair, firmly sealed in an evidence bag.

Gardener placed them on one of the tables and addressed his squad. Without wasting any time, he took them through what he and Reilly had witnessed at the station, and concluded by showing them the ICD.

He opened the two envelopes found at the scene and held them aloft for the team to make notes. The first card he pointed to was another tarot: The Papess, or High Priestess. In many ways, it was very similar to any one of the queens in a normal pack of playing cards. She was sitting on a throne between two columns, one white, one black. On one side of the card was the letter B, on the other, the letter J.

"Sean, can you give Laura a call and see what she can tell us about this one?" Reilly nodded and retreated to the far end of the room to speak to his wife.

The second card he held up was almost certainly part of the set that included Inspector Catcher. It was identical in size, and on the reverse was the same logo, the word 'Murder' in a very fancy font. The hourglass and the patent number were also there, and when compared with the Catcher card, their similarities were evident.

The front of the card bore the name 'Nurse Willing', and had a woman in hospital uniform holding a stethoscope in one hand, and a needle in the other. There were no slogans on the card. The nurse's outfit was prim and proper, portraying a style similar to that worn in the late Sixties or early Seventies.

Reilly returned to the front of the room. Gardener nodded, and he told them what he'd found out.

"It has dual meanings. All of them have. Upright means we're looking at wisdom and secret knowledge, something that is yet to be revealed."

"And the reverse?"

"Equally as bad. Lack of personal harmony, problems which could be the result of one not looking into things properly. Ignorance of true facts and feelings."

"Once again," said Gardener, "the killer is playing games with us. He knows his victims better than we do. He's letting us know how much he knows about them, and that he's got a very good reason – as far as he's concerned – for killing them."

"In other words, it's the tail wagging the dog," said Thornton.

"Probably. Unfortunately, we still don't know who the hell is in the frame. That means we have to step up our game. So, on top of everything else we have to do today, I have some more actions."

Gardener glanced at Maurice Cragg. "All of us must keep an open mind from now on. What I'd like you to do is get me a background on Sonia Knight and Lance Hobson. I want everything you can find out about them."

"Will do, sir."

Gardener readdressed his own men. "I also want someone looking into the last movements of those two. Hobson we know for a fact is either still missing, or still at large depending on how you look at it. Someone somewhere knows these two very well. We need to find them. I appreciate that means we're going to be talking to the scum of the big city, and it's very unlikely they'll want anything to do with us, but it has to be done."

"Why don't we run the bastards in?" Reilly asked.

"It's a bloody good idea, Sean, but we don't have the room or the manpower, and I doubt we could make anything stick. No, I think we need the softly, softly approach first. If that doesn't work, then we'll run the bastards in no matter how small the station is."

Gardener was about to speak again when the door opened and Gary Close limped in, obviously in tremendous pain.

"Is everything okay, Gary?" Gardener asked.

Close dropped into a chair. "I'm okay, sir. Some days are worse than others, is all."

"In what way?"

"The doc says my leg's still knitting together, and while it's doing that, it might give me some real gip."

Gardener suspected that Gary was about to say more, but instead winced. He reached down and rubbed the affected part of his leg.

"Has he given you anything?"

"Yes sir, but I don't like taking 'em."

"Maybe you should, especially when it's this bad. You certainly look like you could use some of it now. When did you last take any?"

"A couple of days ago, sir. But it's worse today than it has been for a long time."

Gardener glanced at Cragg. "Maurice, would you fetch him a glass of water, please?"

While the desk sergeant did as he was asked, Gardener spoke to the young PC again. "Have you been working a night shift?"

"No, sir. Mr Cragg let me go a lot earlier than usual."

"How's your mum?"

Close seemed to brighten up with that question. "She's doing fine, sir. I spoke with Mr Sinclair this morning. He said she's had a really comfortable night, and he thinks she's responding to the treatment."

That surprised Gardener after everything he'd heard. He would have to bring the subject up in the presence of Robert Sinclair.

"That's great news, Gary. Have you been to see her?" Maurice Cragg returned with a glass of water.

"No. Mr Sinclair said she was sleeping, and it was best to let her rest."

"I'm pleased to hear that, as I'm sure we all are. With that in mind, I'd like you to take this 'Nurse Willing' card, continue your research and see if you can find out which board game these cards are from."

Gardener reached into his jacket pocket and pulled out the pad with the registration numbers of the cars parked at the Bursley Bridge train station.

"I want someone to chase up these cars and their owners, and take statements from them. Colin Sharp is at the pub in town at the moment getting a list of names and addresses of their paying guests. I also want a couple of you over there on house-to-house inquiries.

"Thornton, Anderson, you two continue with what you were doing. Go and speak to the person who runs the computer shop, see what you can find out. Take the pictures of the cards with you.

"Benson, Edwards, can you go and talk to Iain Ross and get his opinion on everything we've found?

"Sean and I are going to speak to Robert Sinclair today. We need a line on these implantable things that keep popping up. And we also intend to go to Ronson's office and find out why he's not there."

Gardener requested Reilly organize photocopies of the cards and the pumps for the officers to take with them. A few minutes after he left, Dave Rawson entered the room.

"Sir, I think you ought to take a look at these."

"What are they?"

Reilly returned, munching a couple of biscuits.

"We've just finished a search of Pollard's place." Rawson placed what resembled diaries on the table.

"What are they?" asked Gardener.

"I'm not sure, sir. They're full of names, and sums of money."

Gardener picked one up and skimmed through it. He couldn't understand what they represented, but he did recognize names. Some were local, and most respectable.

"Is that all? Nothing else to suggest he was our man?"

"No, sir."

Gardener was not happy. Although the mystery was deepening, they were as much in the dark now as when they had started at three o'clock yesterday morning.

Chapter Twenty-eight

Before Jackie Pollard even sat down, he started shouting at both officers.

"You're taking bloody liberties, you lot. I've been here far longer than you're allowed to keep me. You've got no bloody evidence of me having done anything, least of all murdering someone. Is my solicitor back yet?"

"Have you finished?" Reilly asked.

"I asked you a question."

Reilly stood up. Gardener remained seated, glancing through a file.

"You're not listening to me, son. I said, have you finished?"

"How long do you intend to keep me here?"

"That depends on you," said Reilly.

Pollard snorted, and finally sat down. He was still dressed in the standard issue holding clothing, but the Irishman could see he had recently showered. His hair was damp. Reilly also noticed that he was very agitated.

"Is Ronson back yet?" asked Pollard.

"I've no idea, son, he's *your* solicitor. You told us yesterday he wouldn't be back until tomorrow, so I guess the answer is no."

"This isn't good enough. You are breaching my civil rights."

"You were offered a duty solicitor and you declined," said Gardener. "Would you like to change your mind?"

"You must be joking. If he's a duty solicitor, he'll be in your pockets."

"I'll ignore that," said Reilly. "We have a few more questions for you, Jackie lad. Quicker we get the answers, quicker you get out of here."

"Why don't I trust you?"

"Probably the same reason we don't trust you," answered Reilly.

"Can I have a coffee, please?"

"Of course."

Reilly arranged for the drink and returned to the table.

"I'd like a cigarette as well."

"You're out of luck there, son."

When the drinks were delivered, Reilly started the tapes and introduced everyone.

Pollard glanced at Gardener. "I thought *you* were the senior officer."

"I am."

"So why aren't you interviewing me?"

"Does it make any difference? Would you prefer me?"

"Anything's better than him," answered Pollard.

"Well, he's all you've got. Today, I'm on listening duty. You'd be surprised how much you learn when you don't say anything."

Pollard sighed.

"How do you earn a living, son?" asked Reilly.

"What?"

"Don't mess me about, Pollard. I was pretty fed up with you evading questions yesterday. It's not going to happen today. I want an answer."

"It's not relevant, so I'm not going to tell you," said Pollard, smiling. "Not without my brief."

Both officers rose immediately and walked towards the door, to the annoyance of Pollard.

"Where the hell are you going?"

"See you in the morning." Reilly opened the door.

"Wait," shouted Pollard. "Okay, okay, perhaps I was a little hasty."

Reilly had had enough. He slammed the door and marched over to the table so fast that Pollard shrank back and nearly fell over his seat.

"Game over, sunshine. We're conducting this interview my way. Just one more snide comment like that, and we're out of here until your brief shows up, and you can shout all you like about civil rights because no one will be listening."

Reilly and Gardener sat down.

"Answer the question!"

"I'm a legitimate businessman."

"Where do you think you are, Jackie lad? *The Apprentice*?"

"What?" Pollard replied.

"This is not national television. We're not asking that question so we can give you a loan and set you up in business on your own. You're in a shit load of trouble, so you are."

Gardener threw Pollard's diaries on the table, but didn't say anything.

"So tell me, Jackie lad, what are these?"

"Where the hell did you get them? Have you searched my house without a warrant?"

Reilly ignored him and continued.

"We've had a good look at these, and we're not quite sure what to make of them. We can think of one thing. It looks like a protection racket. Maybe you're not involved in drugs like we first thought. Maybe you're running a nice little earner by intimidating people. You get money out of them, and you leave their businesses alone. Only, we can't quite figure out where Hobson and Knight fit in."

"You're way off the mark, Irishman. By the time I've finished with you two, you'll need the solicitor, not me."

"If you say so. Now, if we're that far off the mark, why don't you put us straight?"

"It's not a protection racket at all. And it's nothing to do with drugs. Those are my private diaries. You have no right—"

"Will you stop your bleating and just answer the question, son?" shouted Reilly. "We're in the middle of a very serious murder investigation. Do you honestly think we would have searched your house if we didn't have reasonable suspicion of your involvement?"

When Pollard didn't answer, Reilly continued. "If you're innocent, now's the time to tell us why. Believe me, we are far from over here today, and this is just the first shock coming your way."

Pollard stood up. "What's that supposed to mean?"

"Sit down," ordered Reilly. "And answer the question. What do these books represent? Books that have names, with large sums of money against them?"

Pollard finished his coffee, then sat down at the table, clenching and unclenching his fists. He seemed to be wrestling with his conscience. Reilly couldn't work out why. If the man was innocent, why not tell them and save everybody some time? He noticed Pollard was sweating, wondering if a lack of nicotine was playing havoc with his system.

Pollard lifted his hands in resignation. "Okay."

Gardener stopped going through the file and put it on the table.

"I'll tell you what I know, but when I've done, I want out of here."

"We don't make bargains, Jackie lad," said Reilly. "But I'll tell you this and I'll tell you no more, if you convince me of your innocence, we'll review your situation. So, maybe you won't be here much longer."

"I won't be anywhere much longer if you don't give me some kind of protection."

Reilly folded his arms and continued staring at Pollard.

"You say you're not a murderer. If you know who the murderer is, then you have a duty to tell us. Once we have him, you won't have to worry about protection, will you?"

"That's just it. According to your desk sergeant, no one has seen him for a month."

"Are you saying Lance Hobson is responsible for Alex Wilson's murder?" Gardener asked.

"I have no idea who did that, but I'll tell you what I do know, and you can make up your own mind. I've been clean since I came out of Armley. But I know what people round here think of me. They're very quick to point the finger. They don't trust me. I learned a long time ago to ignore them, let them think what they want. I know what I'm doing is right."

"And what *are* you doing?"

"Those diaries contain the names of sponsors. It's taken years for people to trust me when I say that I want to rid the city of this filth. Carrion, like Lance Hobson, that feed off the flesh of what's left when they've converted them.

"The names in those books are sponsoring a massive drug rehabilitation program. They're giving me money so that we can set up premises and clean people up, keep them clean, and at the same time, try to stamp out the likes of Hobson."

"Why didn't you tell us this yesterday?"

"Because I'm leaving myself open to arrest. You think I killed Wilson, and you think I've made Knight disappear."

"Not to mention Hobson."

"I lost my brother to drugs a few years ago. Sonia Knight lost her cousin more recently. They were addicts, and the man responsible is Lance Hobson. Sonia Knight has been double-crossing him for a long time now."

"How?"

"She runs his empire. Takes care of all the finance. Invests money where he tells her. Has done for years. Now I'm not saying that she's an angel. She started out like

145

all of us. It's bloody hard to resist the luxuries that the profit from drugs can bring you. But Hobson's a bastard, just like my father was. He likes to intimidate people, threaten them. And he has a number of henchmen to do his dirty work, and snitching little bastards like Alex Wilson. If he'd got wind of what was happening, he'd have shopped Knight to Hobson, no mistake."

"So, what part has she been playing?"

"She's been filtering off the profits from his drug business for ages, putting the money into a bank account for the rehab centre. He thinks she's been investing where he's told her to, but she hasn't. She's been giving me the money. It's all in those diaries there, every penny that she and everyone else has given me."

"And to do that, I had to get Hobson on my side. I had to get him to trust me. It took a long time, but bit by bit I handed over all my customers to Hobson, and I made sure he knew about it."

"That must have been tricky. On the one hand, you were making people believe you were straight, and on the other hand you were still involved with drugs. I mean, how the hell did you feel when you realized that although you wanted no part of the business, you were giving Hobson customers and allowing him to make massive profits from something you hated so much?"

"The investments I'm talking about had nothing to do with drugs. The people who've been sponsoring the rehab centre are businessmen; they've been feeding me with lucrative stock market information, which I've been feeding to Hobson. Everyone's happy when we make a killing. What I like the most is Hobson thinks I'm on his side completely. I give him the information. He gives the money to Knight to invest. She filters some of it off. He makes a profit and then pays me a bonus, which also goes into the rehab centre fund."

Reilly mulled over the information.

"If he's making so much money from the drugs, why is he bothering with what you're telling him?"

"Because he's greedy. People like him can never have too much money. They simply want more and more."

"And when was the last time you saw him, exactly?" asked Gardener.

"Around the time he disappeared. I was staying at The Harrogate Arms. We met in the bar for a quick drink. I gave him what he needed, and he went."

"And hasn't been seen since," said Reilly.

"That's nothing to do with me."

"And we know that because?" asked Gardener.

"Why would I tell you all this if I was responsible?" Pollard replied.

"Murderers do strange things, Mr Pollard," said Gardener. "They bask in the glory of everything they are doing, and quite often they like to think they can outwit us by talking openly. They think they are more intelligent than we are."

"Well, I'm not basking in any glory. What you're forgetting here is that my business partner is also missing."

"Sonia Knight," said Reilly.

"Yes, no one's seen her for a month, either. I'd hardly drop her in it, would I?"

"Actually, Mr Pollard, you're mistaken there," said Gardener.

"What about?"

"Sonia Knight has been seen. The Railway Station at Bursley Bridge, this morning."

Jackie Pollard breathed a huge sigh of relief. It seemed as if the world had been lifted from his shoulders. "Thank God for that. I wonder where the hell she's been. But at least she's okay, yes?"

"You just hold your horses, Jackie lad. We never said she was okay."

Chapter Twenty-nine

The small market town of Bursley Bridge was under siege. Not – as one might expect – from tourists, but the police and the media. Scene tape had been extended to the whole perimeter of the railway station, with officers scurrying like ants around a hill. Reporters were out in force, snapping their cameras at anything that moved. And the locals were starting to gather, asking the usual stupid questions.

Standing outside the railway station, the scene reminded Frank Thornton of a circus, and a badly managed one at that. He was pleased his boss wasn't there.

As well as trying to run an investigation, organize all the other officers and the POLSA team, Frank had been keeping his eye on the computer shop for any sign of life.

The exterior of the building was not maintained to the standard of the town's other shops. The windows were clean and the brickwork was in reasonable condition, but the paintwork was dull. Either the owner didn't care, or didn't have enough work to support the upkeep, or was far too busy to notice. He doubted the reason was the latter one. The shop was closed yesterday, and he had not seen a customer today.

But what he had seen within the last thirty seconds was movement in the window, and that was enough for him.

He informed his partner, Bob Anderson, and they both made a move.

Thornton opened the door, and the sight that met him made him think that the man had very little work. He had never seen so much junk in his life. There must have been a hundred carcasses of redundant machines littering every surface available.

Although he could not see the owner, Thornton could hear a conversation in the back. In the front of the shop, he noticed a cup of tea on the bench, in front of a stool next to a radio, which was switched on. He recognized a Robbie Williams tune, but he couldn't say what it was.

The owner appeared, waving a packet of biscuits.

"Isn't this typical, eh? Pretty quiet all morning, and the minute I start listening to my pop quiz, the phone goes and I have customers in my shop. But who am I to complain? I should count myself lucky that people demand my services."

Thornton guessed the man's weight at possibly sixteen stone, but he carried it well because he was tall. His hair was mousy brown, quickly going grey. He had brown eyes, thin lips, and a very determined walk.

Both men displayed their warrant cards.

"You'll have to excuse us. We don't have the luxury of being able to drop everything for tea and biscuits and quizzes. DCs Frank Thornton and Bob Anderson. We'd like to ask you a few questions, sir."

"Oh God, I'm sorry, fire away."

The man behind the counter lurched forward to switch off the radio, but disappeared under a cloud of dust with a crash. Frank Thornton heard the word "fuck," and managed to catch the packet of biscuits that had come his way.

In a scene straight out of Monty Python, the shop owner was quickly on his feet and switched off the radio, after which he dusted off his brown smock.

"Sorry about that."

"It's okay," replied Thornton. "And you are?"

"Graham Johnson. I own the place."

Bob Anderson had not said anything as yet. He remained near the door, glancing out the window.

Thornton passed the biscuits back. "We'd like to ask you a few questions about an incident that may have taken place on either late evening Sunday, or early hours Monday morning."

"Guess that's why the place is swarming with cops. Has someone been killed?"

"It is a pretty serious matter," replied Thornton. "Were you around the town during those hours?"

"Probably. I live here, above the shop."

"How long have you lived here?"

"About eight or nine years now."

"So you pretty much know everyone in the town?"

"I'd say so."

"Do you keep late hours?"

"I reckon. That's the thing about computers. They're unpredictable. Repairs can take minutes or hours. Once you're in the zone... well, I've sometimes been up all night. Lost track of time."

"Didn't happen to be up all night on Sunday, did you?"

"No. I have been really busy of late, but no all-nighters."

"And you haven't noticed anything unusual going on at the station?"

There was a slight pause before Johnson answered. Thornton reckoned he was probably a nervous person by nature. He could tell the man constantly bit his nails.

"Not really, but that station is bloody busy. Napoleon's always got something going on."

"Napoleon?" Thornton asked.

"You know, Major Middleton, or whatever title it is he's given himself. Thinks he runs the town, never mind the station. Napoleon is my little joke. He reminds me of Captain Mainwaring out of *Dad's Army*. The warden used to hate him, and always called him Napoleon. That's what I call Middleton. He's a bit pompous."

Amused, Thornton pressed on. "So you haven't seen any unusual activities outside of normal hours?"

Johnson appeared to think about it, then said he hadn't.

"Notice any strangers around, recently? I realise the pub runs a bed and breakfast, so I suppose there'll always be strangers of some description around."

"No, but I know what you mean," Johnson replied. "Most of the people we get here are train-spotters, or people who are really into steam, up for the weekend. You can spot 'em a mile off. They're the only people I've seen."

"You haven't noticed a white van hanging around the place?"

"White vans are pretty common, aren't they? I dare say I have seen one or two."

"You might notice this one, Mr Johnson. The driver's side brake light wasn't working."

After a moment's thought, Johnson replied that he hadn't.

Thornton decided to move on, figuring there was nothing further to be gained on that subject. So far, very few people they had spoken to had come up with anything concrete they could follow up. But that wasn't unusual.

"I noticed you were closed yesterday."

"Yes, I had to go out and collect computers that needed repairing. I have contracts with a lot of the major businesses around Leeds and West Yorkshire, so there's always enough work."

"Good to hear it. For a minute when I walked in, I thought you might have been having a closing down sale."

Johnson seemed confused for a few seconds, then laughed.

"Oh, the mess." He pointed to the piles of machines. "I'm too busy to clean up, but I know where everything is, don't let that fool you."

"It doesn't," replied Thornton.

Bob Anderson had stopped staring out of the window and was now pacing the floor, lifting the odd carcass, as if he was trying to work out what the hell was wrong with them. Thornton knew that wouldn't be the case. His partner was a bit of a technophobe. Kept well away from things he didn't understand. Thornton noticed Graham Johnson frown as he watched Anderson. Perhaps he didn't approve of having his shop casually searched.

Frank pulled out a blown-up photocopy of the SIM card taken from the implantable insulin pump. "Know anything about these?"

Johnson leaned forward. "I'll say. It's a subscriber identification module."

"Pardon," said Thornton.

"A SIM card."

"I know what it is. I just wondered if you knew anything about them."

"How big was it? Do you have a life-size photo, or any dimensions?"

"What for?"

"They come in different sizes. Which one have you got?"

Thornton suddenly felt out of place, and consulted all his notes before saying it was the micro SIM card.

"The first SIM card was made in 1991 by Munich smart card maker Giesecke & Devrient, who sold them to the Finnish wireless network operator Radiolinja," continued Graham Johnson whilst staring at the photocopy. "It securely stores the service subscriber key used to identify a subscriber on mobile telephony devices such as mobile phones and computers. The SIM card allows users to change phones by simply removing it from one mobile phone and inserting it into another mobile phone, or broadband telephony device."

Thornton quickly realized he had to be very careful with Graham Johnson. His manner indicated he was a logical person who displayed little or no emotion. He would probably answer all Thornton's questions honestly, but if he started to ask Johnson about his specialised field, he would simply swamp them with his knowledge, unaware that he was doing it.

"What I meant, Mr Johnson, was do you recognise it?"

"As it is, no. I could stand here all day and talk technical but it won't mean anything to you, and I'll end up boring you to death. You're in my territory now.

"All I will say is SIM cards are identified on their individual operator networks by a unique IMSI. Mobile operators connect mobile phone calls and communicate with their market SIM cards using their IMSIs. The first three digits represent the mobile country code. The next two or three digits represent the mobile network code. The final digits represent the mobile station identification number. Normally there will be ten digits, but there could be fewer in the case of a three-digit MNC, or if national regulations indicate that the total length of the IMSI should be less than fifteen digits."

Thornton was beginning to wish he hadn't started the conversation. He had, however, picked up something useful.

"Are you saying that there is a way to identify this particular card?"

"I doubt it. Cards are very unique. I suspect that the mobile companies who issue brand new phones have records of all the serial numbers of the cards and the phones and be able match them in an instant, but your serial number has been wiped out. Take a look." Johnson handed back the photocopy. "Someone has very carefully obliterated it."

Thornton sighed, thinking about the pump inside Alex Wilson, and how the serial number on that had been removed. He supposed that he was hoping for too much, but one never knew when the break would come, and for that reason he could not give up.

Thornton turned and noticed Bob Anderson was still completely engrossed with all the scrap machines. He was beginning to wonder if his partner had found something.

A crash diverted his attention back to Graham Johnson, who was busy cursing the stool for being in his way. Where he'd been going and what he'd been trying to do, Thornton wasn't sure. One thing he did know, the man seemed to be a little accident-prone.

"Are you okay?"

"I'm fine, don't worry about me."

He'd answered a little too quickly for Thornton's liking, which made the DC wonder if it hadn't been an accident, and more a diversion tactic for Bob Anderson, who had now joined Thornton at the front counter.

"Well, thank you for your time, Mr Johnson. I'm sorry to have spoiled your morning routine. Before I go, can I ask, are you into games?"

"Computer games? Yes, love my online games. Just don't get much chance to visit the sites these days, what with the pressure of work."

"What about the older ones? You know, the board games from years ago?"

"When I was younger, I think I probably had most of them."

Thornton produced the copies of the Inspector Catcher and Nurse Willing cards and passed them over.

"Recognize those?"

"Christ, these are old." Johnson studied them for a few moments, turning them round and round. "I've absolutely no idea. Where the hell did you get these?"

"Oh well, thanks for your time," replied Thornton, passing over his own card. "If you do think of anything, give me a call. Or just pop over to the station and ask for either of us, we'll be there all day."

Chapter Thirty

Eighteen hours after the shock of finding himself humiliated and trussed up in a wooden frame, Lance Hobson felt so disgusting that death was becoming the preferred option.

Shortly after the computer monitor had fired up, he had either fallen asleep due to a lack of energy, or passed out through sheer pain.

He'd woken up earlier in the day, sometime around five o'clock. The computer had been active and had informed him of the time. He could remember excruciating pain enveloping his body, his stomach rumbling, and filling the bucket.

He was awake now and it was midday. Glancing down, the bucket had been changed, and a toilet seat had been placed on the top. Hobson wondered what kind of a bastard was holding him captive, because he didn't find it amusing. He had no control over his aim, so narrowing the gap was of no real advantage. Still, it was simply more mess for someone to clean up. He was sure they'd grow bored in the end.

What would happen then?

The monitor screen changed to bright green, and his whole body suddenly felt as if it had been turned inside out. As though large needles on the inside were trying to force their way through. Perhaps if they were, the end he craved would soon come. He had little strength left in his vocal chords, so what should have been a scream came out as nothing more than a strangulated yelp. When the pain subsided, his body went limp against his restraints. As he reopened his eyes and tried to focus, he became aware of two things.

First, a small frame had been connected to the wall, housing five vials, each containing a liquid. One was clear, the others blue, green, amber, and red. He had no idea what they were.

Second, there was something wrong with his skin. Seriously fucking wrong!

It was red and patchy, and covered with small bumps. If he didn't know any better, he would say he had measles. But he did know better; he'd had them. It could be a heat rash, but he doubted it. He didn't have any clothes on, for a start.

He'd killed people for less. But that was when he *was* someone, a force to be reckoned with. No one messed with Lance Hobson. As far as he was concerned, he'd been the king of the underworld. He'd had the biggest patch, the most affluent income. Flash car, big house, the lot. He'd been the man.

But someone somewhere had obviously not paid the slightest attention to any of that.

A noise from behind the frame halted his thoughts. He heard footsteps, and someone appeared at the corner of his vision, before finally stepping all the way round.

Despite the position he was in, Hobson noticed certain things.

The man was wearing a business suit with a pair of new leather shoes. He was slim, with long, slender fingers, and a very expensive watch, possibly a Cartier. He also had a mask over his face.

Despite Hobson's lack of energy, and a general unwillingness to enter into a long, drawn-out conversation, he wanted to know who the man was, and what it was all about. Given his disadvantage, however, he was not going to let his captor see that he was frightened.

"Who the fuck are you?" asked Hobson.

"That's no way to speak to me," replied the hooded man. "But, despite my dislike of you, Mr Hobson, it would be rather remiss of me not to treat you like a guest in my house."

"A fucking guest?" shouted Hobson, but before he could continue, he felt enormous pressure on his body, as if a train had run over it. He tried to scream, but couldn't. He hadn't enough strength left.

As normality returned, he realized that the hooded man had placed a hand inside his jacket pocket seconds before the pain engulfed him. So it had to be something remote he was using. But what?

Hobson glanced down at his body. Everything seemed to be intact. He couldn't see anything connected to him, although he only had the front view. So, what was delivering the pain?

"Where am I?" asked Hobson.

"Who *I* am and where *you* are is not really that important." The man's voice was clear-cut and without any trace of accent, his diction precise.

"It fucking well is to me," shouted Hobson, still the fighter despite not having the upper hand. "People will be looking for me."

His captor calmly placed his hands in his pockets and said, "I doubt that very much."

Hobson had to find a way of unsettling him. If the man knew of his reputation, maybe he would start to think about the type of person he was dealing with. "Of course they will. I have friends, dangerous friends."

"And who might they be?"

"Never you mind. But they'll be out there, and they won't stop looking."

The man put a finger to his mouth, as if he was thinking.

"Like I said, Mr Hobson, I doubt it. You see, the problem is, I actually have all your friends. Alex Wilson, Sonia Knight. Do either of those names ring any bells?"

That was enough for Hobson. His growling stomach finally erupted, and he hoped the bucket would receive accordingly.

"Thought they might," replied the man, when Hobson's bowels settled down.

The wave of diarrhoea had not only depleted what little energy he'd had, but had started the pains in his body again. The boot was certainly on the other foot. Hobson had tried to gain a little bit of respect for fighting back despite his predicament, but he'd achieved nothing.

"You can't put your trust in either of those two, and they are about all you have. Unless, of course, you count your bent solicitor Wilfred Ronson, but I wouldn't bank on him coming to your aid, either. Not unless you were paying, and you're in no position."

The man *had* done his homework.

"You've given me something, haven't you?"

The man smiled. "I certainly have."

Hobson didn't know what to do or say. He had no idea who the man was, or what he had done to him. Surely, there had to be a drug connection. Was he a dealer? He certainly seemed to have the expensive lifestyle that went with it. Dealers, however, rarely did their own dirty work. Hobson was lost.

"What have you done to me?"

The man stepped back, and seemed as if he was going to walk away before he answered.

"I like puzzles, Mr Hobson. I've spent my whole life studying puzzles, setting them, working them out. Games as well. Did you ever play games when you were young?"

"Games? What kind of fucking games? Not the type you play, by the look of it."

"Board games. Monopoly, Cluedo, that sort of thing."

"Probably did, but I grew out of them. Have you?"

"I don't think you ever do. Anyway, let me answer your questions. It would be rather unfair of me not to. I'm going to be honest with you. Because by being honest, it means that I can create a more horrifying environment, much more frightening than if I lie. So I want you to think about one thing when you ask me a question. Make absolutely sure that you want to know the answer."

Hobson did think about that, and the man was right. There *was* something terrifying about having lost all control, only then to be told exactly what the outcome was going to be.

But Hobson was a fighter, if nothing else. "Go on."

"You're connected to a mainframe, and when I say that, I mean it sincerely. It's a wooden frame with a number of locks and levers and electric cables."

Hobson's heart sunk. The bastard was going to electrocute him.

"If you want to get out alive," continued the man, "you will notice a computer in front of you, which will randomly generate questions to which you either know the answer, or you don't. Each time you answer correctly, a lever will be released, which will free a part of your body.

"Should you successfully get out of the main frame, fastened to the wall is another, much smaller frame, with an antidote to your condition. There are five vials, but only one of them will cure you. All you have to do is choose it. You may have to consult the computer to work it out, should you be in the fortunate enough position of having the luxury of time."

Hobson felt hollow inside. He grew cold at the thought of what he'd been infected with. It could be anything. Even worse, how was he to know that the man who held him captive was telling the truth?

As if in response, the man suddenly removed his mask. He had a square face, with silver hair, but he wasn't old. His nose was long, and he had a silver moustache.

But for all that, Lance still had no idea who he was.

"What have I done to you?" repeated Hobson.

The man leaned in a little closer. "That's for another time, Mr Hobson."

159

A period of silence followed, and when Lance Hobson thought the conversation had ended, the man spoke again.

"As for what I've given you, Mr Hobson, well, that's a rather nasty little piece of work. It's a virus that interferes with the endothelial cells, lining the interior surface of blood vessels. As the vessel walls become damaged, the platelets are unable to coagulate. Subjects tend to succumb to hypovolemic shock.

"It has the highest case fatality rate, up to 90% in some epidemics, with an average case fatality rate of approximately 83% over twenty-seven years.

"You may be clever enough to work out for yourself what it is. If not, the next time we meet, I shall tell you."

It wasn't a question of whether Hobson was clever enough or not, it was more a case of being allowed to think rationally. Which, at the moment, was out of the question.

"It may surprise you to know, Mr Hobson, that I have studied you for four years. I know everything about you, where you go, who you see, who your friends are, what car you drive, what food you like. Everything, to the point that I probably know you better than you know yourself.

"I'm a very sporting man. The answers required for the questions designed to free you are well within the bounds of your limited knowledge.

"Once you are out of the frame, you need to make a decision on which liquid to drink. The computer will help you there, with a variety of clues. Once the correct answer is given, and you have found the necessary liquid to save your life, you can occupy your free time by trying to find the key to unlock that door in the corner, also hidden somewhere in this room."

Chapter Thirty-one

In Reilly's car on the way to Robert Sinclair's house, Gardener sat in the passenger seat, trying to make sense of what was happening. Within twenty-four hours, the victims had doubled, and the suspects had diminished.

Although willing to accept that Jackie Pollard could be their killer, he was unhappy with the lack of evidence. There had certainly been enough to detain Pollard for a further twelve hours, but he'd soon turned around any thoughts of another extension. The necessary paperwork had duly been signed, and a very despondent Pollard had left the police station pending further inquiries.

The news of Sonia Knight's demise now meant that instead of being a suspect, Pollard could possibly be the next victim.

The whereabouts of Lance Hobson was paramount in the investigation. Had he discovered what Knight and Pollard had been up to? If so, why would he have killed Alex Wilson? Unless Wilson was in on the deception.

Despite what Jackie Pollard thought about Wilson being a major snitch, maybe he had turned and was blackmailing Knight. Had Knight killed Wilson? Had Wilson threatened to tell Hobson, leaving Knight with no option? Either way, it was unlikely that Gardener and his partner would actually find that out, with Knight having been disposed of.

Which led him back to Hobson, who had not been seen for a month. He'd met Pollard at The Harrogate Arms, had a drink, and then left. Where had he gone from there? Probably not home. The building seemed as if it had been empty for all of that time. Gardener had sent Dave Rawson over to the Harrogate Arms to interview the staff and the owners, which would hopefully reveal something. CCTV footage would be handy, but he doubted anyone kept recordings that long.

The other problem with Lance Hobson being involved was that he was not a doctor. If *he* was running things, then there had to be someone else working with him. But that made it a three-man operation. There was nothing to say it wasn't a whole gang, but Gardener did not think a large number could operate on such a scale and keep everything under wraps. Someone somewhere would be seen or would let something slip. No, his money was on a smaller number.

Frank Thornton had called him as he was leaving the station to tell him about the interview with Graham Johnson, the owner of the computer shop.

Gardener couldn't work out whether or not the cards were, in fact, red herrings. He certainly didn't think the tarot cards were meant to point him in any direction other than the killer telling them he knew the victims extremely well. That led Gardener to surmise that the level of success the killer had was due to extensive planning, which would also indicate that he or she – he couldn't rule out the possibility their killer was female – had been harbouring a grudge for a while.

The board game cards were completely baffling to him. He'd had board games when he was young, and he'd also bought them for his own son, Chris. Like everyone else, he had the popular ones: Monopoly, Cluedo, Scrabble, and even some of the less popular games like Exploration and Campaign. The cards that were being left at the scene he could not recognize. Nor could anyone else, for that matter.

Had the cards been specifically printed by the killer for no other purpose than to throw them off the scent? Make them think outside the box, allowing him to buy time? He figured anyone who was clever enough to use Photoshop and had a decent enough imagination would be able to knock out a few cards that would resemble a board game from the past, but never actually exist in the first place.

All these possibilities were beginning to make his head hurt. Given that he was paid to produce results, he did not feel like he was earning his money. They needed a break. Maybe they would find one here, thought Gardener, as the car pulled up at the house of Robert Sinclair.

A wall had been constructed all around the house, with two wrought iron gates leading onto a red brick drive. As Reilly drove the car in, Gardener noticed a black sports car – a Peugeot RCZ – parked in front of the double door garage.

An array of potted plants enhanced the exterior of the building – not that it needed any. Apart from the predominant green, other colours were out in abundance: russet, purple, yellow, white, all of which added to the splendour of the environment. Extremely healthy Dutch elms and oaks stood across the grounds. Gardener was beginning to wonder if Sinclair was a tree surgeon as well. The whole of the drive was spotless.

Despite being a large house, it was only two-storeys high. The entrance had a curved arch with double doors, and carriage lamps. Most of the building was Yorkshire stone, a good portion of it covered with ivy and a variety of other creeping plants. The roof was thatched.

They stepped up to the entrance and rang the bell. The housekeeper answered and let them in.

Gardener glanced around the hall. The sound of a train chugging round a track from the first level of the staircase took his attention. Nothing in the house could have been described as cheap, and the item that drew his attention to the model train was absolutely no exception.

The grandfather clock was an impressive six feet tall. The face was centred between two gold columns, featuring a commemorative image of The Flying Scotsman on its plate. A plaque beneath the clock displayed the train's number, 4472. The pendulum was reminiscent of the original wooden half-way signpost between London and Edinburgh. A miniature of the locomotive encircled the base of the clock on a track, with several model buildings positioned between them. Amongst them were a Tudor-fronted pub, a post office, a garage, a railway station, and a church, the diorama complete with trees, lawns, lampposts and street lighting. On the top, above the clock face were a number of figures, which included a ticket inspector, railway porter, a driver, and a few passengers. A gold bell on the top of the clock chimed the hour.

Sean Reilly whistled through his teeth. "What do you think something like that would be costing, boss?"

"I shudder to think, Sean. What would all of this place cost?"

"Doubt you'd have any change from a million."

"He must be good," said Gardener.

"I think we're about to find out."

Miss Bradshaw had appeared at the foot of the stairs. "The doctor has a window for you. If you'd like to go into his study?" She pointed to the door. "Would you both like afternoon tea?"

"Thank you," said Gardener. "That would be nice."

"I don't suppose you could manage a few biscuits with that, could you now?"

The Irishman placed an arm around the housekeeper's shoulder. "Or maybe some fine home-baking. I bet you're a dab wee hand at that, so you are. You look to me like a woman who could bake a grand scone, and no mistake."

Gardener chuckled. He wasn't sure which was funnier, the fact that Sean Reilly could charm the birds from the trees, or he'd never forget his stomach no matter what the occasion.

It had quite clearly worked. "I'm sure I can, Mr Reilly. You go on through, and I'll be along shortly."

Both men entered the study and drew out their warrant cards as they approached one of the largest desks Gardener had ever seen.

Rising from the chair was the doctor they had heard so much about, Robert Sinclair, dressed in a pale blue suit that was definitely designer and no doubt cost more than Gardener's. He wore a white shirt and blue tie. His hair was immaculately groomed, and his fingers well-manicured. Gardener noticed the wedding band. He felt compassionate towards the man, because he still wore his own despite having lost Sarah.

"Please, gentleman, take a seat," said Sinclair. "I'm afraid I don't have a lot of time, but it's a pleasure to see you all the same."

"Thank you, Mr Sinclair," replied Gardener after the introductions. In the background he could hear music at a very low volume, something classical. The speakers were well hidden and must have been of exceptional quality, because he could hear every single instrument.

"What can I help you with?" asked Sinclair as he sat down.

"It's your technical expertise that we need, but before I get into that, can I ask how Christine Close is? I'm not prying, and I understand patient confidentiality, but at the moment, Gary works as part of my team. I'm asking as a friend and colleague."

Sinclair clasped his hands together in front of him and rested them on the desk. "She's doing as well as can be expected, Mr Gardener. You'll no doubt be aware that her condition is very serious, but we have her at the Ross & Sinclair Foundation, and she is receiving the best care."

"I'm sure Gary is grateful for what you're doing, but surely the cost of such treatment is out of his league?"

"Very definitely. My late wife's dream had been to set up a private clinic to care for cancer patients. After she'd died, I continued with her plans, and opened up the Foundation with my very good friend, Iain Ross. I won't bore you with the details, but we do receive some government funding, which we can use for some people who cannot afford the cost like most of our clients.

"PC Close and his mother Christine are a very deserving case. I've known them all their lives. I've never met harder working people, or two people who have had their fair share of tragedy. I suppose I also feel quite an affinity to Gary, because I was there when he was born. I've watched him grow up into a fine young man."

The door to the study opened and Miss Bradshaw wheeled in a hostess trolley, which she left at the side of the desk. She handed each person a drink and a small plate, and then put a tower of cakes on the edge of the desk, much to the delight of Sean Reilly.

"Miss Bradshaw, you're a treasure, so you are."

She smiled and left the room.

"Help yourselves to pastries and biscuits," said Sinclair.

"Are you not having any?" asked Reilly.

"No, Mr Reilly, I'm afraid I have a very strict diet."

When they had all settled themselves, Gardener explained briefly what had brought them to the surgeon's door, and drew out both the pump and ICD from an inside pocket.

"I wondered if you could tell us anything about these items? I understand this is an implantable insulin pump, used to treat diabetes."

He pushed it forward for Sinclair to gain a better view, although it was unlikely he would need it.

Sinclair studied the pump before he started talking. "Originally, yes. They are surgically implanted under the skin of someone who has diabetes. The pump then delivers a continuous dose through a catheter, usually into the patient's abdominal cavity. Where did you find yours?"

"Inside the patient, but it wasn't being used for its intended purpose. The pathology results tell that it had been filled with caustic soda."

"Good grief," said Sinclair. "That wouldn't have been pleasurable. And the victim is obviously dead because you mentioned the word 'pathology'. How horrific, it would have damaged the blood vessels without question, not to mention the blood. Very few of the major organs would have survived. I don't envy your job, Mr Gardener."

"Can you tell us who makes them?"

Sinclair's expression was pretty tormented. "You're going to have a problem with that, Mr Gardener."

"Tell us something we don't know," said Reilly. "We're having our fair share of those things you call problems."

Sinclair sat back and sighed. "I can imagine. Under normal circumstances, you could find out that information from the pump itself. I can see that this one has no markings. They always have a serial number. It might be recorded as sold or supplied in one country, but used in another. It's a very grey import market.

"The manufacturer's records may show a pump as being sold or supplied to a customer in Brazil, but if it eventually turns up in England, they would most likely refuse to acknowledge that serial number. They do not want any liabilities, like giving a guarantee, if it's used in a different country to the one intended. You have to remember, Mr Gardener, that these liabilities might be in the region of several million pounds, should a case go to court and damages be awarded against the company."

Sinclair continued. "However, reps will give goods away as 'loss leaders' to try and gain lucrative contracts. This is another grey area as far as the companies are concerned. They may condone it without acknowledging that it happens, then if something goes wrong, the rep is sacked or sued, and the company denies all knowledge of the transaction.

"The serial number on this pump has been removed. Maybe it's a demonstrator that it's been stolen, which is another possible scenario. I can't see any identification marks on it at all. And even if I could, we'd have a devil of

167

a job getting the company to cooperate with us, depending on whether or not it implicates them in dodgy supply deals."

Gardener was beginning to realize how intelligent their killer had been.

Reilly pushed forward the ICD. "Is it same in this case, with the defibrillator?"

Sinclair examined it and expressed the same conclusion.

"How was this used, if you don't mind me asking?"

Gardener told him.

"That's awful," replied Sinclair. "I can't imagine the pain that poor girl was going through. And you say that all the cables were leading into her teeth?"

"Yes," replied Gardener.

"What kind of monster are you trying to catch?"

"You're the second person to ask us that in a matter of hours."

"Who was the first?"

"A doctor at St. James's Hospital in Leeds, where our victim ended up. Andrew Jackson. Do you know him?"

"I certainly do. He's a very good orthopaedic specialist. I imagine this stuff is a little out of his league – as it is mine, to be perfectly honest."

"Is the likelihood of it being a doctor quite high?" asked Gardener.

"I would say so, Mr Gardener, although I'd like to think not. Doctors are supposed to save lives. I would think the person who has done this has extensive medical knowledge. They have known exactly where to place both devices, and how to modify them in order to achieve the maximum result. In the latter case, especially with the teeth, I think you should speak to my colleague, Iain Ross, he is a very gifted neurosurgeon and may be able to help."

"We're also looking for any leads on manufacturers. Can you help?" Reilly asked, having finished his scones and biscuits and no doubt eaten enough for all three of them.

Sinclair studied them both. "As I've told you, it won't be easy. I'll write down a couple of names."

He did so while he continued talking. "One of them is local, a company called KarGen, operating in Hunslet, a large industrial estate. The other company, called Hospitech, is just outside Stockton in the North East. I've also added the name of the company director. You may find it carries more clout to know that. And by all means, mention my name if it helps."

He passed over the paper with the names and addresses. "As I said, gentlemen, I really don't hold out much hope after what I've told you. Naturally, I don't expect to tell them what you've told me, but they're still going to be very cautious."

"On the contrary, Mr Sinclair, you've given us more than anyone else."

"There is always the possibility that neither pump belongs to them, and should that be the case, don't hesitate to contact me, and I'll try and point you in another direction." Sinclair glanced at his watch. "I would love to allow you more time, Mr Gardener, but I do have an afternoon surgery to run."

"You've been more than helpful," said Gardener, rising from his chair. "Nice place you have here."

"A lot of hard work. After my wife died, I wasn't sure I wanted to continue living here. Too many memories, you understand. But there was a lot more at stake than just the house. My practice, my reputation, but most of all, the fact that Theresa would have wanted me to continue."

It was something Gardener understood all too well. He was about to turn and leave when he noticed a trophy in a cabinet behind Sinclair.

"Sporting man?" he asked.

Sinclair followed his line of sight. "Not really. Take a closer look, I was the Junior Scrabble Champion, sometime back in 1972."

Gardener wandered over. There were more trophies, awards for crossword puzzles, and other word related games. A name that Gardener had almost forgotten popped out at him: Walker Brothers. He mentioned it to Sinclair.

"The crossword trophies are my mother's. She compiles them, but at one time she actually used to work for Walker's, here in Leeds."

"That must have been beneficial for a young man who had such an interest in Scrabble."

"You could say. Though Scrabble wasn't one of theirs. I must have had a copy of everything they ever released. Before anyone else, I might add."

"Really?"

Gardener wondered if he was on to something. He decided to draw out the game cards. He was probably hoping for too much, but one never knew. He passed them over to Sinclair.

"Wouldn't happen to recognize those, would you?"

Sinclair stared quite hard at the cards. "They ring a bell, though I'm not sure from what game."

"So you recognise them?"

"Only vaguely, Mr Gardener. It's the kind of thing that was around in the Seventies. Look at the cheeky innuendoes, almost as if they were from a 'Carry On' film. But I'm afraid that's as far as my knowledge extends."

"So, it isn't a game that came from the Walker Brothers' stable?" asked Reilly.

"Not as far as I can remember," said Sinclair, checking his watch. "Now, if there isn't anything else, maybe you will excuse me."

Both detectives thanked Sinclair for his time before leaving.

At the door, Gardener turned. "You wouldn't still have a copy of all those old games, would you?"

Sinclair smiled. "I wish."

Chapter Thirty-two

Gardener and Reilly pulled up at the mortuary. After having left Sinclair's house, Gardener telephoned Gary Close and asked him to concentrate his Internet search on the local game manufacturer, Walker Brothers. He asked Close to find out everything he could about the company, and whether or not any of the directors were still around. More importantly, did any of them live in or around Leeds, and were they available for an interview.

After that, he spoke to Cragg and gave him the names of the two companies who made and supplied the pumps and ICDs. He then asked for two men to be sent over to the local office in Hunslet.

Gardener and Reilly entered the building and walked down the corridor leading to the pathologist's work quarters, the sound of their heels bouncing off the walls. Gardener nodded to the receptionist as they passed. The warmth of the building was welcoming, but there was an air of trepidation. The SIO knew all too well that he had in fact tampered with a crime scene by demanding that Andrew Jackson remove the ICD. A reprimand from Fitz would be imminent.

Both men continued towards the silver steel door at the end of the corridor. Before going through, Gardener checked his reflection, adjusting his tie slightly. He glanced down. His suit now bore the hallmarks of a day's work, and his shoes were in need of a polish. All his life, he had taken a pride in his appearance. Despite the rigours of the scenes he had to visit in his job, he still wore clean clothes and a pressed shirt and tie every day, something Sarah would have demanded.

Fitz was working on Sonia Knight. He was dressed in a green surgical gown and gloves. He wore a mask, and his glasses were incongruously perched on the end of his nose, very close to joining whatever else was in Knight's chest cavity. Above him were a camera and a microphone. Fitz glanced up at the two men as they entered.

"I'd like a word with you two."

Here it comes, thought Gardener.

The pathologist switched off the microphone and camera, and asked his lanky assistant Richard to clean up. He removed his work gear, and disposed of everything except the gown, which he threw into a laundry basket.

After washing his hands, he beckoned them to his office.

"What *were* you thinking of?" Fitz asked Gardener.

"I know what you're going to say. I tampered with a crime scene. But I had good reason, Fitz."

"I could understand it of him." Fitz pointed to Reilly.

"Oh, that's right, go on, have a go at me. What have I ever done to you to earn such a low opinion?"

"How long have you got?"

"Never mind all that now. Let's have a cup of that lovely coffee you keep brewing." Reilly stood up and poured three cups without the approval of the pathologist, then started poking around.

"Now what are you after?"

"I'm trying to find a wee snack. I know you have them."

"My God, is nothing sacred?" Fitz handed out the biscuits from his desk drawer as he continued to speak to Gardener.

"It's definitely the same hallmark. I spoke to Andrew Jackson at St. James's Hospital. He told me it was an ICD in her throat. What I did find out was that all of the wires except one went into her teeth."

"And where did he lead that one?" Gardener asked.

"The spinal cord. The cables in the teeth probably wouldn't have killed her. They would almost certainly have caused diabolical pain, but once they had been removed and she was talking again, she would quite naturally tell us everything.

"He somehow managed to split the charge, so that her teeth received a separate jolt to the brain. That must have come last, because when it did, it caused the brain to explode. Literally."

"Jesus Christ! Her brain actually blew up?" asked Reilly.

"As good as. It certainly isn't in a position to be weighed, and the details recorded. It's very unlikely I can take a biopsy, either, although I shouldn't think you'll need it."

"Did you find anything else, Fitz?" Gardener asked. "Any clues left on the body?"

No. She's naked, and she's hairless. There are no further clues, and nothing else seems to have been tampered with. If you want the technical stuff on what it would do to her brain, you'll have to ask Robert Sinclair, or his partner, Iain Ross."

"We've just come from there."

"Did he tell you anything useful?"

"You could say that."

Gardener's phone chimed, cutting the conversation short. "DI Gardener."

"Mr Gardener? It's Andrew Jackson here."

"What can I do for you, Dr Jackson?"

"It's about the defibrillator we found inside the mouth of your victim."

"Go on."

"We've checked all the stock here at the hospital. It's all present and correct."

Gardener was disappointed. "Well, thanks for checking."

"Oh, that's not all. I do recognize your ICD. It's part of a number to be returned to the manufacturer, a company called KarGen, here in Leeds. We had a faulty batch, maybe four or five. I'm not quite sure what the problem was, but they should all have been returned over a month ago.

"I've checked the returns forms and there appears to be a discrepancy. You see, the same man always signs for returns at KarGen, only this time it was someone else. I cannot read the signature, which suggests something is amiss. I have the feeling that they were not returned at all."

"Unless the person who normally signs off was on holiday, Dr Jackson. But that said, I want a list of all the staff, including directors, and the man responsible for returning them."

There was a pause where Gardener could almost hear the cogs spinning round in Andrew Jackson's mind.

"That's a bit of a tall order," he replied.

"I appreciate that, but this is a murder investigation."

Chapter Thirty-three

Reilly pulled the car to a halt outside the railway station in Bursley Bridge. It was another warm day with a blue sky unspoiled by clouds. Members of the public were still present, trying to breach the scene. Even though their police car was unmarked, reporters had spotted it, converging on them before Gardener had his hand on the door handle.

As he and Reilly exited, the questions started.

"Sir, Darren Smith, Yorkshire Post. Can you tell us anything?"

Gardener ignored him and made his way to the station entrance.

"Geoff Hughes, Yorkshire Echo. Has someone been killed? The public has a right to know."

Gardener stopped and stared at the man. He was no more than five-foot tall, and almost as round. His head desperately clung to what hair remained, and he wore half-lens spectacles.

"What they have, Mr Hughes, is a right to the truth, something you lot seem to know very little about."

"That's a bit strong," shouted the reporter.

"Truth hurts, does it?" replied Gardener. "Oh, I'm sorry, you wouldn't know, would you?"

The reporter was about to protest further when Gardener turned and walked away.

"You heard him," said Reilly. "Now when we have something, we'll tell you."

Both men flashed their warrant cards to the officer guarding the entrance before continuing up the steps and into the station. Gardener was pleased he hadn't seen Giles Middleton standing vigil.

Everywhere he stared, the POLSA team – plus his own officers – were on their hands and knees conducting a painstaking fingertip search, which must be rankling *them* as much as him. It was a thankless, painstaking task that was unlikely to yield any result, but it had to be done.

Gardener was encouraged by the information he'd received during the last few hours. Though it didn't constitute hard evidence, he was pretty sure it could only lead somewhere positive once followed up. After what Sinclair had told them about the pump and ICD manufacturers, he figured that could be the only fly in the ointment. If they proved uncooperative, he would come down on them so hard they would have to reach up to tie their shoelaces.

"Christ, I wouldn't like this job, boss," said Reilly.

"Well, you wouldn't get down there, would you? All the biscuits you eat."

Reilly smiled and glanced around the platform. "At least my age wouldn't come into it."

Gardener spotted Frank Thornton and called him over. "How are things?"

"Pretty quiet at the moment. These lads must be pretty pissed off."

"It's part of the job. Where's Bob?"

"Had a call from a woman called Hillary Easterby, lives on Middleton Road. He's just gone to see her. Says she has some information which might help."

Gardener's mobile rang. "DI Gardener speaking."

"Mr Gardener, it's Maurice Cragg. Where are you?"

"The railway station at Bursley Bridge."

"Perfect," replied Cragg. "We've had a call from Graham Johnson, runs the computer shop. He's found something that he doesn't like the look of."

"Relating to the case?"

"Apparently, no. Something he doesn't like the look of on a laptop that he's repairing. Now I know it's not strictly in your field, but I just thought if you were there you might want to check it out, save me sending any of my men."

"Okay, Maurice. Sean and I will pop across the road."

"Thank you. Thought you might like to know, young Gary's had a breakthrough with Walker Brothers, got some good information for you. Still no news on KarGen."

"Okay," Gardener glanced at his watch. "Thank you. See you back at the incident room later."

"Will do, sir."

Gardener broke the connection and related to Reilly and Thornton what Cragg had told him. As they were about to move, Bob Anderson came up the station entrance steps.

"Sir, got something you'll want to hear."

They were all ears.

"Just been to see a woman called Hillary Easterby. She was out and about on both nights, Sunday and Monday. She's recently recovering from an operation and she can't sleep, so she goes for walks. It's very quiet in the early hours. She saw Graham Johnson's van on both occasions. It left the railway station around four o'clock, and headed off in the direction of Harrogate."

Gardener glanced at Thornton. "He never said anything to you about having a van, did he?"

"No." Thornton glanced at his partner, Bob Anderson. "Did she give you a reg and a colour?"

"White," replied Anderson. "And it's an 06 plate."

"Have the DVLA supplied the numbers for all those in the area?"

"I haven't seen the list if they have."

Gardener rang Cragg, who read the numbers out to him. In total there had been an original list of two hundred within a fifty-mile radius. Cragg had narrowed that down to ten within ten miles, and three within five miles. One of which was Graham Johnson's.

He told Anderson, who then gave him a piece of gold.

"She also said the driver's side brake light was out."

Chapter Thirty-four

Gardener stepped into the shop, recoiling immediately. He felt his partner bump into him.

The SIO had never seen such a mess in his life. His immediate first thought was that Graham Johnson had had an accident; perhaps he'd survived a gas explosion, and the resulting heap was how everything had landed. Gardener hated filth and dust and mess and everything that went with it. He'd seen better living conditions in war zones.

"Jesus Christ! How the hell does he find anything?" asked Reilly over Gardener's shoulder.

Gardener moved further in, if only to let his sergeant make some headway. He could hear a radio playing, and a voice in the back of the shop.

"You can't believe that anyone could work like this," he replied.

"Some people actually do, boss. There's probably some kind of organization to his chaos."

"So, what does it say about his mind?" asked Gardener.

"It's probably full of shit, like this place. I reckon he'd be great in a pub quiz. He's probably one of these people that stores all sorts of crap in his head."

"Thornton reckoned he was a bit of a specialist with electronics."

"The type of person we're looking for."

"It doesn't look good for him, does it? If you'd been in his position and you had nothing to hide, wouldn't you have told us that you had a white van, even let us have a look at the lights, just so we could eliminate you?"

"You're talking about the general public here, boss, most of whom go around with their eyes shut and their ears closed. We've had posters up outside the station and around the town asking for help, but how many have come forward and told us anything?"

"Yet they expect us to clean their backyard up. If the next victim was one of their own, they'd soon come running."

"Too right."

Reilly lifted one tower carcass and glanced underneath. Gardener couldn't help but notice the layer of dust.

Gardener studied Graham Johnson as he walked through to see who was in his shop. He was as tall as the SIO, with unruly hair, peppered grey and brown. He had brown eyes, thin lips, and a very straight walk. He was wearing a brown smock. Underneath, Gardener could see a black T-shirt.

"Can I help you gentleman?"

The two officers showed their warrant cards and introduced themselves. "I believe you called the station about a laptop, Mr Johnson," said Gardener.

"Christ, that was quick. I only called about five minutes ago. Guess you guys really must take this seriously."

"We just happened to be across the road."

"Nasty business, that."

"What is?" Gardener wondered how much he really knew.

"Whatever's happened. You guys have been round it like a swarm of flies and now it's covered in scene tape. It can't be a case of shoplifting."

Graham Johnson glanced over Gardener's shoulder, watching Sean Reilly sift his way through the debris. His manner suggested he was a little nervous. That could be due to either what he'd found on the laptop, or that he had something to hide. If it was the latter, then he probably couldn't have picked a better place than his shop, judging by the mess.

"You wanna watch you're doing, mate? You never know what's lurking under there."

"I'll bet you do," replied Reilly.

"Funny you should say that."

"About the laptop, Mr Johnson?"

"Oh right, I'll bring it through."

Johnson went into the back of the shop, returning immediately. He placed the laptop on a bench in front of him, hooked it up to some kind of electrical testing equipment, and powered up the machine.

"Couple of young guys brought it in yesterday. I just want to say that I don't think they're responsible for what I've found."

"What did they bring it in for?" asked Gardener.

179

"Usual thing, machine has a virus. They told me their dad's away, and they'd been using it to do their homework. Likely story. Cut a long story short, they'd been surfing a little porn, nothing bad, but the machine got a virus and then the Blue Screen of Death, and they couldn't do another thing with it."

Gardener knew better than to probe further. He didn't fully understand what Johnson had said, but suspected he'd be there all night if he asked the man to explain it.

The tune on the radio changed, but it was nothing that Gardener recognized. A noise behind him, followed by a curse, suggested that Reilly had dropped something. Johnson glanced over at him.

"And what have you found on the laptop?"

"I found what they'd been looking at. All the usual stuff. It's only when I located and removed the virus and powered the machine up again that my software discovered a load of hidden files. And when I say hidden, I mean hidden. The encryption system was better than the one they have in the Pentagon." Johnson stopped talking and fiddled with the laptop.

"Here they are, Inspector. They're not very nice."

Gardener took one glance. Reilly had joined him. The material was very extreme, most of it connected to the National Front.

"How much is on there?"

"I don't think I've discovered all of it."

"Okay, Mr Johnson. If you'd like to switch off the machine and let us have all the details. I take it you keep documents relating to whose machine you're repairing?"

"Oh, yes, got it right here."

Gardener was relieved. At least there was some organization within the place.

"We'll pass this on to the relevant authorities."

"Oh, are you not connected with that branch, then?"

"No, as I said, we were across the road at the station. We're with the Major Crime Team."

"Isn't this a major crime?" asked Johnson.

"It is, but not our jurisdiction."

"When we said major crime, we were talking about murder, son," said Reilly.

"We actually came to talk to you about something else."

"Oh?" said Johnson.

Gardener was beginning to suspect that Johnson was very unhappy about them being there, now that their interest in the laptop was not a high priority. He'd started biting his nails and moving his tools from one place to another.

"Two of our officers were in here earlier today, questioning you about the incident."

"I remember that."

"Do you remember what they asked you?"

"Most of it."

"Let's jog your memory a little, son," said Reilly. "Did they mention a white van to you?"

"I believe so."

"A large white van that had been seen around here and Bramfield, one that has a driver's side brake light out?" pressed Reilly.

"I can't recall the exact details."

"Maybe you were having trouble with your memory, Mr Johnson," said Gardener.

"How so?"

"You failed to let the officers know that you had a white van. It's come to our attention that your van also has a brake light out. We've been around the back, Mr Johnson, and we see that your van has been reversed into the premises. Would you like to do us a favour and drive it out on to the street in front of the shop, so we can check the lights?"

Johnson almost seemed relieved. "Oh God, for one shitty minute there I thought you were going to say that someone had fingered my van in whatever's going on over there. Christ, if that's all it is, give us a minute to find the keys and I'll be right with you."

"Thank you," said Gardener.

Johnson went into the back. Gardener could hear him rummaging in drawers.

"Took that a bit well, didn't he?" asked Reilly. "Maybe he's fixed it – thinks he can fool us."

Johnson shouted he'd be through in one second, and that he had the keys.

Although Gardener heard him, he was glancing at something that had caught his attention on the floor, between the bench and the wall.

"Sean, will you give me a hand to move this bench?"

"What have you seen?"

Gardener pointed. "Is that a SIM card?"

"Looks like it," said Reilly.

Both men managed to move into a position that was not perfect, but would do. They dragged the bench out, and Reilly retrieved the SIM card.

"Well, look what we have here."

He passed it over to Gardener, whose skin prickled. It was a micro SIM card, and the serial number had been removed.

Gardener glanced towards the back of the shop. "Where the hell is he?"

Reilly didn't wait. He cleared the shop in seconds, and Gardener could hear him stomping around in the back.

Without warning, an engine burst into life, and Gardener saw the white van screech around the corner of the shop and out on to the road. Graham Johnson was at the wheel.

"Sean, out here, now!"

As both men exited the shop, Gardener glanced in the direction the van was going, towards Harrogate. Graham Johnson was paying no attention to speed limits. By that time, Thornton and Anderson had joined them.

"What happened?" asked Thornton.

"I'm not sure, but let's say Johnson's just climbed the ladder of suspects. Frank, Bob, jump in your car and see if you can follow him. Whichever one of you is not driving, get on the phone and see if you can set up a series of roadblocks."

Chapter Thirty-five

Gardener was late for the incident room meeting. He wasn't happy, but his team was in good spirits. The ANACAPA chart was huge, with spider's legs going in all directions, and Maurice Cragg had updated it with Graham Johnson's name at the top of the tree.

Tea and coffee had been laid on, and Gardener grabbed a cup whilst the men sorted through their notes and took seats. It had been another long day, and though they'd had some encouraging results, there was still a lot of work ahead of them.

He stood at the front and addressed the team.

"As you all know, we found Sonia Knight this morning at the railway station in Bursley Bridge. She was alive when we arrived, but has subsequently died.

"This afternoon, Fitz confirmed for us that although she had cables into her teeth controlled by the ICD, that wasn't what killed her. She also had a cable running directly into her spinal cord. Apparently, the charge from that simply overloaded the brain, and it exploded."

"Same man, then, sir?" asked Rawson.

"Almost certainly," replied Gardener.

"This morning, at the hospital, Sean and I spoke to a surgeon called Andrew Jackson. He thought the ICD looked familiar, and has since called to tell us that he recognizes it as part of a faulty batch that should have been returned to the manufacturer. He suspects they were not, in spite of the relevant paperwork being signed."

"Have we spoken to the man responsible?" asked Bob Anderson.

"We have. I asked Andrew Jackson for a list of staff at the hospital, including directors. About an hour ago we had a brief meeting with the storeman, Percy Slater. He says that the pumps and ICDs were returned, but it wasn't the normal driver who collected them. Apparently, that man was on holiday, so it was a relief driver."

"What was his name?" asked Thornton.

"We don't know. Mr Slater gave us a good description, though. The most important thing he did was record the registration of the white van."

"Nice one," said Sharp. "Anyone we know?"

"As a matter of fact, yes. It belongs to Graham Johnson, the man who runs the computer shop in Bursley Bridge."

"Excellent," said Benson. "Let's get him lifted."

"We'd love to, Paul, but it's not that simple." Gardener nodded to Reilly while he sipped his tea.

"Our man with the van has done a runner. Graham Johnson called Maurice Cragg earlier and reported some nasty stuff on a laptop he was fixing – all sorts of political crap connected to the National Front. We've passed that over to the relevant department. While we were in his shop, we also needed to discuss the fact that he owned a white van with a brake light out, something Bob had said one of the locals mentioned. When we tackled him about it, he managed to slip the net. What we did find in his shop was a micro SIM card with the serial number scratched out."

"Does anyone know where he is?" asked PC Patrick Edwards.

"Not yet, Patrick," replied Gardener, "but we're on to it. I put a marker on the PNC against the vehicle number. Any officer who finds him will stop him, detain him, and call me immediately. I've also put the van on the ANPR database. If he drives through a camera and it pings on the system, we'll know about it."

"We might be able to check his phone location," Edwards added.

"Good point, Patrick." Gardener turned and addressed the desk sergeant. "Maurice, would you get me a complete background on Graham Johnson, everything you can find?"

"Yes, Mr Gardener. I'll get on to it as soon as we finish here."

Dave Rawson coughed and stuck his hand in the air, as if he was back in the classroom.

"Yes, Dave," said Gardener.

"That might tie in with something I've found out. The people who run The Harrogate Arms recognized the shots of Pollard and Hobson. Said both men were in there on the night that Pollard says they were. They were drinking for about an hour before Hobson left. Pollard stayed for another two hours, he had a meal and a couple more drinks, and then a blonde-haired girl came in and collected him. Owners reckon the girl was Sonia Knight.

"The owners mentioned a couple who were out with their dogs who claim they saw someone bundling something into the back of a white van the same night that Hobson and Pollard were there. They thought it looked like a carpet and said no more about it."

"Good work, Dave. Have the owners supplied names and an address for the couple?"

"No, but I'm going back in the morning. He says the couple are there as regular as clockwork, about nine-thirty every two days. They weren't there today, but they should be tomorrow. I'll see if I can talk to them."

"Good. If we can get a registration, we could probably tie this up if it's Johnson's van. That brings me to Jackie Pollard. We have released him pending further enquiries. I have to be honest here. My gut feeling is that Pollard is not involved. He's explained to Sean and me why he was outside the shop on the night Alex Wilson was killed, and we're quite happy to accept what he said as truth for the moment."

"Which still leaves Lance Hobson," said Sharp. "Any news on him?"

"Nothing yet. As Dave just said, he was last seen at The Harrogate Arms a month ago and has not been seen since. All these people are tied into something. They've upset someone. Wilson and Knight are dead. Hobson is missing. For what it's worth, I don't think he's pulling strings."

"What about Ronson, Pollard's brief? He's also Hobson's brief. Do you reckon he's involved?"

Gardener turned to Cragg. "Maurice, anything on Ronson?"

"Yes, sir. Ronson lives in Shipston. Seems he's spent most of his lifetime on the right side of the law, but has skirted over to the wrong side when it suited him. He nearly always turns up to represent criminals with a drug background. If a client had no solicitor, he was always on hand.

"Robson's biggest failing is that he's a drunk. The most interesting thing I found out is that he's had a history of heart problems. Seems he had surgery recently, and some say that's why he hasn't been seen for a while. Probably why he's on holiday."

"Do you know anything about the surgery?"

"No, sir. I'm only going by what I've managed to pick up, but I bet his secretary knows."

"In that case, do you have an office address for him?"

"Yes, sir." Cragg passed it over.

"Thank you," said Gardener. "Tomorrow morning we're paying his secretary a visit. We'll find out exactly where he is, when he's due back – which I believe is tomorrow, anyway – and whether or not he's implicated in any way."

"There is another thing, boss," said Reilly.

"Go on."

"If he's had any surgery involving his heart, he could be the next victim."

"It's always possible, especially if he's had an ICD fitted."

Gardener glanced around the room. "Thornton, Anderson, got something for you. We went to see Robert Sinclair this afternoon, and he also recognised the pumps and the ICD, told us exactly what they did. He even suggested a manufacturer for us, a company called KarGen in Hunslet.

"Seems their reps are sometimes involved in unscrupulous deals, leaving free samples, and pumps being recorded as sold in one country and then turning up in another. I want you to speak to the top men and rattle some heads. As we have no serial numbers, they may well deny the pump came from them. Read them the riot act. Tell them that if they don't cooperate, I will arrest every last one of them for withholding information in a major crime investigation. See how they like that."

Bob Anderson's face lit up. He was an old-fashioned copper who liked old-fashioned methods, and Gardener could tell his last statement was right up Anderson's street. He rubbed his hands together. "Get in. I'm going to enjoy that."

The rest of the team laughed. They may have had a tough two days, but information was beginning to filter in, and they were making headway. That always lightened the mood.

"Colin, are you still working your way through the names and addresses of the pub guests?"

"Yes, I've spoken to a lot of them, they're still there. Most are train-spotters a bit disappointed about the weekend being spoiled by a murder."

"Oh, I'm so sorry," said Reilly with a couple of biscuits in his hand. "Next time we'll try and work around them." His comment raised more levity.

Sharp continued. "I need to speak to two more couples. Apparently, they left early."

"Okay," said Gardener, with the full confidence that Sharp would see it through to the end.

"There is one more thing," said Gardener, noticing the board game card stuck to the ANACAPA chart. "We've had a lead on the cards."

PC Close nodded, as much to say that he had as well.

"We got a lot more than we bargained for when we spoke to Robert Sinclair. Seems his mother used to work for Walker Brothers, a games manufacturer here in Leeds."

"Bloody hell, I remember them," said Thornton. "I think I had quite a few myself... still, don't remember anything with cards like we've got."

"You might not," replied Gardener. "Sinclair's mother used to bring him a copy of every brand-new game."

"Doesn't still have them, does he?" asked Thornton.

"No," said Gardener. "At least he inferred he didn't."

"But you think otherwise?" asked Bob Anderson.

"Not really, Bob. You know the old saying, once a copper, always a copper. Sometimes you never trust anything that anyone says, but they can't all be lying."

"What did you think of Sinclair, sir?" asked Cragg.

"Seemed okay to me, Maurice," replied Gardener. "A bit of a control freak, maybe."

"And a bit of OCD, if you ask me," said Reilly. "Did you notice the light switches?"

Everyone roared with laughter. "Fuck me, Reilly," said Anderson. "Only you could go and interview someone and come out with a statement like that."

"That's 'cause I pay attention."

Even Gardener was laughing. "Go on, then, Sean. What's with the light switches?"

"They were all the same way up, including the double and triple switches. Have you any idea how hard it is to control light switches so that they all face the same way?"

"Tried, have you?" laughed Thornton. "Wouldn't surprise me, it's obviously another sign of madness, and they don't come any madder than you."

Another roar of laughter erupted.

"You mark my words," shouted Reilly to Thornton. "Something will come of it."

As the laughter subsided, Gardener continued. "Anyway, Sinclair felt that he recognised the game cards: figured that they may have been from a game released in the Seventies but couldn't tell us a great deal more."

He glanced at PC Close. "Gary, did you find out anything on Walker Brothers? I'm not after a chequered history, just someone we can talk to."

"Yes, sir," said Close. "This game called Murder was developed and distributed in 1968. The man you want to talk to is Simon Walker, the founder's grandson. He had a seat on the board from 1980, until it was sold to Hasbro in 1994. Anyway, he lives in Shipston, west side of Leeds going towards Bradford. Said he'd be happy to speak to you tomorrow morning, if you have the time."

"Isn't that where Ronson lives?" Reilly asked. "We can probably kill two birds with one stone."

"You're right, Sean."

Gardener turned back to PC Close. "Excellent work, Gary. I've been meaning to ask, how's your mum?"

"Comfortable, according to Sinclair. He reckons I should be able to go and see her tomorrow morning. She's heavily sedated at the moment."

"That's good to hear." Gardener did not want to tell him anything about his meeting with Sinclair, and the fact that he had also asked about Gary's mother. He didn't particularly want to betray client confidentiality.

"And your leg?"

"Improving, sir. Now you've made me take the tablets."

Gardener smiled. He turned to Rawson. "Dave, anything on Ross, did you manage to speak to him?"

"Yes, sir. But not for long."

"How come?"

"He sounds just like Sinclair from what you've described, a bit of a control freak but I didn't check his light switches."

Another roar of laughter erupted before Patrick Edwards took over. "We went to see him, had to speak to his wife first. She said he followed his morning rituals quite closely: another one with OCD."

"One of his rituals was the Times crossword," said Rawson. "Anyway, I remember seeing a film with Roger Moore once. He was doing the Times crossword, and someone asked if he could do it in ten minutes, and he replied, I have never taken ten minutes. Which was exactly what Ross said when he came out of his study as I was asking his wife."

"Everything about him reeks of money," said Edwards, "posh house, fancy car, a watch that probably cost more than I earn in a year... not that I'm complaining about my salary."

"To cut a long story short, sir," said Rawson, "he told us pretty much the same story you got from Sinclair. He reckoned you have to know what the hell you were doing to get away with what the killer did to Sonia Knight: more importantly, you would have to have somewhere accommodating to carry it out. It wasn't an afternoon fix – something like that takes time."

"They certainly had the time if she's been missing a month," said Cragg.

"Somewhere accommodating," repeated Gardener, "like a big house, or a foundation?"

"Or a hospital," suggested Reilly, "but I doubt you could get away with that."

"Food for thought," replied Gardener. "It doesn't really move us on except to put two people into the frame who are probably not the ones you'd suspect."

"Sinclair and Ross?" suggested Colin Sharp.

"I really can't see either of those two being involved," said Cragg.

"You wouldn't think so, Maurice," said Gardener. "And I would doubt it myself, unless we find a connection with Graham Johnson."

"There's always Andrew Jackson at the hospital," said Reilly.

"Time would be his problem," said Gardener, "he only breathes because it's automatic."

Further topics discussed included the PolSA team at Bursley Bridge, the house-to-house, the pub guests, train-spotters and, finally, the station manager Giles Middleton, but most of the comments brought nothing new to the table.

"Still a bit of an open playing field," Dave Rawson finally offered.

"Yes, but I do feel we're getting somewhere." Gardener smiled. The meeting had been a good one. The team had their actions; perhaps it was time to wind down a little earlier than last night.

He was about to say as much when Cragg demanded their attention.

"There is one more thing, sir. It's pretty serious." Judging by the expression on the desk sergeant's face, he meant it.

"Go on," said the SIO.

"We've had a call from a gentleman whose son has apparently gone missing."

"Missing? Where's he calling from?"

"Churchaven, sir."

Gardener thought about that for the moment. "Well, that's where I live. Who is it?"

All eyes were on Gardener now. Children going missing was a serious business, especially as Gardener had had first-hand experience during the Christmas murders case.

A smile cracked Cragg's face as he started laughing.

"A gentleman called Malcolm Gardener, sir. Said he hasn't seen his son Stewart since Sunday night, and if I came across him, will I send him home early for his tea?"

Reilly's infectious laughter instigated the entire room, and Gardener could feel his face reddening. He knew he would never live it down.

Chapter Thirty-six

Lance Hobson was confused on a number of levels.

Sitting on the toilet seat on top of the bucket with his legs still shackled, he wondered if that had been its sole purpose all along: somewhere to rest his weary body if he found he could play the game and become a winner.

The first hint that he would ever walk free from it all came five hours ago, when he'd actually managed to answer one of the random questions thrown out by the computer. The man holding him captive had obviously been right when he said he knew Lance. Despite feeling so crap, it hadn't taken Hobson long to work out that the ones he was able to answer with relative ease were all about his favourite childhood football team, Leeds United.

Hobson had been an ardent follower since he'd been taken to the Elland Road stadium in 1982, when he was five years old. His father had bought him everything he needed to become a true supporter: shirt, hat, gloves, scarf; even strip to play on outside.

He couldn't remember too much about those early matches, but the game and the club had started to make a real impact in 1985, when former player Billy Bremner took over the team. During that year, Lance, eight at the time, had managed to secure a place in the youth team, and had spent more time at the ground, taking any odd jobs he was given, acquiring first-hand knowledge about his pride and joy. Within three years, everything had changed. He'd fallen in with the wrong crowd, and found a life of crime far more attractive. His love for the club did not wane, but his ability to play the game did. The rest – as they say – is history. Despite his extensive knowledge, however, the questions his captor had fed into the computer were not as easy as he would have wanted.

At two o'clock in the morning, Hobson had woken up with every joint in his body engulfed by pain. The computer was on, still throwing out conundrums for him to work on. The time limit on the questions meant that they were refreshed every two or three minutes. He'd lost interest early on, and had stopped trying to answer questions on subjects he felt he had little or no knowledge of, despite what his captor had told him.

Then he'd noticed something. The subject of Leeds United was raised, and with it the possibility that he may be able to work his way out his mess. The first two questions remained unanswered because they were too far back in team history for his memory, and he ran out of time. He'd realized he would have to do better if anything was going to happen. Thankfully, his newfound interest allowed him to forget about his mystery virus, and any pain it brought.

The first question that he had been able to answer was: "Leeds United's predecessor team, Leeds City FC, was formed in 1904, but was forcibly disbanded by The

Football League in 1919 for what?" He'd heard about the reason, and somehow managed to scream out the answer on the very edge of the time limit. It concerned allegations of illegal payments to players during the First World War.

When the loud creaking noise came, it had startled the life out of him. The frame in which he was held suddenly moved, allowing his right arm to drop by his side. The pins and needles as the blood returned made him feel sick.

The second question, and the subsequent release of his left arm, came at four-thirty. "One of Leeds United's first nicknames, the Peacocks, came from the original name of Elland Road, 'The Old Peacock Ground', which was named by the original owners of the ground. Who were they, and what was it named after?"

That one had been pretty easy: Bentley's Brewery. The nickname came from their pub 'The Old Peacock', which still faces the site.

That answer had allowed him to sit down for the first time in forty-eight hours. Even then, it had been an extremely slow process, because he was still in the dark. The only time the cellar light burst into life was when his captor came to talk to him. Aware of what was in the bucket below him, Lance had been very careful when lowering his body to the seat.

He had spent his time since with his eyes either on the screen or the vials in the frame on the wall, his last obstacles to freedom.

God help the bastard keeping him when that happened.

Eventually the questions about Leeds United had dried up, allowing him further time to figure out his predicament.

He'd wondered if the man who had him was making his escape easy. If so, why? Surely if he had gone to such lengths to abduct him, make him disappear, torture him, and very likely do the same to his colleagues, why the hell would he make escape an easy thing? The only answer Hobson could come up with was that the man had something far more serious in mind. Perhaps Hobson was only playing round one of his game. Should that be the case, he was in trouble. The opening round of any game was usually pretty easy.

And what reason did the man have for everything he'd done to him? Yesterday, the man had told him that he'd been studying him for four years. How had he done that without Hobson knowing? He'd obviously infiltrated his life in some way, but Hobson did not recognize him when he'd had his first glimpse. He still didn't have a clue about the man's identity. What had he done to the man four years ago that had created such animosity?

The more he'd thought about it, the more convinced he became that the answer had its roots in drugs. Because that's all Hobson had been involved in since he had left school. His life of crime had started when he was twelve, stealing cars and burning them out. But he seriously doubted it had anything to do with that. Anyway, whatever the reason, it was something that had happened four years ago, and he had certainly given up stealing cars by then.

With so much time on his hands, he'd also considered the state of his health. At the moment, he was no worse than yesterday, but he was no better, either. He thought back to what he'd been told about the virus, and tried to rack his brains. What the fuck had he been infected with? He was fully aware of the things you could pick up from dirty needles: AIDS, hepatitis, possibly HPV. None of those made someone feel so bad so quickly, though. Whatever he'd been given was far more lethal.

One thought frightened him even more: was his captor lying about the vials on the wall? Did they really contain an antidote? Or something even worse?

Hobson did not want to think about that. He tried to put any thoughts of freedom, or an antidote, to the back of his mind. He was in the game now for one reason. He was determined to free himself and take his revenge. He was going to kill the man who had him, irrespective of whatever he was supposed to have done four years ago. According to his captor, Hobson had started it. Well, Hobson had news for him. He was damned well going to finish it, too.

The light coming on nearly blinded him. He felt a sudden wave of nausea and wrapped his arms around his torso, pressing his hands against his stomach.

He almost jumped out of his skin when those same hands passed over a very rough piece of skin. Fighting the shock of discovering he glanced down his body. There was no mistaking the fresh, clean stitching on his abdomen, about six inches long.

He struggled and tried to concentrate, quickly feeling the rest of his torso. He did not come across any more wounds, but what he did find was a small oval-shaped lump on his chest. He ran his hands over the object, and his skin was extremely sensitive to the touch. It felt blistered, and hurt him as he pressed on it. It had a very hard, metallic feel to it, and was, in fact, underneath the skin.

Once again, not being a doctor, he had no idea what it was. He doubted very much it would come out, though.

Hobson was revolted by the fact that the monster who had him seemed to be turning him into a freak.

The basement door suddenly opened, and the very man he was thinking about walked in, wearing a tracksuit and trainers. He had a towel draped around his shoulders, sweating profusely and breathing a little heavy. Hobson thought it was a pity that he was unable to take advantage right now.

"Good morning, Mr Hobson. I see we've made some progress."

The man's condescending manner was really beginning to wind Hobson up.

"You'd better hope I don't make any more, sunshine," Hobson replied.

"If you say so."

Christ, he was a smug bastard. Lance had to give him that. He wished he could stand up and take a pop at the man.

"I'm pleased to see that you've figured out which questions you can answer. Makes things more interesting, don't you think?"

"For who?" replied Hobson.

"Both of us, of course. Tell me, have you worked out yet what I've infected you with?"

Hobson gripped the sides of the toilet seat. It was all he could do to control his emotions, but he realised he might well gain more satisfaction if he could. But despite trying to fool himself into thinking he didn't care what the man had given him, deep down, he did. He ignored the question and went on the attack.

"I will get out of here," replied Hobson, "make no mistake. Then I'm going to kill you."

"Are you really? Don't tell me, you're going to do that because of what I've done to you?" asked the man in front of him.

"No. As a matter of fact," replied Hobson, desperately fighting to keep his feelings in line, "what *I've* done to you is more important to me. You must have a fucking good reason for all of this, so let's hear it. What exactly have I done to you?"

The man walked around the room, removing the towel from his shoulders, wiping his face and forehead. Eventually he stood before Lance and leaned over, but not close enough to come within striking distance. He obviously knew that Hobson's legs were still locked up, as he stood far enough away to be able to keep his captive out of harm's reach.

"To me personally, nothing," replied the man. "But you and low life scum like you were responsible for my son's death. I swore blind that I would hunt you down and I would get even with you. It's taken me four years, but I wasn't going anywhere. It simply gave me more time to prepare a very satisfactory revenge."

Suddenly, despite all the bravado, the courage, the staring into the face of adversity, the boot was on the other foot again. Hobson had obviously been fooling himself if he'd thought it could ever be any other way.

His mind whirled like a roller coaster. There were so many questions. The most prominent being who the hell had he killed four years ago?

Chapter Thirty-seven

Reilly parked the car at the back of The Corn Exchange and switched off the engine. He activated the central locking, and both he and Gardener set off to find Ronson's office.

"You never did tell me the punishment your dad metered out," commented the Irishman. "So what happened, then? A slap on the back of your legs and off to bed without any supper?"

Gardener smiled. "Oh, the wit of the Irish. So, what happened to you, a personality transplant?"

"God, no, I didn't get off so lightly. I started working with you."

Gardener laughed as they crossed the road in front of the circular building, heading towards the pedestrian access of Kirkgate.

"Well, he had to have his say, you know what he's like. I think he thinks I'm still a child."

"Only natural, boss," replied Reilly. "You'll always be his boy no matter what age you are."

"He must have had forgiveness in his soul. He'd made a nice shepherd's pie, which we had with honey-roast parsnips, vegetables, and roast potatoes. It was the first cooked meal I'd had in three days. And we also had homemade bread and butter pudding."

"Jesus wept. I don't know how you can eat that stuff."

"That coming from a human garbage disposal."

"Even we have standards!"

Gardener spared a thought for his father, Malcolm. Following Sarah's death, he'd offered his help, and had moved into their home temporarily. The house was detached and large enough, centrally located in the small but picturesque village of Churchaven. The relationship had worked out so well that the arrangement had become permanent, which pleased his son Chris, who was now considering a career in law.

Malcolm was always available for his grandson, especially when Gardener could not be there for one reason or another. He helped Chris with his homework, cooked his meals, catered to most of his whims in general, and regularly took him to the cinema. They shared a great love of films.

The streets of Leeds were full of people on their way to work, hopping on and off buses. The market traders were busy with their stalls, something that always pleased Gardener. He noticed a window cleaner plying his trade early. The food stalls were up and running, smells of cooked breakfast permeating the air, mingling with the aroma from the local bakers. Gardener knew which he preferred, which no doubt differed to his partner's tastes.

They entered a small side street off Kirkgate, where Wilfred Ronson's offices were situated. Both men glanced up at an exterior that had seen better days. A lot of the buildings had been cleaned by the council over the last few years and were much smarter for it. Ronson's had obviously been missed.

There were four brass plaques on the wall at the side of the door. Three of them were highly polished: one belonged to a shipping office, another an accountant, and the third an interior designer. The fourth had a dull, tarnished finish. That was Ronson's.

Gardener pushed the door open and was greeted with a long, winding staircase. He caught an odour of lavender and beeswax. A deep blue carpet covered the floor. Adorning the walls were a number of oils featuring ships and seascapes. The building had two offices upstairs and two on the ground floor, one of which was Ronson's. The place was as silent as the grave.

Gardener did not bother to knock, but simply opened the door and entered, surprised to find it actually open. He suspected most solicitors didn't start before ten.

Ronson's office was large, accommodating two desks and an inordinate number of files, which were conveniently stored on shelves with the overspill left on desks and chairs. The place resembled a burglary.

In the corner he noticed tea and coffee facilities. The enclosed space smelled musty, and he suspected from the grime on the windows that they had never been opened. What he couldn't understand was why the door was unlocked, and the office unoccupied.

"Christ," said Reilly. "You'd think with the money he made he'd be able to afford something better than this."

"Even if he couldn't," replied Gardener, "cleaners don't cost much, do they?"

Gardener heard a door open and close in the hall they had recently been standing in. The solicitor's door then creaked, and a woman jumped and screeched when she saw them both standing there.

"Oh my word, you gave me such a fright." She held her hand to her chest as if to prove the point.

She was very frumpily dressed in a brown skirt and tweed jacket, with a white blouse and a square-shaped hat on her head. Her face was long and angular, and she had grey hair and a deep voice. He saw no wedding ring. Gardener guessed her age around, or possibly past, retirement.

"I'm very sorry, but we're not open yet." She then went off on a tangent. "I don't know what Mr Ronson will think. I had a few days off last week. We had a temp in. I thought I'd come in early and catch up. Never realized I'd have the whole place to clean. What on earth do these temps do all day?" Her head was constantly bobbing up and down. "Not a great deal by the looks of things. Still, it's not as if he's actually starting work today."

Gardener flashed his warrant card and made the introductions. "It's Mr Ronson we came to see."

"Oh dear, he's still on holiday, I'm afraid. Won't be back to work until next Monday."

"We know that, but we also know that officially he's due back today. How long has he been away, Miss..."

"A month now. It's Miss White. The doctor said it would be good for him. He's been working too hard, you see. That's Mr Ronson for you. I tried to tell him all those hours are no good for you."

Gardener could see they were going to have a hard time with the secretary. She seemed nice enough, but she was the type that always answered questions with her own opinions, and she had plenty of them. He wondered if she knew anything about the solicitor's drink problem.

"We're investigating a double murder, Miss White. Can you tell us where he's been and how long he's been there?"

"A double murder! Oh my word, you people have to look at some awful things. I don't know how you do it, really, I don't. He's been recuperating in Madeira."

"But he is due back today?"

"Yes, he is."

She moved around the room, having removed her hat and coat and hung them on a peg behind the office door. She made her way over to the other side of the office and started making tea.

"Would you gentleman like one? I always think you should start the day with a cup of tea. Never did my father any harm, and he lived till he was ninety-five."

"We could be in for a long wait, boss," said Reilly.

"I was beginning to think that. But at least she's not being evasive."

When the secretary had finished making her drink and was sitting comfortably behind her desk, he addressed her again. "Can you tell us anything about his surgery, Miss White?"

She put her hands to her chest. "That was an awful business. I came in one morning, about three months ago, and found Mr Ronson slumped over his desk, right there." She pointed at the desk opposite hers. "I called an ambulance immediately. He'd had a heart attack. They kept him in the hospital for weeks, checking him out, doing their tests."

"And what was the outcome?" Reilly asked.

She took a sip of tea and clasped her hands around the cup. Gardener wondered why. It wasn't cold out.

"He had something fitted, but I'm not sure what. I certainly don't think it was a pacemaker, because I remember them saying his heart was good, had a steady rhythm."

Gardener's own heart sank. He didn't like what he was hearing. Instead of Ronson being involved, he could be another victim. The SIO was convinced that something big had gone down somewhere, involving all these people. He was determined to figure out what it was.

"Do you have any details of his surgery? Where it was done, doctor's name?"

"I'm afraid I don't know the doctor, officer, but I know he had his operation at St. James's Hospital here in Leeds."

Not again, thought Gardener. Odd how that name seemed to be cropping up a lot.

"When was that?" asked Reilly.

"Let me see…" She placed one hand on her head and started rubbing it, as if that would help. "I found him at the beginning of June. I think he had his operation at the end of the month, and then spent some time in there afterwards. He then went on holiday when he got out, and he's due back today. I've spoken to him a number of times and he sounds like he's doing really well."

"Can you tell us where and when he's due to land, and where he's going from there?"

She opened a drawer and consulted a schedule. "He should have landed at seven o'clock in Manchester. His train is due into Shipston in about twenty minutes."

"In that case, we'll meet him off the train," said Gardener. "I'd like his mobile number."

"Is all this necessary? The man *has* recently had heart surgery. I'm sure he won't want you lot meeting him off the train and questioning him about murders that he probably knows nothing about."

"I never said we were going to question him about murders, Miss White. Now, if he calls you and he hasn't heard from us, tell him we will be meeting him at the station, and to stay put in the waiting room till we arrive."

Both officers left without giving the secretary the opportunity to say anything further. But she did have her mouth open at the ready.

* * *

It took them only twenty minutes to reach Shipston. In that time, Gardener made three calls to Ronson's phone. All were unanswered. The SIO had to be content with leaving messages, each more urgent than the last. When he'd asked at the ticket office about the train, he was told it was due in on Platform 1 within the next five minutes.

Shipston was a Grade II listed station that had been restored to its Lancashire and Yorkshire Railway appearance, with huge wooden name boards and raised lettering. There was, Gardener noticed, a heated waiting room with a well-stocked bookcase, a working signal box, and a staggered platform linked by a subway. On any other day, the place would have been beautiful and well worth a visit. Given his recent contact with stations and the reason he was here, his surroundings only served to diminish his patience by the second.

Gardener turned to see where his partner was and couldn't help but smile when he saw him with two coffees and a small packet of biscuits.

Reilly shrugged. "Got to keep your strength up."

"Keep going and you'll make Geoff Capes look small," said Gardener.

"What time's the train due?"

"Anytime now, according to the ticket inspector. I have a bad feeling about this, Sean."

"Can't blame you after what we've seen. Has he not answered his phone, then?"

"No. All I've done is leave messages."

"Do you reckon something's happened to him? On the train, maybe?"

Gardener glanced around. Both platforms had about thirty people on them despite it being early morning. No doubt some were commuters, but a lot of them had cameras and were photographing everything in sight.

"I hope not, for all our sakes."

Gardener suddenly heard a siren, not unlike the one heard from leaving a phone off the hook. A loudspeaker announced the arrival of the train from Manchester.

"Guess we're about to find out," said Reilly.

The tracks vibrated, and Gardener heard the noise of the train letting loose steam. In the distance, he could see the locomotive approaching.

The train stopped. People jumped off. Others stepped on. There seemed to be no sign of the man they were there to meet.

The conductor walked up and down the platform with a flag in one hand, and a whistle in the other. Gardener was about to give up when he noticed a porter leaning towards one of the windows. He appeared to be having a conversation with someone when the door suddenly opened. A man reached out and placed a suitcase on the platform.

Gardener breathed a sigh of relief when Ronson stepped down from the train. He shook hands with the porter. The conductor blew the whistle and raised his flag. The train slowly departed.

Ronson walked towards them, wearing a long coat and a deerstalker. In one hand he carried a briefcase, with the other he dragged his suitcase. He had a pipe in his mouth.

"Thought it was too good to be true," said Reilly. "Take a bit more than a dodgy ICD to kill that bent bastard."

Gardener silently agreed.

"Mr Ronson," Gardener greeted him.

"I thought it was you ringing my phone. Can't get away from you lot no matter where I end up."

"Why didn't you answer it?" Reilly asked.

"I'm on holiday. Not back till Monday. Whatever it is, it can wait!"

"Maybe not," replied Gardener. "We wouldn't be here if it wasn't a matter of life and death."

Ronson's mobile rang again, the trill sound coming from within his coat.

The solicitor rolled his eyes into his head and threw his hands in the air in exasperation.

But Ronson's eyes never came back round to face Gardener. Instead, he hit the platform like a solid block, his briefcase landing about ten feet away. The woman whose leg it hit started screaming as Gardener knelt and felt for a pulse.

There wasn't one.

Chapter Thirty-eight

Gardener stood up and immediately assessed the situation, scanning the station for all possible exits, trying to work out how many people were present.

Sean Reilly had his back to him, also glancing around. The train had pulled out of the station, but it was not so far down the track that it couldn't be stopped.

"Sean, get on the phone and arrange for the team to meet us here. Request extra back-up. As of now, this place is shut."

Gardener ran across the platform to the booking hall.

As he reached the hall, the clerk was already out of his booth and craning his neck down the track to obtain a better view. He flashed his warrant card.

"What's your name?"

"Ian, sir. Ian Kelsey."

"Is the manager around?"

"He's got an office at the back of the ticket booth."

"Good, go and get him and do not leave the hall to go out onto the platform. And while you're at it, get him to stop the train that's just left."

Gardener glanced back in Reilly's direction. He could see his sergeant multi-tasking already. He had his phone in one hand, whilst talking to the porter and pointing at the corpse with the other. At the same time, he was also herding people like sheep towards the waiting room.

Gardener reached the entrance to the station and saw around a dozen people, expectantly waiting, wondering what was going on. Warrant card in hand, he addressed them.

"I'd like each and every one of you to step into the booking hall and remain there until I say so." Not wanting to waste time waiting for them to do it voluntarily, he began ushering them in himself.

He noted a mixture of expressions, fear, wonder, concern, and annoyance. One person made a comment about police harassment. Gardener swore to himself that if he heard another word about that, he would show them exactly what police harassment really meant.

As he was about to close the door, he noticed a couple of Panda cars turn up. Six constables jumped out, so he led two of them into the booking hall, then closed and locked the door behind them.

As he turned, he saw Ian Kelsey with the manager. He was perhaps the tallest man Gardener had ever seen, not to mention the thinnest. He had a pale complexion. In fact, Gardener thought Ronson was in better condition, and he'd died within the last five minutes. Gardener showed his card yet again.

"DI Gardener. And your name is?"

"Darren Rafferty, I'm the station manager."

"There's been an incident out on the platform. I'm closing your station until further notice."

"What kind of incident?"

"A man has died, and I have every reason to suspect foul play."

"Oh my God!" exclaimed Rafferty, bringing his hands to his mouth.

"How many exits are there on the station?"

Rafferty thought for a moment before replying there were four, including the booking hall. He then ran back into his office.

Gardener turned to the remaining police constables. "You two grab a couple more constables and go and cover those exits. Which one of you is the most senior?"

"I am, sir. Colin Wilson." The man stepped forward. He was big and beefy, built very similar to Dave Rawson on his own team.

"Okay, Colin. I want you to take the details of everyone here, including their mobile phone numbers. My team will soon be arriving, so you'll have some more help. No one comes into the station, and no one leaves until you know exactly who they are and why they are here. If you have any spare men out there, ask them to cover the platform opposite. Do you understand?"

"Yes, sir."

Gardener addressed Rafferty as he came back into the booking hall. "Have you stopped the train that's just left?"

"Yes. In fact, if you walk out there, you should be able to see it."

"I want you to call upon as many staff as you have and block the tracks both sides of the station. I want no more trains in or out of this place until I say so."

"Anything else?"

"Yes. I want a list of all the staff that work here, names and addresses."

The man scurried back into his office like a mouse heading for a cheese mountain.

Gardener returned to the desolate platform. There were no trains, and very few people. Reilly had somehow managed to usher everyone into the waiting room and shut the door. He stood guard outside. Gardener glanced across to the opposite platform. The two local policemen were doing the same.

"Do you think he's here?" asked Reilly as Gardener approached.

Gardener glanced around. "I can't see why he'd need to be. We already know he's using the phones to set things in motion."

"But killers love to watch their victims die. You know that as well as I do."

"Fair comment. So if he is, we'll have him. No one's getting out of here until I know who they are."

"We have to find out who did the operation on Ronson."

"We will, believe me," said Gardener.

The SIO noticed that one of the people in the waiting room was opening the door and glancing around.

Gardener pointed. "Can you sort that lot out? Get everyone's name and details. I'm going across that side to see if those lads can keep everyone there under control."

Gardener used the subway to reach the other platform. He instructed the two officers there to collect information, before returning to his side of the station.

There was no doubt in his mind that Ronson, like Wilson, had been deliberately killed. He wondered if Ronson's death had been planned first, only to be completed when an opportunity presented itself. The secretary told them that he'd had his operation at the end of June. That was over a month ago. What the hell had happened, and when?

How long had their killer been harbouring his grudge? And for what? It had to be something serious.

He was grateful to see that Steve Fenton, the CSM, was standing on the platform when he returned.

"Steve, good to see you."

"What happened?"

"It's Wilfred Ronson, the solicitor."

"I gathered that much. I think I've seen him before."

"We came to meet him off the train. Neither Sean nor I could work out whether or not he was implicated, so we needed to talk to him. His secretary told us this morning that he'd had heart surgery at the end of June."

"So he's a victim?" Fenton rolled his eyes, much like Ronson had done. Only the CSM's came back down.

"Exactly. Ronson stepped off the train, and his mobile rang. Then he simply dropped dead. Funny thing is, I'd called him three times on the way here, and each call went to voicemail. And before his phone rang, he spoke to us and said he knew I'd been ringing him, so whoever is controlling all of this is clever enough to program the SIM cards to react to whatever numbers he wishes."

At his own mention of SIM cards, Gardener made a mental note to contact the police station in Bramfield to see if there was any news on Graham Johnson.

More of the crime scene team arrived. Steve Fenton told them he wanted a marquee around the body.

"Steve?" Gardener said. "I want his phone sent off immediately for testing. I want to know who rang him." Gardener glanced along the platform and saw Ronson's briefcase. "And can you also check through his briefcase, see if you can find anything we need to know?"

"Will do."

Wasting no further time, Gardener used his mobile to call Desk Sergeant Williams at Bramfield and ask if he could action one of his men to identify the cell masts covering Shipston station, and do a cell dump on each. He told Williams he needed all the phone numbers in the area within the last hour. Williams, in turn, told him there was still no news on Graham Johnson.

Before Gardener had the chance to do anything else, most of his team arrived at the platform, having the good sense to stand outside the booking hall and move no further.

He instructed Frank Thornton and Bob Anderson to put together a question set for potential witnesses, and to assist the local constables on the other platform in gathering all names and addresses. Gardener then ordered Paul Benson and Patrick Edwards to take over for Sean Reilly and do the same. He tasked Dave Rawson to help Colin Wilson in the booking hall with the people there. He also told Rawson to call The Harrogate Arms and have the landlord take the dog walkers' names and address if they showed up, so that Rawson could head over there after his station duties. It would please him no end if they could confirm the number plate of the van on the night Lance Hobson went missing.

Gardener then addressed his DC, Colin Sharp. "I'd like you to oversee this operation in my absence. Sean and I need to go to St. James's Hospital and follow up on Ronson's operation. Can you organize action teams to visit all of the people here at the station today? Frank and Bob are putting a question set together that they can all use. Someone might have seen something. For what it's worth, I don't think the killer is here. He doesn't need to be."

"What about that train, sir, over there? He could be on that. He may have been watching as Ronson got off, and knew he could get away easy enough."

"That has gone through my mind, Colin. As soon as we have all names and addresses from everyone here, and you're satisfied, let them all go. Then you can start on the train. The station manager has had specific instructions that no one leaves the train until we say so. In fact, whilst they're organizing questions to ask, you go down there and tell them why they're waiting. But first of all, come with me."

As Gardener glanced down the track, he could see workmen in orange protective clothing putting out the blockades as he'd asked.

The three officers entered the booking hall. Colin Wilson and Dave Rawson had everything under control. Most of the people were now seated and seemed a little calmer. He left them to it, and he and Reilly entered the ticket office and went through to the manager's room, where Rafferty was currently barking orders into the phone.

The small room was very clean and smelled of leather and beeswax. A wine-coloured Chesterfield settee matched a dark red carpet. The walls were pastel colours and had a variety of paintings. Rafferty was sitting at a desk that housed a computer, and what Gardener took to be photos of his family. When he placed the phone in its cradle, he seemed very harassed.

"My God, I never realized how hard it was to cancel and reroute trains. I've spoken to some pretty unhelpful people in the last few minutes, Mr Gardener, I don't mind telling you."

"We appreciate what you're doing." Gardener pointed to Colin Sharp. "This is DC Sharp. He's going to be in charge in my absence. I know this incident is rather unfortunate, but we really are needed somewhere else."

"What actually happened out there?" asked Rafferty. He gestured for them to sit down, but each man remained standing.

"I'm afraid I can't go into too much detail, other than to say a man died after exiting the train."

"Oh my word, I hope he hadn't eaten a National Rail sandwich."

"That's a good one," scoffed Reilly. "But I don't think you've anything to worry about on that score."

Rafferty managed a smile.

"Where were you, Mr Rafferty, when all this happened?" asked Gardener.

"In my office. I've been here all morning." He then glanced at his watch. "Well, since eight o'clock, anyway. I came in through the booking hall. My ticket clerk, Ian, was already here. He made me a cup of tea, and I came in here to get on with some work. Next thing I knew, he was back in here telling me the police were on my platform and a man was dead. I couldn't believe it."

"Do you have CCTV on the station?"

"Yes, we do. I know it's a country station, but you can't be too careful all the same."

"I'd like the recordings covering the last twenty-four hours. Just give them to DC Sharp."

Gardener didn't see a lot of point in going much further back. With all the technology being used, he did not think the killer had entered the station that day, or any other for that matter.

Gardener stared out of window and down the track. The men in orange uniforms were still busy. He sighed heavily. There was so much to do. He couldn't believe how much had happened in such a short space of time. Three o'clock Monday morning was when it had all started, and Gardener felt like he'd been on duty ever since, without sleep. So much havoc had been caused within fifty-four hours. Suspects were thin on the ground, and the one man vital to their investigation – namely Lance Hobson – remained at large. It was doubly important to find him because Gardener wasn't certain if he was a suspect, or a victim.

He knew that Ronson's death was going to exhaust an already overstretched team. Last night, when he had left the incident room, he felt a glimmer of hope that they were heading in a positive direction. Now, he had a mountain the size of Ben Nevis to climb, especially with what he needed to know today. The hardest job would be capturing transmission signals in the area and trying to trace their origin.

Gardener and Reilly stepped out of the office and back into the booking hall. They were about to leave, when Steve Fenton came after them.

"Sir, found these."

He had two plain white envelopes in a clear evidence bag.

"Where were they?"

"In the briefcase. But someone had been clever. They were sewn into the lining. The stitching had been left unfinished at the end. You had to look closely to spot it."

Gardener thanked him and took them. If he'd actually needed more proof that it was the same man, here it was.

"Come on, Sean, let's get to the hospital."

Reilly drove. Gardener produced a pair of latex gloves and removed and opened the envelopes. In the first, he had a tarot card known as Judgment. The top part of the card had an angel with wings against a blue background, blowing a trumpet with a St. George flag attached. Below the angel were a number of naked people with their arms outstretched. What that meant, he had no idea. But as soon as they arrived at the hospital, he would have Sean telephone Laura for an explanation.

The second envelope revealed yet another game card. The really disturbing part about it was the character on the card, 'Barrister Bent', was the spitting image of Wilfred Ronson as they had seen him on the platform, right down to the coat and the deerstalker. He even held a similar briefcase. Like the Inspector Catcher card, Barrister Bent also had a balloon coming from his mouth, with a phrase written in: "Don't worry about a thing, son."

Chapter Thirty-nine

Reilly brought the car to a halt in the hospital car park and switched off the engine.

Inside the hospital, it took them nearly fifteen minutes to track down Andrew Jackson. Gardener had to have the staff put out a call; they found he had finished up in theatre within the last five minutes, and would be with them in the next five.

They waited in his office. Jackson seemed equally as harassed as they had seen him yesterday.

"Gentlemen," he greeted them, striding across to his desk and sitting in the chair. "How can I help you this time?"

Gardener came to the point. He was in no mood for the doctor trying to close ranks on him. "Wilfred Ronson is a solicitor whose name has come up more than once during our investigation. We met him off a train this morning, and he dropped dead in front of us."

"Oh, dear," said Jackson.

"Yes, oh dear," repeated Gardener. "Turns out he had an ICD fitted here at the end of June."

"What are you suggesting?" asked Jackson, standing.

"Can you tell us who operated on him?"

"I don't think I can. Ever heard of client confidentiality, Mr Gardener?"

"Never mind all that bollocks," replied Reilly. "This is a murder investigation. We want to know who fitted the ICD, and the exact date."

"I think it's best if I consult a solicitor before I say another word."

"The next words you speak will be from the inside of a cell if you carry on," said Gardener. "Now, as my sergeant has pointed out, we're investigating murder and we are trying to get to the truth: we are not breaking confidentiality codes here. We are simply asking for the name of the doctor. I can, if you'd like, shut this place, and keep you rooted here to your desk until I get a warrant, but I don't think you want that inconvenience any more than I do. So please, just do as we ask."

Jackson seemed to think Gardener's speech made sense, and tapped a few keys on his keyboard. "When did you say?"

"Sometime around the end of June." It took another few minutes, but the doctor found what they were after.

"Mr Ross. A Mr Iain Ross, spelling the first name with two 'I's. June 28th."

"Thank you," said Gardener. "Is he here today?"

"No, but you will find him at the Ross & Sinclair Foundation. He's a part owner and works with Robert Sinclair."

That was all he needed but another thought struck him as he turned leave the office. He spotted the edge of the collector's magazine he'd seen last time. Moving all the papers for a better view, he studied the cover. The issue had a big spread about retro games and the Cluedo board was on the front.

"Is this yours?"

"Well it's on my desk, so it must be," replied Jackson.

Gardener ignored the sarcasm. He picked up the magazine and leafed through it. The ten-page article he found on games covered most everything but the one he wanted.

"Are you into games?" he asked Jackson.

"My grandfather introduced me to them a few years back before he died. He had a huge collection, even some from his childhood. He left them to me. As you can imagine I don't have a great deal of time to play them but I intend to one day. I'm quite fascinated how popular they were. And still are, according to that magazine."

Gardener sifted through his pocket and pulled out the game card sealed in the polythene bag. "Ever seen this one?"

Jackson stared at it. "Christ, where did you get that?"

"Did your granddad have an edition of this game?"

"No," replied Jackson, "but I didn't think one existed. I just thought it was a myth."

"What do you know about it?"

"Only that it's a bit of a holy grail of games, very collectible, very limited. There was something in the magazine about six months ago."

"Do you still have it?" asked Reilly.

Jackson glowered at the desk and then at the detectives. "Somewhere, but I doubt I could lay my hands on it."

"Can you try for us, please, Dr Jackson? It could prove very invaluable. Give me a call if you do."

Leaving Jackson's office, Gardener had his phone in his hand, talking to Sergeant Williams at Bramfield. He wanted background information on Robert Sinclair, Iain Ross and Andrew Jackson.

He left the hospital with mixed feelings. He was elated that they were heading out with something positive, but disappointed that Ross's name had cropped up again. Maybe he could kill two birds with one stone, however.

It took another half an hour before they arrived at the Foundation, a gigantic, high-tech building that resembled something out of Star Trek.

"Jesus Christ," said Reilly, parking the car. "There's some money here."

The pair of them entered the air-conditioned reception. A blonde receptionist sat in front of a glass and chrome desk, and Gardener wondered if they were plastic surgeons as well. She had to be the most perfect specimen he'd ever seen. The girl didn't have a visible blemish on her.

Both men showed their cards, and Gardener felt as if that's all he'd done all morning. He told her they wanted to speak to Dr Ross immediately, before asking if Robert Sinclair was in office as well. The receptionist corrected him, telling him it was "mister," not doctor, and that Sinclair wasn't but Ross was in attendance.

Within two minutes, they were in an office furnished to the highest standards. Leather suite, dark oak furniture, and a brick-built fireplace with an open log fire ready for a match to strike. The ceiling had a chandelier, and the walls had a variety of oils that were, in Gardener's opinion, out of place – especially the one above the fireplace.

Ross was as smooth as Sinclair. He was wearing a grey Italian designer suit and shoes that matched the colour of his hair – which was damp. He was slim and handsome, and spoke with a deep, resonant voice. He was the type of person who gestured with his hands as he spoke. "How can I help you? Do you mind if I sit down, I've just recently had an intense workout?"

Gardener glanced to the chair, and he and Reilly also took one.

"I knew the Times crossword was tough but I didn't realize it was that hard," said Reilly.

Ross simply smiled.

"That's an unusual painting above the desk," said Gardener.

Ross turned and glanced at it. "It represents strength."

"Is it a tarot card?" asked Reilly.

"I couldn't tell you," replied Ross.

Gardener doubted that. The painting depicted a woman calmly holding the jaws of a lion. She was cool and collected. At the bottom of the frame was the word 'strength'.

"It's something my wife is into. It means that you have inner strength and fortitude during moments of danger and distress: that you have the ability to remain calm and strong, even when your life is going through immense struggle," Ross said.

"And are you?" asked Gardener.

Ross turned to face the officers. "No, but my wife has over the course of her life – none of which I have the desire to go into. It shows that you are a compassionate person and you always have time for other people even if it's at your own expense. That sums up my wife perfectly. If it wasn't for her, I wouldn't be where I am today. Now, I'm very sure that you have not come to talk to me about this painting or my office, so would you please tell me why you are here? My time is valuable, even if yours isn't."

"We'd like to talk to you about Wilfred Ronson," said Gardener.

"Who?"

"A solicitor who had ICD surgery at St. James's Hospital in Leeds."

"I'm sorry, gentlemen, I don't know anyone called Wilfred Ronson."

"Oh my God," said Reilly. "Is this what you get for paying thousands for private surgery? A doctor who can't even remember your name?"

Ross seemed a little short on patience, thought Gardener, judging by his expression. "I can remember the names of all my patients, Mr Reilly. So if I'd operated on someone called Wilfred Ronson, I would know. When was this?"

"The end of June," said Gardener.

The man in front of them seemed to relax slightly. Gardener did not like that. "What date?"

"The 28th."

"In that case, it wasn't me," replied Ross. "Which is why I don't know what you're talking about."

"The records show it *was* you, Mr Ross."

"The records are wrong, detective. On the 15th of June, my wife and I flew to Florida for a month. We have an apartment there. Didn't return until July 17th. You can check with the airline if you like. We flew business class with BA from Manchester airport. I can also give you the names and addresses of the people we saw in Florida while we were there. Before you leave this office, I would like to know who says I have operated on Ronson, and why. Then I will telephone my own solicitor and have the matter investigated."

That was a bolt out of the blue that Gardener never expected.

Chapter Forty

"The problem is one of your own making, Graham. You've created it, no one else."

"How the hell have I done that?" Johnson was tired of the lectures. No one was perfect, including the man dishing out the sermons.

"You left! You were out at the first sign of trouble."

It was easy for him to say, sitting at his desk, living the lifestyle of a lord.

"What the hell was I supposed to do?"

"Stay, front it out. What did they have on us, anyway?"

"My van," shouted Johnson. "They came to see my van because a white van had been seen all around Bramfield at odd times in the morning, when strange things were happening. People reported the van as having a brake light out. My van has a brake light out."

"There's probably a hundred white vans out there with a brake light out. Did anyone say they had seen your van in particular? Did they give out your registration number?"

Graham Johnson was growing more frustrated by the minute, unlike the man in front of him, who had yet to raise his voice despite the mounting tension.

"Well, not exactly."

"So, you had a vehicle similar to the one seen around Bramfield and Bursley Bridge at strange times in the morning, and you also had a brake light out. That still doesn't mean they had anything on you. They were clutching at straws, Graham."

"But how would I have explained my way out of it?"

"You're a computer geek. You people are awake all hours. You could have told them you had been making deliveries, or that you'd been out collecting computers for repair. You could have told them anything to get them off your back, while you thought of something more positive to give them."

"Well, what about forensics? What if they wanted to keep the van and do those tests on it?" Graham Johnson was unable to keep his hands and feet still. He stormed around the room, shouting and panicking.

"What would they have found? The floor of the van had been covered with a tarpaulin for each person we put in there. They themselves were wrapped in clear polythene bags with their hands and feet tied. They were gagged. What possible evidence could they have left?"

"Haven't you watched those CSI programs, for God's sake? They could probably find a speck of fly shit in the aftermath of the apocalypse."

"Don't you talk to me about forensics, Graham. I know all about keeping things clean. I'm a doctor."

Graham Johnson sighed heavily and chewed on the fingernails of his right hand. Not one in particular, but all of them. It had all sounded so good in theory, but now the situation was way beyond his control.

"Jesus Christ! I never wanted to get into this in the first place. I told you!" shouted Johnson, pointing at the man. "I told you we couldn't pull it off. The police are too clever."

"I beg to differ. I seem to remember it was you who came up with the original idea. I'm certainly not capable of working out something so intricate."

"Don't lay all the blame at my door. You wanted revenge as much as I did."

Graham Johnson was beginning to realize how far things had spiralled out of control. He was in so much trouble. He couldn't go back. The police would be watching his shop. They'd be all over it like a rash, probably had been all night while he'd been here.

"You needed me as much as I needed you." Johnson was almost hyperventilating.

"You need to stop getting agitated, Graham. It's not good for your health. I've treated you on more than one occasion for blood pressure."

"How can I calm down? What am I going to do, where am I going to go? They're onto me now!"

The doctor rose from his desk, and came and placed his arm on Graham's shoulder.

"Please, sit down, calm down."

Johnson was too agitated and turned away from the man. He'd had enough. He had to leave here. As big as the house may have been, he could feel the walls closing in on him.

"Graham, sit down and let me give you something for your nerves. If you carry on like this, you'll end up with heart trouble as well."

"Calm my nerves? You can fuck off. I've seen what happens to people when you operate on them!"

Before the doctor reached him, Johnson produced a gun from the inside pocket of his jacket. The doctor stopped mid-stride. "What the hell do you think you're doing?"

"Putting an end to this mess you started."

"Graham, for God's sake think about what you're doing. Please put the gun down."

Johnson waved the gun around. "Oh, not so big now, are we? It's okay to dish out death in large doses, but when you're facing it yourself it's a different matter."

"You know why we started this. We wanted justice, pure and simple. The police were powerless, because they had nothing on the scum that walk our streets. The reptiles we have to put up with are too clever by half. Take a long look at the people we put away. Hardly doing society any harm, were we?"

"I don't have a problem with that!" shouted Johnson. "It what's happening now that I'm worried about. The police are on to us. We have nowhere to go. *We* might see what we did as justice, but they won't."

The doctor ran towards Johnson with his arms outstretched. Instinctively, he dropped the gun and threw a punch, followed by a second in quick succession. He chose not to shoot because he was not a killer; he'd never had any intention of firing the gun in the first place.

His fist connected with the doctor's right eye, and his second punch landed square on the chin, taking the man clean into the air. The doctor flew back, catching the back of his head on the side of his desk.

Graham Johnson turned and ran out of the study, pulled open the front door, and headed for the van. Once in, he gunned the engine, and he wheel-spun all the way around the front path and out of the gate.

Chapter Forty-one

Hobson was feeling worse now than he had twenty-four hours ago. In fact, worse than he'd felt since he'd been held captive. God only knew how long that had been.

He couldn't be sure what it was. The fact that he had not had any food for quite some time didn't help. Since he'd spoken to his captor yesterday, he had suffered at least three serious bouts of stomach cramps, all of which had ultimately led to the shits. As he'd had no food it was mostly liquid; but the bucket must be full. The smell was awful.

The light had been left on overnight, and Hobson had thought long and hard about the metallic object under his skin, and the suture on his abdomen. They couldn't be helping him any, either.

For the last half hour, he'd simply sat on his toilet and held his head in his hands, defeated by the manipulation, as much as anything else. If there had been any further questions on his beloved Leeds United, he had almost certainly missed them.

Hobson figured he must have fallen asleep at some time during the night, because when he'd finally woken up, a bottle of water had been placed within reach. He didn't care whether or not it had been tampered with; he simply unscrewed the top and started drinking. It tasted fine to him.

Hobson ran his hands over his face, and glanced upwards. He saw the computer monitor change question. It took him longer than normal to read it, but when he'd done so, he realized straight away that he knew the answer.

"Name the author of the bestselling books, *Paint It White: Following Leeds Everywhere* and *Leeds United: The Second Coat,* a man who has missed only one game, including friendlies, since he started watching Leeds United in 1968?"

Hobson was so excited, he leaned back a little too far, nearly tipping the bucket. That would have been a mistake.

He reached up as far as the frame would allow and shouted, "Gary Edwards."

His reward came with a creaking sound, and the release of his left leg.

Hobson reached down and rubbed his ankle with both hands. There was a red band around the joint where the clamp had been too tight; all colour had drained from it. It felt funny, and although he wanted to try and stand up, he thought it best not to. One thing at a time.

He glanced at the PC screen again, but the topic of the next question was something entirely different, and he couldn't hope to answer it in a million years. But however crap he'd been feeling, the release of one of his legs was beginning to make up for it.

Wouldn't be long now.

What he had not noticed, however, was that the door to his basement had been opened, and the man holding him captive was standing in front of him.

"Well done, Mr Hobson."

Something had happened to the man. He was normally suave and sophisticated, and almost always dressed in a clean, pressed suit. He may well have been in a suit today, but his right eye was bruised, and starting to swell. His hair was uncombed, and although Hobson couldn't be sure, it appeared to have a streak of blood in it. When the man had spoken to him, he didn't appear to be as calm and calculating as usual.

"What's happened to you?"

"You need to worry about yourself, not me."

Hobson was about to make another remark when a surge of pain equivalent to what felt like ten thousand volts engulfed his abdomen, pulsating upwards into his head.

Hobson screamed so loud his voice broke. His left leg involuntarily hit the bucket, and he ended up on the floor covered in his own excrement.

"Dear me, Mr Hobson. Now look what we've done."

Hobson's breathing was erratic. He was sucking in air at an alarming rate, but he was also struggling for breath.

His left hand went to the stitches, where the pain had originated. With his right hand, he was doing his best to support himself. Given the fact that his right leg was still trapped, he thought he was very lucky not to have broken his ankle.

Hobson did not want to do that. When – if – he finally managed to walk out of the frame, not to mention the basement, he wanted all his limbs in as good a condition as he could hope for. He was going to kill the bastard in front of him. And he wasn't even sure he was going to stop and ask his name.

When his breath returned, he glared up at his captor. "What the fuck have you given me?"

The man stepped backwards, studying the vials before facing Hobson again. "You remember our little talk about honesty?"

"Not likely to forget that, am I?"

"Good. Look at the PC screen."

Hobson did as he was told. At first he had no idea what he was staring at, so he struggled to reach a standing position in order to see the screen, trying to keep from putting too much pressure on his right leg, which was still clamped in the frame. As he drew level with the image, it finally dawned on him that he was staring at an X-ray. He could see the top half of a body. But he couldn't quite work out what was going on inside.

"What the hell is this?"

"Take a closer look."

He did, but he still didn't understand. The body on the screen appeared to have wires going all over the place: across the chest cavity, up into the head, and down towards the legs that he couldn't see. It was like an atlas.

"Can't you see your name underneath?"

He hadn't done, but when he did, the realization hit home. Hobson's knees buckled, and he had to grab the side of the frame to remain upright.

He studied the two objects inside the body on the monitor. They were in the very same place as the bump and the stitching on his body. The metallic thing in his chest had to be the one with the wires going off in all directions. There was also something very similar in the area behind where he had the suture.

"Please tell me that isn't me."

Losing face was the last thing he wanted, his voice came out like that of a begging child's, he didn't know what else to say.

"Of course it's you." The doctor's attitude was matter of fact.

Each time Hobson thought he was managing to gain some confidence, the bastard came in and knocked the wind out of his sails. He stared hard at the doctor.

"What have you done to me? What are those things?"

"Here's why I asked you about our little chat on honesty. If you remember, I said I would always tell you the truth, because I thought it was more frightening than lying to you."

Hobson closed his eyes, wanting and praying for his nightmare to end.

"In your chest cavity you have an ICD. In layman's terms, it's a defibrillator. It's something we doctors use to stop or start a heart. In your case, it's been modified. You can see a number of electrical cables all leading outwards from it. Each one of those cables has been attached to a nerve end in your body, which is why you feel great pain when I want you to."

From inside his jacket pocket, the doctor withdrew what resembled a TV remote control unit. In order to prove his point, he pressed a button, and Lance Hobson hit the floor like a ton of concrete, writhing around in the excrement once again.

When the pain stopped, Hobson was convulsing, and covered in his own filth. It took him five minutes to regain some composure. Despite his situation, and with great difficulty, he made himself stand up again.

He concentrated on one thought: *may the Lord have mercy on the doctor's soul.* It really would be better if he killed Hobson, because if he didn't, and Hobson freed himself, the bastard was going to suffer like no man ever had.

"What's behind the stitches?" Not that he wanted to know.

"An implantable insulin pump."

"What the fuck do I need one of those for? I'm not a diabetic."

"You're right, you're not. Once again, it's modified. I desperately wanted to get even with you, Mr Hobson, for what you did to me. You are a drug dealer. You prey on innocent victims. You, and people like you, are a virus, stripping society of innocent people like a flesh-eating bug."

The doctor pulled a phone out of his pocket and held it in front of Hobson. The drug dealer did not recognize the photo of the person on the phone.

"You've no idea, have you?" asked the doctor.

He was right, Hobson hadn't a clue who the person was. The only thing he knew was that the phone was pretty old, by today's standards.

The doctor flicked to another photo, one that Hobson instantly recognized.

"How did you get a photo of me?"

"The phone belongs to my son, Adam. Or should I say, used to belong to him, before you killed him. The photo I first showed you *was* my son.

"It happened four years ago, Mr Hobson. Seems that you and Alex Wilson had my son cornered in the alley on Market Street, leading to the indoor market. Adam was given a massive dose of drugs, a lethal cocktail from which he would never recover. His body was doused in alcohol and wrapped in a blanket, to make it look as if he was either a down-and-out, or a drunk. One of the market traders found his body at five o'clock in the morning.

"At some point during the confrontation, he managed to take a photo of you on his phone, and, in fact, record what you did to him. After you left – and before he died – he very luckily dumped it in a skip nearby. I say luckily, because the police never found it. I did. Now, what I did not find out was what had happened to cause all this, or why. I'm sure you know the answer. So, I'm going to give you some more time alone to think about it. The next time we meet, I'd like you to tell me. You know enough about me now to realise that it would not be in your own interest to withhold the information I require."

The doctor placed the phone and the remote-control unit back in his jacket pocket.

"I think that about concludes our business for the time being. I'm going to leave you now, Mr Hobson, because I have work to do. I will be back." He turned to walk away.

"Just a minute," shouted Hobson.

The doctor faced the drug baron.

"The pump. What's in the pump if it isn't insulin?"

"Oh yes," said the doctor. "The pump. Well, I was looking for something that would eat away at your tissues like you and your friends were eating away at society. It took me some time, but I finally found it.

"It contains a genetically modified strain of the Ebola virus. For it to work in the timescale I wanted, and to have any noticeable effect, it had to be held in a liquid suspension and injected into the tissue where the effect was desired. Anything going straight into the bloodstream tends to cause septicaemia, high temperature, circulation collapse, and maybe even generalized clotting. Which could have killed you, possibly painfully, but very rapidly.

"And whilst I want you to die in agony, I do not want you to die very quickly."

The doctor stopped talking and left the room.

Chapter Forty-two

Back in the incident room, Gardener was still rocked by what he'd discovered at the Ross & Sinclair Foundation. They had questioned Ross further about the computer records. During that time, he'd used his PC and telephone to verify for them he had not been in the country. British Airways had been more than cooperative.

The two officers then drove back to St. James's Hospital, where they encountered a pretty hostile Andrew Jackson, whom they had actually dragged out of an appointment with a patient. Jackson said he would have Gardener's badge. The SIO said he didn't care what threats Jackson made, he wanted information about the computers and the log-in details and who had access, and he wanted it today. Having spoken to the IT team, Gardener left the hospital satisfied that they would meet his demands within two to three hours.

The SIO glanced up at the ANACAPA chart, wondering where the hell to start with it all. He placed the two cards discovered in Ronson's briefcase onto the board and stood back.

Sergeant Williams came into the room with a cup of tea in his hand, taking a brief sip. "I thought I'd help out for a few minutes, it's pretty quiet out there."

"How's Gary? Have we heard anything about his mother?" Gardener asked.

"I've given him some time off. He's going to see her this afternoon. Apparently she's doing as well as can be expected."

"Which is more than can be said for us."

"I hear things didn't go too well at the train station this morning."

"That's one way of putting it," said Reilly. "Ronson stepped off the train and dropped down dead in front of us, which suggests he wasn't our man."

"Did you find out anything about the three doctors?"

"We have a couple of officers on it now, sir. I did come across something interesting regarding Sinclair's parents."

"His parents?" questioned Gardener.

"Yes, you mentioned after going to see Sinclair that he was a bit of a word puzzle buff, and that his mother compiled crosswords and won trophies for it, and that she worked for Walker Brothers games."

Gardener nodded: all of it was true.

"I took the liberty of checking his parents out. Seems they have retired to a small country estate in Ilkley. I have the address if you need it."

Gardener was curious. "And I would need it for what reason?"

"I just thought if he was one of the doctors in the frame, who better to ask about him than his parents?"

Gardener was beginning to think he had found two really good officers in Cragg and Williams: he would have liked both of them on his team. "Thank you, David. Good work. Anything on Graham Johnson?"

"Not yet, sir. No one has seen him since yesterday, and we have nothing from ANPR. He must be somewhere. When he shows his face, we'll have him."

Williams pointed to the cards on the chart. "I see we have two new additions."

"Yes, but they don't tell us very much. It's obviously the same killer, but we've had a lot of trouble interpreting the tarot card."

"Couldn't you help, Sergeant Reilly?" asked Williams.

"It's not as straightforward as you think. Me and my wee wife had a long conversation earlier. So far, all the other cards have indicated the reverse meanings. If we go with the reversed meaning here, it doesn't make too much sense: fear of change or death, or lack of progress when making important decisions. That wasn't Ronson. Guilt is also associated with the card, and that could well be him."

"What about the upright position?"

"Well now, that could have a bearing: satisfactory outcome to a specific matter or period of life."

"A satisfactory outcome for our killer," offered Williams. "Meaning that our friendly solicitor has made some dodgy decisions, the outcome of which has gone against the law – and maybe even the killer."

"That's pretty much what we're thinking," replied Gardener, "that Ronson was as bent as they come. He defended the scum of the earth, mostly drug dealers. On more than one occasion, he managed to keep Hobson out of prison. Maybe his reward for that satisfactory outcome was plenty of money."

Gardener pinched the bridge of his nose. "This is so bloody frustrating. The entire investigation has been nothing but a series of puzzles the killer has been feeding us."

"Question is," replied Williams, "have we worked out the answers?"

Gardener sighed heavily. "Judging by our achievements, I'd say not. Three people dead, one missing. Four possible people in the frame, all with some connection but no concrete evidence against any of them: one of whom we can't find."

Gardener stepped back, staring at an aerial map of the county on the board next to the ANACAPA chart. There had to be answer. The chances were it was probably something mundane and simple that they were overlooking. They had been running all over the place, trying their best to solve intricate puzzles, and had probably missed one vital clue sitting right under their noses.

Gardener sighed again when a thought came to mind. If he wanted to think like Sherlock Holmes, maybe he should start acting like him.

"Have we got any pins and some string, maybe some cotton, anything?"

David Williams left the room and came back with the items he'd requested.

"Okay, let's do something very simple. Alan Radford was the DI in charge when I joined the force, and he took me under his wing. He was succinct and to-the-point, almost as if he spoke in bullet points, and he was damn good at what he did.

"We were struggling once with robbery and violence in Leeds. I remember it dragging on for months. All we had were bits of information. Someone had seen this or that, a van at the scene, a car at another. One woman said she thought a local gang was involved. She fingered one or two of them, but there was no concrete evidence.

"Radford was studying an aerial map, like we have here, when he started putting pins in various places. Then he crossed the pins with the cotton. Eventually the points

232

overlapped, and we came up with an answer. Not straight away, but one that finally led us to an arrest."

"I remember Radford," said Reilly. "I had a lot of respect for that man."

Gardener stepped up to the map. "Okay, so what do we have?"

"We can start with Bramfield, sir," said Williams. "That was the first murder."

Williams put a pin in the map.

"Then we had Bursley Bridge," said Reilly, taking a pin and pushing it into position.

"Shipston this morning," said Gardener. After he'd put that one in, he ran the cotton through the three points, forming a straight line.

"So where now?"

"What about the hospital in Leeds?" Reilly offered. "That place seems to be well involved. And Andrew Jackson works there."

"Okay. Put a pin in."

"What about Ilkley?" added Williams.

"Ilkley?" questioned Reilly.

"Sinclair's parents live there."

"But his parents are not really involved," Gardener countered.

"I realize that, sir," replied Williams, "and I know it's a long shot, but maybe you can satisfy my curiosity by putting a pin there and seeing where that leads us. It is close by, after all."

Gardener glanced at the map. Following the line through from the hospital in Leeds, he realized that it crossed over Burley in Wharfedale, running alongside the Foundation and the home of Iain Ross.

"That may not be as long a shot as you think, David."

Gardener pointed out why.

When they had finished with pinning that location and running the cotton through, the two points formed a line that gave them a perfect cross with their previously marked locations. Sitting dead centre was Bursley Bridge, the home of the second murder, Graham Johnson's computer shop, and Robert Sinclair. The connections were there. Although they had no proof that either of these men was responsible for the crimes committed, it was pretty bloody suspicious that both had a connection to the locations.

Gardener thought for a moment. Was Bursley Bridge the hub of activity? Had something happened there that they needed to know about?

He turned to Sergeant Williams. "David? Anything come to mind?"

"Not straight away, but I'm probably not the man you want. I've only been the desk sergeant here for four years. Transferred from a force in Northampton."

Gardener didn't think he was going to add anything else, but he did. "If I remember correctly, though, something had happened shortly before I came here, caused a bit of a stink."

"Can you recall anything?"

"Not really, but I know a man who will. We both do."

Chapter Forty-three

Since leaving the doctor's house, Graham Johnson's mind had been a complete jumble of thoughts. What to do and where to go were his primary concerns. He couldn't go home because the police were onto him. The shop would most likely be closed, blue and white tape all over it. Everybody in the town would have gathered outside, suspecting that he had something to do with the recent murders.

Not that they'd be wrong, but he didn't want them knowing his business. Why was it that small towns and villages bred the nosiest of bastards? They all knew everyone's business. Didn't they have lives in these small communities? He supposed that's what came of being inbred. Most of them probably were.

As for somewhere to go, that was another problem. He wasn't married, which was probably a good thing. He doubted any woman would understand what they had done, despite having sound reason. Being single meant he didn't have a large family.

His sister, who *had* been married to the doctor, had died two years back. That had been a terrible affair. She had basically lost her mind after the death of their son Adam two years previous. She was finally admitted to a clinic, where she died under mysterious circumstances. That bitch of a nurse, Sonia Knight, had had something to do with that. He was damned sure.

Graham Johnson had a brother who lived in London. But he couldn't really go there. For one thing, the police were well known for using all the latest technology. They would more than likely have his van on the Automatic Number Plate Recognition system, which meant major motorways were out. He had to stick to local roads, but there could be roadblocks.

Johnson glanced at the van speedometer. He was within the thirty miles per hour limit and the road was pretty clear. But it was a major route. If the police had set up blocks along the way, the road he was on would be one of them. He drove for another fifty yards and took a small winding lane, which led out to Burley in Wharfedale, and eventually Ilkley and Skipton.

His parents lived in that direction; he *could* head out that way. They were always an option. But would they understand? He doubted it. They had been gutted, naturally, at the loss of their daughter. Like all people of their generation, they had sought justice, but not in the way Graham had. In an ideal world, the police would have caught who was responsible and put them behind bars.

Imagine how they would feel if it all came out, that their son was the one going to prison for exacting revenge for his unavenged sister.

Johnson took a left and drove through Main Street. Burley was a lovely village that maintained an olde-worlde charm, with buildings made mostly of Yorkshire stone, including the pub. The whole place spoke of money. The problem was, it was very small, so he was exiting before he had realized.

His thoughts went back to what he and the doctor had done. Why had he been so stupid as to allow himself to be talked into such drastic measures? It wasn't fair to blame the doctor completely. To exact revenge in such an intricate way certainly did need both of them.

The road in front of him was open and straight. Johnson was so frustrated by his limited options that he floored the accelerator, increasing the van's speed. Perhaps he should live on the edge for a mile or two, see if he could replace his venom with a touch of adrenaline.

He went back over the conversation he'd had with the doctor, particularly about the police having nothing on him. That wasn't true. They had the white van with the brake light out. They had his registration number, which must have been spotted for them to even consider consulting him in the first place. So they definitely had *something* on him.

The doctor had said that he could have told them anything to remove the tension for a while, till he thought of something better. What benefit would that be? It would have given him breathing space, but then they would have come back, and they'd have more on him because he'd have been lying.

The van crept up to seventy miles per hour. He'd need to slow down soon because of a bend up ahead. But for now, it felt fucking great!

Then a sudden thought hit him. One that nearly finished him off.

A vision entered his mind. Two days previous, before the young ginger twins had brought the laptop in, he had lost his temper with the machine he was working on. The screwdriver had slipped and damaged a SIM card. In a fit of anger, he had thrown it across the shop. He did not go and search for it. But the police were in the shop. If they found the card, he was toast.

His mobile phone chirped into life. It was lodged in a hands-free cradle. Johnson was so furious that he swiped his left arm across the dashboard, and sent the phone towards the footwell, immediately regretting his action. What if it was the doctor?

He tried to think if there had been any opportunity whatsoever for the doctor to have modified *him* in any way.

Jesus! He'd treated him for blood pressure. Johnson panicked, trying to think what he'd given him. He had to retrieve the phone.

Johnson reached down to make a grab for it. Luckily his foot came away from the throttle pedal, reducing his speed now that he had his eyes off the road.

He picked up the phone and saw it was a withheld number. Probably the cops. The bastards were on to him.

As his eyes focused on the road again, the bend was suddenly upon him. Although he had spotted a yellow sign at the side of the grass verge, he had no idea what it had said.

He hit the brakes, and the tyres screeched as he spun the steering wheel. He was pretty sure that the van was on two wheels going round the corner.

The van returned to the road surface with a loud bang, and for a fraction of a second, he felt relieved.

Until he saw the trailer full of steel less than ten yards away, and the shocked expressions of the men working at the side of the road.

He had no time to brake or swerve. The last thing he saw was the red and white triangle letting him know that more than one of the lengths of steel overlapped the bed of the trailer.

It was the longest one that crashed through his windscreen, taking his head through the rear window.

Johnson's foot was still on the throttle pedal as the van was lifted off the ground, leaving the engine to scream and the back wheels to spin out of control.

His head bounced and rolled for at least twenty yards before disappearing into a ditch.

Chapter Forty-four

Williams had been right. They definitely knew a man who would know exactly what had happened four years ago in Bursley Bridge.

Gardener approached Cragg and told him everything that had happened, bringing him up to date on Ronson and the cards.

"Ronson? I thought that old soak was invincible."

"Seems not," said Gardener. He then mentioned the reason he was there to see him, about the possible unsolved crime from four years ago.

"Four years ago?" said Cragg, his face wrinkled up.

"Yes, Sergeant Williams seems to think something had happened, and that you may remember."

Cragg snapped his fingers, and Gardener thought he had the answer, when the desk sergeant suddenly said, "I know what I did forget to tell you. You asked me about it yesterday."

"What?"

"Sonia Knight. There was something involving her a couple of years ago."

"Go on."

"She was a duty nurse at an institute near Harrogate. I can't remember the name of the place, but it wouldn't be that hard to find. She used to care for patients on the night shift. She was relieved of her duties. There was talk of patient neglect at the time, especially after one of them died."

"Can you remember anything more?"

Cragg rose from his chair and put his empty glass on a small coffee table. "Let's go downstairs. I know where I can lay my hands on the story."

The two men left the upstairs quarters. Gardener returned to the incident room, noticing Williams as he entered.

"Did you find Sergeant Cragg?" he asked.

"Yes, he's in the back room digging out some files. Have you got anything on Graham Johnson yet?"

"No sir, no one's seen him."

"Any idea where Sergeant Reilly is?"

"Mr Reilly is outside with the local police from Ilkley. Apparently there's been an accident out on the road between Burley in Wharfedale, and there. Pretty bad, by all accounts."

Cragg came rushing into the room with an old, faded newspaper in his hand.

"I'm sorry, it's a macabre hobby of mine. I tend to keep stories of crimes that we're linked with. You never know when you might need to refer to something."

Cragg put the paper on a desk and rifled through it.

"Here it is."

Gardener noticed the headline: 'Local Nurse On Murder Charge'.

Whilst Cragg read the details, Gardener walked over to the ANACAPA chart, and did his best to draw more lines and add whatever information the desk sergeant came up with.

The door opened, and Reilly walked back in with the traffic police from Ilkley.

"Oh my God," Cragg said suddenly.

Gardener turned, not sure who to speak to first.

"Boss," said Reilly, making Gardener's choice for him. "We've found Graham Johnson. It's not good, I'm afraid."

"Go on," said Gardener, a sinking feeling in his stomach.

"He's just been killed in a road traffic accident."

"What happened?"

"We're not sure just yet, sir," said one of the traffic squad "Apparently, he took a bend too fast, didn't see the roadworks, and ended up running into a flatbed full of steel. I'm afraid he was decapitated."

Gardener couldn't really say anything about that. Had they lost a suspect, or a victim? Had something premeditated happened, causing the accident? And why the bloody hell would you not see a flatbed full of steel?

"Are the police at the scene now?"

"Yes sir, we've cordoned off the road while we clean up."

"Check his van for a phone," said Gardener. "If you find it, I want it back here. I also want his body taking straight to the mortuary. DS Reilly will give you the details." Gardener started at Reilly. "Sean, can you ring Fitz and brief him?"

"I'd rather not," said Reilly.

He turned to Cragg. "Maurice, pull up everything you have on Graham Johnson, in particular, a medical history."

Could Graham Johnson have been a victim of his own involvement? Did he have a device inside his body with a

Bluetooth chip simply waiting for the right moment? Even if Johnson had been involved, Gardener felt that they had yet to find the main man.

Cragg drew his attention. "I haven't got much better news, either, sir."

"Go on."

"One of the patients in Sonia Knight's care died from an overdose of a drug she should never have been given. At the very least, it should have been manslaughter, but Ronson was her brief and he somehow got her off."

"How the hell did he manage that?"

"Anything was possible with Ronson," said Reilly. "Who was the patient?"

Cragg glanced around the room solemnly. "Theresa Sinclair, wife of Robert, and sister of Graham Johnson."

Gardener was busy trying to take everything in when Maurice Cragg dropped another bombshell.

"I remember now what happened four years ago. Young lad was found dead at five o'clock in the morning by one of the local traders, covered up with an alcohol-soaked blanket. That was your unsolved crime. Local folk say it had a lot to do with drugs, but no one's ever been brought to justice."

"Unless what we've seen recently contradicts that. Who was the victim?"

"Robert Sinclair's son, Adam."

Chapter Forty-five

Gardener put the pens on the table and decided not to bother with the chart for the moment. Instead, he crossed the room and took the newspaper from Cragg, sat down, and read the article about Sonia Knight. When he'd finished, he asked Cragg to try and remember exactly what he could about the unsolved crime surrounding Adam Sinclair's death.

"It's my opinion that Adam Sinclair was killed for being in the wrong place at the wrong time. I'm sure we had witnesses that say he was coming home through the town by himself one night. It was late. I think he'd been to a party.

"I don't know exactly what happened, but a few last-minute revellers leaving a lock-in say they saw a chase. Three men running from what looked like Smiddy Hill through to Birdgate, two men after one. There wasn't any shouting or cursing, but they were going at it pretty fast. No one seemed to think it was serious, so no one bothered to see where it ended up. We see that sort of thing all the time. Not all of it leads to crime."

"On Monday morning we find Alex Wilson crucified in his uncle's shop. Was Alex Wilson involved in this fracas four years ago?" Gardener asked.

"I think so," replied Cragg.

Gardener continued. "On Tuesday morning, we find Sonia Knight glued to a chair in the waiting room of the Bursley Bridge railway station, who subsequently dies when we get her to the hospital."

Gardener stopped talking and called Fitz on his mobile, inquiring about Wilfred Ronson. Despite the fact that the elderly pathologist couldn't tell him a great deal, he did confirm that he had found an ICD in Ronson's chest, with external wires going into his heart and elsewhere on his body. From what Fitz could see, Ronson's heart had been fried.

Gardener ended the call and continued with his summary.

"This morning, we meet a solicitor off the train at Shipston. We now know he was victim number three. Fitz found an ICD in his chest, which delivered a massive electrical charge to his heart, killing him instantly.

"We have an idea that two people are involved, one of whom – Graham Johnson, the electronics genius – is now dead. That leaves us with the medical man."

Reilly took over. "And your man here tells us that we have one very respected medical man whose wife and son have died in mysterious circumstances, and our victims are involved. Doesn't take a genius to work out that when we dig a little deeper into this, we might find they're all implicated."

"I agree, Sean, but we still need to connect all the dots."

The traffic cop coughed and drew Gardener's attention. "If you'll excuse me, sir, I have to get back to the scene."

"Yes, thanks for letting us know. Can you make sure you follow up on what I asked?"

"Yes, sir."

The man left the room and nearly collided with Steve Fenton, the CSM.

"A couple of important things for you, sir."

"I hope so," said Gardener, rising out of his chair. He didn't really like talking to any of his team from a sitting position, unless they were seated as well. Apart from the fact that he felt at a distinct disadvantage, he saw it as bad manners.

"The call to Ronson's phone came from a mobile owned by Graham Johnson."

"Johnson?" replied Gardener, astounded. "Have you any idea where he was?"

"Not exactly," replied Fenton. "We've traced all the masts in the area. Nearest we can get it is Bursley Bridge."

Gardener wondered where. He couldn't possibly have been back in the shop, because they had it sealed off and it was currently being searched. A man had been posted outside all night, and he hadn't reported anything. So where the hell had Johnson been?

"Any chance you could really narrow it down? Tell us to maybe within fifty yards where it came from?"

"It's a tall order, but we can try."

Gardener thought about what Cragg had told them. Graham Johnson was Robert Sinclair's brother-in-law. Perhaps that's where Johnson had been. The case against Sinclair was building, but there were still things he needed to know.

"You said you had a couple of things. What's the other?"

"I can't work this one out. The call to Sonia Knight's phone yesterday morning at the station came from a pay-as-you-go mobile that hasn't been used for four years. There have been no calls to or from this phone in all that time."

"Don't tell me," said Reilly. "You've found out the phone belongs to a dead man."

The CSM stared at Reilly with a strange expression.

"Adam Sinclair?" asked the Irishman.

"How did you know?"

"Call me psychic," said Reilly.

"I can think of a lot of things to call you, but that wouldn't be one of them."

It was the only comment of the whole morning to raise a smile.

"Maybe Johnson and Sinclair have been in it together all along," said Reilly to Gardener.

"I was just thinking the same thing. Perhaps Johnson spent the night with Sinclair so they could plan what to do next."

"Or get their stories right," said Reilly. "Have you thought that Johnson crashing his van was no accident?"

"That's why I asked Maurice for his medical records."

"You think Sinclair might have put a small insurance policy in place?"

"Wouldn't you?"

"I can't believe it," said Maurice Cragg. "Not Robert Sinclair. With all due respect, sir, I think there must be some mistake. I know the man's been through a lot, but he's a pillar of the community."

"I hope you're right, Maurice, but even respectable people can fall from grace."

"Especially with what he's been through," said Reilly. "It'd be enough to unbalance anyone."

"But he's been a brick to Gary and his mum. He operated on Gary's leg. And all his mum's treatment would have sent anyone bankrupt, but I haven't heard of any payment being made."

Gardener wondered about the young constable. "Has anyone been in touch with Gary, just to see how things are?"

"I'll get on to that, sir," said Williams.

Gardener did not like the idea of Gary Close having been operated on by Robert Sinclair. He started to wonder what their relationship really was. It was a thought he wanted to keep at bay for the time being.

"When did all this happen, Maurice?"

"Well, Sinclair lost his wife two years ago, in the nursing home. But his son was found four years ago."

"Why was his wife in a nursing home?" asked Reilly.

"I believe she had a breakdown, sir. After Adam's death, they do say she never fully recovered."

"What about Sinclair?" Gardener asked.

"He took it bad, naturally. But rumour has it they were given treatment by Robert's father, Peter. He's something of a psychologist."

"Is he really?" Gardener thought about that, and the death of Adam. "So, we had an unsolved crime on my patch four years ago, possibly murder. Why can't I remember anything about it?"

Gardener turned his attention to the ANACAPA chart. It really did need updating now. But there were other avenues he needed to pursue. They had still to find Lance Hobson, and he was beginning to wonder if they ever would. He had decisions to make.

He turned to the team. "Maurice, I'd like you to find me everything on the two cases. All the files you can lay your hands on, and I wouldn't mind betting they're upstairs. Can you also move mountains, and find that medical history for Graham Johnson?" Gardener glanced at his watch. "I appreciate I'm asking a lot, but can you have them all here in one hour?"

He turned to Sergeant Williams. "David, can you call everyone in my team, with the exception of Colin Sharp, and get them all back here to study those files? Ask Colin to go and see Robert Sinclair's mother and father over in Ilkley. I'd like to know about her life at Walker Brothers, and how her son benefited. I'd also like to know a little bit about Robert Sinclair, especially from his father. How he coped with the loss of his son and his wife, in particular. Can you also get in touch with Gary Close? If nothing else, to make sure he's okay."

"Yes sir," Williams left the room. Cragg followed.

Steve Fenton said he was going back to the station at Shipston. As far as the CSM was aware, Sharp pretty much had everything under control and there was nothing to report. Most witnesses had been logged and allowed to leave. That left Gardener and his partner in the room.

"Bit of a mess, Sean, but we're seeing some results. A clearer picture."

Reilly was staring at the chart. "I wish we had a clearer picture on the game cards."

Gardener glanced at his watch again. "Maybe it's time we went and found out. There's just enough time to talk to the man from Walker Brothers, and get back here to sort through those files."

Chapter Forty-six

Simon Walker was not at all what Gardener had expected. He was short, fat, and ginger. What was left of his hair resembled tightly bunched coil springs. He had a monocle, which he continually kept placing against his right eye. His teeth were a little crooked, with a gap in the middle of the lower set. He was dressed in a tweed jacket and plus fours.

They were in the living room of a small, detached cottage. The enclosed space was stuffy, because all the windows were closed, and he had a Parkray stove pretty well cranked up. Walker was wedged into an armchair that was too small. Gardener and Reilly had chosen a settee to park themselves. An elderly maid had served tea. References to the games manufacturer were evident all over the walls, posters adorning them alongside certificates of accomplishment and recognition. A version of Cluedo was set up on a small coffee table.

"Now, how the devil can I help you gentlemen? It's not often I have a visit from the police." At that point, he shoved the monocle back in place before continuing. "I say, you haven't come up with a new idea for a game, have you? That would be terribly exciting."

"Nothing like that, Mr Walker, but we would like some help with our inquiries," said Gardener. "Can you tell us a little about the company?"

The monocle slipped; the man obviously disappointed. "I'm sure I can."

Walker started to search around inside his jacket. What the hell for, Gardener wasn't sure, but from where he was sitting, it seemed as if he'd let a ferret run riot. He'd never seen so much movement inside one piece of clothing. Walker eventually removed a pipe.

"I'm not going to light it until you've gone. That would be bad manners, and I was not brought up to display bad behaviour in any form, Mr Gardener."

The two detectives merely nodded, but Gardener suspected his partner was busting a gut to remain composed.

"Now, what would you like, a blow by blow account, warts and all, or the edited version?"

"We haven't much time I'm afraid, so best be brief. We may need to ask questions about former employees."

"Oh, my good God, what have people been up to? I do hope no one has brought the company into disrepute. I might not own it, but I still think very fondly of the old place."

In went the monocle once more and he leaned forward, so much so that he had to struggle with the sides of the armchair to do so, and even then still nearly fell out. "Have we got a real life Cluedo going on?"

"The particular game we wanted to talk about was called Murder."

"Murder?" repeated Walker, as if he hadn't heard correctly.

"You look a little confused, Mr Walker. Is the game not one of yours?" asked Gardener.

"Well, it doesn't ring any bells. What is it about?"

Gardener was surprised that he had to go into great detail before the man could recall anything.

"Oh, that game. I really had no idea what you were talking about, gentlemen. Yes, I do remember that."

"Anything specific?"

"It was never a commercial game. That's why I wasn't sure."

"What do you mean, never commercial?" asked Reilly.

"It was never a game that we developed and distributed. I think it first made an appearance in 1970."

"If you didn't develop or distribute it, who did?"

"Well, when I say we didn't develop it, we did, of course, but we didn't distribute it. We never sold it to Europe or America. It was a very limited edition. I think there were about 500 copies. You have to understand, it was a very complicated game, all about justice. Not the British judicial system, but justice in general. You couldn't get away with anything in that game. The puzzles would always be solved. The criminals would always be caught."

"Can you tell us more about the game? Do you have a copy?" asked Gardener.

"I most certainly do, Mr Gardener. Come with me." He pointed, but Gardener wasn't sure where to. Walker struggled intensely to remove himself from the chair.

Finally, he said, "It's no good."

He shoved a hand in Reilly's direction. The Irishman helped, but it took two or three heaves to remove him. Once out, Walker turned and stared at the chair.

"Do you know, I think my housekeeper likes to play games with me? There is a sister chair to that one, and do I believe she swaps them around."

Gardener thought that Walker actually believed what he was saying.

The three of them shuffled into an adjoining room, which was a study. A number of boxes appeared to have been abandoned around an already cluttered desk. The room had shelves and books of every description, and a door in the corner, which housed a cupboard, but it was bigger than any that Gardener had ever seen.

Walker leaned in and shoved the monocle into the orbit of his right eye. He started to rummage, boxes flying around the cupboard at all angles. Most of them opened up, scattering pieces everywhere. Suddenly, when Gardener thought they were out of luck, Walker jumped up with the board game in his hand.

He shuffled towards the desk and removed the lid, emptying the contents, which included the board itself, dice, and a large number of cards.

"The game, Mr Gardener," said Walker, "was based around the concept of law and order. A murder is committed, and you have to solve it."

He separated some of the cards. "As you can see, characters in the game include the police, solicitors, doctors, storeowners, other professional people, and criminals. It uses dice and cards: character cards, weapon cards, location cards, instruction cards, witness cards, punishment cards, every bloody card you can think of. You use money to trade and buy information."

Gardener was very pleased to see all of the cards their killer had used: Inspector Catcher, Nurse Willing, and Barrister Bent, as well as a number of others. At the same time, it was a very weird feeling.

"So, what kind of a game was it?" asked Reilly. "I know you said law and order, but how did you play it?"

The monocle dropped out of Walker's eye. "Good lord, Mr Reilly, you don't want much for your money, do you?"

The big man dropped into the chair behind the desk. He quickly scanned the instruction document.

"I need a refresher. Not played this in years."

Walker was the type of person who could not read silently. Add to that the facial expressions, and you had a walking one-man sitcom.

"I remember now. It's a cross between Cluedo and Whodunit. All the cards have the same design on the back, but they are categorised on the front." He started to lay them out to prove his point. He also continued talking whilst consulting the instruction document.

"At the start of the game each set – and there are six different sets in total – is turned face down. The game should not be played with any less than four players. One of each card type is then placed in an envelope, still face down so no one knows what it is. The judge card is placed in one, and a murder scenario card in another. The envelopes are sealed and then shuffled, and each player picks one. No one at that point knows the identity of the judge or the murderer. Are you with me so far?"

Both detectives nodded, even though Gardener wasn't.

Walker went on. "Players roll the dice and move around the board, giving each the opportunity to question every other player, in an effort to find out whatever information he needs.

"Now then, certain locations have access to further cards, which can be obtained by entering a building and trading information. Cards and money can be used as a trade-off for information. When a player thinks he has solved the mystery, he needs to involve the police and take the criminal to court, where the judge will hold a trial."

Gardener leaned over and glanced at the board, noticing a number of buildings: The Railway Station; The Courthouse; The Council Offices; The Butcher; The Baker; The Market; The Mill; The Pub; The Library; The Police Station; The Fire Station.

Once again, he struggled with the street layout, but he finally noticed something he'd failed to work out the first time he'd seen it: the board was based on the town of Bursley Bridge. Gardener actually recognised some of the streets in relation to where the buildings were. He wondered why.

Walker distracted him when he started talking again. "It was an exciting game in some respects, but we didn't think it would catch on. We basically did it as a favour to the inventor, and only then because his mother worked for us."

"His *mother* worked for you?" Gardener asked.

"So how old was the inventor?" asked Reilly.

"When it was finally developed, eleven, but I believe his brainchild had been in progress for two years. He was ever such a particular little man. An absolute stickler for seeing justice done, even at that young age.

"I did once hear that three young bullies – or should I say, little thugs – gave him a beating in the playground, over something and nothing. He exacted his revenge in a variety of ways. He wasn't a violent child, gentlemen. No, he wouldn't lay a finger on anyone. Didn't like fighting. He always said: 'You could solve anything by talking.' So, he set a number of puzzles, and ran them all over town for no reward whatsoever, just for the sake of seeing those young men frustrated. To my knowledge, they never found out who was responsible for running them ragged.

"His mother used to bring him to work in the school summer holidays, after school, or on a weekend. He was here more than most people we employed. He'd spend hours in the creative department. Proper little puzzle setter was our Robert. Oh, I remember him well. Always wanting to know about the puzzles in the games and how they were set, and what kind of a mind had created them. He even helped develop some of our commercial games. He couldn't get enough of it."

I bet he couldn't, thought Gardener.

Chapter Forty-seven

Gary was feeling pretty edgy as he drove his car into the car park at the Ross & Sinclair Foundation. He pulled it to a stop two spaces away from where Mr Sinclair normally parked his sports car, surprised to see it wasn't there.

Gary switched off the engine and, as usual, it ran on for a few seconds. He hadn't a clue what was wrong with it, apart from the fact that it was bloody old. Someone had mentioned valve timing, but he had no idea about things like that. He was a copper.

The car was a thirteen-year-old Vauxhall Corsa, and it was all he and his mother had been able to afford. They had both realized that as her condition worsened – and it inevitably would – he would need a car to ferry her around. Eventually she may become housebound, and very probably more dependent on it.

But according to Mr Sinclair, she was on the mend. Her dependency might be a lifetime away. At least far enough away for him to consider having something of a normal life with his mother for a while longer.

Gary had not seen her for a couple of days, and he was pretty nervous about doing so now. He glanced at the passenger seat of the car, where he had a fresh bunch of flowers. He wasn't sure what they were, but the colours were nice. He'd also bought Thornton's chocolates. She loved those. She would probably scold him for that. But not for the latest Tom Jones CD.

The Voice from the Valleys had been her favourite singer for years. Gary thought back to when he had first started working at the police station. He'd saved up his wages for a number of weeks to send her down to London to The Wembley Arena to see him live. She hadn't stopped going on about it for three months. How happy she'd been. It was some time since he'd seen her like that.

He'd spoken to Mr Sinclair twice yesterday, and had been told that her condition was stable. Or was it comfortable? He couldn't remember, but suspected they both meant the same thing. He'd also had a word with him earlier today. Mr Sinclair had said that she was still not up to visitors, that his mother was still sedated, and that it would probably be of no benefit to either of them if he called.

But Gary felt he could not go another day without seeing her, whether she was awake or not. At least if he paid a visit and she was not conscious he could leave the gifts, and when she woke up she would know he'd been. She would know he cared. Not that he doubted that for a minute. He knew if the position were reversed that she would probably never leave his hospital bed whether he was awake or not.

He jumped out of the car, and as he brought his foot down, a severe pain flared up the entire length of his leg, leaving Gary momentarily grounded on his knees at the side of the car, struggling for breath.

He twisted around so his legs were straight out in front of him. He rubbed the back of his left leg and suddenly felt something. The young PC located the object and pinched his fingers closer together. It was small, perhaps an inch long, narrow, with a metallic feel to it, almost like a capsule. He had absolutely no idea what it was; neither could he work out why he hadn't come across it before. Unless, of course, it was something that had only recently surfaced. He would have to ask Mr Sinclair.

He stood up, limped around to the passenger side, collected the gifts, and locked the vehicle. As Gary walked into the building, he breathed in the rich aromatic scents of wood, leather, and beeswax. It spoke of the volumes of money that had been spent on the place. The blonde receptionist at the desk smiled as he walked past. She didn't say anything, but he figured she knew him well enough by now. He didn't need directions.

As he walked down the corridor to his mother's side ward, the only thing he could hear was his own footsteps. The mood in the clinic was sombre and hushed. He couldn't even hear a conversation. He'd expect a radio, or a television at the very least, or even catch a glimpse of the odd nurse walking around. Today seemed very different. Still, everyone had off-days, he supposed.

Outside his mother's room, he composed himself. Why was he so nervous? He guessed it was because he had no idea what he would find. The last time he saw her – two days ago – she was being carted off in an ambulance after nearly screaming the house down. At least there was no pain at the moment.

But he didn't like the thought of her wired up to all those machines. There was something final about seeing a person in that situation, as if somehow they were never coming back from the world they were inhabiting. It was hard to imagine where they were, and what they were experiencing. Could they see, hear, or feel anything at all? In their world, were they talking to their friends? Did they think they were with you? What did they think? Did they feel lost and isolated and desperate to return to what they knew?

Gary put the thoughts at bay and stepped inside. His mum wasn't there. The bed was empty. The room was bare. None of her belongings were evident.

Gary couldn't work it out. He stepped back out of the room and checked the number, to see if he had somehow entered the wrong one. No, it was definitely his mother's.

He walked back in, laid his gifts on the bed and checked the cupboards. There had to be something wrong. It was as if she had never been here.

He checked the bathroom. It was the same. Had they taken her home? He couldn't see how that was possible.

As Gary turned and glanced around, his stomach started swelling. His vision narrowed, making the room appear smaller.

He walked towards the door when a nurse in white uniform entered. Her hand went to her mouth and she gave an involuntary shriek, not loud, but enough to show he had startled her.

"I'm sorry, I didn't realize anyone was here."

He could see from her name badge that she was called Carla, and she had a north-eastern accent. She was small. Her short black hair was tied up in a bun.

Gary apologized as well. "I'm sorry. I was looking for me mum."

"Your mother?" she questioned.

"Yes. Christine Close. She was admitted on Monday. Mr Ross was looking after her."

Carla's face seemed to drop as far as the floor, and her eyes took on a vacant expression.

"Are you Gary?"

Even before she'd replied, he did not like the feeling that washed over him. His stomach now felt like it had a football in it. His legs were weakening, and he was starting to tremble. He thought he'd said yes, but he couldn't be sure.

Carla glanced at the flowers and the other gifts, and he knew at once a serious situation had developed.

"I'm so sorry," she said.

Sorry for what? thought Gary.

He lifted his hands to his mouth, and then put them in his pockets, then brought them back out again, unsure what the hell to do with them. Whatever else she was going to say, he didn't think he wanted to hear it, but still had to ask.

"What are you talking about?"

"Gary... I, er..." She was stumbling over her words now.

"Can you tell me where me mum is?" He couldn't think of anything else to say.

"I think I'd better go and get Mr Ross."

"Just a minute," said Gary. "Where's Mr Sinclair?"

"He's not here at the moment. Has he not spoken to you? I thought he'd phoned you yesterday... last night."

Gary's insides were starting to churn so bad he thought he was going to be sick.

"What about? Why was he calling me last night?" Gary was in a state of panic. "Don't you know where my mum is? Has she gone for an operation? Is that it?"

Carla put her hands out in front of her. "Please, Gary... just wait there, please. I'll go and get Mr Ross."

Before he had the chance to ask her anything else, she swiftly left the room.

Gary had no idea what was happening, but it obviously wasn't good. Where the hell was his mother? If something really bad had happened, he would have been told. Maybe she *had* taken a turn for the worse, and she was having another op. Maybe that's why Mr Sinclair was not around. He was over at the St. James's Hospital, operating on her.

Carla returned with Mr Ross, whose expression was as grave as hers.

"Gary, are you okay?" asked Ross.

"No, not really."

"It must have been a great shock to you."

"What? What must have been a shock to me? Where's my mum? I just want to see my mum. Do you know where she is?" Gary was losing control. Someone had better tell him something. Right then.

He noticed Mr Ross step towards him.

"Gary... have you not been told?"

"Told? Told what? What the hell are you talking about?"

Gary fell towards the bed, feeling faint and sick.

Ross caught him in time and eased him onto the bed. "Please, sit down, Gary."

He turned to Carla. "Would you fetch him a glass of water, please?" She did as she was asked. Ross turned back to him.

"Gary, I'm so sorry. I thought Robert had telephoned you last night. I really don't know what to say, but we did everything we could."

Gary's eyes were full of tears, and the football had now moved into his throat.

"What do you mean, phone me last night... did everything you could?"

The nurse returned with the water. Ross put it on the table near the bed.

"I'm so sorry, Gary, but your mother passed away last night."

Chapter Forty-eight

Back at the incident room, Gardener sensed mixed emotions. His team was busy. Some were reading through the files that Cragg had managed to find. Others were updating the ANACAPA chart and making telephone calls.

He felt an air of excitement. He also realized how tired his men were. Despite the fact that it had not been a long investigation in so far as man-hours were concerned, it had felt like it. The days had been exhausting, and they had been made to fight for every piece of information.

He drew everyone's attention, informing his officers of what he and Reilly had been told by Simon Walker.

"Sinclair invented the game?" asked Bob Anderson, when Gardener had finished.

"He did more than that," said Reilly. "According to Walker, he spent his entire life – apart from school hours – in that place. He even got himself involved in some of the commercial games."

"What kind of a mind puts together a game as complicated as that at nine years old?" Thornton asked.

"What I'd like to know is why," said Gardener. "At that age, most of us are playing football, or hide and seek."

"Or watching the telly," said Reilly. "Given the timescale. It *was* the early Seventies."

"Or *playing* board games," added Anderson.

Gardener smiled at the irony, and then continued. "Walker showed us a copy of the game, with the cards that we have here on the chart. Told us a bit about how it worked, before dropping the bombshell.

"After we left Walker, we went across to the Foundation, but Sinclair was nowhere to be found. They *were* trying to raise him. Apparently they lost a patient last night. We also tried his home, but he wasn't there either."

"So, what are we going to do?" asked Paul Benson.

"Continue with the files. Let's find every piece of evidence we can, make a water-tight case. Sean and I will concentrate on trying to locate him, and then pick him up for questioning."

Cragg raised his hand. "I have some information about Adam's death that might help."

"Go on," said Gardener.

"According to witness statements, Adam Sinclair was chased through the town by two people that were never identified. Alex Wilson was fingered, but no one was prepared to state that on oath. The two that chased him had been seen earlier at the crossroads of Bridge Street and Park Street, outside the station gates. It's a bit of a local haunt for drugs.

"Adam had been walking home from a party, texting his girlfriend. Maybe the two drug dealers thought he was filming them. Anyway, whatever they thought, they chased Adam and caught him, finally cornering him in the alley on Market Street leading to the indoor market.

"Later that same night, Lance Hobson was seen in and around the town. The next thing we know, Adam's body was found doused in alcohol and wrapped in a blanket, either to make it look as if he was a down-and-out, or a drunk. One of the market traders found him around five o'clock in the morning.

"Estimated time of death was between midnight and two o'clock. The post-mortem revealed he'd been given a massive dose of drugs, a lethal cocktail from which he would never recover."

Gardener sighed. Lance Hobson again. Where the hell was that man?

"It's highly likely then that Hobson and Wilson had been involved in Adam's death?"

"Yes, but it was never proven," replied Cragg. "No one was prepared to testify against them. We simply didn't have enough evidence to prosecute. And even if we had, chances are, Ronson would have got them off."

"But that wouldn't matter to Sinclair, would it now?" said Reilly. "He didn't need to know whether we could prove it or not. He had enough evidence, as far as he was concerned."

"He must have carried out his own investigations," said Gardener. "What happened to Adam's phone? If he was texting his girlfriend, he must have had it with him. So where did it end up?"

"We don't know, sir. The phone was the one thing we never recovered."

"Sinclair obviously found it," said Reilly. "He must have done. If the call to Sonia Knight's phone came from Adam Sinclair's phone, which hadn't been used for four years, he must have somehow gotten hold of it."

"It was probably quite easy for him," said Gardener. "Think about it, leading surgeon, must have had contacts everywhere. He probably used that to break the scene. What disturbs me is that he found something we didn't. Why couldn't SOCO find the phone?"

"Well, that's not something we're going to find out now," replied Cragg, "but we have enough to go on where Sinclair's concerned."

"Something else bothers me," said Gardener. "He seems to have been so careful with all the phones up to now. Why did he use Adam's to activate one of the devices? He must have known that we would find out eventually."

No one offered an answer to that question.

"I've got another problem, as well, sir," said Cragg. "Gary Close."

"What about him?"

"According to this," Cragg held up a witness statement, "he and Adam Sinclair were friends."

"Really? Were they at the same party that night?"

"No. But Gary *was* interviewed to see if he knew anything."

"And did he?"

"No. Seems they were quite close. Went to the same school together, played football for the school team, and a local junior team."

"Hang on a wee minute," said Reilly. "Close and Sinclair attended the same schools? Wouldn't you think the son of a surgeon would go to a public school?"

"You would have thought so," said Gardener. "So why didn't he? Does it say anything in the files about that?"

"Not that we've come across."

"Has anyone heard from Gary today?" asked Gardener.

"No, sir," replied Williams. "I've called a couple of times, but I think he must have his mobile switched off."

Gardener turned around and glanced at the ANACAPA chart, studying where all the lines went to: who was implicated, and who was connected to whom. Admittedly, Gary Close was not on the chart, but when Gardener added him, an idea came to mind. He turned back to face Cragg.

"Maurice, you were in the station two nights ago when the initial call came in at three o'clock in the morning. Who answered the phone?"

"Gary did. He had to, it was his mobile."

"The call came to Gary's mobile?" Gardener asked, surprised. "Not the station landline?"

"No sir, not the landline, that rang afterwards."

"So at the time, you probably didn't think it strange, him receiving a personal call. What was said?"

"Well, I let him answer personal calls on account of his mother's condition. Gary didn't say a great deal. He asked, 'Three hours to what?', and then I think he said, 'Who is this?'" Cragg seemed to have finished, but then added: "He also told me it was a withheld number."

"And what about the call to the station landline? That was straight after?"

"Yes, sir. That was from one of our witnesses, Richard Jones, telling us about the hardware shop, and the fact there was a light on."

"Now you've had time to think about it, doesn't it strike you as odd? It should have been police business if it concerned the shop. So why didn't it come in on the station phone?"

Gardener didn't wait for an answer before continuing.

"Fitz told us that Alex Wilson had probably died around six o'clock that morning, and even if we *had* found him within the time allotted to us, we couldn't have saved him. Do the math. Gary gets a personal call at three o'clock telling him he has three hours. Or should I say, we have three hours. Alex Wilson dies at six, which is probably the exact time he was meant to die. What conclusion does that leave us?"

The question remained unanswered. The SIO realized that everyone in the room had to be thinking about the implications of what he'd said.

Cragg sat down, an expression of defeat on his face. "Don't tell me that Gary is involved in all of this as well."

"I'm not saying he is Maurice, but it doesn't look very promising, does it? I'd like a history of all Gary's calls to and from his mobile in the last month. And I also want a list of calls made to and from the hardware shop for the same period."

Gardener could tell the case was beginning to affect Cragg personally. He felt as if he had physically kicked the desk sergeant in the stomach. Two people that he must have thought were pretty solid, reliable characters for quite some time, were now involved in a pretty vicious serial killing.

The door opened and Colin Sharp rolled in. He greeted everyone and took a cold drink from the tray. He threw a file on the table, and quickly munched on a biscuit.

"You go easy with them, mind," said Reilly.

"Surprised we have any left," retorted Sharp.

Gardener smiled. Whatever happened, the team remained solid, and still had a sense of humour.

"What have you got, Colin?"

"Quite a lot." He stood next to his senior officer, consulting his notes.

"I won't bore you with a lot of the details but Robert Sinclair is quite an achiever. His work mostly involves mending nerves damaged in accidents – severed limbs, digits, that sort of thing. He operates on backs in patients with chronic back pain and collapsed discs.

"He also had a hand in the pioneering of a new machine, something you attach to the outside of a patient's arm to stimulate the motor nerves with small electrical impulses. Apparently, it's designed to make the muscles twitch, to test whether the nerve-muscle path is complete.

"He's a keep-fit fanatic, sees his body as a temple. Come rain or shine, he's always jogging along the river and through the town near where he lives. He has a gymnasium in his house. He only drinks green tea, and eats very healthy foods."

"Another nail in the old coffin, there?" said Reilly.

"What else did his parents have to say about him?" asked Gardener.

"Apart from working for Walker's, his mother compiles crosswords for newspapers and magazines. She's very intelligent.

"She says that Robert loves puzzles. Plays cards, particularly Bridge, but he loves word games."

"Was there any mention of the tarot?" asked Reilly.

"Tarot?" repeated Sharp, "No, nothing about that."

"Maybe the use of the tarot cards was a way of implicating someone else," said Gardener, "namely Ross. After all, Ross was in the town on Monday morning, seeing to Christine Close."

"And a mix up on the computer files at the hospital," added Reilly, "another way of implicating his colleague."

Sharp finished his drink and then said, "Apparently, he has OCD pretty bad."

"What did I tell you?" said Reilly. "Light switches."

"When he was young, his fascination with puzzles mixed with his OCD in such a way that when he earned money, he bought two copies of everything he wanted. One to play, and one to keep in pristine condition, unopened. Naturally, she got him all the stuff that Walker's brought out. His mother's really nice, but I reckon she's in denial."

"What do you mean?" asked Gardener.

"She reads the papers, listens to the news. I think she suspects what's happening, but doesn't want to admit it."

"You think she knows her son is behind the murders?"

"Suspects, maybe. She didn't say it in so many words, but it's the impression I got."

"What about his father?"

"That man is a totally different kettle of fish. After Adam died, Robert's father Peter spent a lot of time with them both. He visited Theresa, Robert's wife, sometimes two and three times a week at the clinic in Harrogate. She couldn't accept the death of their son, and had a breakdown. He helped her to come to terms with it. Just when he thought they were making headway, she died in mysterious circumstances. Something to do with the wrong drugs."

"I'm just throwing something out here," offered Reilly, "but you don't think Sinclair had anything to do with that, do you?"

"It's unlikely," said Gardener. "Unless he was implicated. But why would he have anything to do with his son's death?"

"I don't think he did," said Sharp. "Peter reckoned that the family were a pretty devoted one. The parents would have done anything for their son.

"As for Robert, his father could not get through to him. He has the ability to put up a front no matter what the situation. Somehow, he seems to block out everything he does not want to deal with until he's ready. He also has an obsession for seeing justice prevail, right is right and all that."

"That would answer for the game he produced."

"What game?" Sharp asked.

Gardener briefed him on what Simon Walker had told them.

"That's interesting. His father mentioned that he hates being the centre of attention. He also said that more than anything, he hates losing control of any situation. He is an absolute control freak."

Sharp picked up another two or three sheets of paper. "Peter also told me about a situation between Robert and Theresa. She could not forgive herself for what happened on the night Adam died.

"Apparently, Adam and his parents had argued that night. All his friends had been going out to the cinema, and then on to a party in Bursley Bridge. Robert and Theresa said they had wanted him home by eleven o'clock, and Adam had said it was too early. Robert said he would only allow Adam to stay later if he had agreed to his father meeting him.

"As it turned out, Robert had been called to the hospital on an emergency, which had taken him through the night and into the next morning. He was about to leave the hospital sometime around six-thirty, when Adam's body had been taken into the mortuary. The attending pathologist had recognised Robert's son, and called him immediately."

"Stupid question time: how did he take the death of his son?"

"Like his father said, he just seemed to withdraw, block everything out. Within a couple of days he was back at work, and completely refused to talk about it. His father knew that he was thinking about it, and that it was weighing heavily on his mind, because he was so obsessed with blocking it out. As if, because he wasn't thinking about it or acknowledging it, the whole thing had never happened."

"Jesus Christ!" said Reilly. "I wouldn't like to be there when he finally does."

"I have a feeling we will be," replied Gardener.

Silence filled the room. Gardener needed to plan a course of action for his officers.

Steve Fenton the CSM barged in. He'd removed his white paper suit, and was dressed casually in jeans and a T-shirt.

"Bit more on Graham Johnson for you, sir. The cell sites put him in Bursley Bridge at the time that he called the solicitor, Ronson. The best we can narrow it down to is a postcode, which could very well put him at Sinclair's house."

"So either of them could have made the call," said Reilly.

"Assuming he was at Sinclair's house," said Gardener, "But I don't think he could have been anywhere else."

Gardener turned to Sergeant Williams. "David, will you call Sinclair, see if he's at home? You'll probably end up speaking to his housekeeper. Just tell her your investigating something that's happened to Graham Johnson, and you're trying to piece together his movements for the morning. Ask her if he was there."

Williams nodded and left the room.

"Anything else?" asked Gardener.

"I think it's safe to assume he will have been," said Fenton. "Just before the crash, Johnson received a phone call from Sinclair. That might have had something to do with his death."

Gardener turned to Cragg. "Maurice, anything on a medical history for Johnson?"

"Not yet, sir."

"I could do to know whether or not Johnson has had any operations recently. Judging what we've learned about Sinclair today, I wouldn't put it past him to have a little insurance policy on everyone involved. If the heat in the kitchen became too much, he could simply pull the plug on them all."

"I'll get onto it, sir."

"That leaves us with another problem," said Thornton. "If Gary is involved, has Sinclair taken out an insurance policy on him? After all, he was the one who fixed Gary's leg."

"Maybe that's why he isn't answering his phone?" added Anderson.

The situation was growing worse. Gardener sincerely hoped not. He liked Gary Close. But bent coppers were no good to anyone. When and if they found the evidence to support it, he would love to know what had driven the young PC. The only conclusion Gardener could come to was his mother Christine.

Gardener's mobile rang. He recognised the number as Andrew Jackson's.

"Dr Jackson?" he answered.

"Mr Gardener. I'm just calling about the computers at the hospital. I'm afraid I have no good news for you."

"I'd still like to hear it."

"Well, it seems that our machines have been tampered with in some way. The IT guys are still trying to get to the bottom of it. But at the moment, I cannot give you a definite answer as to who performed the surgery on Mr Ronson."

Gardener was not about to play his hand and let Jackson know that he probably knew already.

"Okay, keep trying. I appreciate what you're doing."

The call ended.

Mike Sands, the officer in charge of HOLMES, entered the room.

"Mike?" said Gardener.

He had a piece of paper in his hand. "Something here you might want to see that HOLMES has just thrown out. It's a receipt from the shop that shows Robert Sinclair bought a stack of wood, fixings, and tools from Armitage about five weeks ago."

Chapter Forty-nine

Albert Armitage and his wife lived in a dormer bungalow out on the old Bramfield Road, halfway between Bramfield and Bursley Bridge. Gardener and Reilly had to negotiate a tree-lined drive, which eventually led to a double garage before they saw the place. To their left was a well-maintained garden with a colourful display of flowers and shrubs. Each window of the bungalow had blinds, and Gardener suspected that being in the business, he would see a lot of Armitage's handiwork inside.

The old man opened the front door and greeted them. He was dressed in a plain blue shirt, paisley patterned jumper, and a pair of cream trousers.

"Mr Gardener, Mr Reilly. Come on through, the wife and me were just having us afternoon glass of wine in the conservatory."

They followed him through the house and, as Gardener had suspected, unique, hand-crafted furniture was evident in each of the rooms. They were offered a seat on cane furniture, and the view from the conservatory was pleasant: another large garden full of shrubs and flowers and, at the back, apple and pear trees.

Mrs Armitage nodded and poured them both a cold soft drink whether they wanted it or not and left the room, informing her husband she was going to put the dinner on.

"Lovely place, Mr Armitage," said Gardener. "I can see it's very well kept."

Armitage sipped his wine, and then sat back and folded his arms.

"Any nearer to catching the killer? It's not that Lance bloke, is it?" he said.

"We are following a number of leads, one of which has brought us here."

"And what might that be?" asked Armitage.

"The last time we spoke to you, one of the questions we asked was whether or not you'd had any people asking for strange or unusual tools."

"I remember you asking, but like I said, I hadn't. There's that many tools on the market these days that are strange and unusual in their design, but at the end of the day, they're made that way for a reason. What are you getting at?"

Gardener passed over a copy of the receipt he'd taken from Mike Sands of the HOLMES team. Everything was itemized, and the list ranged from basic screws and nuts and bolts, to all manner of fancy brackets and hinges. There was a lot of wood, and a number of power tools. The final figure came to a little under seven hundred and fifty pounds.

Armitage studied it and then handed it back.

"I do remember that."

"Do you remember who purchased it all?"

"Mr Sinclair."

"Did you not think it unusual for a doctor to ask for such stuff?" asked Reilly.

"I wouldn't have thought so. Perhaps he had a DIY hobby. Why do you ask?"

"Doctors are pretty rich by most standards, surely they could just employ other people to do that kind of work for them?" offered Gardener.

"I think you'll find junior doctors disagreeing with you, Mr Gardener."

"Did you ask him what it was for?"

"Well, as a matter of fact, I did, a big order like that."

"What did he tell you?" asked Reilly.

"It was for a patient of his who suffered chronic back pain. He'd had it for years. Most of the national health doctors couldn't be bothered to spend the time to really find out what it was. Going private was beyond his pockets, but someone suggested Sinclair."

"He volunteered all this information? Did he give you the patient's name?"

"No. And I didn't ask. You know what they're like, all this patient confidentiality claptrap. I can understand that for a lot of things. I wouldn't have thought he'd be giving away any secrets. I might even have known the bloke, but I couldn't think of anyone local who fitted the bill.

"Anyway, we got talking, and he'd designed this machine... contraption would be a better word for it, to relieve the pain. It was remote control as well. I could see from the drawings—"

"He showed you drawings?"

"Yes. He told me how it worked and how it was designed, and he wanted my opinion, wanted to know if I could spot anything that he'd missed."

"And could you?"

"Not really. But I'm not a doctor. As far as I could see it *was* well designed and would probably do what he wanted."

"What did it look like?" asked Gardener.

"A bloody great frame. Looked to me like you stood up in it. There was nothing to lay down on, so I don't really see how it could help someone with back pain. But, like I said, I'm not a doctor, and a mind like his is something you can't argue with."

Gardener wouldn't disagree. "Did he say where he was taking it, once it was finished?"

"No, but it was probably his private clinic. It didn't look the sort of thing to me that you could have in your house. Not in a normal house, anyway."

Armitage had made a good point. The clinic was one obvious place, but then again so was Sinclair's house. A number of people had indicated how big it was. If it had a big cellar, then that might be the perfect place to keep someone. Especially if they were trussed up in a frame.

Lance Hobson came to mind. Gardener figured it was a logical conclusion now to think that Sinclair was their murderer, and that he had Hobson, who'd probably had nothing to do with the death of Knight, Wilson, or Ronson.

"Thank you, Mr Armitage, you've been most helpful."

Both detectives rose to leave, and Armitage showed them to the front door.

Gardener turned. "Just one more question. Did you deliver the material, or did he have it collected?"

"He had it collected, Mr Gardener."

"Did he collect it himself?"

"No. A friend of his, white van, big enough for everything in one go. I remember saying to Alex at the time to be careful with it all."

How ironic, thought Gardener. Alex had even helped with his own demise.

"Thank you, Mr Armitage. We know where to find you if we need anything else."

"Before you go, it's my turn for one more question. Do you really think Sinclair is behind my nephew's death?"

"Right now, Mr Armitage, he's just helping us with our inquiries."

Gardener and Reilly left the shopkeeper at his front door and jumped in the car. Within ten minutes they were back at the station.

* * *

Cragg and Williams were sitting together in the incident room, each holding a cup of tea in one hand, and a sandwich in the other. Both men were chewing in silence, probably thinking about everything that had happened in the space of two days.

Gardener's team had also chosen to take five minutes. He noticed Thornton and Anderson outside, both smoking. The rest had succumbed to the afternoon cup of tea ritual. But he couldn't blame them. Once again, he realized he had not eaten since breakfast. It's funny how he could go about his daily business without a thought for food, until he saw someone else eating.

"Mr Gardener," said Cragg. "Come and help yourself, sir."

He pointed to a tray of tea with one or two remaining sandwiches. "I know your sergeant won't need telling twice."

Gardener did as he was asked. The tea was only warm at best, but the sandwich was roast beef and top quality, judging by the taste.

Gardener told them what Armitage had to say. He then asked what they had come up with.

David Williams went first. "Graham Johnson had stayed the night at Sinclair's house. But the housekeeper thinks they parted on bad terms. She heard raised voices, a slamming door, and a few minutes later, his van start up. When she next saw Robert Sinclair, he had a nasty bruise on the side of his face. She thought better than to ask."

"Another piece of evidence," said Gardener, enjoying the sandwich. "Johnson spending the night with Sinclair goes some way to proving that they were in it together, as far as I'm concerned."

"It certainly looks like it," said Williams. "As far as I can see, Graham Johnson was the electrical genius, and Robert Sinclair the medical man. Both had a motive to kill. One had lost a sister, and the other a wife."

"And when you put Adam's death into the equation," said Cragg, taking a gulp of his tea, "both of them had lost another family member."

"Both had the knowledge and could help each other out," added Williams.

"The only unusual thing about that was Sinclair allowing Johnson to help," said Gardener.

"What makes you say that?" asked Williams.

"If you consider everything that's happened, in my opinion, it would take a true psychopath to invest the time and the money in research and development to kidnap and operate on potential targets."

"And if anyone had the time, the money, and everything he needed, it was Sinclair," said Reilly.

"Maurice? Phone calls?" he asked, changing the subject.

"Yes. We've pulled out all the stops." He consulted his notes. "The one that Gary got at three o'clock came from Armitage's landline in the shop."

"That pretty much seals it for me."

"It will when I play you these."

"Play me what?"

Cragg moved over to an ancient tape recorder. It was an old mono ITT machine like Gardener used to have when he was a child. Very basic, but it did the job.

"Armitage had an answering machine installed. It took some time to find because it wasn't next to the phone. It was hidden in one of the cupboards in that bloody great unit across the back wall."

Cragg switched on the machine. The first voice they heard was Sinclair, informing Gary Close that it had all been taken care of, and Gary could start the ball rolling.

They heard Gary's part of the conversation when he was asking three hours to what, and demanding to know who was calling him.

He'd acted well. Each man in the room seemed as gutted as Gardener.

"The second conversation is when Gary called Sinclair from the landline in the shop, while he was investigating. That was around 3:40 in the morning."

They listened to Gary Close informing Sinclair that he'd done his part.

The writing was on the wall. The evidence was all there for them.

"SOCO found that tape recorder and brought it straight here, just after you'd left to go and see Armitage. I called him myself a few minutes ago. You two were on your way back. He told me he'd installed the machine so as he didn't miss any calls, but also so as he could listen back in case of discrepancies. It was just a better way of keeping the customer happy, he reckoned."

"Good old Armitage," said Gardener.

Thornton and Anderson had returned to the incident room, a slight smell of cigarettes enshrouding them. He had Cragg play the tape again for their benefit.

He had all the team together. "Full steam ahead lads. We need to find Gary Close and Robert Sinclair. Who knows, we might even find Lance Hobson in the middle of all this mess."

Chapter Fifty

"I want a word with you!"

Gary Close had spent three hours at the Foundation. He'd been in terrible shock when he'd first heard the news that his mother had actually died. Guilt followed. He'd begun to wonder whether or not he could have done more himself. Had he let her down? Even if he hadn't let *her* down, *he* had certainly been let down by the one man who'd said he could save her.

Anger now replaced any other emotion.

The staff had been terrific with him, but he'd told them about an hour ago that he would like to go home. What he *had* done instead was sit in his car in the car park and wait for Robert Sinclair, the man who'd led him to believe that everything would be okay. He'd known the surgeon would return at some point, and he'd been prepared to wait all night if necessary. The longer he'd waited, the more infuriated he'd become.

After he stepped out and locked his car, Sinclair turned to meet Gary's intense stare.

"Gary. I'm sorry."

Gary Close thought he must have been hearing things. His mother had died yesterday – not today, but last night – and no attempt had been made to inform him of that. And all Sinclair could say was sorry. That didn't cut any ice with Gary.

In fact, the man hadn't even called and asked him to make a mercy dash so he could be at his dying mother's bedside, like any normal surgeon in any other hospital would have done. He'd told Gary that she was still asleep, and there would be no point in visitors. How bad, not to mention unethical, was that?

While Gary's thoughts had festered in his mind, he failed to notice that Sinclair had walked towards the building.

Gary followed him. "Hey, I'm talking to you."

Sinclair stopped and faced him. "Then have the common decency to do so inside."

"And you'd know all about decency, wouldn't you? My mother dies, and you don't tell me till the day after. In fact, come to think of it, you never told me at all. Still want to preach about common decency?"

Sinclair kept walking, leaving Gary to talk to his back. Gary stopped and stared as Sinclair kept walking through the front door, closing it on Gary behind him.

What the fuck is he on, thought Gary. But then, what could he expect?

The young PC followed Sinclair all the way down the corridor, past glaring, disbelieving staff, into the surgeon's office. Sinclair laid his suitcase on his desk before turning to face Close.

"Don't you dare walk away from me anymore!" shouted Gary.

"And don't raise your voice to me, Mr Close."

Gary noted the change immediately. The surgeon had not used his first name. Suddenly, it was Mr Close. Now he had what he wanted.

Gary took a step towards the desk.

"Didn't you hear me? My mother died. Do you have anything to say for yourself?"

"Should I?" replied Sinclair.

That sentence stopped Gary's thought processes. If he didn't know any better, he'd say that he had been taken over by some alien life force. He was a totally different man.

"Should I?" repeated Gary. "What's that supposed to mean? You were looking after her, and now you're talking to me as if neither of us counted for anything. What the fuck's wrong with you?"

Sinclair opened his suitcase and pulled out a number of files, which he placed in a variety of drawers either in his desk, or in a filing cabinet, going about his business as if Gary wasn't even in the room.

"There are always casualties in war," Sinclair said eventually.

Gary didn't know what he meant.

"What are you talking about?" he screamed. "Who the hell are you at war with? Not me!"

"We've been in a war from the beginning, young man. Against the drug dealers, the people who killed my wife and son. Casualties, Gary, all of them; my wife, my son, your mother. We have to expect casualties when we are fighting a war."

"You're a doctor for God's sake, where's your compassion?"

Sinclair stared at Gary. "You're allowing your emotions to cloud your judgment. You must not let your emotions enter into this."

Gary Close fell back into one of the leather armchairs, totally defeated by what he was up against.

"Your mother was never going to recover anyway."

That comment brought Gary to his feet again, running on adrenaline. "You didn't tell me that when we started this, did you?"

The door to the surgeon's office opened, and Iain Ross popped his head around the frame.

"Is everything okay, Robert?"

"It's fine, Iain," replied Sinclair, walking towards the door. "Gary is upset, naturally. And who wouldn't be, he's just lost his mother."

"Is there anything I can do?" asked Ross.

"No, I'll be perfectly fine. I'm quite capable of dealing with the situation. Please, go back to whatever you were doing."

Mr Ross didn't seem too happy about the decision, but left anyway. Gary didn't think he would leave the building altogether, which was good as far as he was concerned, because they may well need a witness before too long.

Sinclair closed the door and returned to his desk. "Please keep the noise down, Mr Close. Shouting will not help either of us."

"I can't believe you. Someone's died, and you don't care."

"Of course I care. I don't like losing patients. I take it personally when I do, but I can't save them all. If I allowed my emotions to come into it every time I lost a patient, I would have given up practicing a long time ago."

Gary had had enough. "I risked my career for you. I got you what you wanted, all the information on the druggies, where they were, what they were up to. I even managed to get a set of keys to the shop so as you could carry out your work. And all for what? Nothing, by the looks of things. Your part of the bargain was that you would treat my mother."

"And we did."

"You said you would save her."

"No I didn't," replied Sinclair, standing opposite the young PC, meeting his glare. "I said I would try. But you were not the only one taking the risks."

"What risks did you take?" asked Gary.

"Without me, your mother would not have lasted as long as she did, nor would she have been as comfortable. The drugs and the medication she needed cost a fortune. And what you have to remember is that no NHS hospital would supply them. But because of the position I was in, I was able to make sure she got the best of everything. And she did. But I could not guarantee it would save her."

"You led me to believe you could."

"No, I did not. I told you from the start I would do everything I could, and I did."

Gary ran his hands though his hair, and down his face. He didn't know what to do, what to say. He wasn't sure how to deal with what was happening.

"Why didn't you tell me she'd died last night?"

Sinclair didn't reply immediately. In fact, Gary thought he was going to ignore the question altogether.

The surgeon let out a defeated sigh, which, as far as Gary was concerned, was the first bit of human compassion he'd shown since driving into the car park.

"That was just one risk too many."

"What the fuck's that supposed to mean?" shouted Gary.

"I couldn't have had this argument last night. I couldn't take the risk of you informing your colleagues."

"What?" Gary was stunned by the admission. "Go to my colleagues? And tell them what? That all the crimes during the last few days were down to me?"

"You're not taking it too well now, are you? I needed a little more time to complete things before you went running off. I never leave anything incomplete, Gary. You should know me by now."

Gary walked over to the window, clenching and unclenching his fists.

He was confused, but he did realize one thing: he was through talking. It was like having a conversation with a brick wall. The surgeon was hiding behind a force field of some kind, unable to see any wrong in what they had done. All Gary really wanted was to knock seven shades of shit out of him.

Gary thought about what Sinclair had said. Maybe he'd given him a clue, and the way to deal with it *was* to come clean. After all, what did he have to lose? His father had died; so had his mother. There was nothing left to lose.

He turned and raced towards the surgeon, stopping short by a matter of inches, pointing a warning finger. "I'm going to finish you, Sinclair. You're right, I should go to the police. I will. I'll tell them everything."

"That's your prerogative."

Gary backed away slightly. Something told him that Sinclair was still far too calm. After everything that had happened, the threats Gary had made, and still he had not put up a fight. Most people would have panicked, tried to talk him out of it. But the surgeon had acted like a robot.

Gary had no idea what was going through his mind. The man was a psychopath. The calm ones always were.

The young PC needed to leave, and soon.

"You really aren't bothered, are you?"

"I wouldn't say that, Gary," said Sinclair.

They were back to first name terms. Gary definitely had to go, come clean to the police as soon as he could. He'd serve time, but what the hell did that matter?

Gary backed away and headed for the door. As he turned the handle and opened it, Sinclair spoke.

"How is your leg, Gary?"

Chapter Fifty-one

Questions: Which two players were sent off in the scandal-ridden Charity Shield match against FA Cup Champions Liverpool, during Don Revie's last season as manager? Who took over the team and lasted only 44 days, and which England Captain replaced him?

Answers: Billy Bremner & Kevin Keegan. Brian Clough. Jimmy Armfield.

His remaining leg was finally free. Hobson had shouted the answers with what little strength he had left.

He felt disgusting. He had no idea how long it had been since he'd seen the monster who'd held him captive. A few hours maybe, but in that time his health had deteriorated.

He was sure now that he had succumbed to a fever of some description, brought on by the effect of the Ebola virus. His body was in total discomfort all the time. Each and every one of his muscles ached. His head pounded, and his nasal passage and throat felt closed in, obviously inflamed. The rash covered much more of his body, and he was beginning to resemble a burn victim. The diarrhoea had grown worse, and he'd noticed traces of blood in it.

But he was free.

And now, no matter how fucking crap he felt, he was going to fight the remainder of the battle on his terms.

He glanced at the vials on the wall. What was it the surgeon had said?

There were five vials, but only one would cure him. How did he know that to be true?

He didn't.

But the surgeon had also mentioned a key, hidden somewhere within the four walls.

Hobson glanced around. The door to the basement was shut, and there was very little else apart from a central heating boiler. Certainly very few places to hide a key.

That would be another statement without a grain of truth.

He stared at the vials again, debating what to do, when he noticed two plain white envelopes on the floor beneath them.

It took every ounce of strength he had to move. Finally, he bent down and retrieved them.

He opened both envelopes.

In the first he came across a card. He hadn't the faintest idea what it was or what it meant.

Against a white background, he saw a king sitting on a throne between two columns, holding a sword in his right hand, and a pair of scales in his left. The king's robe was red. Behind him was a purple backdrop – curtains maybe. Above his crown were the Roman numerals XI. Along the bottom of the card was one word: Justice.

Hobson understood that the card was meant for him because of the one word, although he had no idea where the card had come from. It didn't matter. He would, however, make sure the surgeon understood his version of the word justice.

Breathing heavily, he took a card out of the second envelope.

He had no idea what that was either. It had a figure on the front, obviously a judge because his name was The Lord Chief Justice Dunne. He held a gavel in his right hand, and pointed his finger at the viewer of the card with his left, no doubt for the benefit of whoever held it.

Losing interest, he threw both cards onto the floor, glancing at the vials yet again.

Hobson made a decision. He'd been given no reason to trust the monster at all.

Fuck the vials. He was no longer prepared to play the game for anyone else. He was a dead man anyway. So, with what little time he had left, he was playing it his way.

He walked slowly towards the basement door.

Chapter Fifty-two

The ringing phone startled him.

Gary stole a glance at the dashboard. His mobile was lodged in a hands-free cradle, and he could see from the display that it was Sinclair.

He pushed the button and immediately went on the attack.

"You're not going to talk me out of it, Sinclair!"

"I have no intention, Gary."

"Good. Then why have you called me?"

"To ask you to think about what you're doing."

"So you are trying to talk me out of it." Gary slowed down as he approached the bend. As a policeman, he should know better than anyone else the dangers of using a phone while driving, hands free or not.

"On the contrary, Gary, I'm simply asking you to be careful."

Gary couldn't understand what Sinclair was doing. Fifteen minutes ago he'd shown no remorse whatsoever, hadn't even tried to stop him leaving the Foundation. So what was he playing at now?

"Just fuck off, Sinclair," shouted Gary. "You had your chance. Too late now."

"Like I said, Gary, take care. Dusk is approaching. Roads can be treacherous."

Gary hurled further abuse at the phone, but it was too late. The connection had been cut.

"Bastard," he shouted, and then screamed again due to the pain in his left leg.

Chapter Fifty-three

Gardener and Reilly were on the A65 heading towards the Ross & Sinclair Foundation. After having digested all the information from the incident room, they had only one option: arrest Robert Sinclair.

Dave Rawson had been the final member to join them, and he'd informed them that he'd spoken to the dog-walking couple at the Harrogate Arms. Although they hadn't remembered all of the registration of the white van, they had supplied the first two letters and numbers.

The husband had also stopped and tried to engage Graham Johnson in conversation about the vehicle that night, because he was currently in the market for one. The dogs had been uneasy around the carpet that Johnson claimed he and his colleague had recently bought and were shoving into the back of the van. He had seemed nervous and unwilling to talk, fidgety, biting his nails. His colleague had remained at the rear of the van without speaking a word. The couple hadn't been able to describe him.

Gardener had put a marker on the PNC against Sinclair's vehicle: 'to be stopped and detained if found.' The vehicle was also on the ANPR database. A number of the local officers had been posted in and around Bursley Bridge. Before he'd left the station he'd called Sinclair's housekeeper, but the phone remained unanswered. Staff at the Foundation said he had been there.

He suddenly realized the car was slowing down.

"We've got a problem, boss," said Reilly.

Ahead of them, Gardener noticed three cars parked at the side of the road at odd angles.

Reilly brought their pool car to a stop, and both officers jumped out. As Gardener walked towards the small gathering of motorists, he flashed his warrant card. He glanced past the broken fencing and saw a silver Vauxhall Corsa wrapped around a tree. The front of the car had a huge V-shaped dent going back almost to the dashboard. The wheels were splayed outwards. The windscreen was smashed, the driver's door open, with a body dangling out of the car.

Gardener's heart sunk when he saw Gary Close.

Whilst Reilly controlled the crowd and used his phone for back-up and an ambulance, Gardener walked through the fence and over to the body.

He checked for a pulse. Gary Close was dead. His skin was tinged blue, and his swollen tongue lolled out of the right side of his mouth. He was clutching his mobile phone.

"Jesus Christ! What's happened to him?" asked Reilly, as he joined his SIO.

"I've no idea, Sean. It looks to me like he's suffocated, but how the hell that's happened is anyone's guess."

Reilly glanced past Gardener in the direction of the A65 and the Foundation. "Seems to me like he was driving at high speed. Look at the state of the car. You reckon he's been to see Sinclair?"

"Probably," said Gardener. "According to a report earlier, Sinclair was supposed to have been there."

"I wonder if young Gary here has had an attack of conscience. Maybe he confronted the doc about it all."

"That would be enough to cause an argument, send tempers flaring."

"They have a fight, Gary leaves in a rage and doesn't pay attention to what he's doing, ends up smashing into a tree."

"I'd go along with that, Sean, if Gary wasn't blue. Something's happened to him. You don't suffocate without a reason."

The approaching sirens halted their conversation. Along with an ambulance, Thornton and Anderson arrived in one car, and Fitz in another.

"I might have known you two would be involved," said Fitz, walking towards them with a case in one hand and wearing an overcoat. "If anyone's going to disturb me at odd hours, it's usually you two."

Fitz glanced at Close. "Oh my word, what's happened here, then?"

"Why do you always ask *us* what's happened?" asked Reilly.

"The Lord only knows. Makes you wonder, doesn't it? Perhaps it's a senior moment. I'm sure it will pass."

"I doubt it."

Gardener noticed Thornton and Anderson closing off the road with scene tape. Two officers from traffic division had turned up and were helping.

Steve Fenton, the CSM, was the next to arrive. Gardener put on a set of latex gloves, and handed him Gary's mobile phone as he approached.

"I need the results as fast as possible, Steve."

"He's died within the last fifteen minutes," said Fitz, glancing up at the SIO as he knelt over Gary's body. "Respiratory failure judging by the colour of his skin."

"Fitz, I'm going to need the post-mortem done immediately, I need those results, like yesterday."

"You're going to have a lot to answer for when my wife sees you next."

Gardener oversaw the removal of the body. Once Fitz had left, he asked the traffic cops to remain at the scene and coordinate a diversion for the time being.

Steve Fenton stood behind him, finishing a call on his mobile.

"Good news," he said to Gardener. "We've located the signal from Johnson's mobile when he called Ronson. He was at Sinclair's house."

"Good work, Steve. Can you get all the information off Gary's mobile for me? Give me a call when you have it."

Fenton nodded and returned to his car.

Gardener addressed his partner. "Let's get to the Foundation. I doubt he's still there, but you never know."

"I've just had a thought," said Reilly. "We were there earlier and the staff were all a bit down, they said they'd lost a patient. You don't think that was Gary's mother, do you?"

Gardener sighed. "I sincerely hope not, but it might explain what happened to Gary."

"Only partly. Wrapping his car around a tree through grief might be one option, but he wouldn't have suffocated."

Gardener could only nod in agreement. He turned his attention to Thornton and Anderson. "You two follow us. If Sinclair isn't at the Foundation, I'd like you both to wait there while we go to his house."

On arrival at the Foundation, Sinclair's car was not in the car park. The receptionist said he had been there, but he'd left about ten minutes ago.

Iain Ross was walking towards the reception desk when he saw the two officers. "Can I help you gentlemen?"

"Not unless you can tell us where Sinclair is," said Reilly.

"I'm afraid I can't. He was here earlier."

"We know that. Did you speak to him?"

"Only briefly. He was with Mr Close."

"And how did they seem?" asked Gardener.

"Mr Close was upset, naturally."

"Why do you say that?"

"His mother died yesterday, last night to be precise."

Gardener's heart sank.

"Due to a terrible mix-up," continued Ross, "he didn't find out until this afternoon. I had to tell him."

"Who should have told him?" asked Reilly.

"Although I was the surgeon in charge of Christine Close, I asked Robert if he would speak to Gary because he knew him much better than I did."

"In which case, you'll probably find it was no mix-up," said Reilly.

"What are you trying to say?" asked Ross with a hint of a challenge.

"Mr Ross," said Gardener, "are you staying here for the remainder of the evening?"

"I hadn't intended to."

"I'd appreciate it if you did. And if Robert Sinclair makes an appearance, I want you to call me immediately." Gardener handed over a card.

"What's going on?" demanded Ross. "Is Robert in some sort of trouble?"

"Just do as I ask, Mr Ross. And to see that you do, I am posting two of my officers on the door."

"Do I need to call my solicitor?"

"We're not arresting or detaining you. It's Sinclair we want to talk to. All we're asking for is your cooperation."

"What's he supposed to have done?"

Gardener didn't answer the question. He had more important matters to attend to.

Chapter Fifty-four

The two detectives entered the theatre in the mortuary. There were four steel gurneys, and although three were occupied, Fitz was working alone on the body of Gary Close. The young man had been opened up in the usual manner, with a Y-shaped incision into the chest cavity.

As Gardener closed the door he could smell the formaldehyde, and chose to remain near Fitz's office door, where he could smell something much better in the form of fresh coffee.

The pathologist turned and greeted them both. "Are you joining me over here?"

"No," replied both men in unison.

Gardener had had his fill of these places. He'd seen the inside of more dead bodies than he cared to remember and had no desire to see another. Especially one so young as Gary Close, who, despite his age, had had more than his fair share of tragedy. If ever Gardener thought he was hard done by, he would only have to stop and think about Gary Close.

Fitz moved away from the body and disrobed, throwing his green gown and gloves in the bin. He washed his hands at the sink and guided them both into his office.

He poured three coffees and placed them on the desk.

"What have you found?" asked Gardener.

"I removed this from his leg." Fitz passed over a tiny capsule that was not really much bigger than a standard antibiotic. It was transparent, and Gardener could quite clearly see a micro SIM card inserted in one half. He couldn't imagine what compound the other half would have been filled with. Why else would Gary Close have suffocated?

"As you can see, our friend with his devastating Bluetooth technique has been up to his tricks again."

"What's happened? What was in there?"

"I wondered at first whether or not it was acute cyanide poisoning, but that usually takes a lot longer, and causes a red or ruddy complexion because the tissues are not able to use the oxygen in the blood.

"However, just before you arrived, I managed to run a couple of tests, and I'm pretty sure it's botulinum toxin, a protein produced by the bacterium clostridium botulinum. It's extremely neurotoxic."

"What the hell is that?" asked Reilly.

"You or I would know it by the trade names, Botox or Dysport."

"Botox?" repeated Gardener. "I thought that was used to treat wrinkles."

"It is used for various cosmetic and medical procedures. It's also one of the most powerful poisons known to man. A tiny amount used in the wrong place would cause respiratory failure due to the paralysis of the respiratory muscles, which is exactly what happened to young Close out there. And I reckon it will have killed him within five to ten minutes."

"So, Gary's driving along in his car, going where, we're not sure, when his phone rings. That sets off the Bluetooth signal, activates the chip, which sends out the poison. The killer doesn't have to lift a finger other than call him."

"I think you're on the right line," replied the pathologist, sipping his coffee.

Gardener sighed. "Which brings us back to Robert Sinclair and his insurance policy."

"Looks that way," said Reilly. "Close and Sinclair were working together. I wouldn't mind betting Sinclair had a hold over Gary through his mother."

"Especially when you consider Adam and Gary were friends. It must have been a bonus to Sinclair to have someone so close, and be a policeman as well."

"Would one of you mind telling me what you're talking about?"

Gardener briefly outlined their thoughts and the evidence they had found. Fitz sat back in his chair.

"That takes some believing. I often wondered what the effect of losing two close family members in such a short space of time would do to the man. But, if you're looking for suspects, Sinclair certainly had the knowledge. Have you caught Sinclair yet?"

Gardener rose from his chair. "No, but we will before the night's out."

Chapter Fifty-five

Lance Hobson had had the house to himself for two hours.

He'd left the basement. Unaware that he was alone, he'd crept around the place very carefully, glancing into every nook and cranny, leaving no stone unturned. He'd started at the top and worked his way down.

An attic room had provided him with a good insight into the man he was dealing with. Sinclair had kept a shrine to his family. Hobson had recognized Adam. He'd remembered the incident four years previously. It had had something to do with that idiot, Wilson.

He'd been scoring drugs in the middle of Bursley Bridge – against Hobson's express wishes – when he'd suspected he was being filmed. He'd chased young Sinclair and cornered him in the alley leading to the market before calling Hobson. No amount of searching had revealed the so-called phone that he was supposed to have been filming them with. However, the matter had to be put to bed. But Hobson hadn't known about Adam's death until a couple of days later.

There were also family photos in the attic, many of Sinclair's wife, and the three of them as a family unit. That death he did know about, because he'd ordered it. Sinclair's wife had been in the clinic near Harrogate: the one that Knight had worked her way into with the express purpose of keeping her eye on the woman, whose name, for the life of him, he couldn't remember. Sinclair's father had been treating her. Knight was uneasy that Sinclair's wife, growing in confidence with each passing day, had gone to great lengths to obtain anything she could relating to the death of her son, which could have spelled disaster for them. She'd had to go.

Whilst Hobson had understood Sinclair's feelings about everything, a score still had to be settled. Hobson may well have been a bad lot, with very few excuses for the things he'd done but in his world it was dog eat dog. And even though he sympathized with the surgeon, he could not allow the man to treat him the way he had done and walk away. Hobson may well have considered trying to bargain with Sinclair, had he not figured he was a dead man himself.

Down in the bedroom, Hobson had used the en suite toilet on more than one occasion, which also gave him the excuse to have his first shower in at least a month. He'd cleaned his teeth, which had hurt. He chose one of Sinclair's own running suits to wear.

Then he'd glanced in a mirror. He'd wished he hadn't. God knew how much weight he had lost. His hair had thinned out. His face and his cheekbones had sunk inwards, leaving his eyes bulbous, with dark circles underneath. His teeth had gaps between them – no wonder brushing them had nearly killed him. His body was skin and bone; he could quite clearly see his ribs. There was no wonder he'd felt so bad.

On the ground floor, he'd found further evidence of where he was being holed up. In the study were a number of envelopes with Sinclair's name and address. He'd found it hard to believe that he had been in Bursley Bridge from the beginning, not too far from his own home in Harrogate.

Leaning on the desk for support, he'd thought about his home and his life, and Sonia Knight, which had caused a tear or two. He'd had everything: big house, conservatory, pool. Flash car. More money than he needed. Why the hell hadn't he called it a day before now? In retrospect, it wouldn't have mattered. He'd have needed to call it a day before Adam Sinclair's death in order to escape what had been coming to him.

Before leaving the study, an unexpected bonus had presented itself on the floor underneath the desk. He wouldn't have known but for a coughing fit, which had rendered him helpless and on his knees, fighting to breathe.

In the kitchen he had found food. He hadn't eaten for a few days, so he'd taken it easy. He'd scrambled some eggs and made fresh coffee in the percolator, completely at ease, unfazed by the fact that he had not seen a soul since his escape from the basement. People would have to show eventually, especially the man he wanted.

Hobson finished the last of the coffee and placed his cup on the empty plate. The eggs and the coffee had been good. He didn't feel any better. His body was racked with pain now, from head to toe. His breathing was heavier than it had been in recent days. He suspected that his body was now prone to infection. Earlier, in the study, the coughing fit had resulted in a small amount of blood in his hand after he removed it from covering his mouth.

He was about to investigate the house further when he heard a lock turn. The front door opened, and eventually slammed shut.

Hobson rose from his chair very slowly, not that he had much choice.

Whoever was home went straight up the stairs.

He made his way to the kitchen door and stood behind it, with his hands behind his back.

Eventually, a petite woman with grey hair waltzed into the kitchen, stopping dead at the sight of an empty cup and plate. She was obviously confused, and spoke to herself whilst removing the crockery from the table and into the sink. She muttered something about the doctor knowing better. From that, Hobson worked out that the woman was not his second wife. Maybe she was a housekeeper. Not so good for him. Not as much bargaining power.

The woman turned.

Hobson blocked the doorway.

Her hands flew to her mouth. "Who are you? What do you want? There's no money here."

"I don't want money," replied Hobson, calmly.

"We have no drugs on the premises. Mr Sinclair doesn't believe in that sort of thing."

"I don't want drugs," said Hobson. He knew she had lied about the drugs. God knew what he'd been given in the time he'd been held captive. He could tell that his two simple statements had really unsettled the woman.

"Why are you wearing Mr Sinclair's clothes?" she asked him.

"What's your name?" he asked her. "Who are you?"

She seemed to have lost her tongue.

Hobson helped her to find it by taking a couple of steps into the room, and raising the gun he'd found in the study level with her head.

The woman let out an involuntary yelp and went into a faint. She held on to the side of the table and eased herself into a chair.

"I'm waiting," said Hobson.

"I'm his housekeeper," she eventually said. "Would you please put that thing down?"

"Why? Am I making you nervous?"

"Oh, dear," she cried, once again burying her head in her hands.

"Name!" shouted Hobson, banging the gun on the table.

She jumped so quickly she nearly fell out of the chair.

"Mabel Bradshaw."

Hobson could see that it took every ounce of effort she had to utter those words, which meant he wasn't going to obtain much information out of her by brute force.

He lowered the gun.

"Thank you, Mabel. You can calm down. It's not you I'm after. I don't want money, and I don't want drugs. Don't reckon either of those would be much use to me in my condition."

"Is it medical help you're after?"

"You could say that."

She placed her hands on the table, continually twisting a handkerchief she had removed from the sleeve of her cardigan.

"If it's Dr Sinclair you want, I'm sure he won't be far away."

"Now you're talking my language."

"I'm sure he can help you. What is it? What's wrong with you?"

"You'd better ask the good doctor that."

"Pardon?" replied Mabel Bradshaw, quite clearly not grasping the situation.

"Surprise you, that, does it?"

"I really don't follow you, Mr…?"

"Hobson. I said, you'd better ask your boss, the doctor, just what the hell it is he's done to me."

Mabel Bradshaw blew her nose. "Done to you?"

"Yes, done to me," said Hobson. "Quite the man, your Mr Sinclair. I've been here a bloody long time."

The housekeeper made no reply. Perhaps she was beginning to think the man in front of her was deluded. Maybe that he'd escaped from a local asylum. Well, she wouldn't be far wrong with that one, would she?

He leaned in close to her, tiring of the game. He had no idea how much time he had left, but of one thing he was certain: he would make damn sure he lived long enough to finish off every last member of the Sinclair family, starting with psycho surgeon.

"Yes. I've been here some time. I've been holed up in the fucking basement while your boss did exactly as he wanted with me."

Hobson pulled out a chair and sat down.

"So, I'm going to sit here and wait for him, and you can keep me amused. And you'd better hope that he comes back soon, because my patience is running out!"

"We can't have that, can we, Mr Hobson?" said a voice from behind.

Chapter Fifty-six

"He said what?"

"He said they were being held at gunpoint."

"Where?" Gardener asked.

"At his home," replied Cragg.

Gardener and Reilly had tried the Foundation once more after leaving Fitz at the mortuary. Before returning to the police station in Bramfield, Gardener had made a quick call to the Sinclair residence, which had once again gone unanswered. Now he had Maurice Cragg telling him that Sinclair had called them to say they were being held at gunpoint in his own home.

"How do you have the time to make a phone call to the police if someone has a gun on you?" Gardener asked Cragg, glancing at Sean Reilly, who had brought the car to a halt in a lay-by.

"He said he'd just returned home from an important meeting, sir. When he opened the front door, he could hear raised voices. One was his housekeeper, and the other a male with a deep voice that he didn't recognize. So he sneaked down the passage and glanced around the doorframe in the kitchen. His housekeeper was sitting at the table, held at gunpoint."

"We're on our way. And Maurice, call for an armed response unit and have them meet us there as soon as possible."

"Will do, sir."

Gardener thought he had finished his conversation with Cragg when the desk sergeant suddenly shouted down the phone, "Please be careful, Mr Gardener."

Gardener turned to Reilly. "That was Cragg. You've probably guessed by now that Sinclair is at home. He's walked in on his housekeeper and an unidentified male. Looks like a hostage situation."

"Do we know who's holding the gun and why?" replied Reilly.

"Cragg hasn't said so."

"I wonder if it's Hobson."

"That's what I was thinking."

"And where are they?"

"In the kitchen, apparently."

Reilly checked his rear-view mirror, then turned the car around.

Gardener glanced at his watch. They were five minutes away from Sinclair's place. It had been yet another long, demanding day, that was now nowhere near over. Finding Sinclair at his house and arresting him would have been too much to ask. Walking into an explosive situation like the one that was developing wasn't something you would like at the *beginning* of the day, never mind the end.

Reilly had decided to park the car approximately a hundred yards from the house.

"Not much point in letting everyone know we're here."

"Good thinking, Sean."

"That's why you're still alive," replied the Irishman. "I'm like your presidential bodyguard. You know, the man who takes the bullet."

"In that case, you can go in first."

"I only said I was like him. There is a limit, even for friends."

Gardener laughed. He could always count on the Irishman for that. He knew from past experience that Sean Reilly had seen things in Ulster that would make his hair fall out, never mind curl up. As far as he was concerned, he could not walk into the current situation with a better man. Assuming he was actually telling the truth.

The night was warm and clear. The tree-lined road was a pleasure to walk. There were no cars on the road, and the only sound Gardener could hear were their footsteps. By the time they walked through the gates onto the drive, the whole situation had been turned upside down.

Floodlights lit up the entire front of the house. Sinclair was standing near his car. Mabel Bradshaw was backed up against the wall of the house about three feet from the front door, a hand clamped around her throat by a man holding a gun, which he had pointed at Sinclair.

"Who the fuck are you?" shouted the man with the gun.

Gardener kept his hands in front of him where the gunman could see them. "Are you Lance Hobson?"

"What of it? You look like pigs to me."

Gardener was horrified at the state of Hobson. He did not resemble any of the photographs that Gardener had seen. The man was a mere shell of himself. Where had he been, and what the hell had happened to him?

"Come on now, son. Put the gun down. You don't want to do anything stupid."

"He did that when he broke into my property and threatened us," said Sinclair.

"Fuck off, Sinclair. Why don't you tell them the truth? You and me have a score to settle." Hobson glanced at Gardener. "And it doesn't involve you lot, or anybody else for that matter."

"Then why are you holding her hostage?" asked Reilly.

"That's my business."

"Mr Hobson, you've already told us your argument is with Mr Sinclair, and it involves no one else," said Gardener. "In which case, you should let your hostage go."

Hobson glanced at Sinclair. "I'm waiting."

Sinclair glanced at Gardener. "I have no idea what he's talking about, Mr Gardener. I've had a very long and tiring day, and I returned home from an important meeting to find this lunatic in my house, brandishing a gun."

"Lying bastard," shouted Hobson, leaving Mabel Bradshaw and taking a step towards the surgeon.

"Calm down, Hobson," shouted Reilly. "Whatever's going on here, we can talk about it."

Hobson pointed the gun at Reilly, which, as far as Gardener was concerned, was the wrong thing to do, even if it was loaded and you were a crack shot. The Irishman was so unpredictable, he could turn almost any situation to his own advantage.

"Keep out of it."

Mabel Bradshaw had not moved. She was obviously too frightened.

Gardener took a step in her direction, only to discover that *he* was now facing the gun.

"I don't want to have to blow your head off, copper."

"I don't want you to, either," said Gardener. He glanced at Sinclair, and then at Hobson. "Seeing as he isn't going to talk, maybe you can tell us your version of events."

Gardener heard a car behind him. The armed response unit had arrived. Four officers all wearing protective Kevlar clothing, and each with his own rifle.

Gardener held up his right hand and waved slightly to signal that he did not want them any further than the gate.

Reilly must have read his intentions, because he backed away from Gardener – never taking his eyes from the situation – and spoke to the officers.

Gardener turned back to Hobson. "I'm waiting."

"For what?"

"Tell me what's happened. He clearly isn't going to," said Gardener, pointing to Sinclair. "And you're claiming you did not break in. So, tell me what's happened."

Sinclair stepped forward. "Are you going to believe him over me?"

Hobson raised the gun at the doctor. "Stay right where you are!"

"I might," said Gardener to Sinclair.

"This is outrageous," said Sinclair. "Do you know who I am?"

"I know who you think you are," said Gardener.

"I am a leading member of the community. I'll have your badge when this is over."

"Assuming you're still alive. As for who you are, it's my guess from what's been happening that you think you're The Lord Chief Justice Dunne. Ring any bells?"

Sinclair's expression remained unchanged, but his eyes flamed. Gardener felt he'd touched a nerve.

"You can cut out the act, Mr Sinclair. We know all about your wife and son."

"Hey," shouted Hobson. "I know who that is." He reached inside his running suit.

Gardener backed away slightly.

Hobson pulled out an envelope and tossed it to the ground. "In there."

Gardener glanced at the envelope, then back at Hobson.

"Go on, pick it up."

He was about to, but Reilly rejoined him. He retrieved it and showed Gardener the card inside. Although they had not seen it used on any of the victims, Gardener remembered it from the game in Simon Walker's study.

"Your shout, Mr Hobson. Tell me what you know."

Hobson seemed to be having trouble. Gardener could see the terrified expression in his eyes, which turned to tears as his bottom jaw started to quiver. Perhaps it had all become too much.

"I've been here fucking ages. I don't even know how long." He stared at Gardener. "What date is it?"

"August 3rd," he replied.

"Oh Christ," said Hobson, defeated, trying to compose himself. "That bastard took me from outside my house back in May."

Sinclair said nothing. He continued to stare at Hobson.

Gardener noticed that the armed response unit had taken positions, their rifles raised. He stepped to one side, trying to make sure they had a clear shot at Hobson.

"Do you know what he's done to me?"

"Judging by what he's done to others, I can imagine," said Gardener, sensing the situation was defusing.

"He kept me in his basement, locked in a wooden frame."

Gardener could see that Hobson was close to breaking point when he heard another car pull up. Officers Thornton and Anderson jumped out. They joined the armed response unit.

He glanced at the house. Mabel Bradshaw had gone. Where, he wasn't sure. Hopefully inside, if she had any sense.

Hobson had actually lowered the gun. "He had a computer wired up to my body, and the frame. I had to answer questions in order to free myself. He also had me wired up to some fucking pacemaker, with wires running all over my body, touching nerves, so that when he wanted, he could press a button and give me pain like I've never had."

Hobson turned to Sinclair and screamed, "So where is it you bastard? How come you haven't given me a blast?"

Sinclair remained calm. "Lucky for you, it's in the house."

"So you're not denying it?" Gardener asked the surgeon.

"What would be the point?"

Hobson pulled his running suit top upwards. "And look at this! What do you think that is hiding?"

Gardener saw the scar, a mirror image of Alex Wilson's.

"An implantable insulin pump at a guess."

Hobson's head shot up. "How did you know that?"

"Alex Wilson had one in the same place."

"Bet he didn't have his filled with the fucking Ebola virus."

Everyone took a step back with that sentence.

"Ebola?" said Reilly.

"Not quite, Mr Hobson," said Sinclair, his arms folded across his chest.

"What?" Reilly asked. "So he hasn't got the Ebola virus?"

"Oh yes, he has," replied Sinclair. "But his is modified, it acts much quicker than the standard virus."

Gardener was lost for words.

Hobson suddenly sunk to his knees. In his left hand he held the gun, which was pointed at the ground. His right hand was across his chest, and he had the most horrific grimace on his face.

"Jesus Christ!" he exclaimed.

Gardener could see the man was in serious pain. He shouted to Frank Thornton. "Ambulance, now!"

Hobson screamed, and let loose with a horrible bowel movement.

"You can't save him, Mr Gardener," said Sinclair.

The screaming subsided. Hobson glared at the surgeon. "I know what you think of me, Sinclair, but I'm not like you. I never intentionally killed anyone in my life. I didn't even know about your son's death until a day or so later."

Sinclair snorted.

"I really don't give a fuck what you think of me, Sinclair, but I reckon I've paid the price, and you probably think we're even now."

Hobson grimaced again, holding his chest.

"But we're not, not in my book. You're one up on me, and I have a score to settle," he rasped. "Only then can I save myself."

Gardener stepped forward.

Hobson raised the gun. "Get back, you bastards!" He continued to raise the gun towards the sky and let off a round.

Everyone hit the deck instantly, giving the armed response unit every opportunity.

The second shot came immediately afterwards.

When the dust had settled, Gardener raised his head, only to find that Hobson had shoved the gun inside his own mouth and blown his brains halfway across the drive.

Sinclair was on his feet, wiping down the front of his suit.

Mabel Bradshaw had come out of the house. She had covered her face with her hands. If she'd seen that, she would have nightmares for the rest of her life, thought Gardener.

Reilly was on his feet and had already covered the ground between him and Sinclair.

"Are you satisfied now?" he asked the surgeon.

"Very," replied Sinclair. "Mission complete."

Gardener glanced at his partner. "Sean, the cuffs?" He suddenly remembered the comment Simon Walker had made earlier in the day: 'He was ever such a particular little man. An absolute stickler for seeing justice done.'

Gardener faced Sinclair.

"Robert Sinclair. I'm arresting you on suspicion of murder. You do not have to say anything, but it may harm your defence if you do not mention when questioned something you later rely on in court. Anything you do say may be given in evidence."

"Pardon?" replied the surgeon.

"If you're having hearing problems, Mr Sinclair, I can recommend a doctor."

What happened next did not shock Gardener at all.

Sinclair started to cry like a baby.

"He killed my wife and son, Mr Gardener."

The sobs were like a storm breaking on the mainland. You could wait for days, but when it came, you were not prepared. His whole body buckled under the emotional pressure, and he fell to his knees.

"What did you expect me to do? Sit back and let him take the lives of the people I loved?" sobbed Sinclair. The tears flowed freely, given the fact that he was handcuffed.

"I had nothing left."

Sinclair glanced towards the heavens, whispering, "And now... now..." He glanced back at Gardener, "I have nothing."

Gardener led Sinclair to the car, thinking how many other people had nothing left: Wilson, Knight, Hobson, Ronson, Johnson – possibly even the innocent bystanders like Albert Armitage, and one of their own, Gary Close. How many lives had been ruined for the sake of a mistake? The fact that someone happened to be in the wrong place at the wrong time? How destinies can change in a fraction of a second.

Sinclair apologized to his housekeeper. What for, Gardener wasn't sure.

As he lowered Sinclair into the car, Gardener said, "I can understand your grief, Mr Sinclair, but what I would have expected you to do was call us, the police, and let us deal with it."

Sinclair stared at Gardener. It was an intense glare, and made him feel like he was staring down the barrel of a gun for the second time tonight.

"You lot couldn't even find the phone."

Sinclair then stared down his chest.

"It's in my inside pocket... if you want it."

Epilogue

Maurice Cragg was sitting alone at the desk in the back room. On the table in front of him, he had a cup of tea, and a couple of digestive biscuits.

He picked up the tea, clasping the cup between both hands, desperately trying to make sense of something that didn't make any at all. Three days ago, everything appeared fine on the surface. Since then, six people had been killed, one of which was a policeman, a young man he had known for some years. And one of the county's most respected surgeons, someone he'd known even longer, had been arrested.

He was alone in the station. The HOLMES lads had gone home for the day. They would be returning tomorrow to collect everything. Two of his men were out attending to a burglary. DI Gardener and DS Reilly had taken their suspect to Millgarth in Leeds.

He simply couldn't begin to work out what had gone wrong, and when it had all started.

In the corner of the room, the desktop PC that Maurice liked to think was Gary's machine – because he didn't really know how to work them – pinged. The screen saver disappeared, and the computer seemed to be going into self-destruct mode as far as he could see: flashing lights and beeping noises all over the bloody place.

But then something else happened.

The screen cleared, the machine calmed, and Maurice could see a document.

He placed his cup on the table, lifted himself out of the chair, and put on a pair of reading glasses before reaching the machine.

Glancing at the monitor, he saw a letter written to him. The only thing Maurice knew how to do was print, so he did.

When the printer had finished, he collected the paper and sat back in his armchair.

Dear Maurice,

If you're reading this, something serious has happened, probably to me.

I won't waste time telling you why I've done it, but I do owe you some kind of an explanation.

Since my dad died, I've been lucky enough to have two father figures in my life: you were one. You investigated his death, and eventually put the coked-up arsehole who ran him over behind bars.

I spent time with you, and I realized the one thing I wanted to do was join the force, protect people, put the bad guys away like the bastard who killed my dad. I know it sounds like a cliché, but there it is. So working with you was an added bonus. The other person who influenced me was Adam's dad, Robert.

Me and Adam were big mates. When he died I was well gutted. Not as much as when my dad died, though. Adam was also killed by a pair of drug-crazed lunatics, who chased him through the town because they thought he was filming them. He wasn't. Thing was, he did actually film his own death. He shoved the phone into a crack in the wall and left it on record. Although Lance Hobson didn't do it, he was involved. Don't ask me how, but his father Robert, had the phone (still has, for all I know), and he knew what had happened.

It seems that Adam's mother was also killed by one of Hobson's gang, Sonia Knight. I don't know much about that.

Robert Sinclair had probably lost out bigger than me. He was the only person who understood what I was facing when my mam was diagnosed with the brain tumour. There was no chance I could afford what it was going to take to treat her. But Sinclair came up with a once in a lifetime offer, one that was really non-negotiable.

He said he would authorize my mam's treatment to be covered by a hospital grant. I don't understand everything, but what it meant was she would have the only treatment available that would help her lead a normal life, and I didn't have to pay for it. Well... not with my own money anyway.

Sinclair told me all about Hobson, Ronson, Wilson, and Knight. He told me what they had done, and he wanted revenge, like you could never understand. All I had to do was help him. I had to feed him everything I knew about them: everywhere they hung out, where they went, who they saw, who they were *selling to, everything. And I also had to get hold of copies of the keys to Armitage's shop.*

The rest is history. But at least you know now what I've done. I've let you down, Maurice, but try looking at it from my point of view. In my position, what would you have done? Would you have upheld the law and let the drug dealers that we couldn't run to ground carry on, or would you have helped? You know how much I hate drugs, and the bastards that peddle them. Look at all the misery they've caused us. It was either them or my mam. As far as I was concerned, it was no contest.

But I didn't do it without a conscience. I recorded every last detail of everything we did, and I placed it upstairs in the file room. You can't miss it. It's in a bright orange folder.

As I said at the start, if you're reading this, something has gone wrong, and it's possible that I'm dead. Let's face it, if I was still alive, you wouldn't be reading this anyway. It's also possible that Sinclair may have gotten away with everything, and even though he deserves to, the law is the law. So I want you to go upstairs and grab the file and give it to DI Gardener. It has everything he needs to do his job.

Don't be sad, Maurice. Things may not have worked out for me, and whatever else seemed bad to me, you got me through it.

Yours, Gary

Maurice put the file on the desk, removed his glasses, and wiped his eyes.

Gary Close was one unlucky man. Why did the worst things always happen to the nicest people?

Maurice Cragg felt as if he had lost everything as well. The last three days had been the most intense investigation he had ever been involved in, but the senior officers had made him feel more alive than he had done in years.

He had a feeling that things were never going to be the same again.

ACKNOWLEDGEMENTS

It's time to thank a few people for a lot of help, especially with this book. Iain Ross for his technical help and also for looking after my website. Andrew Gardener, the author of a number of crime novels, and someone always willing to listen and offer advice. Darrin Knight, my real life Gardener who does a great job on the streets and in the pages of my books. Bob Armitage, a valued friend and a great chemist. Boy, does he know some stuff! David Johnson, a very keen editor and now, a really good friend – we get on really well. To Will and Harry of Edge Waes for producing superb trailers (Implant was no exception), and continually pushing the world of Ray Clark forward. To Peter James, fellow author and friend, who writes great books and keeps me on my toes – for all the help he's given me. It's an honour to have such a close friend. And to the team at The Book Folks, they're all very good at what they do.

If you enjoyed this book, please let others know by leaving a quick review on Amazon. Also, if you spot anything untoward in the paperback, get in touch. We strive for the best quality and appreciate reader feedback.

editor@thebookfolks.com

www.thebookfolks.com

ALSO AVAILABLE

If you enjoyed IMPLANT, the third book, check out the others in the series:

IMPURITY – *Book 1*

Someone is out for revenge. A grotto worker is murdered in the lead up to Christmas. He won't be the first. Can DI Gardener stop the killer, or is he saving his biggest gift till last?

IMPERFECTION – *Book 2*

When theatre-goers are treated to the gruesome spectacle of an actor's lifeless body hanging on the stage, DI Stewart Gardener is called in to investigate. Is the killer still in the audience? A lockdown is set in motion but it is soon apparent that the murderer is able to come and go unnoticed. Identifying and capturing the culprit will mean establishing the motive for their crimes, but perhaps not before more victims meet their fate.

IMPRESSION – *Book 4*

Police are stumped by the case of a missing five-year-old girl until her photograph turns up under the body of a murdered woman. It is the first lead they have and is quickly followed by the discovery of another body connected to the case. Can DI Stewart Gardener find the connection between the individuals before the abducted child becomes another statistic?

IMPOSITION – *Book 5*

When a woman's battered body is reported to police by her husband, it looks like a bungled robbery. But the investigation begins to turn up disturbing links with past crimes. They are dealing with a killer who is expert at concealing his identity. Will they get to him before a vigilante set on revenge?

IMPOSTURE – *Book 6*

When a hit and run claims the lives of two people, DI Gardener begins to realize it was not a random incident. But when he begins to track down the elusive suspects he discovers that a vigilante is getting to them first. Can the detective work out the mystery before more lives are lost?

IMPASSIVE – *Book 7*

A publisher racked with debts is found strung up in a ruined Yorkshire abbey. Has a disgruntled author taken their revenge? DI Stewart Gardener is on the case but maybe a hypnotist has the key to the puzzle. Can the cop muster his team to work some magic and catch a cunning killer?

IMPIOUS – *Book 8*

It could be detectives Gardener and Reilly's most disturbing case yet when a body with head, limbs and torso assembled from different victims is discovered. Alongside this grotesque being is a cryptic message and a chess piece. A killer wants to take the cops on a journey. And force their hand.

IMPLICATION – *Book 9*

When a body is found in a burned out car, DI Stewart Gardener quickly establishes that a murder has been concealed. But with a missing person case and a spate of robberies occupying the force, he will struggle to identify the victim. When the investigations overlap, he'll have to work out which of the suspects is implicated in which crime.

All FREE with Kindle Unlimited and available in paperback.

www.thebookfolks.com

Printed in Great Britain
by Amazon